THE
BITE
OF
WINTER

ALSO BY BETHANY HELWIG

International Monster Slayers:
The Curse of Moose Lake

~

Darkest Light

INTERNATIONAL MONSTER SLAYERS
BOOK TWO

THE BITE OF WINTER

BETHANY HELWIG

BRIGHTWAY BOOKS

Copyright © 2017 by Bethany Helwig
Published by Brightway Books, LLC

THE BITE OF WINTER, characters, names and related indicia are trademarks of and © Bethany Helwig.

Cover Illustration: Bethany Helwig

First Edition: April 2017

ISBN-10: 0-9981247-3-7
ISBN-13: 978-0-9981247-3-5

For my dear friend, caffeine.
I love you.

The salty ocean spray feels like flecks of ice against his freezing skin. He grasps onto the railing of the *Nauti Buoy*, his uncle's forty-foot yacht, and fights the vomit rising in his throat yet again. His insides are a churning pot as the Atlantic Ocean rocks the vessel up and down, side to side, rolling it ever on the waves scaling up in size. A yacht trip will be fun, his uncle said. Take a vacation before you go to college, he said. The sea's great, he said. His uncle's a liar.

"Gene!" His uncle thunders his name from where he stands on the opposite side of the yacht. He waves his bear paw of a hand and Gene staggers over to him, working to gain his sea legs across the yawing deck while clutching onto his life preserver that he refuses to take off.

"Give us a hand, boy," his uncle says. "There's trouble."

His hope of not being asked to help is crushed as his uncle grabs his arm and pulls him down into the motor launch with him. Gene nearly falls flat on his face getting in but his uncle and the deckhands hardly seem to notice. One grabs him under the arm and hauls him onto the seat next to the others. His uncle's best friend starts up the motor and they come alongside the lifeless triple-decker yacht they stumbled across on their "super fun" trip. There are no lights, no sign of people, no nothing. A chill runs down Gene's spine. They came across it by accident when it almost ran into their yacht. No one has responded to his uncle's hails. The men around him are quiet and not a sound is heard apart from the roar of the Atlantic Ocean.

The deckhands manage to tie onto the transom at the back of the yacht and they clamber onboard. For a long moment they all stand there and no one moves except to sweep the beams of their flashlights over the deck. With the storm and twilight falling around them, everything is bleary, gray, and dim—like all those horror movies Gene loves to watch. In real life, it's a lot less cool.

"Hello?" his uncle calls.

Once his voice breaks the silence, the others start to spread out. Gene's uncle takes his arm, dragging him along, and together they head below deck into the belly of the craft. He lags behind his uncle and continues to clutch his life preserver to his chest. He doesn't like to think of himself as a coward but he's terrified. There's nothing like walking through a ghost ship to make you jumpy. The muffled calls of the others sound across the vessel as they walk through the levels above. With the power off it's near pitch black down in the hold. Why didn't anyone bother to give *him* a flashlight? His uncle's beam is the only light now.

"Hello? Anyone here?" his uncle calls again. There's no response. Just the echo of his own voice. Suddenly he freezes and Gene takes a cautious step forward to see what his light is resting on.

A woman lies on her stomach, stretched out and unmoving, her splayed hair hiding her face. There's a dark pool beneath her that looks suspiciously like blood. Gene's heart leaps into his throat along with another swell of nausea. His uncle, a man of stronger countenance, bends down to hold two fingers to the woman's neck. Gene stays frozen where he is, soaking up the nightmare of finding a dead body in the darkened hold of a mystery ship. After a few seconds, his uncle shakes his head to confirm the woman is dead. Is the killer still on board? What happened? Where's the rest of the crew? Are they dead too? Is their crew going to die next?

"Gene, go get the others," his uncle orders, his face grim.

Gene glances over his shoulder to the dark hallway that leads back to the door. He can't see a thing. There's no way he's going by himself. He shakes his head and pulls the edges of the life preserver closer to his chest.

"You've got to be kidding."

His uncle opens his mouth to respond, but he never gets to make a sound as a white hand shoots out of the darkness to clutch his throat. His uncle's eyes bulge as the woman thought to be a corpse on the floor rises, her hold tightening on his uncle's throat. The beam of the flashlight catches the woman's snake eyes and razor sharp teeth like a shark's maw opening out of the darkness. Gene can't shout, can't move. Warmth soaks his pants.

There's a loud crack of bone and his uncle suddenly falls lifeless to the floor, his neck broken. The flashlight drops and with it the light. The monster of a woman disappears in the void of darkness.

Fear engulfs everything. Gene's survival instincts make him turn heel and run as hard as he can back the way he had come. He stumbles blindly into the walls and nearly trips over the hatch but find the stairs and keeps running, screaming the whole way. He reaches the deck and keeps running until he comes to a jerky halt at the railing where the motor launch is still tied.

A single shout is all that's heard behind him and then silence. No screams, no calls for help from the others, just silence. He spins about and scans the ship. There's not a soul in sight. Frantically turning back to the single means of escape, his hands fumble with the rope holding the launch in place. That monster will be coming for him. He has to escape. He has to get back to the *Nauti Buoy.* God, his uncle. His uncle is dead. He's *dead* and Gene will be next.

The rope in his hand suddenly goes taut and his hand is almost caught in the knot he had been loosening. The launch below inexplicably sinks—no, it doesn't sink. It gets *dragged* down. It disappears below the waves and then bubbles are all that's left. Lightning flashes across the sky and if he wasn't terrified before, he is now. Below the surface, for just that split second of lightning, he sees a massive shape moving beneath the waves. The mass of it stretches on and on, impossibly large. There's more than one monster out here?

The hairs on the back of his neck rise. There are no footsteps, no slapping of shoes or feet, no breathing, no sound of movement along the deck, but he knows there's someone—*something*—directly behind him.

A cold white hand grabs his shoulder.

1

Snarls and howls echo in the wintery air. If not for the cold, I would be overwhelmed by the smell of wet dog. As it is, it's strong enough. My breath mists before me and I hug my winter jacket closer to myself in the freezing temperature. Werewolves race back and forth through the snow, jaws snapping and saliva flying. I keep my distance so I don't get run over but one purposefully veers in my direction at full speed. I jump back just in time so I'm not flattened and almost lose my balance on the slippery field.

I cup my hands around my mouth and shout, "Ben, do that again and I'll red card you!"

He barks at me and keeps running, his blue jersey sticking to his damp fur. He races after the soccer ball being pushed along by Hawk in wolf form moving towards the makeshift goal at the other end of the field in a red jersey. Other wolves in red jerseys team up around Hawk and protect his charge. The atmosphere is rich with adrenaline as Ben and the rest of the blue team rush to cut him off. When they get in close, Ben snaps at the ball and grabs it with his teeth. Before he can make a dash for the opposite goal, he's hit from the side and the pair of blue and red jerseys go tumbling.

A yellow flag flies into the air and Deputy Graham jogs out onto the field in his Carlton County Sheriff's jacket. His towering frame makes him seem like a giant amongst the wolves spread out around him. Strands of his chin length hair peek out from a dark beanie on his head as it starts to slip off. "Hey, hey! No biting the ball! This is soccer, not Frisbee!"

The soccer game pauses and the werewolves stand still, breathing hard. Ben and a werewolf I recognize as Jason untangle themselves. The deputy has to pull Ben's paw out of Jason's twisted jersey before they are completely extricated. He picks up the ball, shaking his head, and tosses it to me. It's punctured and bleeding air fast, turning into a limp mass in my hands. I hold it up for Ben to see.

"This is why we can't have nice things!" I shout and toss the ruined ball aside. A line of others, loaned out by players in the game, sits behind me. I pick up the closest non-mangled one and place it on the edge of the field.

Hawk trots over and stands perfectly still behind the ball, paw pointed. His reddish fur pokes through the jersey around his torso and gleams in the fading winter light. His team automatically starts spreading out between the blue jerseys.

I hold up my hands and call, "Resume!"

My brother nudges the ball with his nose and races back into the fold. The wolves dive around each other, fighting to get the ball to the goal. I may be prejudiced but Hawk is one of the best players on the field. He's the captain of the red team and they've won four consecutive games so far. If he makes this next goal, it'll be their fifth. I'm supposed to be refereeing along with Deputy Graham but I start cheering my brother on.

Mrs. Ferguson guards the goal, furry head bent low as she paces back and forth. The wolves pound across the snow packed down by their many trampling paws. Ben slides forward to block Hawk's drive but overshoots and ends up running into one of his own teammates. The way is clear. Hawk tosses the ball into the air with his nose, launches skywards, and gives the ball an almighty kick with both back legs to send it towards the goal. Mrs. Ferguson slides.

"Goal!" I shout and jump up and down with my hands in the air.

The red team howls and they throw themselves into a literal dog pile on top of Hawk. I laugh and want to jump in to congratulate him, give him a noogie maybe, but there's a crowd of wolves between me and my brother. I hold off and stand on the outskirts. I know better than to get into the middle of a pack of excited werewolves.

Since Hawk and I started our campaign to turn the werewolves into more of a community rather than a loose smattering of loners, our job has become more like herding puppies than corralling wolves. The sight before me is evidence enough of that. Several are now jumping around like antelopes and eating snow simply because they can. It's almost easy to forget what they are and what this city went through three months ago. I subconsciously rub the spot on my forearm that bears the scar from having my first life-threatening encounter with a werewolf. It doesn't have the same silver sheen as your typical werewolf bite but I'm still marked where teeth punctured the skin. As a force of habit, I find Jason's slinky gray wolf form in the crowd, always conscious of where he is. Jason had been under an alpha's compulsion at the time he bit me, but still.

I heave a sigh and push the thought out of my mind. Dwelling on something like that will only give me a headache. Dasc, Lycaon—whatever his name is—is gone along with his influence. None of the werewolves gathered here would ever hurt someone like that now.

"I thought you were supposed to be keeping them in check," a grouchy voice says behind me. "What is this? 101 Dalmatians?"

Jefferson stamps out from the trees, a black stocking cap over his shaggy gray hair and the collar of his fleece jacket pulled up to his ears. He's let his scruff grow out into a thick beard since winter started. It's his "extra layer of protection" as he puts it. His beady eyes appraise the werewolves with disapproval.

I just smile and rub my cold hands together. "Hawk won again in case you were wondering."

"Shocker."

"Any trouble out there?"

Jefferson heaves a sigh and frowns at the tangle of werewolves still running around and playing tag with each other. "Surprisingly, no, considering the racket they're making. I could hear them howling all the way out at the road."

"They were just having fun."

"Yeah, well." He rolls his shoulders and gives me a sideways look. "Too much fun and too much noise and they'll end up drawing more attention than we can handle. Do you want them winning soccer games, or safe?"

I scowl at him and kick at the snow under my feet. He always has to be the downer of the group. "They can't have both?"

"They can play soccer like normal people. They don't have to wolf out for it."

"They need this," I say and throw a hand out to the werewolves finally settling down and tugging their jerseys off each other with their teeth. "It lets them blow off steam and get all that instinctual crap out of the way. We've cut way back on the number of incidents Moose Lake used to have."

He rolls his eyes. "It's only been three months, Phoenix. Don't let it go to your head, and never let your guard down. Come on. We've got probation duties to attend to."

The werewolves have started to shift and people stagger to their feet panting after the exertion of the game and the pain of transformation. Hawk stands on his tiptoes over the group and waves to me with a big smile before one of his teammates tackles him. I laugh and watch as a few boys wrestle with him for a bit.

I've always wanted this for Hawk, for him to fit in completely and have friends. I mean, we had friends back in Underground but none that were like him, none that knew intimately all the things a werewolf goes through. Even I can't fill that void for my brother. After his alpha display when we took down Dasc, the werewolves flocked to him. They look up to him and I've never seen him happier.

But I also realize I'm standing on the outskirts now, looking on instead of being in the thick of it with him. I'm not a part of the pack, and never will be, but at least I'll always be his sister when he needs me.

The teams disperse and everyone walks off the field into the sparse woods down a narrow path to an impressive colonial style house. Cows and horses fenced in near the enormous red barn shy away from the werewolves walking as humans. Animals must be able to sense the danger lurking beneath on some level. It makes them nervous but not terrified. Their owner, Mr. Wick, who's a werewolf himself, still handles them just fine. He's been kind enough to allow us to use his land on the far outskirts of Moose Lake to host these kinds of events. Thanks to soccer games, capture the flag, races, and whatever other games we feel like, the werewolves have been far more willing to comply with probation.

Jefferson and I catch up to the tail end of the werewolves and I pat Ben on the shoulder.

"Ready for your checkup?" I ask, and Jefferson moves on to talk to another boy.

Ben's red in the face and still breathing hard. The front of his black hair is plastered to his forehead and when he tries to fix it, he ends up making it stick out in every direction. He smiles and heaves a little sigh before holding out his hand palm down.

"Sure thing," he says and waits.

I pull out my bio-mech scanner, that looks like little more than a handheld video game, from my jacket pocket and switch it on. Ben holds his hand steady while I scan the probation ring on his finger. The ring doesn't look like much but that's kind of the whole point. It's just an ordinary silver band until the bio-mech scanner does its thing. Then the whole band glows faintly blue while it transmits data to the scanner. Four seconds later and it's back to being a regular old ring. Ben lets his hand drop and gives me another smile but I'm paying attention to the readings on my scanner, not him. Data displays in a line graph and each spike shows when Ben has transformed. Today's transformation for the soccer game shows up in two sharp spikes—one for turning into a wolf, and one for turning back. The rest of the line is flat.

"How've you been, Ben?" I ask, eyes glued to the screen as I scroll back in time to the last time I tested his ring.

"I've been great!" he says enthusiastically and starts to stretch his arms. "School's fine, I'm fine. I've been wanting to go see a movie though."

I speed through the rest of the data and mark him as all clear. "Oh yeah?"

"Yeah, do you want to go?"

My mind draws a blank and I look up, finally finished with the probationary report. "Go where?"

"To a movie. With me."

"Sure. What movie, what time, and who else is going?"

His entire face turns the shade of my hair. "I meant, you and me. You with me."

"Yeah, I got that part. And who else is coming with?"

He runs a hand through the back of his hair and I frown at him, trying to figure out what his problem is. It takes me a moment before it clicks in my head. He's asking me on a date. Duh. Now *my* face flushes and I panic.

"I think I hear Jefferson calling me," I say in a rush and start jogging away. "Gotta go!"

Ben remains where he is as I flee. I'm such an idiot. Jefferson is already onto his second probation ring check when I slide to a stop next to him. Matt Jones keeps his hand steady for the check and gives me a curt nod—yet another werewolf that almost bit me. He's also the boy I punched on my first day at Moose Lake High School. Then he later tried to hit on me. Our standing relationship hasn't exactly been friendly and we tend to avoid each other to prevent awkward conversations. As soon as Jefferson gives him the okay, Matt hurries away.

"What's with you?" Jefferson says and gives me a once over.

"Nothing," I say a bit shrill, so I clear my throat. "Nothing at all. I'm as fantastic as a unicorn on a rainbow."

He raises an eyebrow. "You realize that's not a good thing, right? Unicorns hate rainbows."

"Oh, I know."

His eyes dart over my shoulder to Ben skulking away into the farmhouse. "What did you do now? Break that kid's heart?"

I lean back in shock. "What?"

"Don't play coy. That boy's been trying to hold your hand since you got to town." He shakes his head and studies some data on his scanner before continuing to mutter, "The number of times I've had to listen to Ashley fawn over his looks during your stupid werewolf Olympics . . ."

"Well, I ran away."

At that, he throws his head back and laughs. Something must occur to him, though, because he quickly stops and gives me a piercing stare. "He asked you out and you just ran?"

"I panicked!"

"You've faced down a berserker, a shapeshifter, a pack of werewolves, a deranged psychopath, and *now* you run? Mrs. Ferguson's going to filet you alive. And she was finally starting to be nice to all of us."

I throw up my hands. "What was I supposed to do?"

"How about not run away? You could have just said no." He pinches the bridge of his nose between his thumb and forefinger. "Okay, I'm probably going to regret asking this, but have you ever been in a relationship before? Aren't you teenagers always dating someone?"

Out of nowhere Hawk appears and throws his arm around my shoulders. "You kidding? Fifi here's never been on a date, unless you count that centaur from Ireland—"

I shove him away. "Shut up! That wasn't a date!"

He gives a bark of a laugh. "Well, what would you classify a night at the movies and dinner as?"

"A free movie ticket and free food," I say flatly. "I couldn't pass that up. And I'm not the one that kissed a water sprite—"

"*You* dared me to!"

Jefferson lets out a disgusted noise and starts to walk away. We jog after him to keep up and enter the farmhouse together. Hawk punches my shoulder and flees further into the house before I can hit him back. I lose him near the stairs as he slips between the werewolves crowded inside the house. Annoyed, I get back to work and move clockwise through the house scanning everyone with a ring on, which is just about every werewolf inside. After the fiasco with Dasc, the IMS wanted to keep a closer eye on those exposed to his powers of persuasion just to make sure there weren't any aftereffects. So far that doesn't seem to be the case.

When I turn a corner and bump into Jason, my hand instantly reaches around to the back of my waistband before the jolt of panic subsides. I let my hand slide off the handle of my mother's gun that I always carry now, and try to pass off the motion as if it was nothing. It's a reaction I don't seem to be able to control. Sure, Jason bit me but he wasn't in control then. He also attacked people at a high school dance while under Dasc's persuasion, but so did a lot of other people. He's the only one I react to like this, though.

I even out my breathing and urge my heart to stop racing. It's just Jason and just a stupid reaction. I force myself to look him in the eye. He's pale and seems to be getting paler all the time. Shadows paint the underside of his eyes and I swear he's wearing eyeliner to match his black wrist cuffs and shirt. I haven't really spoken to him since we bagged Dasc and no words come to mind now. Jason must feel the same because he doesn't say a word either.

Fortunately, Hawk materializes beside me and takes the scanner out of my hands. He gives me a knowing smile and nods, giving me the okay to leave the awkward encounter.

"Hey, Jason, time for your checkup," Hawk says and nudges me with his elbow so I back away and turn down the hall so I don't have to deal with Jason. Every time I do my probation rounds Hawk comes to my rescue and deals with Jason himself. He's been keeping a close eye on him ever since Jason bit me. I'm thankful for it.

A minute later, Hawk turns the corner and passes the scanner back with that same smile before slipping away to talk with some of his other friends. I heave a sigh and continue on, trying to clear the frustration from my mind.

I enter the living room where Mrs. Ferguson and Mr. Wick are watching the evening news. Some report about ships missing off the east coast has them glued to the screen. I knock lightly on the side of the television to get their attention and hold up the scanner.

Mrs. Ferguson gives a little dignified huff and her short curly hair wiggles side to side. She holds out her hand like a princess waiting for a knight to kiss the back of her hand. I try not to cringe as I scan the ring on her finger.

Trying to make polite conversation, I say, "You did some great goalie work out there today. Nice save against Matt earlier."

"Hmph. I still wasn't good enough to stop your brother." She lifts her chin.

"We'll have to work on that," I say and scan through her data quickly. "He's going to float away in a high wind if we don't deflate his ego."

"I appreciate all that you and your brother have done for my son. Truly."

For the first time she gives me a real, full on smile. My face flushes again. I appreciate the high praise but I can only imagine what her temper will be once she finds out I ran away from Ben, even though I'm sure I didn't "break his heart." He'll be fine, but Mrs. Ferguson's fury when it comes to someone messing with her son is terrifying.

"Thanks, Mrs. Ferguson. We do our best."

Just then Hawk reappears with an entourage. "Where's the food? I thought Ashley was supposed to be back an hour ago."

I shrug and walk casually over. "I'm sure she just got caught up shopping in Duluth. She's probably on her way back now." I'm only a foot away and while his guard's down I slug him in the shoulder. He topples to the side from the force of the blow and falls into a tangle on the sofa. I race back out of the house as fast as I can, laughing the whole way. I just manage to make it outside when he tackles me to the ground from behind. I throw out my hands and catch myself before I face plant in the snow.

"Truce! Truce!" I shout. Hawk's laughing and I'm laughing and a few others gather at the door cheering us on to fight. My brother tries to kick out the back of my knees to make me crumple. I go down on one knee, grab his arms, and yank us both hard to the side. We fall into the snow but I roll onto my stomach faster than he can get up and push a handful of snow into his face.

I jump away and shout, "Winner!"

A sweeping bow to the crowd gets everyone laughing, but then I get a big wet snowball to the back of the head and almost fall over again. Hawk caws and starts to charge again when Jefferson pushes his way through the crowd and gives us the stink eye.

"Come on, Phoenix," he growls. "We should get moving."

"All right, I'm coming, I'm coming." I evade Hawk's attempt to give me a noogie and trot after Jefferson to our black SUV covered in road salt.

"Have fun!" I shout over my shoulder. Hawk waves and disappears back inside with the others. Jefferson tosses the keys to me over the hood of the SUV and I catch them lightly before sliding into the driver's seat.

"Don't crash," Jefferson says, the same thing he says to me every time I drive, ever since his old truck turned into a wreck. I never say *I* wrecked it because it really wasn't my fault. I can blame that one on Dasc—one in a very long list—for sending a werewolf with a semi to turn me into roadkill.

The playfulness bleeds out of my bones and I change into a different person driving back to the Moose Lake Field Office. I don't let Hawk see this part of me. I can be regular old me with my brother but there's a dark shadow of a person in me now ever since I emptied a clip of bullets into a man's chest. Yes, he was a werewolf, the worst there is, but at that moment he was just a man. I shot to kill. I *meant* to kill him. Only Dasc, the first of all werewolves, could have managed to survive that many bullets coated in wolfsbane. It scares me what I did. Part of me is glad that it didn't work and he survived. The other part of me—well . . .

Jefferson knows. He's always known. He's always had that dark part, the void left in place of his family. He understands. He would have pulled that trigger a thousand times, and he's told me that, too, when he's found me sitting alone in the middle of the night cleaning my mother's gun, as if I could clean the shots I fired from my memory. *You stopped a monster*, he says. *You saved an entire city*. Then why do my hands shake when I hold a gun? I need to make it all worth it. I need to get answers from Dasc.

We make it home and I park outside the cabin. Together we trek through the half-foot of snow to the barn and Jefferson turns on the lights. The Green Monster remains dormant under its tarp to protect it from the salt and snow on the roads, like a bear in hibernation until spring comes. I move past it and take the stairs two at a time to the loft.

It's hard to remember when there were only bookshelves, a map on the wall, and a rough table. After our successful capture of Dasc, the IMS was in a generous mood and gave us a major technology overhaul. Jefferson finally insulated the walls, brought the electrical up to code, and then the IMS technicians came. The map of Moose Lake is now rolled up and gathering dust in a corner. In its place on the wall is a list of all those people still missing—Jefferson's daughter is at the top and not far below is Deputy Graham's sister. Next to that is a weapon rack, an ammo cache, and a mounted television. Jefferson turns the TV on to a news feed for background noise before settling in front of one of our two computers.

I take the swivel chair next to him at the other computer setup with two widescreen monitors. After logging into the IMS remote servers, I upload the probation ring data we collected at the farmhouse before moving on to what I really want to see. Witty's been emailing me constantly—because I harass him if he doesn't—with updates on Dasc's condition and ongoing interrogation. Today's email is thin with the same line he's been repeating for the last four weeks.

"Any change?" Jefferson asks, leaning back in his chair to see my screens.

I read off Witty's message in a dry monotone. "*Dasc is nearly recovered. Still refusing to talk. Will send another update in a few days.*"

"So another boatload of nothing."

"Yup. There's a P.S., though."

"Yeah?" Jefferson's eyes widen hopefully.

"Says, *No, you still can't come see him. Stop asking.* Real charmer, that Witty."

He sighs and raps his fingers on the arms of his swivel chair. "I guess we can't blame them for not letting us interrogate him ourselves. You tried to kill him. I *would* kill him."

"But answers first, right?"

"Right. Then I'd kill him."

We say it casually like we're discussing the weather or what we want for supper. We come off like we're joking but we're really not. I run a hand through my hair that's damp thanks to Hawk.

"Anything interesting in the feeds?" I ask to change the subject.

He shrugs and clicks through a few browser windows. "Not really, just some gossip from one of the teams afloat that got information on a possible leviathan sighting."

That certainly catches my attention. "Really?"

"Don't get so excited," he grouses. "They're baseless rumors. All the leviathans and a lot of other monsters died out hundreds of years ago, but every now and then people will claim they saw one of the old favorites. There was a story just last month where a senile retired agent claimed he saw a lamia—you know, one of those serpent-lady-demon-things—consorting with Big Foot in the sewers of Paris."

"Did they ever figure out what he really saw?"

"Turns out it was a regular human girl meeting up with a really hairy guy. And that leviathan sighting? It was probably a whale."

"Yeah, I guess you're right."

He gives me a sharp look. "Trust me, you wouldn't want those rumors to be true."

I shrug my shoulders and stand when my stomach rumbles.

"You want anything from the fridge?" I ask.

He shakes his head and starts typing away, intensely focused on his task. I know what he's doing but I don't say a word. Instead, I take the stairs and move into the cabin. The stacks of paper that once flooded the place are gone. The dinosaur of a computer that used to sit on the table is now a burned out hull on Jefferson's makeshift gun range. Once we had gotten the new computer equipment, we celebrated by smashing the old one to pieces and roasting marshmallows over the fire we set inside its corpse. That was a fun night. The kitchen is clean and tidy nowadays—thanks to yours truly.

I open the fridge and absently scan what's available. The beer bottles have been replaced with 12-packs of Dr. Pepper. Jefferson stopped drinking once Dasc was in custody and has been sober ever since. Soda and coffee fuel our work these days. I start inspecting a foam container of venison—the staple of our field office—when my phone buzzes in my pocket.

When I pull it out, Hawk's cross-eyed mug displays on my phone.

"Miss me already?" I say by way of greeting.

"Have you heard anything from Ashley?" he asks.

"She still hasn't shown up?"

"No, and she won't pick up for me. Maybe you'll have better luck."

I frown. "That's not like her. I'll give her a ring."

He hangs up and I dial Ashley's number, listening to it ring while I pick out my dinner. Eventually I get her voicemail. That's odd. She's normally glued to her phone and hates missing out on parties. For her to not show up is unthinkable. I dial again and then a third time until the line is finally picked up.

"Hello?" It's an unfamiliar male voice. "To whom am I speaking?"

Instantly suspicious and on the defensive, I say, "I could ask you the same thing."

"You came up as the I.C.E. contact when you called." There's a moment of silence. What, is he letting that sink in or something? Who the *pixies* is this? "Nosce te ipsum."

My training kicks in and the dinner I've picked out is quickly forgotten. *Nosce te ipsum* is the Latin code phrase used when IMS agents are trying to identify each other. It means "know thyself." The only reason this guy would know I'm an agent is if he knows Ashley is a werewolf because all werewolves must have an agent listed as their "in case of emergency" contact. But how would he know Ashley is a werewolf, unless . . . she transformed in front of him?

I respond with the appropriate phrase. "Timendi causa est nescire." *Ignorance is the cause of fear.*

"This is Junior Agent Charlie Jaeger," the male voice says. "We have your friend here in custody."

Oh, crap.

2

"Come again?" I say. "In custody? What's going on? Where is she? Is she okay?"

His irritated sigh issues through the phone. "Can I get your name?"

"Junior Agent Phoenix Mason. Moose Lake Field Office. Now, where is Ashley and what's going on?" My brain goes into overdrive. If Ashley has been taken into custody by other IMS agents, she must have done something seriously wrong. She was just supposed to be getting food for the party after shopping in Duluth. What kind of mess has she gotten herself into?

"Can I speak to your supervising agent?" the junior agent asks.

My anger is quick to flare. "How about I speak to *your* supervising agent. What field office are you with?"

"The one that doesn't care for conservations going in circles," he says dryly. A woman's voice reprimands him in the background, there's some shuffling, protests from the junior agent, and eventually a female comes on the line.

"Sorry about him. I'm the supervising agent for the Duluth Field Office." She has a distinct British accent that I'm not expecting. "We've got your girl in our office but she's not calming down. Maybe if she sees a familiar face she'll consent to transforming back. I'd rather not hit her with a bio-mech pulse or tranquilizer if I can help it."

"She wolfed out?" I clap a hand to my forehead.

"And ran like a lost husky through Canal Park during a busy shopping hour. Spare some time to come down here?"

Ashley was out in the open in wolf form during daylight in a populated area? This is bad. This is very bad.

"Of course," I say quickly. "We'll head up straight away."

"Ta!" she says and hangs up.

I stare at the phone a moment before running out to the barn. Jefferson is watching his computer screen intently but turns it off as soon as he sees me. There must be something of panic in my face because he practically launches out of his chair.

"It's Ashley," I say before he can ask what's wrong. "We've got a problem."

The second I finish relaying what I was told, Jefferson throws on his jacket and hustles down the stairs. We hop into the SUV, Jefferson takes the wheel, guns it, and I dial Hawk. He picks up on the first ring.

"You reach her?" he asks immediately. "We're starving here."

"Umm, yeah, slight change of plans. You need to man the field office until Jefferson and I get back. Ashley's been arrested and they need us to go up to Duluth to calm her down enough so she can shift. Oh, and she was running around in daylight as White Fang."

Silence follows, filled in only by muted voices in the background. I already know what he'll say next when he regains his composure so I cut him off before he has the chance.

"You can't come with, Hawk," I say. "We can't all go running off. Someone needs to stay behind."

"If they need someone to calm her down, I should be there."

"Hawk, don't you think *I* have the best chance of calming her down? I've got a little more in me than sassy remarks and movie quotes, remember?" We don't talk about it often, more to make sure it stays secret than anything else, but we all know it's there. The magic in my blood made me Dasc's target because what's in me has the potential to cure werewolves. Sure, it needs to mature like wine—or so I'm told—but ample power runs through my veins. I used it before to calm the frantic and anxious werewolves in school back when Dasc was using his own power to put them under his sway.

"Your magic doesn't make a frantic person calm," Hawk continues to argue.

"And what, that's your superpower? I'm her friend, too. I can get her to calm down. We'll be back soon enough. I'll keep you updated."

"You better," he says and hangs up.

I purse my lips and tuck my phone into my pocket. Jefferson gives me a sideways look.

"He'll be fine on his own?" he asks.

I know he's asking about more than being left behind. I'm also the thing that keeps Hawk from going dark side. We've been stretching the limits of how far and how long we can be apart before his werewolf instincts really kick in. Hawk can handle being on his own for stretches of time. Jefferson's been keeping a close eye on our progress.

"He's fine," I assure him and focus on the road, worrying my lower lip.

We reach the interstate and journey northeast to Duluth on icy roads. It grows dark and the headlights pierce through the evening gloom. I stare mindlessly out the windshield. This sort of thing wouldn't have even happened if I could just cure werewolves now. I can tame and diminish the strength of the magical disease in their blood but I haven't been able to rid them of it yet. We gave samples of my blood to Jefferson's expert but the only word I've gotten on progress towards a cure is Jefferson telling me it'll take time. How much time? I have no idea and it drives me crazy.

Exit ramps flash by to cities I can't make out from the interstate. Half an hour passes and the SUV begins to climb hills until we finally reach civilization again. We crest the final hill and the view takes my breath away. A city of lights stretches out below us from the ice covered shores of Lake Superior to the heights of the hills to the northwest. Across the harbor and river, the lights of Superior in Wisconsin twinkle in competition. I haven't been in what I would consider a big city since my time living in Minneapolis before I moved to Moose Lake. Hawk and I haven't traveled much at all. Now the streetlights, tall buildings, and packed in suburbs feel like returning to my past.

The SUV curves along the side of the hill, making its way slowly down until we enter a twisty maze of bridges and roads. Factories, mills, and huge mounds of minerals line the shore on our right but to the left are retail shops, big box stores, supermarkets, and tightly packed in residential neighborhoods. We wind through traffic until Jefferson takes an exit on our right, and we enter an industrial area. Warehouses box us in until we're practically at the lake's edge.

Jefferson stops in front of a nondescript building with commercial red siding and hardly any windows. It's at least double the size of Jefferson's barn, boasts a heavy-duty steel door, and has a down sloping ramp that leads to a pair of closed garage doors.

"This is their field office?" I ask, peering up through the windshield at the array of antennas on the roof.

"No, I just stopped here because I like the color," Jefferson says gruffly and gets out.

I sigh and follow after him. Hawk and I haven't managed to smooth out Jefferson's grouchy sass since we met. Not that we've really tried. It adds to his charm.

We stop beneath a floodlight outside the building's front door. Jefferson buzzes the doorbell and we wait.

"Do you know them?" I ask offhand.

"Not really. You've meet them already, though."

"I have?"

He rubs his hands together. "They were some of the agents that showed up to pull our butts out of the fire when we took down Dasc."

"Oh. I didn't know," is all I can say. You think I'd remember someone as rude as Junior Agent Jaeger. Granted,

I didn't really chat with many of the agents that showed up that night. I was exhausted and out of it at the time. Being in a car crash and fighting for your life the rest of the night tends to have that effect.

The door finally opens and a woman stands in the way. My first impression of her is a safari guide like from the movies. She's wearing tall brown boots, khakis, a matching shirt, and brown leather jacket. All she's missing is one of those round kaki hats. Her curly blonde hair is tied loosely in a ponytail and stray wisps frame her sharp brown eyes. Built taller than both me and Jefferson, she makes an imposing figure.

"Can I help you two?" she asks. "It's a little late to be sniffing around the warehouses."

"We're here for Ashley," I say.

Her face brightens into a smile and she grasps my hand to shake it. "Just had to make sure. We have some random gents show up now and again. Junior Agent Mason, I presume?"

"That's me."

Jefferson leans in to make himself known. "Agent Jefferson Barnes."

"Welcome, welcome. Do come in," she says and steps aside to allow us entrance before shutting the door behind us.

The Duluth Field Office looks like an average living space with off-white plaster walls, an open kitchen, and dining area. It's all one big room that looks out at the lake through tinted windows. It's quaint.

The woman that let us in stands with her hands clasped behind her back next to the kitchen counter nearest us. "I'm Agent Melody Boyd, the supervising agent of this field office. If you'll follow me, I'll take you to Ashley."

She trots down stairs against the right wall and we follow. The lower level changes into something reminiscent of the armory in Underground. The off-white walls are replaced with light gray and imbedded with blue LED lights to outline the massive room we enter. There's a stand of computers back to back in the center, then numerous weapons on display along the walls next to mounted televisions and metal cabinets. It makes Jefferson's loft look like, well, a barn. We pass through the main room into a hallway with a couple of closed doors that I assume could be living quarters, an open door to the garage where several SUVs sit, and to the last door at the end of the hallway with bars on its single window. That gives me a bad feeling straightaway. Waiting just outside the door is a man I can only presume is Charlie.

"This is Junior Agent Charlie Jaeger," Melody says and introduces us.

He's taller than I'm expecting, as in at least six feet tall, and better looking, too. Part of me associates a bad attitude with a face to match when I hear someone over the phone. He should be more crone-like, sneering, wretched, and smelly. Instead he's got intense green eyes, charming freckles, a face out of a magazine, and hair that can't decide if it's really blonde or brunette styled short and fluffed up on top. He's got sharp fashion sense too, to the point I almost feel shabby by comparison—corduroy jeans, a white button down shirt rolled to the elbows and a dark blue suit vest. He's handsome. It makes me angry.

He cocks his head to the side as he sizes me up. "Finally come to grace us with your presence?"

"Charlie," Melody sighs.

I glare at him and push past to open the door. The inside is basically a cement cell with brackets on the walls where I suppose chains could be linked to hold down monsters. And huddled in the corner shaking and letting out the weirdest sort of whine is a wolf. Its muzzle turns towards me and great big tears roll down its furry cheeks. When Ashley the wolf sees me, she lets out a keen howl.

"Ash, what did you get yourself into?" I say and go to kneel beside her. Her whole body is shaking so I put both hands on her shoulders to hold her steady. "You gotta calm down, okay? We can't help you like this."

"You sure that's safe?" Charlie asks from the doorway.

I throw him a dark look over my shoulder. "She's under the serum. She's not going to bite me."

He holds up his hands with a sarcastic smile. "Well, as long as you're sure. Shall I put your doctor on hold while we wait?"

Melody smacks him upside the head so he gives her a dark look but finally shuts up. With him quiet I can finally focus all of my attention on Ashley. I want her to stop shaking and be okay. I will that urge to protect my friend to pulse off my skin. Her shakes slow until she simply sits there breathing deeply in and out. Hawk was right, though. It's not enough. Now I need to be her friend.

"I'm going to protect you, Ash," I say with as much confidence as I can muster. "It's going to be all right. You believe me, don't you? You know I'll stick up for you. Remember when I punched Matt for picking on you and your friends? I won't let you down."

At that Ashley nods and signals with one paw for me to move back. I get up and give her space. She crouches and lets out a low whine as her body changes shape and the fur recedes until she's a human again on all fours. Her winter jacket is muddy and when she inspects her soiled superhero shirt, she lets out a soft cry. I quickly give her a hand up. As soon as she's on her feet she gives me a bone-breaking hug and starts sobbing in earnest. I pat her back awkwardly as the other three look on.

"It'll be okay," I try to reassure her. "Just tell us what happened."

She pulls back and takes several long, shaky breaths until she stops crying. She runs a hand over her disarrayed hair then grasps my upper arms, her eyes wide.

"I was attacked, Phoenix," she says dramatically.

"Attacked?" I glance to the others and they all seem to be paying much keener attention. "Attacked by who?"

"Not a *who*. A *what*."

"Come again?"

"It was a—a *vampire*."

There's a loud sigh from the back of the room, its source none other than Charlie. "Oh, for crying out loud—"

"You got a problem?" I snap.

He gestures to Ashley, whose grip on my arms is starting to hurt. "Come on, she's got *Love Moon* fan girl written all over her. She saw what she wanted to see or she's making up a story to cover for wolfing out in public."

"You calling her a liar?" I step away from Ashley, and both Charlie and I start closing the distance between each other. My hands curl into fists and I see Jefferson tense to the side.

"There hasn't been a vampire in Minnesota for fifty years," he counters. "Try Wisconsin, but not here. Minnesota is werewolf territory. They don't mix and match."

"Oh, that's funny. I must have imagined that shapeshifter working under a werewolf's orders in Moose Lake then. They *do* mix."

"That's different. Apples and oranges."

"Why the *flaming hydra dung* are we talking about fruit now!" I shout.

"Enough!" Melody slaps a hand on the metal door and the loud reverberation startles us both into silence. She glares at us and moves to place a hand on Ashley's shoulder. "Where and how were you attacked, Ashley?"

Ashley runs a hand under the edge of her nose, her eyes darting between all of us. "Canal Park. I was heading between some of the restaurants when I was jumped by a vampire."

"What did it look like?"

"Pale. Really pale. Sharp teeth. Weird eyes. When he tried to grab me I panicked. I didn't mean to transform, I promise!"

We IMS agents share looks—actually, I avoid Charlie's gaze completely—because Ashley has roughly described your typical vampire—pale, sharp incisors, bloodshot eyes, ragged. Vampires usually don't feed off people with any type of magic though, diseased or regular. It's like playing Russian roulette. Maybe they get a high off the magic in the blood, or maybe their head explodes. Every person's magic is different and affects vampires differently, but usually their heads just explode. It's not pretty so they usually aren't dumb enough to try it.

"And then what happened?" Melody says, her voice soft and comforting. I determine I really like Melody and really don't like Charlie. How on earth do they stand to work together?

"I wolfed out." Ashley sniffles. "I don't really remember what happened next. I ran and kept running. I don't think the vampire tried to follow me."

"Yeah, well," Charlie says in that same sarcastic tone. "Once this vamp figured out dinner wasn't quite the treat he thought, he probably thought better than to run after you. That, or there wasn't a vampire at all."

I'm inclined to start another argument, and Jefferson must sense that, too, because he quickly puts a hand on my shoulder and says, "Why don't we go back to the scene? We should figure out what exactly we're dealing with here. Ashley can show us where she was attacked."

She nods, but her fingers knead the bottom of her shirt anxiously. Melody agrees and leads Ashley out of the room. Charlie and I hang back a second longer to glare at each other before following after behind Jefferson. While everyone moves into the garage to hop into one of the Duluth team's black SUVs, my phone buzzes in my pocket. Hawk's mug displays on the screen.

"Hey, what's going on?" he asks the second I pick up.

"Ashley's fine, for the moment," I say. "She says she was attacked by a vampire so we're going to check it out. I'll call when I know more."

"Are they going to be pressing any charges?" he asks.

I glance at everyone waiting in the car for me. Charlie gives me the stink eye before looking away. "I don't know. I'll call you back," I say and hang up before he can keep pestering me. I don't have anything for him, despite how much I'd like to.

I hop into the second row seat next to Ashley and Jefferson while Melody takes the wheel and Charlie sits shotgun. The garage door lifts and we pull out into the dark wintery night. Ashley fidgets constantly next to me so I pat her awkwardly on the shoulder. I'm not so great with words of comfort, not like my brother, so I don't say anything at all. We wind down a road alongside the interstate, passing warehouses and shipping yards, an aquarium, a huge convention complex, and some old ship docked as a museum until we turn into a stretch of shops and restaurants that line the road all the way to a massive lift bridge.

"Well, this is Canal Park," Melody says from the front and signals a right turn to join the throng of creeping traffic. It's crammed here. Must be a hot spot. "Which way, Ashley?"

"Up on the right in a couple of blocks," she says subdued. "Near the Blue Comet."

"That's a nightclub," Charlie says. "Aren't you underage?"

"I wasn't *in* the Blue Comet," Ashley shoots back defensively. "I was walking down the alleyway to the parking lot. I *had* been at the Chocolate Factory." She stares down at her hands morosely and says in a sad undertone. "It was delicious."

The SUV moves an inch at a time in the traffic. If I didn't know any better, I'd say we were in rush hour traffic in Minneapolis. This is ridiculous.

"I could walk there faster," I say.

"Want to grab me a coffee while you're at it?" Jefferson grumbles.

I keep a hand on the handle of the door, ready to hop out as soon as possible. Cars fill every parking spot, people walk in groups on the sidewalks laughing and talking, stores display bright signs and throw out welcoming warm light. Ahead in the distance, beneath a neon sign that proclaims

Blue Comet, a lady stands holding a mic in front of a video camera held by a squat man.

"Reporter," Charlie says and points out the window. "Who's ready for their fifteen minutes of fame?"

Before waiting for permission, I throw open the door and hop out. I try to blend in with the crowds and come up behind the reporter and cameraman along with a group of other onlookers. The next second Charlie is there, an arm stretched out in front of me.

"And where are you going?" he asks casually and looks down his nose at me.

I shove his arm away harder than I mean to and he stumbles to the side. When he straightens his look changes from condescending to surprised and wary. Yeah, that's right. I've got power in my veins. Don't underestimate me.

"I'm going to listen to the report," I growl. "I'm not a rampaging berserker, you know."

"That's debatable," he says under his breath.

Instead of arguing, we both stop and listen as the reporter starts to talk.

"That's right, Jim," she says, flashing brilliant white teeth. "Locals reported seeing what appeared to be a timber wolf running behind the shops here in Canal Park. At first glance a few thought it was a dog that had gotten loose from its owner but it was confirmed to be a wolf after reviewing footage taken by an eyewitness. I'm here with Kevin Rogers who managed to capture the sighting on his phone. Mr. Rogers, in your own words, what did you witness tonight?"

"Oh, *sweet piping Pan,*" I mutter under my breath. If they had actual footage of Ashley turning—

A lanky teenager wearing just a ragged hoodie despite the temperature eases into the spotlight with a goofy grin, waving at the camera like a fool.

"Hi, mom!" he says. As far as introductions go for your first time on camera, I think he hits the top of the stupid list. "Yeah, so, like, I was just hanging with my buddies and I saw this huge thing out of the corner of my eye. I thought it was a pitbull or something. I started following at the other end of the alleyway here—" He saw a possibly dangerous dog and decided to follow it? Moron. "—and it stopped and looked straight at me. I pulled out my phone and started recording because it was a *wolf*. No lie!"

"And there you have it," the reporter says to draw the attention back to herself. "Authorities have not been able to locate the animal and commented this is very unusual behavior for wolves who tend to shy away from human contact—"

She drones on but it's clear no one actually saw Ashley change—well, except for the vampire. And why was a vampire here in the first place? On top of being out where it could be seen, it attacked someone in a very busy part of town? Was everyone drinking a glass of stupid here?

"I'm going for that alley," I say. "You're welcome to try and stop—"

Charlie isn't there. I glance around and spot him already receding into the shadows of the alleyway. How did he get there so fast? I push my way through the crowd, bypass the reporter, and jog into the alley after him. Steam issues from the restaurant on the right and billows in the cramped space shared by dumpsters and recycle bins. A cold breeze off the lake scoops up the foul odor of the trash and carries it away.

Next to the last dumpster at the end of the alley I find Charlie kneeling on the ground, a massive purse in his hands.

"Uh, what are you doing?" I ask.

Instead of answering, he pulls from the depths of the purse a long, glossy looking wrap the color of ash. The more he hauls it up, the less like cloth it appears to be. The light from the restaurant's floodlight catches it and I realize it's not cloth at all. It's *skin*. The skin from a seal to be more precise. I know exactly what that is.

"There might not have been a vampire here," Charlie says and heaves a heavy sigh. "But there was definitely a selkie."

3

At the word "selkie," all the facts I know about them pop into my mind like hits from a web search.

Selkie—a seal that sheds its skin to become human, then puts that same skin on again to transform back. They come mainly from Scotland and Ireland, and it's a rare occurrence to see one in the States. Take a selkie's skin and they can't transform back. People have stolen skins before as blackmail to keep a selkie under their control, so selkies guard the skins with their lives. Finding one here must mean there's a selkie nearby.

"But . . ." My brain comes to a stop when I put that knowledge in context with what's before me. "A selkie wouldn't attack Ashley. They're not monsters, and they don't look like vampires."

"I know that," Charlie says irritably. "But whoever this belongs to probably knows something about what happened. I'm not buying it as a coincidence that there was an attack and a selkie skin in the same alleyway. This is the most solid lead we have. I'll believe a selkie was here but I'm still holding off on accepting a vampire was waltzing around in the middle of a busy city hub."

"But Ashley—"

"Wouldn't be able to tell the difference between a stranger accosting her in an alleyway and a freakin' movie star painted with glitter." He gestures between the pair of us. "*We* have training. We can tell what's what. She doesn't. She saw what she *wanted* to see."

"Why would anyone *want* to see a vampire in an alleyway as opposed to a regular guy?"

He nods thoughtfully, a rueful look on his face. "You know, I've been asking myself the same question ever since Anne Rice starting writing vampire novels."

"Who?"

He rolls his eyes. "Forget it. We still have to figure out who this skin belongs to and why they dumped it in an alley. A selkie would never do that."

I don't want to admit it but he's right. Even if it wasn't a selkie that attacked Ashley—and it's highly unlikely that one did—maybe the selkie saw what happened, or knows where we might find that vampire. The fact we found a skin just lying around is a very bad sign.

Charlie tucks the skin back into the purse, stands, and shoves the bag into my hands.

"Carry this," he orders and stalks out of the alleyway.

"Why can't *you* carry this?" I snap back. I've known Charlie for less than an hour and my automatic response is already to start an argument with him.

"Seriously?" he calls back without stopping. "*I'm* not going to carry a purse."

I sling the strap over my shoulder and clutch it tight to my side. I'm not going to be the one to lose something this precious.

The reporter and cameraman are packing up so the crowd is quick to disperse now that the camera's off. Charlie walks back to the street and hails Melody who is on foot on the sidewalk. There's no sign of Jefferson, Ashley, or the SUV anymore. The three of us meet outside the entrance to the nightclub.

"Ashley freaked out after she saw the reporter here," she explains. "Jefferson's trying to calm her down, but she's in a right state. I need to drop them off so they can wait at our office until we're done here. Did you two find anything?"

I hold out the purse. Melody discreetly examines the contents and purses her lips. She and Charlie share a look that is a conversation all on its own. Melody stares him down and he goes from angry to irritated to resigned.

"Okay, fine," he says without any context at all. "I'll go."

"Good," Melody says and smiles.

I hold up my hand to get their attention. "Sorry, what just happened?"

Melody passes the purse to Charlie who promptly shoves it into my arms again. He huffs and explains in an undertone, "A group of selkies came to town on one of the salties at the beginning of fall and they tend to hang out at the Blue Comet."

"Saltie?" I interrupt.

"Ocean-faring vessel. Selkies would never come this way by plane so they rode through the St. Lawrence Seaway, across the Great Lakes, and parked in Duluth," he rolls off then continues as if I hadn't said a word. "But Melody and the selkies don't exactly get along—"

"Threatening to skin one alive tends to elicit that sort of reaction," she comments offhand. "But they just *love* Charlie, don't they?" She gives him a crooked smile and he goes rigid. "They'll talk to him but they won't even let me in the club. Phoenix, why don't you go with him and see if they know who this skin belongs to?"

"What?" Charlie and I protest at the same time. We glance at each other before avoiding any more eye contact.

"You could use more hands-on experience, Phoenix," she says. "And Charlie could use some backup."

"I don't need help," he says flatly.

Melody tosses her hair back. "Just like you didn't need a hand when one tried to drag you into the lake with her?"

His face turns brilliant red and he stalks away into the Blue Comet without another word. Melody shoos me after him.

"Well, go on then!" she says and pushes me towards the door.

I swing the purse onto my shoulder and push in the black door Charlie disappeared through. The wintery chill outside disappears into heat and a thick atmosphere inside. A neon sign above my head announces Blue Comet with a flashing picture of an actual comet below. The walls are black but decorated with florescent splashes of orange, green, and blue. Black lights overhead turn the paint vibrant. The air is heavy with the smell of sweat, cheap cologne, and alcohol. I walk carefully down the short entrance and into a large room pulsing to a techno beat. Flashing strobe lights make my head dizzy and I pause on the edge of the dancers filling up every crevice of the club.

A hand lands on my shoulder and I flinch away, spinning about to grab the person's wrist before they can make another move.

Charlie jerks his arm out of my grip with a grimace and shakes out his hand. "Nice reflexes, psycho. Come on, it's this way."

He pushes through the dancers, past a bar with an illuminated glass countertop, and to another black door hardly visible in the far wall. A huge man larger than the door itself stands before it, arms crossed, tattoos up and down his forearms, no neck, no hair, and a massive jaw. I don't see any tusks poking out between his lips, otherwise I would think he's a troll.

"Heya, Quincy!" Charlie says with a wide smile and smacks the big guy on the arm.

The guy doesn't move an inch but his tiny eyes narrow on Charlie who, despite being tall himself, is at least a foot shorter than him. "Charlie," he says with no inflection whatsoever. "The girls have missed you."

Charlie's smile never dims but his face turns a brighter shade of red. He shrugs like it's no big deal but there's a bit of a twitch in his left eye as big-man-Quincy lets Charlie through. I make to follow after but find an arm the size of a tree trunk blocking my path.

Quincy squints down his thick nose at me. "Who are you?"

"She's with me," Charlie says and pushes the huge arm out of the way. He grabs my shoulder and starts tugging me down a flight of steps before there's any argument. As soon as the door shuts behind us the stairwell becomes dead silent except for the clunk of our shoes on the metal steps. I look back and see a flickering blue, transparent light covering the door like some kind of florescent plastic wrap.

"There's a dragon's barrier on the door?" I ask, surprised. "For a place like this?"

"Yeah, duh. When there's a dragon around they like to put up barriers."

I pause on the steps and brace a hand on the wall. "There's a *dragon* here?"

Charlie stops and turns about to face me a few steps down. "Did I stutter? Pretty sure there's been one in the area for a while now."

My jaw pops as I shift it back and forth. "Okay, what's your problem with me? Stop dancing around whatever it is and just spit it out, will you?"

We both remain where we are, glaring each other down. He half turns like he's about to ignore the question and keep walking, but apparently changes his mind and charges up the steps. He stops directly below me and puts his hands on both walls, leaning in so much I'm forced to tilt back. Despite myself, I actually find him sort of intimidating.

"When I first told you Ashley was under arrest," he says in a low, very serious tone, "your only concern was what had happened to *her*."

"Is that supposed to be a bad thing?"

"The first thing that pops to mind when I hear someone is arrested is *who did they hurt?* We don't arrest werewolves because someone hurt *them*. You never even bothered to consider potential victims. She's a werewolf, Mason. Part of them is human, sure, but part of them will always be an animal, no matter how much serum you pump into them."

I open my mouth to argue but he cuts me off before I even get the chance.

"Before you try and tell me that's not what happened tonight," he says, his eyes dark and dangerous, "let me tell you something you should try and remember. Werewolves never want to be exposed. What happened with Ashley was a fluke accident. They normally guard themselves so well that exposure is a nonissue. Ninety-five percent of all werewolf arrests are because they bite someone. Whose defense should you really be jumping to?"

The words to defend my actions fall flat in my mouth. I went to Ashley's defense because she's my friend. Innocent before proven guilty, right? But if she hadn't been my friend, then would my first thought be about the safety of others? Have I gotten too close to the issue to be able to see objectively? Granted, I don't know if I've ever been able to. If it had been Hawk in Ashley's place today, I would have already broken him out of custody and not listened to a word from Charlie or Melody. What kind of IMS agent does that make me?

Charlie finally pulls away and continues down the stairs. I follow after with lead feet, considering what he said. I wonder if he took my defensive attitude about Ashley so strongly because he's been affected personally by something of the same nature. Maybe someone he cared about had been a victim of a werewolf or monster before. Everyone gets into the business somehow, right? If it hadn't been for my own parents being murdered by a werewolf, I might not be where I am today.

The stairs continue for three floors until I hear music coming from below and we arrive at another black door.

Charlie yanks it open, clearly ready to get away from me, and reveals a rather different scene from the one upstairs.

The walls inside are made completely of aquariums but no aquariums I've ever seen. There are no fish or sea critters inside but different colors of water swirling through the thin panes. Regular people have a miniature version of these—what are they called . . . *lava lamps*. Right, like giant thin lava lamps of bright red, blue, green, purple, and orange water slipping past and around each other in endless loops. Concrete channels crisscross the room and flow with the same water creating vivid streams between the feet of the people inside. The lighting is low and I almost stumble on a boulder sticking out of the floor. There are larger ones like it around the room used as chairs. It would be almost beach like if not for the bizarre water.

Women—tall, tan, athletic, and beautiful—are having drinks and dancing to a mellow techno-beat laced with the sound of waves and seagulls. Even though it's winter outside, they're all wearing short skirts and tank tops with sequins. I note no one except me and Charlie are wearing shoes. My winter jacket is becoming unbearably warm so I quickly unzip it to air myself out.

"Stay close," Charlie warns. "They tend to get a little competitive with other women."

I snort. "I can handle myself."

"Trust me, they—"

"No, trust *me*."

He rolls his eyes. "Whatever."

We move forward together and the second the dancing women spot Charlie, they smile and rush over like he's a long lost best friend. He holds out his hands to try and keep them back but they're running their hands through his hair, touching his arms, trying to hug him, and eventually start dragging him over to a rock in the middle of the room. They forcefully set him down and corral him so he can't get up any more. He tries to keep up a cocky pretense but his face is flushed and there's desperation in his eyes. The whole thing makes me uncomfortable but I also have to bite my lip to keep from laughing.

"Ladies, ladies!" Charlie shouts over the music. "Please, I'm on business."

"But yer always on business!" a particularly tall blonde croons in a heavy Scottish accent. "Don't you ever just come for comfort?"

I've heard stories of selkies being seductive but this is just ridiculous. They're throwing themselves at him. It's then I realize he's also the only guy in the room. Even the DJ in the back is a woman wearing a backwards ball cap. I guess it's a good thing they don't hang around in the general public, for everyone's sake.

"I need to ask you a few questions," Charlie continues, trying to talk around a selkie stroking the side of his face.

"You can ask us *anything*, Hunter."

Hunter? I think it's a pet name or something before it dawns on me. I almost forgot Charlie's last name is Jaeger, German for hunter. I've heard that name before. There's a famous IMS agent with the last name Jaeger but a lot of people just refer to him as the Hunter. It can't be Charlie himself, of course. The Hunter is no junior agent and I've heard stories about him for a while. Charlie could be related though.

"Is anyone missing from your party?" he asks, and startles when the blonde plants a kiss on his check.

"Well, you are every night," she says and gives him a wide smile.

Oh, for the love of—this is getting old *really* fast. I can't take this anymore. I swing around the purse and haul out the selkie skin, holding it high so everyone in the room can see it.

"I think one of you left your pajamas outside," I say loudly.

The music screeches to a halt and everyone falls silent. All eyes turn to me. The women in the room don't look even remotely friendly now. Maybe I should have heeded Charlie's warning. I clench my jaw and hold my ground against the burning glares I receive from every corner of the room. Then from the very back someone bursts out in laughter. The angry eyes veer and bodies part so I can see a single girl with black hair that falls to her waist. Her head is thrown back and she's holding her stomach she's laughing so hard.

"Shut up, mercow!" the blonde next to Charlie shouts.

Mercow? I look at the black-haired girl's feet and realize there's webbing between her toes. Selkies don't have that feature when they shed their skin. The girl must be a mermaid, transformed. Oh, boy. Selkies and mermaids have some of the worst love-hate relationships known to the legendary community. Getting in the middle of one of their fights is the last thing I want to do. They've been known to haul people into the ocean for interrupting their spats. You'd think they can't stand the sight of each other, and yet for some reason they always hang out together.

The blonde spins about on me. I'm getting the impression she's the leader around here.

"Where did you get that?" she hisses.

"Do you recognize it?"

"Answer the question!"

She's still got a hand on Charlie's shoulder and he's wincing like she's squeezing the life out of him.

"Answer mine first, and then I'll answer yours," I say. "Official IMS business."

The blonde smiles sweetly and finally lets go of Charlie, who starts rubbing his shoulder, then stalks towards me. I lower the skin into the purse and hold it between us. She's a good half-foot taller than me, gorgeous hair, long legs—a super model basically. Nothing like a good blow to the self-esteem when trying to be tough. She suddenly grabs the purse and tries to wrench it out of my grip. I hold on and can hear the fabric start to rip as it's pulled in two different directions.

"I don't think so," I growl. I grab her wrist to wrench her forward and hook my foot around the back of her knee. Unfortunately for me, she does the exact same thing at the same time. We both pull and twist in unison and crumple in on each other, landing in a heap on the floor with the purse between us. No one moves to stop us. Everyone just watches.

"Bad move, Mason!" Charlie shouts.

She snaps a blade hand at my throat but I block with my forearm and shove her off. The blonde tries to roll away with the purse but I snag the strap to wrench it towards me. She plants a foot on my chest and pushes hard. The purse rips in two. The skin falls in a lump onto the floor. Again she lunges for it but I send a well-aimed kick into her shoulder to throw her onto her back. I catch the edge of the skin with the toe of my shoe, fling it upwards, and tumble roll backwards to catch it before it lands on the floor again. I have a fleeting moment of triumph. Unfortunately, that leaves me wide open, one hand stretched up in the air with the skin and the other keeping me balanced on the ground. A bare foot meets the side of my face. Pain shocks through my cheekbones, nose, and teeth and I fall backwards. Miraculously, I still manage to clutch the skin to my chest, keeping it away from the blonde.

I roll out of the way of her next kick coming for my gut and come up on one knee. My entire face pulses and I taste blood in my mouth.

"Not cool!" I shout.

I've been holding back, it's true. I didn't plan on getting into a fight with a selkie, but now she's ticked me off and has assaulted an agent. We both rise to our feet. I hold the bundle of skin and wait for her to make a move. She shifts back and forth on the balls of her feet.

"You really don't want to do this," I warn. "But take your best shot if you're stupid enough."

She leaps, twists in a perfect circle, and her foot comes flying at me in a roundhouse kick. I drop the skin, grab her foot, and effectively drop her face first onto the floor. I keep my hold on her foot and maneuver to put my knee in the middle of her back to pin her to the floor. My other hand grabs her arm to keep her immobile.

"Will you knock it off?" I say. She tries to wiggle out of my hold but my magical strength doesn't allow her to move an inch. "I'm not giving this skin up until I know whose it is. A friend of mine was attacked tonight and whoever that skin belongs to was either involved or a witness. Now you can either help me, or you can drool on the floor until you change your mind. Any questions?"

"Just one," she wheezes, my knee in her back not allowing her a good full breath. "Ye'll give the skin back once I tell ye?"

"I'll give it back to who it belongs, not just anyone. I know the power of a selkie skin. I don't want it falling into hands that'll abuse it."

"Then let me up."

I release my hold and stand. When she rolls onto her back I offer her a hand but she ignores the gesture and gets up on her own.

The mood in the room is drastically different from when we first arrived and the selkies all but ignore Charlie now. He and I follow the blonde to a glass bar along the back of the room where the mermaid that laughed before is sitting. I brush away a trickle of blood coming out of my nose with the back of my hand.

"Thanks for the help," I grumble to Charlie.

"Oh, you clearly had it sorted. My common sense and rationality would have only gotten in the way."

Right, ha-ha, what a charmer. "You freakin' unicorn."

"Berserker."

The blonde snaps her fingers to get our attention and motions to the bartender who sets down three glasses of something dark blue in front of us along with two bags of ice. The blonde downs her drink in one go and presses the ice to the side of her face. I ignore the drink but take the ice and hold it against my throbbing cheek.

"That was some fighting back there," the blonde says. "I'm impressed. What's yer name?"

Now she's impressed? I could have sworn she was furious. "Junior Agent Phoenix Mason."

"You can call me Nessa."

Charlie downs his drink and leans one elbow on the countertop. "What can you tell us about that skin, Nessa?"

She sighs and motions for another drink. "Nothing good, I'm afraid. It belongs to my sister Gillian."

"Do you know where she is now?" I ask.

"She was supposed to meet us here tonight and hasn't showed." Nessa leans in towards us, her dark eyes fierce. "You said yer friend was attacked. Attacked by what?"

"A vampire," I say.

"Or so she thinks," Charlie interrupts.

The selkie laughs and the mermaid behind her joins in. They give each other sharp looks and stop instantly. Nessa flips her hair and turns back to us, giving the mermaid the cold shoulder.

"My sister wouldn't be taken down by a wee whelp the likes of a vampire. We're fighters. We're protectors."

She quickly asks for another drink and keeps her eyes down this time. There's something about the way she says protectors that sounds defensive.

"Are you protecting someone, or something, now?" I ask.

This earns me her best glare yet. "Ye ought to know better than to ask me that. I'd never give up information so private."

Huh. Okay. I consider the dragon's barrier at the door upstairs. A barrier like that is uncommon and very unusual for a place like this. Could the selkies be here protecting a dragon? Granted, dragons don't really need protection. They're the most powerful magical beings on the planet—

well, usually. Hydra are nasty pieces of work that come close to the strength of majestic class dragons. Is there a dragon in this room right now? My eyes scan the women chatting and dancing in groups to a soft melody in the background. I espy more mermaid webbed feet and catch the Scottish accents of the selkies. No one sticks out in this crowd as a dragon in disguise.

"I'm sorry for the way I reacted," Nessa continues, her tone losing its hard edge. "I know it wasn't proper, attacking an agent and all. But it's my sister's. That's the strongest and weakest part of her. I couldn't have it in another person's hands, especially not a stranger. Are you going to press charges? Send me to the penitent cells?"

She waits calmly for an answer. Clearly the threat of the penitent cells doesn't faze her much, but she's put the decision in my hands. Charlie glances between us and his lips part. I cut him off before he can pronounce judgment on my behalf.

"If it were my family," I say, "I would have done the same. I *have* done the same. I want to help find your sister and figure out what happened in that alley. If I leave the skin in your care, will you agree to help our investigation however you can?"

Her lips curl into a smile and she extends her hand. "Aye. I'll abide to it."

"Then you'll be hearing from us. Call if you hear anything or if Gillian shows up."

I give her hand a good shake and pass the skin over. She folds it neatly and sets it in her lap.

The selkies and mermaids part to let us leave. Charlie and I walk silently side by side back up the stairs, through the noisy club, and into the cold outside. A light snow is beginning to fall illuminated by the warm light of the street lamps.

"I'll have to tell Melody what happened, you know," Charlie says. "That decision not to press charges wasn't yours to make."

"Do whatever you want," I grumble.

We trudge along the sidewalk until Melody flags us down from the SUV having returned from dropping Jefferson and Ashley off at the field office. The second we get into the car, Charlie explains what happened in the Blue Comet and doesn't hold back on the details. Both of them give me looks in the rearview mirror.

"But Nessa agreed to help?" Melody asks.

"Yeah, but—"

"Leave it," she warns. "If they don't want to make an issue out of it then neither should we. I don't blame her for trying to start a fight over that skin either. You have no idea how touchy they are about that sort of thing."

I lean forward from the backseat. "Do you know who those selkies are protecting here in Duluth?"

"Does it matter?" Charlie says. We enter the dark area of the docks so I can't see his expression but I'm sure it'd be sour if I could.

My fingers dig into the edge of the seat and the fabric almost starts to tear. "Do you really think it's a coincidence there was an attack right outside the club where a group of selkies were? A group possibly protecting someone or something? What if the attack wasn't random? What if that vampire was waiting for Gillian or one of the other selkies and Ashley was just in the wrong place at the wrong time?"

Melody raises an eyebrow at Charlie. "You know, she's got a point."

The garage door opens and we park inside the field office. We all hop out and follow Melody up the stairs.

"Either way," Melody continues. "We've got a selkie missing and a possible unknown monster running around. Get me eyes on the town, Charlie. Start canvasing. See if you can find anything."

"Of course," he says and hurries back to the SUV.

Jefferson is waiting near the door with Ashley hugging her arms to herself—there are streaks on her cheeks from crying. I pat her on the shoulder and look to Jefferson.

"No charges at this time," he says in an undertone. "But we're recommending she do an hour with a counselor from Underground."

"No penitent cells?" I whisper, surprised.

"Agent Boyd and I will forward our assessments to the Minneapolis Division and they'll make a decision. For now we just need to get her home until we hear back."

I nod and wrap an arm around Ashley's shoulders to guide her to the door. Melody walks us out and gives me a pat on the back before I climb into the passenger seat. Jefferson guns the engine and we fly out of the warehouse district and return to the chaos that is Canal Park so we can pick up Ashley's car. The traffic's as slow as sludge again so I prop my elbow against the window and tuck my chin into my hand to wait it out.

"So, you got into a fight with someone already?" Jefferson asks gruffly.

I give him a sharp look. "How did you—I didn't say anything yet—"

"You've got a fat lip and a shiner coming on."

"Oh. Right." I cross my arms over my chest and stare out the side window. "I didn't get in trouble. It's fine."

"Are *you* fine?"

"Is that concern I hear? I'm touched, Jefferson."

He rolls his eyes. "More like concerned for your sanity."

"Oh, *please*."

I'm working on a witty comeback when my phone buzzes. I pull it out expecting to see Hawk's crossed-eye photo on the screen but it's the number for the Minneapolis Division Headquarters. Nervous, I pick up and press the phone to my ear.

"Hello?"

"Identification please," a bored woman's voice says.

"0919-32, Junior Agent Phoenix Mason."

"Please hold."

When Jefferson gives me a questioning look I just shrug. I have no idea who's calling. Maybe it's Witty with an important update? He usually just emails though. The seconds tick by until the line clicks and a deep baritone comes on.

"Mason, this is Director Knox. We need to talk."

4

I forget how to speak. Director Knox is calling me personally? That's never ever, *ever* happened. Sure, I've been to his office a few times—usually because I was misbehaving—but he's never called before. I haven't done anything wrong. Well, I did just get into a fight with a selkie but even if the director has managed to catch wind of that already, which I highly doubt, he wouldn't be the one reprimanding me.

"Sir," is all I manage to come up with in reply.

"What's your current hearing radius status?" Director Knox asks.

I glance to Jefferson and over my shoulder to Ashley in the seat behind me. "Two, one agent and one civilian," I answer for the appropriate response. At that Jefferson swivels his head sharply in my direction. He clearly knows I'm getting into a serious conversation here. A hearing radius check is only done for highly sensitive information.

"I need you at Underground first thing tomorrow

morning," the director says. "Just you. Your brother and Agent Barnes are strictly forbidden from accompanying you. Check in with Agent Snow at the lifts at 0700 hours. Confirm?"

I've got a thousand questions but I know he won't answer any of them. I've got to follow procedure. "Confirmed."

"Then I'll see you bright and early tomorrow. Good night, Junior Agent Mason." The line cuts out and I'm left stunned, still clutching the phone to my ear expecting more until I finally tuck it back into my pocket.

"Who was that?" Jefferson asks. "What's going on?"

"It was Director Knox," I say numbly. "He wants to meet me tomorrow morning."

"Did he say why?"

There are only two reasons I can think of for why the director would want to see me and only me, without Hawk or Jefferson along for the ride. It could have something to do with the night I plugged Dasc full of bullets. I had been cleared of the shooting, did a couple rounds of counseling, and moved on. Most junior agents never have to deal with something so drastic before becoming full-fledged agents. Lucky me. I'm afraid there's something the counselor might have put in a report to the director saying I'm unfit for duty or some nonsense. Yet, I still can't picture the director talking to me personally for that.

Then there's the only other option, the one that sets my heart hammering in my chest and makes my palms sweaty. The IMS could have discovered what I carry in my blood. They could have found out my magic could be a cure for the werewolves and I'll be in trouble for not revealing it sooner—right before they haul me away to drain that cure out of me, even if it kills me. It's still hard for me to imagine the IMS, the people I work for, could be capable of such things, but Jefferson drilling that scenario into my head each day certainly helps me to picture it. I look to him and see his jaw clench, tension knit between his eyebrows. He's thinking the same thing I am.

"He didn't say why," I say quietly.

Ashley sniffles in the background and doesn't ask what's going on. Maybe she can sense the strain and anxiety filling up the inside of the SUV. I won't have backup when I head to Division per the director's orders. I'll be completely alone. What a day this has been.

We finally get to Ashley's car in the lot and I take the wheel while she sits shotgun. The lights of the SUV follow us as I navigate the prickly traffic. My mind is elsewhere and I almost miss a couple of lights before we begin the ascent up the side of the hill out of Duluth. Dark trees and fields pass around us as we fly down the interstate with nothing but the headlights to guide the way.

The long drive to Moose Lake is done in silence. Ashley doesn't even insist on turning on the radio like she usually does. I take us straight to her house first where her mother stomps outside to greet us. I give Ashley a half-hearted smile, which she doesn't seem to have the energy to return, before she bails out and meets her angry mother. From the shouting, I get the gist that Ashley was supposed to be home a while ago. Her parents don't know what Ashley is—we didn't tell them at Ashley's request—so we can't exactly explain the whole incident in Duluth. Instead, Ashley gloomily says she was at a party and continues to have her ear shouted off.

In the midst of the battle, I sneak out of the driver's seat and hustle to where Jefferson is waiting in the SUV. Ashley gives me a pathetic wave to let me know she's fine and we should take off. I sure hope she doesn't get in too much trouble, but I have bigger worries at the moment. Eventually the two of them go inside and Jefferson drives us home. The floodlights on the barn welcome us back and Hawk stands in the doorway to the cabin.

I climb out of the SUV and walk stiffly to meet him. His face shows alarm and he grasps my shoulders once I'm close enough.

"Hey, are you okay?" he asks. "What's going on?"

Jefferson puts his hands on both our shoulders. "Why don't we take this inside? Then Phoenix can explain."

We do as we're told and I lean against the table in the small kitchen. Hawk hovers nearby with his arms crossed and a frown planted on his face. I relay the short message from the director and then we stand in a triangle pondering our toes.

"I don't like this," Hawk growls. "Why can't I go with you? I don't understand that. There's no reason for them to ban me from Underground. I could still go to visit and—"

"If the director specifically asked us *not* to come," Jefferson interrupts, "then showing up is just going to make things worse. Let's not jump the gun. We don't know what Director Knox wants. It might not have anything to do with Phoenix's ability."

"And if it does?" I say quietly and purse my lips. "Maybe we've been blowing this out of proportion. Who cares if they know? Shouldn't that be a good thing?"

"I've told you a hundred times—" Jefferson says in a very impatient tone but I've heard enough.

"And you've never told me *why* you think they'd bleed me dry," I snap. "What if they just want to help? Jefferson, I *want* to help them find a cure. If I'm it, then why am I hiding? There are millions of werewolves out there that could benefit from my blood!"

"You don't understand," he says darkly and moves in close to glare at me. "You don't understand the lengths they are willing to go."

"Then help me understand!"

He clenches his jaw, walks away into his room without another word, and slams the door behind him.

"That was real informative!" I shout after him. I lift a fist to throw it into the table but stop myself before I punch a hole straight through it. I'm angry and confused and irritated. Why is Jefferson so convinced the worst will happen?

I'm kind of surprised Hawk hasn't said anything more. He leans against the sink with his arms crossed over his chest and shadows fall over his eyes.

"And what about you?" I say, my voice still loud. "Do you think the community that raised us is capable of doing something horrible to me?"

"I don't know," he says softly and his eyes cut through me. "But I'd never be willing to risk your life on anything. You're all I've got, Phoenix."

A pang goes through my chest and I shake my head. "That's not true and you know it. You've got plenty of friends. You're popular, Hawk. People like you."

"And, what? You think that diminishes your own value in my life?" He rolls his eyes and gives a single sad laugh. "Phoenix, no one's ever been there for me the way you have.

You're my sister, and I know you'd do anything for me. You're the only person I really trust."

"But the werewolf disease—" I argue.

"I've dealt with it for fourteen years and I'll keep dealing with it. A cure can wait. For now."

"But that's—it's not—argh!" I throw up my hands and pace away grasping at my hair. I stop in the doorway to our shared room and heave a sigh. "I hate waiting. It makes me feel useless. And I hate hiding when I feel like there's something I could be doing right now to help. To help you, to help everyone in town, to help the *world*. What right do I have to be sitting on this?"

"Phoenix, you almost burned yourself out just calming a bunch of werewolves." He walks around to stand directly behind me. "What makes you think you're ready to cure even one werewolf? The amount of blood they would need from you . . . the magic in you needs to incubate longer, you know? You'll get there eventually, but right now—"

"I'm useless."

"*Hey*," he says sharply and grabs my shoulder to spin me around. He sticks his pointer finger in my face. "I did *not* say that, so stop thinking that. And, as much as I hate to admit it, Jefferson's right. We don't know why the director wants to see you. It might not even be about this. It'll be fine. I'm sure it will."

"You didn't think that about thirty seconds ago."

A ghost of a smile flickers across his face. "Do you need a hug?"

I glower at him. "No."

"Too late. Come here, Fifi." He wraps me up in a bear hug before I can stop him and squeezes so hard that it's difficult to breathe. I start to push him away but he just clings on more tightly. So, instead I allow myself to be rocked side to side like a baby.

"Deep breaths, little sister," he says in a mock soothing voice.

"I'm your twin, you idiot," I wheeze out. "I'm not younger than you."

"Shhhhh. I'm pretty sure I was born first. Deep breaths."

He starts mimicking the breathing pattern people say to use for women in labor in movies. I can't help it. Laughter fights its way up until I'm giggling. Eventually I pull up my arms and hug him back. I close my eyes and we sway like morons together. There are a thousand things I want to say but I don't speak a word. I still haven't told him what happens every time I fire a gun. I don't want him to think I regret shooting Dasc in order to save his life. I want to tell him that I fear what's in my blood will never be enough, and if they have to bleed me dry just to get enough for one cure, I'll do it to save my brother.

"Feel better?" Hawk finally says and draws back to put both his hands on my shoulders. "That's my hugging limit for the month, so—"

I punch him lightly in the arm and he exaggerates grasping his arm in pain. After I reassure him with a nod, we split apart and get ready for bed. I climb into the top bunk once I'm in pajamas and he rolls into the bottom one. It doesn't take long for his snores to fill in the empty silence.

Unfortunately for me, sleep doesn't come so easily and I lie in bed staring up at the dusty ceiling. I'm too anxious and my brain is running through a hundred different scenarios for how tomorrow might go. There isn't much I haven't done with my brother and forcing him out of the equation makes me nervous.

Night ticks by and I close my eyes, drifting asleep eventually. My dreams put me back in that clearing surrounded by werewolves, my mother's gun in my hand, and Dasc shifting into the monster he truly is. Even in my dreams, ferocious anger courses through me along with twisting tendrils of fear. My finger curls around the trigger and the second I fire I jerk awake. I suck down air and exhale slowly to calm my racing heart. I fumble for my phone next to my pillow to check the time. It's 2:00 a.m. I throw an arm over my eyes and try to ease back into sleep but after fifteen minutes of no progress, I slip my hand under my pillow, draw out my mother's gun, then leap to the floor and land lightly on the balls of my feet. Hawk doesn't stir in his sleep, mouth open wide and drool pooling on his pillow. I grab my mother's leather bomber jacket where it hangs on the bedpost, throw it on, tug on some boots, and walk through the chilly winter night to the barn.

As usual, the lights are on inside. I stop to listen and hear what sounds faintly like muted voices before I move lightly up the flight of stairs and pause at the landing. Jefferson is asleep in his chair at his computer so I move around to see what's on his monitors without disturbing him. A video fills up most of the center screen. It's surveillance video from an interrogation room. A man in an IMS uniform sits across a white table from a man I recognize instantly, and one I wish I'd never had the misfortune of knowing.

Dasc sits calmly with his hands clasped before him, his black hair ruffled like it had been when he taught history at

Moose Lake High School. Instead of his usual button down shirt and jeans, he wears white penitent cell garb.

"We'll continue to hold you, you know," the agent says through the speakers set on low volume. "Unless you give us something useful, you'll continue to sit in the penitent cells every day. It'll drive you mad."

"Insanity is relative. It depends on who has who locked in what cage," Dasc counters.

"Clever. You come up with that line yourself?"

Dasc leans forward on the edge of his seat, closing the distance between him and the agent across the table. "Ray Bradbury. You should read more."

I reach carefully over Jefferson and turn the speakers off. I don't want to hear this. I don't want to see Dasc sitting comfortably and healthy after recovering from being shot. He seems fine and cocky in his intellect like before. I still can't sleep at night because of the shooting. Neither should he. The date stamp on the video shows it's a few days old. Technically Jefferson shouldn't even have access to this. Director Knox has really tightened the net on the case. Need to know basis sort of deal. We don't *need* to know anymore but Jefferson has a friend at headquarters that gives him older footage. Jefferson's been watching the videos over and over again, tormenting himself, hoping to find answers where there are none.

He doesn't wake when I pull a blanket off the cot he still keeps in the loft and throw it over his shoulders. Then I tip toe back over to the cot and hold my mother's pearl-handled .45 in my hands. I stare at it a moment, remembering the harsh recoil from each shot I fired, before resting it on the table and pulling out Jefferson's gun cleaning kit. I carefully take the gun apart piece by piece and start cleaning them each separately the way I was taught by Jefferson.

Time passes slowly and I try to let my thoughts taper out into oblivion. The task at hand helps. I check the clock on the wall now and then. Jefferson finally stirs around 3:00 a.m. and runs a hand down his face when he wakes up. When he notices the blanket around his shoulders he searches the room until his eyes find me.

"Can't sleep?" he asks groggily.

"No, I'm sleepwalking," I reply. "Can't you tell?"

He shakes his head but doesn't give me his usually gruff response about me being a smart alec. Instead he gets up, cracks his back, and shuffles over to sit on the edge of the table across from me, pushing aside some of the gun parts to make room for himself.

"Cleaning that gun a thousand times isn't going to make the memory any cleaner, you know," he says gently. Right now I think I'd actually prefer him being gruff.

I exhale sharply and put the slide I'm holding back on the table. With my hands free I don't have anything to control my nervous energy, so I interlace my fingers and set my chin on top of them. There's a sensation in my chest that I can't quite put my finger on.

What Jefferson doesn't understand is that I'm not trying to cleanse the memory. I'm trying to be ready because I always have to be ready. If I'm not, then I'm vulnerable. It's almost become a nervous twitch to make sure I have a weapon on me at all times. I'm pretty sure he still doesn't know I've been carrying my mother's gun around with me everywhere I go, even though it's illegal—I'm underage and don't have a permit. But I don't tell him that.

"I don't understand," I say. "When it first happened, I was shocked, but then I was relieved. I was happy to be alive and my brother to be okay. But now—I don't know. I just feel off, like I'm never going to function normally again."

"You've had time to overthink it."

"Jefferson, how can I be an agent if I can't get my feet back under me?"

He puts a hand on my forearm. "It's not a bad thing to regret having to shoot someone. I'd be more worried if you didn't."

I don't know if I'd call what I'm feeling is *regret*. It's an intense feeling that springs out of my chest and sets my heart hammering when I'm put on edge, but it's not regret. Maybe that's what scares me so much. I'd shoot Dasc all over again if I had to and wouldn't even blink. So, what does that make me?

"But you're the one always saying you'd kill Dasc if you had the chance," I say.

"And I never said that was a good thing, did I?" His eyes are drawn, wrinkles are etched in his face, and he looks like he's aged a hundred years just by saying that single sentence. "We're supposed to be protectors, Phoenix. Sometimes that means being a shield. Sometimes that means being a sword. You have to embrace both. Things will get easier with time."

I worry my lower lip and say what's been eating away at me for the last three months.

"And if they don't?"

He sighs and pats my knee twice before rising to his feet. "Get some sleep."

I nod, pretending I'll follow his advice, but the second the barn door shuts on his way out, I pick up the slide again and continue to clean it. Another fifteen minutes pass and the gun is immaculate. After putting the pieces back together, I rise and move to my computer terminal. In all the terrifying expectations of what will happen in Underground I forgot to put together my report for the incident with the selkies in Duluth. The barn fills with the sound of my numb fingers typing away. As soon as my report is done, I check through the other reports under the same case file number to see what the Duluth Field Office has submitted to take my mind off things.

Charlie's report is very sterile and analytic, hardly giving any room for possible suspicions or speculation of what might have happened in the alleyway behind the Blue Comet. Melody's report is somewhat more enlightening and she gives weight to Ashley's story of events. At the end she gives recommendations to headquarters regarding Ashley. I give a sigh of relief when I see she's only recommending a single session with a counselor to stress the danger of exposure to the general public as a werewolf. Well, that's something.

"Hey."

I jump and my heart tries to leap out of my chest. Hawk stands at the top of the stairs in his plaid pajamas, a thermos and two cups in his hands. His hair is standing up in all directions like he's been struck by lightning and his eyes are half-lidded. He looks about as tired as I feel.

"*Sweet piping Pan,* Hawk!" I press a hand to my heart, my blood pounding in my ears. "You nearly gave me a heart attack."

"Oops." He trudges over, plops down in Jefferson's spot, then sluggishly opens the thermos to pour two cups of steaming coffee. He passes one over while rubbing his eyes and then leans far back in the swivel chair, propping his feet up on the desk. He holds his drink with both hands and blinks so slowly I'm not sure he's going to be able to stay awake another thirty seconds.

"Thanks," I mumble. "You didn't need to come out here, though."

He flops a hand at me. "No, no. I'm good." His mouth stretches for a huge yawn before he sips at his coffee and watches me with bleary eyes. "You never told me what happened in Duluth. You've got a nice shiner, by the way. Did you fight a fish on the lake or something?"

I can always tell how tired Hawk is by his level of wit. He's definitely out of it.

"Funny you should say that," I say. "It was a selkie. So, close enough."

He frowns and holds up a finger. "Wait, seals aren't fish. Are they? Pixies, I need a nap."

I roll my eyes. "Go back to bed, birdie."

"I am a bird of prey, thank you very much. Not a *birdie.*"

"Whatever."

"Hey, no, really." He rubs the sleep from his eyes, takes his feet off the desk, and hunches forward in his seat. "What happened? I want to know if I need to hunt someone down for beating up my twin."

"No hunting anyone down," I say, then rattle off meeting Melody and Charlie, how Ashley was, the possibility of a vampire loose in Duluth, meeting the selkies, and getting into a fight with Nessa.

When I finish, Hawk pours himself another cup. "So, what I'm taking away from all this, is that you really don't like Charlie. At all."

"What? No, the take away is that there is a vampire out there, but a certain moron doesn't even want to *consider* the possibility—"

"Yup. Definitely that you don't like Charlie. I should meet him."

"Why, exactly, would you want to meet him?" I ask.

"So I can say 'My name is Hawk Mason. You insulted my sister. Prepare to die.'"

I almost choke on my coffee and crack a laugh. I guess Hawk has finally woken up. He grins and empties the rest of the thermos into my cup.

"Hey, you think Jefferson has ever watched *The Princess Bride*?" Hawk asks. "We should watch that together. Good bonding time."

"I doubt he's seen it, but he might have read the book," I say. Then Hawk and I say in unison in our best gruff Jefferson impersonation, *"Don't you kids read?"*

Hawk caps the thermos and his smile fades away. "Hey, Phoenix?"

"Yeah?"

"Everything's going to be okay. You know that, right?"

I glance at the clock. It's 4:30 a.m. I'll need to leave in a half-hour if I want to make it on time to Underground. I heave a sigh. "Yeah. Yeah, okay."

"Come on." He gets to his feet and gestures with both hands for me to get up as well. "Time to put on real clothes and pretend to be adults."

I hold out my hands and he tugs me up with an exaggerated grunt. After I grab my mother's pristine gun, we head out of the barn and into the cabin. There's no light underneath Jefferson's door and I hope he's actually getting some sleep, unlike the rest of us. Hawk offers to cook breakfast while I change and make myself presentable to the outside world.

I stand in front of the mirror in the bathroom for a long time just staring at my reflection, wondering and dreading what's to come. My skin's gotten a touch of a tan from being outside so much lately, but today the face looking back at me is pale, making all my little freckles stand out on my nose and cheeks. Shadows hang under my eyes as a testament to months of sleepless nights, and the one black eye, curtesy of Nessa the selkie, has become darkly prominent. There's hardly anything left of that giddy teenager, who dance-battled elves and pulled pranks, in those cold green eyes glaring back at me. I run a hand down the mirror and turn away from the person I'm having trouble recognizing.

By the time Hawk's fried up a pan of scrambled eggs and slathered butter on toast, Jefferson is awake again and we eat together—almost like a family—in the tiny kitchen. We don't say a word but our eyes flicker to the clock on the wall every few seconds like time is going to run away from us and we'll never be able to catch it again. I suddenly remember it's Monday. Hawk will be in school today. He'll have to make an excuse for me again. We begged Jefferson to pull us out for "homeschooling" but he still thinks it's a good idea for us to mingle with the werewolves, earn their trust, and keep them in close proximity to my bubble of anti-werewolf crazy. It makes our other work harder but at least school will be officially over in the spring. No more high school. That cheery thought gets me to my feet.

"I should get going," I say. "I don't want to be late."

Jefferson nods and sets his coffee cup down. "You know the way?"

"Yup." I grab my jacket and sling it on. "I'll see you later."

"Call when you can."

We all smile, casual and forcibly relaxed. Hawk pats me on the back and gives me a low five. I wave goodbye and then I'm out the door. I clamber into the SUV and prepare myself for the long drive to Minneapolis in the dark of an early winter morning. The radio picks up a familiar oldies station and I crank it up to drown out everything else. The headlights dance across the blanket of snow and I'm off.

The next two hours pass with me clenching the steering wheel, tapping my fingers nervously, biting my lip, and barely paying attention to the minimal traffic around me. Once I reach the fringes of Minneapolis the interstate expands lane by lane and the traffic starts to swell. I haven't been back since I first left for the solitary outskirts of Moose Lake. The city feels so familiar and yet so different. It had been my home for so long. It's strange coming back now.

Before I know it, I'm pulling into the power park. I show my junior agent I.D. at the gate and am let through. I park at the end of a row of similar black SUVs and enter the cement bunker nearly hidden in the trees on the edge of the lot. Just like the director said, Agent Snow is waiting inside, leaning against the controls for the lift currently topside and loudly chewing a piece of gum. His hair has receded more since the last time I saw him when he drove me and Hawk to Moose Lake. He's relaxed and that makes me relax a little.

"Agent Snow," I say and step onto the lift beside him.

He presses the button on the control lever and the lift starts to sink down into the cement chute. He stands with his hands in his pockets and gives me a small smile.

"Welcome back, Mason," he says and pops his gum. "How's small town life?"

"Quiet." I shrug and fiddle with my hands. "You know, apart from the occasional uprising, disappearances, and shootings."

"Right. Just another day at the office, eh?"

"Something like that."

His eyes drop to my hands that I'm twisting endlessly over each other. "You look nervous," he says.

I shrug again. "Usually when the director wants to see me, I'm in trouble."

"Hmm," is all he says in response, which doesn't help my nerves. Is that that "hmm" a good sign or a bad sign?

The lift eventually trembles to a stop and Bernie the faun gives me a great big smile at the bottom. I haven't seen him in ages and wouldn't mind hearing how he's been. However, Agent Snow gives him a look to stop any questions or greeting Bernie might give and the faun remains silent, the smile on his face dimming as I'm marched past. I mouth "sorry" to the faun before Agent Snow guides me out of sight. I expect to be led through the middle of Merchant Square but the agent avoids the square altogether, and turns left, following the edge of Underground past the market and living quarters until headquarters looms on our left. Instead of making for it, we enter a door in the massive cement wall that encases Underground with a warning branded on the front that says "IMS AGENT USE ONLY."

Just inside a centaur, unicorn, and two active gargoyles

stand guard. The sight gives me another spike in my blood pressure. The centaur and unicorn are wearing mesh armor reinforced by metal plates. The dappled unicorn even has a diamond tipped cap on its horn. The gargoyles, guardians animated by magic, don't need any armor of their own since they're made of stone. Their flaky wings flex over their gorilla like bodies as they march back and forth across the room. I halt, surprised, and Agent Snow tugs on my arm. The gargoyles stop pacing and stand sentinel at the next massive door. A blue sheen ripples across the surface—a dragon's barrier. Agent Snow pulls me over to a tall white counter on the left behind which the centaur stands. The unicorn paces on the other side of the room, tossing me suspicious glances.

"Agent Snow and Junior Agent Mason, per the director's request," Agent Snow announces to the centaur. I can't even see the centaur's face which is obscured behind a helmet. He taps at a computer and then nods mutely. Agent Snow continues to pull me about towards the door. The dragon's barrier vanishes and the door swings open.

We enter a white walled hallway that is almost too pristine and illuminated by sterile lights that reflect off the glossy walls and floor. Doors line the hall in each direction which splits off into even more hallways. Each door glimmers with the pale blue light of a magical barrier.

"These are the penitent cells," I say out loud, my voice seemingly too loud in the empty, echoing hall.

"Yup," Agent Snow says casually and leads the way to the right.

My breathing hitches and my heart races. Now I'm terrified. Why on earth am I here? The only reason I'd be here is if they want to throw me in a cell. I glance over my shoulder to the door we just came through only to see it's blocked off by a dragon's barrier again. Oh, crap. I don't like this. I don't like this at all.

We turn down one hallway then the next, each and every one the same apart from large bold numbers on the wall in blue to let us know where we are. Out of a survival instinct, I try to memorize them. I almost run into the agent when he finally stops and holds open a door for me. At least this one doesn't have a barrier.

I step very slowly inside to find a long oval table at which four people are already seated. Director Knox sits closest to me in a sharp suit, his bald head reflecting the bright overhead lights. Next is Witty in his wheelchair, his black hair neatly combed, and he gives me a warm smile. Across from them is a heavily built man in reinforced mesh armor like the centaur and unicorn at the entrance. A huge jaw, shortly cut hair, and a scar down one side of his face, he looks like a war hero. His face is set in a scowl.

And standing at the head of the table opposite me is a man I've only seen twice before. Tall, slim, and upright with a gaze that could cut through steel. Right now his eyes are hidden in shadow beneath his ruffled brown hair. He tugs on the cuff of his peculiar all black suit and then that piercing gaze of his meets mine.

"Hello, Phoenix. It's been too long."

He's the only majestic class dragon I've ever met.

Draco.

5

Agent Snow shuts the door behind me, leaving me alone with the four men in the room. I don't know what I'm supposed to say or do. My legs don't seem to work anymore and I stare at Draco. It's probably a rude thing to do but my eyes are drawn to him like a magnet. His expression doesn't betray any emotion as he studies me.

"Have a seat, Mason," Director Knox says, breaking the spell. He nudges out the chair opposite him with his foot.

I slowly sink into it and manage to get out a single word. "Sir."

The director clasps his hands in front of him and gives me his full attention. "I'm sure you're wondering why I called you down here." I nod mutely. "I know Junior Agent Wallowitz has been sending you updates concerning the interrogation of Dasc." At the mention of his name, Witty ducks his head. "I am also aware that a friend of Agent Barnes has been feeding him dated recordings of the interrogations."

I swallow past the lump in my throat. "Am I in trouble?"

He allows himself a small smirk. "For once, no."

If I'm not in trouble for sneaking a glimpse of the interrogations I'm not supposed to be privy to, then why are we talking about Dasc? I clench my sweaty palms together under the menacing black table. Has he told them about me? No, he wouldn't. Why would he? I'm sure he would want to keep my ability a secret as much as I do. My power could destroy his, but maybe being held prisoner changed his mind.

"As I'm sure you are aware, our interrogations have been fruitless," the director continues. I nod again. "He's refusing to give any information as to the whereabouts of the missing residents from Moose Lake and other cities, or the location of Agent Smith whom the shapeshifter you encountered impersonated. We've attempted to crack down on Mr. Webster and the shapeshifter but they have also refused to speak."

That surprises me. I know Mr. Webster originally took the fall as Dasc's patsy before we uncovered Dasc as the real culprit. For some reason I think that would make Mr. Webster angry and want to rat out his boss. I guess not. This still isn't making any sense. Do they want me to explain something more about what happened in Moose Lake? I already put everything—apart from my ability—into my reports. There's nothing left to tell.

"However," the director continues, "yesterday evening Dasc agreed to speak and give us whatever information we want."

"That's great!" I say, the words bursting out of me before I can restrain myself. This is what we've been waiting for. We'll finally have a lead on Jefferson's daughter, Deputy Graham's sister, and all the others.

The director holds up a hand for my silence and looks resigned. "There is a condition for this information."

At that I almost balk. "You can't give him a deal or immunity. He can't walk."

"That's not what he asked for."

Draco finally speaks up again. "He'll only talk to one person."

"What?" I say, caught off guard.

His dark eyes cut through me. "You."

I wait for someone to laugh and say they're joking, but every face in the room is stone cold sober. Words escape me as I try to sort my confusion and revulsion. My face burns and I swallow a few times.

In the silence I leave open, Director Knox continues speaking. "That's why I instructed your brother and Agent Barnes to stay behind. I don't want your brother anywhere near this. I've been keeping as many of the werewolves as I can out of Underground until we know just how far Dasc's influence goes. And as much as I hate to admit it, I can't trust Agent Barnes to be here. He's too close to this and has acted out before. Putting Agent Barnes anywhere near Dasc is asking for trouble."

"You're worried about Jefferson?" I finally manage to say and jab a thumb at my chest. "He killed my parents. *I* am the one that emptied a clip into Dasc. You should be worried about *me*."

"I realize the situation isn't ideal," the director says. "If there was another way I'd take it. Trust me."

I run a hand over the top of my head, trying to hide the fact that I'm shaking. "What about the penitent cells?"

"He's been sitting in one every day but he seems strangely immune to their effect."

Immune? That's not possible. No one is immune to the penitent cells. They're infused with the magic of fauns and cause their captives to relive the terrifying emotions of their victims until they repent for what they've done. I can't even imagine the force of the magic exerted upon Dasc for the countless number of victims I'm sure he's created. My entire family for starters. He would be reliving their last moments of fear and pain over and over again, feeling them as his own. The penitent cells are meant to make criminals truly realize what they've done so they don't do it again. Fauns and a lot of the legendary community think it's a better idea than criminals just sitting in cells with their own thoughts all the time.

I shake my head and knead my knuckles into my thighs. And to think I had been worried all this was going to be about my potential ability. I think I might have actually handled that better.

"Why? Why me?" I ask desperately.

"He won't say," Draco answers, "but Dasc always has a reason for everything he does."

The dragon's eyes narrow and he averts his gaze to the black tabletop. What I still don't get is why Draco is even here. Yeah, so Dasc is the alpha werewolf, but what's that to a dragon? Draco must have better things to do than watch pointless interrogations go round. He could watch recordings later if he really wanted.

"I understand your hesitation and confusion," Director Knox says in the kindest voice he's ever used with me. "But we need your help, Mason."

I close my eyes and press the heels of my palms against them. Each breath I take is ragged and I hate feeling this distressed. Dasc shouldn't affect me like this. I can't let him. I *won't* let him. It takes an effort to level out my breathing, compose myself, and set my hands on the table.

"What do you need me to do?" I ask.

"We'll put him in the interrogation room. Major Lynch will stand guard inside with you." The director nods to the bulky warrior guy on my right. "Junior Agent Wallowitz, Draco, and I will watch through a one-way mirror. We'll guide you through an earpiece if that will make you more comfortable."

More comfortable. Right. As if a lousy little piece of plastic in my ear is going to make this any easier. Then I think of Jefferson. I think of Hawk. I think of my parents. Now's not the time to be a coward. I force myself to take a deep breath and tuck my anxiety deep down, trying to replace it with sterner stuff.

"Okay. I'll do it," I say.

Draco is already sweeping out of the room and his voice booms, "Then we'll start immediately."

The director and major rise. Witty rolls over in his wheelchair and we exit together. I haven't seen him in what feels like ages. It's nice to see a friendly face in the middle of this mess at least.

"Hey," Witty says. "It's good to see you."

"Yeah. Right. Hi, Witty."

"I'm sorry this got sprung on you," he says, hands pumping the wheels of his chair in well-timed, methodical motions.

"And here I thought my biggest worry lately was going to be a selkie holding a grudge against me."

"The one that gave you that shiner?" he asks and grins.

I grimace. "It's that noticeable, huh?"

"A bit, yeah."

He looks away and we follow Draco's lead down the hall behind the director and the major. It feels like I'm being lead to the gallows. I move a little closer to Witty and lower my voice.

"So how come you're a part of this anyway?" I ask.

He shrugs. "I've been working the surveillance feeds, all the tech."

"You're not even a bona fide agent yet."

"I was motivated to help with this in any way I could," he says and gives me a quick sideways glance before staring straight ahead, his ears going red. "And so they let me. I'm qualified to, you know."

"I don't doubt it." I sigh and shake the tension down my arms. "Thanks, Witty. It's good to know I have a friend close by at least."

"And it's fascinating," he says offhand.

"What is?"

"Oh, I mean, umm—" He purses his lips and clams up.

"Witty."

"Dasc. He's fascinating." His expression changes to one of horror when I glare at him. "I mean his abilities. His recovery from those wolfsbane rounds is a thing unheard of. His healing capabilities are far beyond the norm."

"Great," I say flatly. "I'll be sure to shoot him twice as much the next time I feel like killing him then, just to make sure."

Director Knox gives me a cold look over his shoulder so I decide now's a good time to shut up. Next thing I know, Draco has vanished and the director stops me outside a door sealed with a dragon's barrier. From the pocket of his suit Director Knox pulls out an earbud and puts it in the palm of my hand.

"We'll be watching the whole time and will guide you with the questions," he says. "Just try to relax and get the truth from him if you can. You'll be safe. He's restrained and Major Lynch will stay with you in the room."

"I have no idea how to do this," I confess. Some part of me hopes the director will change his mind and let me go. The intelligent part of me knows that's not going to happen.

"Maybe that's what we need," he says. "All the trained interrogators have failed. Perhaps it's time for some unusual methods."

That's really not at all comforting.

He pats me awkwardly on the shoulder and slides away to the observation room with Witty. Major Lynch waits for me to put the earbud in and then the dragon barrier dissolves on its own. The major presses the door open and lets me in.

A small white table sits in the middle of the room, and a pair of chains leading to handcuffs are locked to the center. And shackled in those cuffs, sitting in an equally sterile white chair, is the last person I want to see. When his bright blue eyes find me in the doorway, they widen and he gives me that familiar crooked smile. He's in the same white prison garb from the surveillance feeds Jefferson has been watching, and his black hair is as wild as ever.

The terror that has been building in me leading up to this moment snaps. I'm back at that night squeezing the trigger of my mother's gun, my arm slung around my brother to protect him, Jefferson fighting for his life in the background. Everything becomes so perfectly clear again. There was a reason I put bullet after bullet into Dasc. He's a monster. I stopped him. Now it's time for me to finish the job others couldn't.

I don't take my eyes off him as I walk to the empty chair opposite him and sit down. Major Lynch stands at attention beside the closed door and the dragon's barrier flashes back into place over the entrance. There's silence for a long time and none of us move. Dasc and I just stare at each other, that stupid smile of his never leaving his face.

"Phoenix Mason," are the first words Dasc says, savoring every syllable of my name. It makes me want to cringe. "The girl who tried to kill me."

I don't respond. I don't know what he wants from me but he's not going to get it. I'll be the one getting the information here. A voice comes softly through the link in my ear. It's the director. "Take charge, Mason. Don't let him control this conversation. Don't let him ask any questions. Drill him. He wanted you here so get what you can out of—"

The director feeds me some more advice while I glare at the monster in front of me. Dasc sighs and rolls his head around his shoulders, his eyes locking onto the piece in my ear. "I thought I was going to be talking to Phoenix, not you, Director Knox."

I start and automatically look to the one-way mirror behind me, then to the major who doesn't look impressed, just angry.

"I said I'd only talk to Phoenix," Dasc says and leans over the table, head tucked down so he's looking up through his eyebrows to the mirror over my shoulder. He's deranged, but he also knows what happened to Jefferson's daughter, Deputy Graham's sister, and all the others. I hold onto that thought. It'll get me through.

The director starts to say something else through the earpiece but I pull it out and hold it out for Dasc to see. Then I tuck it into my pocket and lean back in my chair, crossing my arms over my chest.

"I thought I made my feelings about you pretty clear, or did shooting you not get my message across?" I say, trying not to grit my teeth. "Why am I here?"

"You know, up until that point I thought we were getting along rather well."

"Let me make something clear. I'll bury your body in the woods where no one will find you when this is all over," I say, calmer than I thought I could be at this point. "You know what you've taken from me. You know what I'm capable of. You know what I want. So here I am. *Talk.*"

His smile never waivers. I want him to flinch. I want him to tremble. I want him to show he's vulnerable, but he doesn't.

"How about you answer one of my questions and I'll answer one of yours," he says.

"That's not how this is going to work."

"Isn't it?" The muscles in his face tighten and the monster hidden inside him shows through. His eyes flash yellow. "The IMS needs me. They already brought you here at my request. I'm the one holding all the cards."

My breathing becomes shallow and fast. He's infuriating. I want to punch that smug smile off his face and slam his head face first into the tabletop. Everything about him makes me want to turn violent.

"I carry secrets," he says quietly, almost but not quite a whisper. "I learned a lot of interesting things during my time in Moose Lake. Each secret opens a door to intriguing possibilities. Be careful, and I might even open the right one for you. Don't make me pick the wrong door."

The veiled threat is obvious to me. Dasc knows my potential, sure, but what if he also discovered Hawk's secret? What if he learned my brother isn't taking the serum? I can't take that chance. I don't want to play this game but I've been forced to the table. I might as well try my hand at it.

"One question," I say. "I answer *one*, and you tell me what I want to know."

"Agreed."

I remain rigid in my seat as far away from him as possible, so he leans further across the table trying to breach my personal space.

"A little over fourteen years ago I was in Moose Lake," Dasc begins, which isn't what I'm expecting at all. "I'll admit I was there changing the population steadily and growing my numbers. That city is the perfect place for experimentation, you see. It's small but large enough. People know each other but aren't familiar with every face. It's not so well known. Close to a major roadway, yet tucked back in the woods. And they've had numerous sightings of wolves in the area."

I have no idea where he's going with this but I'm intrigued and terrified all the same. I've wanted to know why he did what he did all this time and he's just chatting away like it's something everyone knows.

"I blended in and got to know the kids. People tend to underestimate the younger generation." He nods to himself and smiles a little like he's recalling a pleasant memory instead of turning a bunch of teenagers into monsters. "I didn't think the IMS agents in the area were much of a threat. Mostly they ran around in circles trying to find the cause of what was going on in their quaint little town."

Heat races up my neck and flushes my cheeks. Those agents he's talking about were my parents and Jefferson. How *dare* he.

"I was almost too late to act by the time I realized they were actually rather clever," he continues, inching towards me across the table. "I figured if I changed them, put them under my . . . *sway*, they would be incredibly useful. I planned to change your whole family. I couldn't leave even one of the Masons unturned. They'd feel left out."

My breathing is harsh and my hands tremble as I clench them into fists.

"Your parents were fighters," he says in a soft voice as if trying to console me. "I never meant to end their lives. Then only you and your brother were left. Obviously, I had to change you both. You didn't have any family left, so you'd need a new one." Then he smiles to himself and almost starts to laugh. "I remember you punched me in the nose after I bit your brother. Such spirit! Even then you were doing everything you could to protect your family."

My whole body is shaking. I'm about to react. It's building up inside me like a volcano ready to erupt.

"So my question is, after all that terrible tragedy, how long did it take until Draco showed up to save you? Rather convenient, his timing, don't you think?"

I'm moving before I can stop myself. My chair screeches across the floor as I fling it backwards and rise. My fist plummets into the side of Dasc's face with the full weight of my body and every ounce of magic I've got. I follow through as Dasc's face jerks to the side with the satisfying crunch of bones snapping, abrading the skin across my knuckles.

Something dense and powerful hits me square in the back and I tumble forward onto the table before falling to the floor, stunned. My brain and body decide to stop working and I remain there until someone pulls me up and drags me by the armpits out of the room. It takes a while before I finally come to my senses and find I'm sitting in the white paneled hallway, my back against a wall. My hand throbs—blood has welled beneath the tender, bruising skin of my knuckles. Major Lynch, the director, and Draco stand around me arguing with each other. They might also be occasionally yelling in my direction but my head feels fuzzy. I blink a few times and focus on the conversation at hand.

"I told you she wasn't ready for this kind of confrontation!" Director Knox shouts. He looks furious. Good for him. I'm furious too.

"Our options were limited," Draco says calmly, almost bored. "I accepted the possible risks of putting them in the same room together."

They argue this way back and forth a while longer. My eyes drift to something metallic Major Lynch is holding in his hands. It's a bio-mech gun. I put two and two together—he must have shot me with a bio-mech pulse when I, admittedly, went crazy back there.

I slowly rise to my feet and cradle my painful hand to my chest. All their eyes fall on me.

"You can forget it," I say before they have a chance to yell at me. "I'm done. Discipline me however you like. I'm not going back in there. And unless you decide to stop me, I'm going home."

Director Knox heaves a sigh and steps aside, holding out an arm to let me know I'm free to go. I slip past him and walk away, noting the numeric designation on the walls in order to find my way to the exit. I glance over my shoulder and Draco's eyes follow me all the way until I disappear around the corner. Wheels squeak behind me and eventually Witty catches up.

"Phoenix, I—"

"Don't," I growl. "Don't say a word or I swear I'll punch you too."

At that warning he stops and leaves me to wind back through the maze of hallways to the entrance on my own. I halt before the reinforced door long enough to wonder if I need to say a password or something when the dragon's barrier finally drops and I'm let through. The centaur and unicorn don't say a word as I march out. I enter the main level of Underground and keep walking. I could stop and find my old friends if I wanted to, but I don't. I want to get as far away from here as possible and as soon as possible. I'm practically jogging by the time I reach the lift.

"Phoenix!" Bernie the guard gasps when he sees me. "Your hand—"

"Yeah, it's fine," I say and hop onto the lift.

It can't move fast enough up the chute. The second it levels out at the top I rush past the security guards and jump into my SUV. Now that the adrenaline is starting to ease off, my hand really hurts. I pull the first-aid kit out from under the passenger seat and focus on coiling my knuckles in white gauze as blood starts to seep out between the cracks of my skin. When I'm done I just sit there and stare out the windshield at the ice breaking up on top of the Mississippi River near the edge of the parking lot.

Dasc's voice rings in my head. *How long did it take until Draco showed up to save you? Rather convenient, his timing, don't you think?*

It doesn't even make sense. Is Dasc gloating about my parents not being saved in time? Or is he saying Draco intentionally waited until after my parents were killed and Hawk was turned to show up? How could the dragon even know what was going on in order to plan that? And for what purpose?

My mind reels. Draco gave me a piece of magic as soon as he showed up to save me and Hawk. That magic now could be the key to ending the existence of the werewolf disease.

No. Draco couldn't have known that would happen. I didn't even know it had happened until recently. I can't process this.

I grip the steering wheel with both hands, bend my forehead until it touches the hard leather grip, and start bawling my eyes out. By the time I'm finally embarrassed enough with myself to stop crying, the sun is in the sky and I'm shivering in the cold SUV. My senses flood back and I turn on the vehicle to at least get some heat going. My hands shake as I pull out my cellphone and send off a quick text to Hawk and Jefferson to let them know I'm fine and it wasn't what we thought. I allow myself a few more minutes until I've recovered enough to drive and then peel out of the parking lot.

There's not a lot to occupy my attention for the next couple of hours of driving once I leave Minneapolis so I process everything. I recall all that I learned about magic and the Blessed in Underground. Certain beings are born with magic, like dragons and fauns. They can use it on other people but only dragons discovered how to actually give magic to someone else. That magic then develops into abilities specific to that individual. The last time I faced Dasc he mentioned that very thing, said there was no one else quite like me, that there was no one else with a werewolf sibling that chose to save their sibling.

I try and remember exactly what Dasc had said. Now that I think about it, the way he phrased it was odd. He almost made it sound like there were other Blessed out there that had a werewolf sibling but they chose to ignore them. Ugh! I can't remember exactly. Have there really been others out there in the same position as me who made different choices? Or was that not what Dasc meant at all? I can't believe I'm even considering anything he's said. He's a liar. He manipulated an entire city. He fooled me before.

And yet . . .

My mind runs in circles until I make it to Moose Lake at last. It's not even noon yet. School will still be in session so that's where Hawk will be. Jefferson will most likely be at the cabin. Thinking of Jefferson makes my heart sink and a pit form in my stomach. How am I going to tell him that I had a chance of learning where his daughter is and I blew it, then ran away?

I pull off the main street in Moose Lake and make my way to the field office. A set of tire tracks leads out from the barn. Jefferson must have taken the Green Monster for a spin. I've got to come up with some kind of excuse for ruining our best and only chance of getting answers before he returns. I park in front of the cabin and trudge inside. Once in the quiet retreat of the cabin, I collapse into a chair at the table and hold my face in my hands. This has been a really stressful day.

The growl of an engine outside makes me want to curl up and hide in my bed. Could I not be bothered for a while? I'd appreciate it. The engine dies right outside the cabin. A few seconds later there's a loud forceful knock on the door.

I raise my head. If it were Jefferson, he wouldn't be knocking. I rub at my face, hoping beyond hope I don't look like I've been crying, and move to the door. When I open it, my breath catches in my throat and I stiffen.

Draco fills up the doorway with his presence, hands tucked into the pockets of his black dress pants. He levels his gaze at me and I automatically swallow.

"We need to talk."

6

I don't know what to do, so I stand there like an idiot still gripping the doorknob. It's a good thing I'm holding it gingerly with my injured hand, otherwise I might have crumpled it. Admittedly, I'm terrified. The fact Draco followed me all the way from Underground and didn't just call or something is a really, really bad sign. I shouldn't have run.

"May I come in?" he eventually prompts.

"Oh, I—yeah, of course. Sure thing." I hold the door open wide and he steps around me.

It's a strange sight to see Draco, the leader of the majestic dragons and the IMS, standing in the middle of our tiny kitchen next to the dirty dishes stacked haphazardly in the sink. He takes a slow turn, soaking in the log walls, the cobwebs in the corners, and the marred kitchen table. I reflexively have the urge to clean everything in sight but it's too late. He probably thinks we're a bunch of incompetent slobs.

"Take a seat, Phoenix," he says and pulls out a chair at the table.

He's here two seconds and already giving orders. Crap. I take the offered chair and he sits across from me. Every movement he makes looks carefully controlled like he knows if he moves too quickly he'll break something. Actually, if I think about it, he probably would. Under that slim suit—and I'm not talking about his clothes—is a majestic class dragon. The physics of their transformation is a little hazy to me but it's like they condense down. All that power is concentrated into a body a fraction of its usual size. They're no less dangerous when they strut around looking like humans. They just aren't spewing fire from their mouths, tearing cars in half with their teeth, or flying.

He leans back and rests one arm on the tabletop like a lion relaxing in the comfort of his own domain.

"I knew the risks of putting you in that room," he says evenly. "But sometimes I forget the latitude of human emotions and how adept Dasc is at stirring them."

I don't think he's saying sorry for tossing me in with the devil but it's hard to tell.

"As for what Dasc alluded to—" he continues and lets out a forlorn sigh. My whole body tenses, waiting for him to say it had been his plan all along to let my parents die and Hawk be turned. He holds my gaze and says, "There was no plot, no scheme, no cold calculus in my appearance at your house. My timing, as it was, was coincidental. I received an alert after an agent searched the IMS database for the name Lycaon and came as quickly as I could. Unfortunately, I was not swift enough."

His eyes never waiver and each word is said with such conviction that I believe him. The tension seeps out of me and I wilt in my chair. I'm embarrassed. I let Dasc mess with my head.

"You didn't show up when I had Witty run a search," I grumble. "You only came after we had captured Dasc."

The faintest of smirks crosses his face. Is he impressed I put together the time discrepancy so fast? Or is he smiling at a child stumbling through things she doesn't understand and trying to tie strings together where they don't even exist?

"I was otherwise engaged and not in the country at the time," is his answer.

"Why are you so interested in Dasc?" I blurt out. Since I have Draco here, I'm anxious to get whatever information I can out of him.

His expression never waivers. "He's the first of his race and a powerful adversary obsessed with turning the world into his own personal pack of monsters. Isn't that enough?"

Well . . . yeah. I'm feeling more and more like a toddler next to Draco. I should probably stop talking before I take another blow to my intellect and pride. Then again, I was never one to make smart decisions.

"So, what happens now?" I ask.

"Dasc will need a few days to heal from your attack." He doesn't sound angry about it which makes it a little better. "But then I would implore you to return. Dasc carries more secrets than you can fathom and he's loath to reveal them. I need to know what they are. The fact that he even suggested giving up some of them to you is out of character. So, I suggest you take this time to reflect on what's truly important and what you are willing to do to find the truth. There are countless friends and family members that have gone missing. You could very well hold the key to their rescue. Isn't that worth enduring unpleasantries from a tasteless sadist trapped in a cell without any real power?"

Heat rises in my cheeks and I look away.

He stands and I rise uncertainly as well. "I'll contact you when we're ready to resume the interrogations."

Draco moves to the door and I follow after to see him out. A familiar rumble reaches my ears and we both step out as the Green Monster pulls up the driveway. Jefferson squints at us through the windshield of his green 1970 442 classic and rolls to a stop beside a black, late model Dodge Charger which is obviously Draco's. Wow, that dragon sure loves black. Jefferson steps out and his eyes widen as he finally recognizes Draco. The dragon gives him a rather cold gaze.

"Agent Barnes," he says frostily, then slides into his Charger without another word, not even a polite goodbye, and roars down the driveway.

Jefferson doesn't get out of the open door of his car but his attention finally falls on me, his mouth agape.

"But that was—" he says.

"Yup."

"And he was *here*?"

"Yup."

He shakes his head. "Are you okay?"

I have to think about it for a moment, not really sure myself. "I'm fine."

"Then open the barn doors."

I trudge through the snow and yank open the massive barn doors so Jefferson can park inside. I close the doors behind him and we take the stairs together to the loft. He gestures for me to take a seat on the cot, which I do, and he plops down onto the table opposite me.

"Okay. Talk. What's going on?" he says.

This is even harder than I imagined. Jefferson looks worried about me. *Me*, the one who ran away from our best shot at answers. He's been looking for his daughter for over fourteen years. What's a little insinuation from my parents' murderer compared to that? My parents' case is closed. His is still ongoing.

"It had nothing to do with me, actually," I say, heat crawling up my face. "Well, it *did*, but it wasn't *about* me."

"Phoenix, don't dance around it," he says with a touch of irritation.

"Okay, so here it is." I heave a sigh and rest forward on my elbows. "We both know Dasc hasn't been saying mum about anything. He won't talk to anyone. Now, out of nowhere, he's decided he'll talk but—and here's the pixie in the pie—only to me."

His beady eyes widen, his jaw tightens, and his knuckles turn white as he clenches his hands together. I start talking faster to get it all out in one go before he can say anything.

"So, I went in there and he said I'd have to answer a question first before he'd answer any of mine and he started saying stuff about my parents and you being idiots and implying that Draco let my parents be murdered and Hawk turned, and then I freaked out and punched him and I got shot by the major and then I—" I say this all in rush and then suck in a deep breath before I let the real bomb drop. "And then I ran. I couldn't—I mean, the things he said about my parents. I'm so sorry, Jefferson."

His eyes focus on the bandage wrapped around my knuckles and he holds a hand over his mouth like he's trying to hold in a shout. I'm terrified. What have I done?

"Draco followed me," I say in a timid voice. "Wants me to go back. I have a few days until Dasc is ready to talk again."

He shifts his jaw, then shifts it again, and finally pulls his hand away to speak.

"You should work on your training until Hawk gets back from school," is all he says, then gets up and walks stiffly away.

Well, that went about as well as I expected it would. Part of me wishes he will forgive me and we can just move on, but I know it can never be that simple. If our places were reversed, I would have been yelling. I wait up in the loft as the Green Monster revs to life and Jefferson drives off to who knows where, leaving me alone. I bite down hard on my tongue, punishing myself for my own stupidity, then move into the cabin to hunt for my MP3 player.

I'm still too wound up and tense to even attempt my daily training rounds so I pop in my earbuds and scroll through my playlists to find my parents' old song. I sit on the lower bunk in the room Hawk and I share and let the melody's familiar comfort drown out the rest of the world. My eyes close as I try to block out that awful sensation of guilt, of letting down one of the few people that really matter to me in my life. The song plays on repeat for a solid twenty minutes before I finally change into my exercise clothes, pretend to shrug off my worries, and return to the barn.

Jefferson's been having us get comfortable using the assortment of weapons on our new weapon rack, so I take one collapsible sword off its peg and trot down the loft steps.

The floor of the barn has been cleared for our personal sparring area since we were forced indoors by the heavy snowfall. I stand in the middle, feeling the beat of a techno song, then unlatch the two hooks that hold the blade inside the thick black hilt. The lengths of blade start to drop down one piece at a time. Holding the sword out in front of me, I run my hand along the back of the katana blade to smooth out the segments then give it a good sharp flick to lock them in place to form a single solid blade. It's not the strongest of swords but it's extremely convenient to transport. If I manage to pass the trials this summer and get assigned a slayer position, it'll be one of the weapons I'll always need to keep on hand. Some monsters can only be stopped by a clean beheading.

Thinking of death, the act of killing another being, besieges me with a rush of adrenaline and it's like I'm back on that night firing away into Dasc's chest. My sword hand shakes so I force myself to take slow deep breaths. The shakiness doesn't really go away so I ignore it as best I can and focus on the pounding beat in my ears. I start to move through the simple steps I learned from my days of training in Underground, matching my movements to the rhythm of my music. It's easier to remember what I'm supposed to do if I think of them as steps in a dance. I count out the time by the number of songs I listen to and eventually put the sword back to practice on hand to hand combat against a padded dummy.

When it comes time for target practice, I grab a bio-mech gun and my mother's .45 before heading out to the homemade gun range behind the cabin. My breath clouds before me as I trudge through the half-foot of snow and pin targets to the line before reeling them out. Once in position, I draw up the bio-mech gun and hesitate only briefly before letting off a string of pulses into the paper target. The pulses make the target wave like it's been hit by a strong gust of wind but that's it. No explosion, no holes tearing through the thin paper. It's always easier practicing with the bio-mech gun. I practice shooting while moving side to side, dropping to one knee, moving back, moving forward, and even try a few rolls in the snow before coming up to fire.

Tucking the bio-mech gun into my back pocket, I pull my mother's gun out of the holster Jefferson got for me. I know the gun like the back of my hand, each curve, each component, the weight, the feel. It's a part of me now. I ratchet the slide and take aim at the paper target.

Dasc's face pops into my head, like it does every time I draw my weapon. I can see him sneering at me. I remember how he tried to have Hawk kill me. My face burns thinking of what he put Hawk through and what he did to my family. He said he tried to make Hawk and me *his* family in some perverted, twisted, inhuman way—

I picture his face on the target and fire, and fire again, and again, and again, until the slide locks back because it's out of bullets. My breath is labored as I study the destruction. My tight grouping has blown out the center of the target. I've really taken my firearm training in stride after what happened with Dasc. There's no room for error. I need to be prepared. Yet, despite my level of improvement, the shakes are back in my hand. I flex my fingers several times and shake out my arms. *Pixies*, I hate feeling like this. I'm a junior agent with the International Monster Slayers. How am I supposed to slay anything if I can't even hold a gun steady?

"Well, remind me not to tick you off," a voice says behind me.

I jump and whip about to aim my empty gun at Deputy Graham. He's in his sheriff's uniform holding a box of jerseys in his arms and raises an eyebrow at me. I quickly lower my weapon and run a hand down my face.

"You should know better than to sneak up on someone in the middle of target practice," I say, still catching my breath after getting spooked.

"I do," he says. "That's why I waited to say something until after your gun was empty."

I pinch the bridge of my nose then turn my attention to unlocking the slide and holstering the .45. "Can I help you with something, Deputy?"

"Just dropping off the jerseys from the game." He shrugs the box in his arms. "And wondering if you've heard any more about Mr. Krushnic or Dasc or whatever his name is."

The blood drains out of my face. I should have known Deputy Graham would be coming around again soon. Ever since Dasc was arrested, he's been hounding us for information like we've been hounding Witty for updates. Jefferson isn't the only one who lost someone to Dasc. The deputy's sister disappeared too. I panic and do something really stupid and unfair. I lie.

"No, nothing yet. I'm sorry."

He nods and rolls his lips, clearly disappointed. I pull in my target using the pulleys on the range so I don't have to look him in the eye.

"So, umm," the deputy says uncertainly, appearing to be grasping for a topic for conversation. "Hawk's really a pro. He did great at the game the other day."

"Yeah, that's Hawk for you." I gather the targets in my hand and gesture for the deputy to follow me into the barn. "He's competitive. He works hard to win."

I lead the way up the stairs and Deputy Graham follows, taking off his wide brimmed hat and tucking it under his arm. We reach the loft and I put the targets on Jefferson's desk so he can see I did my firearm training for the day. I was supposed to go through a few rounds but one clip is good enough for me today.

"It's not just that though," the deputy says and leans against the railing at the top of the stairs. "I know some of us are a little awkward as—well, as our other half." The corner of his mouth twitches. "But he's a natural."

I brace my hands on Jefferson's desk and stare at the blank monitor screen. The deputy's comment strikes me as odd. Is he really trying to compliment Hawk on his natural werewolf skills? Skills he should never have had in the first place but was forced into them because a deranged maniac bit him? Am I supposed to say thanks that my brother has gotten so good at becoming one with his inner demon? Any response I might make sounds bitter in my head and I don't want to snap at Deputy Graham. He's a good man.

"It makes me wonder sometimes," the deputy says, his voice trailing off.

"Wonder what, exactly?" I say, a bite to my words.

His hazel eyes meet mine and they aren't accusatory but sad. "If that's why Dasc took my sister," he says quietly. "Because some people adapt to it better than others. I don't know." He combs his shaggy hair back with his fingers and puts his hat on. "Just wish I knew why any of it happened, you know?"

I bite my lip and look away. "Yeah. Me too."

"Take care, Phoenix. Call me if you need anything."

"Will do."

He trots down the stairs and a short while later I hear the growl of an engine as he takes off in his squad car. He's left me with something more to think about. How many more guilt trips am I going to go through today?

I retreat into the cabin and take a shower. Jefferson still isn't back by the time I'm out. He could be anywhere and I'm not inclined to bother him anyway. If he needs space, he can have it. I glance at the clock. It's 2:15. School won't be over for another hour so I'm on my own until Hawk gets out. Time moves too slowly and I've got too much time to think again.

This is probably a bad idea, and an unhealthy obsession, but I leave a note saying I'm gone for whoever returns to the cabin first, then grab the SUV keys and head out. The back roads aren't in great condition, there's not even salt, but I pass someone with a plow on the front of their truck going in the opposite direction clearing off what they can. I take the familiar route that I can drive blindfolded by now and turn onto the long driveway, using the tracks from the last time I came here as a guide. The SUV slides to a stop on a slick of ice right in front of my parents' old house.

Jefferson and Hawk don't know I still come here. I came once with Jefferson and again with my brother, but that was enough for them. Now I always find an excuse to take a quick drive by while on other business or pretend I'm taking my sweet time at the movie rental store while I'm actually walking through the house. For some reason I can't leave this place alone. I dream about it sometimes, about that night when everything changed.

It's definitely seen better days but I've at least fixed the weather door, boarded up the windows, and even installed new locks on the doors. But everything is still peeling paint like bad sunburn. The porch steps are crooked. The roof is in terrible repair and, with the last snowfall, I won't be surprised if it eventually caves in. It's a horrible reminder of what I've lost, but it's also the only place Hawk and I had with our parents. It belongs to us. It has our memories, remembered and forgotten. If I leave it to rot, what does that say about me? Maybe I can't fix the past but I can at least try to fix this stupid house.

I get out of the SUV and wade through the drifts of snow that reach up to my knees. I navigate along the outside edge of the steps to avoid the decayed center and use the only set of keys to enter the front door. There are some fresh signs of creature activity but nothing as bad as the first time I came to this place. A broom sits beside the door where I left it, so I start to sweep up the debris and shrew turds. After a round through the first floor, I unlock the back door and brush it all outside.

It's only then I see a pair of tracks in the thick snow. Small footprints with a deeper imprint in the back, like a little woman wearing boots with a heel, go from the woods to the back deck, to one of the only windows not boarded up looking into the kitchen. Someone's been peeking inside. There's even a little cleared circle on the dirty window where someone could have wiped it with the edge of their sleeve to see inside better. I set the broom aside, heart pounding in my chest, and carefully follow the footprints to the tree line.

There's less snow under the thick branches of the evergreens but there's still enough. I manage to follow the tracks through the trees until they eventually lead out to the road and disappear on the blacktop. I stand on the shoulder looking one way and then the other, even though whoever it was is long gone. The tracks are at least a day old or more by my estimate, which probably isn't a great estimate anyway. That's more Hawk's area of expertise.

What if they had been looking in while I was here before? A chill goes down my spine. I really, *really* don't like the thought of someone watching me, especially when I don't even realize it. I shudder and jog back along my own tracks to the house. I make sure to lock the rear door and then, just to be cautious, check through all the rooms. Nothing's been moved or disturbed recently, so that's something at least. I'm really glad I decided to put locks on the doors.

I exit and lock the front door behind me. It's quiet here and there's hardly ever any traffic on the road. You think I'd notice if someone crept up while I was here. So maybe they didn't come when I was here. Maybe it was some kid just checking out a creepy old house on a dare. It could be nothing. It could be something. It could be everything.

"*Pixies*, I'm paranoid," I mutter to myself and sigh, watching my breath mist before me. "With good reason, I guess."

Before returning to the SUV, I trudge through another drift to sit in the tire swing hanging from the massive oak out front. Ice cracks up the rope when I settle in and try to swing a little. The frigid tire starts to numb my legs but I stay awhile longer, glancing at my phone to check the time every so often.

When my phone buzzes in my hand, I just about jump out of my skin. The number isn't one I recognize but I pick it up anyway.

"Hello?"

"Mason?" It's Charlie. Oh, for the love of humanity. It *had* to be him calling.

"Yeah, it's me," I sigh.

"It's Junior Agent Jaeger." As if I could forget. He sounds a bit stiff, awkward even.

"Can I help you?" I ask, hoping to get this conversation over with as soon as possible.

"We might have found a lead on our vampire and Gillian."

I'm surprised he's actually admitting the existence of a vampire now. "Gillian's still missing?"

"Well, *yeah.*" Through the phone in the background I hear a thud and soft "ow," then some hostile whispering before he continues. "Yes, she is still missing. I did, however, manage to track down a few witnesses who saw Gillian getting hauled off."

I can't help it. I'm extremely curious. "She was taken?"

"I got a description of a car involved and located it abandoned in the middle of a hub of warehouses. I was about to go clear through those buildings but Melody's got her hands full trying to keep the other selkies from barging down there themselves and screwing everything up. And Chip and Rodney still aren't back from the Boundary Waters." He lets out a very audible sigh. Who are Chip and Rodney? "I need your help."

"I'm sorry, I must have misheard you," I say, that inclination to start an argument surfacing again since it's Charlie. "I thought you didn't need help from someone like me."

"Oh, you mean cranky and irresponsible—OW! *Stop hitting me!*" There's shuffling over the line and I can hear Melody hissing something at him. Eventually there's silence and Charlie comes back on.

"I would very much appreciate it if you would come and be my backup." He clears his throat. "Pretty please?"

7

When I call Jefferson to tell him the Duluth team needs us, he hardly says anything at all. He just sort of grunts and acknowledges what I've said. It's like trying to walk on glass and every second of it is painful.

"So, what's the plan? Who should go up there?" I ask, having to forcibly draw an answer from him.

"Grab your brother. You can go up together and watch each other's back. I'll man the office."

"Are you sure?"

"Just go, Phoenix."

The line clicks. I swallow and stare at my phone like it wants to take a bite out of me too. I understand why he's angry but this hurts after everything we've been through. I also can't let this distract me right now. I start up the SUV, work my way to the heart of Moose Lake, and pull into the school parking lot. There's five minutes left until the bell rings so I park facing away from the school to ensure none of the teachers spot me when I'm supposed to be out sick or whatever excuse Hawk made up for me today.

While I wait, I send my brother a text to let him know to head out immediately and look for me. I fiddle with the radio until I hear the distant school bell. Practically seconds later Hawk flies out the door, yards ahead of everyone else. I honk the horn and his head swivels in my direction. He takes off at a jog and wrenches open the passenger door when he reaches me.

"Are we running?" is the first thing he says then tosses his backpack into the footwell and slides inside.

I shake my head and he heaves a sigh. It's probably a bad thing that running is our first instinct. Maybe we wouldn't be so inclined if Hawk was actually using the serum and I wasn't a blossoming nuclear reactor.

As soon as Hawk buckles in, I get us moving towards the interstate. My brother just watches me.

"I know I said I filled my hug quota but I think I need to make an exception for you," he says. "You look like crap, Phoenix. What happened to your hand? Fill me in."

The story spills out of me, starting from my arrival at Underground, to Draco following me to Moose Lake, to Jefferson's reaction, to lying to Deputy Graham. I leave out the bit about visiting our parents' house. I'll keep that secret for a while.

"You should have seen Jefferson's face," I say, voicing my fears. "He hates me."

"He doesn't *hate* you," Hawk says. "He'll come around."

"His missing daughter is at stake. He's not going to just get over that. I screwed up."

"Can anyone really blame you for what happened?" He

shakes his head and gazes out the windshield. "I want to rip Dasc's throat out for saying that crap to you."

The aggression in his voice makes me sneak a look at him. His face is drawn into a deep frown and he has one foot up on the seat, propping up his knee. He looks casually dangerous, if that's even a thing, but Hawk manages to pull it off.

"I don't get why he wanted me there in the first place," I say.

"Phoenix, you almost killed him. He made the IMS desperate enough to give him anything he wanted, so he asked for you to torment you. He's a monster."

I worry my lower lip. "Yeah. I guess you're right."

"Of course I'm right." He slugs me lightly in the arm. "Forget about him for now, okay? Worry about it when you have to go back."

We merge onto the interstate and start the long drive up to Duluth. Despite my brother's advice, I continue to mull over what Dasc said and it makes me angry.

"Hey, frowny face," Hawk says. "Who would win in a fight? Ryūjin or Draco?"

The random question catches me off guard and I laugh. Ryūjin is one of the six majestics that hails from Japan, otherwise known as the Ocean King. Of course Hawk would think to pit the Ocean King against Draco, Europe's Firestorm. "What? What kind of question is that?"

"An honest one."

"Well, it's a dumb question. Both Ryūjin and Draco are majestic class. Their powers are practically equal."

He throws his hands up. "What?! You're crazy. Ryūjin's got crazy awesome water powers. He makes freakin' typhoons for crying out loud."

"Yeah, and Draco makes firestorms."

"Ryūjin would quench them," Hawk argues.

"Not if Draco evaporated the water with the heat of his fires first."

"No way. Ryūjin has the entire ocean at his command. A little fire can't stop all that water."

"Ryūjin doesn't control the *entire* ocean at once."

He presses a finger to my lips and shushes me. "Don't say such horrible things." I shove his hand away but he keeps talking. "Say he gets past Draco's fire."

"There are still dragon's barriers to contend with."

"Well, they both have those. And Ryūjin's are way cooler."

We argue back and forth for most of the ride. Neither of us really wins. We end up laughing too much to form any coherent arguments after a while. It isn't until I pull up in front of the Duluth Field Office that I realize I haven't spared a thought for Dasc in the last forty-five minutes. Before we get out, I grab Hawk's arm.

"Hey. Thanks," I say.

He scrunches up his face into a ridiculous cross-eyed smile. "That's what twinsies are for!"

We're both laughing again as we hop out and I rap my knuckles on the metal door of the Duluth Field Office. After a short wait, I hear a series of locks click and the door swings open with Charlie framed in the doorway. He's looking very posh again in a black overcoat with the collar turned up, leather gloves, and a gray scarf. Seriously, can't he have a bad hair day or something? I resist glancing down at my military green parka I got from a local thrift store.

"Come in before someone sees you," Charlie says briskly.

I roll my eyes and slip inside, Hawk on my heels. Charlie closes the door and the instant he turns around Hawk thrusts out his hand.

"Junior Agent Hawk Mason. You're Junior Agent Jaeger, I take it? It's a pleasure."

Charlie's eyes bounce to me for a second before settling on my brother. He gives Hawk's hand one firm shake and lets go with an expression that makes it clear he's suspicious of Hawk's friendly, easy going introduction after having met me. Honestly, a part of me is wishing Hawk would be more abrasive.

"Where's Agent Barnes?" Charlie asks.

"He stayed back to man our field office," Hawk replies, "but I think Phoenix and I will be suitable backup. How about we move things along and find that selkie? She's already been missing for too long. You found some witnesses, you mentioned?"

Charlie nods, clearly impressed with Hawk's professionalism. Personally, I think my brother's hamming it up pretty good. He's never this professional. Charlie waves us down the flight of steps to stand at the computers in the middle of their command center. Loud voices echo from somewhere deeper inside and they don't sound too friendly.

"Don't mind that," Charlie says and waves a hand before opening up a video on his computer monitor. "Nessa's just ticked Melody is keeping her on the sidelines and stopping her from stomping all over our jurisdiction. Here we go."

He opens a clip of surveillance video situated up high and looking down on what I recognize as the interstate. It's paused on a night shot with the cars illuminated by streetlights set at regular intervals along the road. Charlie circles one car in particular with his pointer finger.

"The couple I spoke to said they saw a woman matching Gillian's description being carried between a guy in a hoodie and a girl with a pink scarf past the Chocolate Factory," he says. "They noticed because Gillian appeared unconscious. When they asked if she needed help, her two *friends* said she was blackout drunk. They got into this car, an older model dark blue Mustang. I managed to spot it while combing through local traffic feeds."

I swallow past the lump in my throat. "So we're dealing with at least two people now, not just our mystery man. Where'd they go?"

Charlie opens up another window on the computer displaying an aerial view of a huge clump of warehouses packed together in a shipping yard along the harbor's edge. Railroad tracks lead right into the mass of buildings, cutting between mounds of minerals covered with tarps for the winter, stacks of crates, and heavy-duty loading equipment. It's a maze and there are a lot of places to hide or hold someone. I get why they want more people to help.

"Melody and I scoured the area and managed to find the vehicle abandoned in the parking lot here." He points to a small lot west of the shipping yard. "It's very possible that Gillian is in one of these warehouses but there's a lot of ground to cover. Nessa wants to barge in with her selkie friends but we can't risk sending a bunch of untrained people in there. One of their own is missing. I don't doubt for a second that one of them might do something stupid or get themselves hurt."

Charlie pulls back the edge of his sleeve to glance at a

shiny wristwatch. "We've already wasted enough time as it is. Now, we know there are two suspects but there could be more."

"Especially if they're vampires," I interject. "They form gangs to fight for territory."

He gives me a flat stare. "Yeah. I know that. If these even *are* vampires."

"There's a strong possibility."

He ignores my comment and says, "I assume you're both armed?"

"We're covered," I say and fight the urge to roll my eyes. I've already got a machete strapped inside the lining of my jacket, a bio-mech gun in my front pocket, and my mother's gun in its hidden holster at the small of my back as always. Hawk's weapons are waiting for him in the SUV.

"Then we need to get moving. Like you said, she's been missing too long. I'll meet you outside. I need to chat with Melody for a second."

He spins away with a flourish—at least it looks like it with his overcoat swishing out around him—and he walks down the hallway out of sight. Hawk lets out a low whistle and we walk outside together. I lean against the side of the SUV as Hawk pops the hatch and pulls out a side panel to reveal a hidden stash of weapons. After a quick look around to make sure no one is nearby, he starts pulling out items and tucking them into his jacket and pockets.

"Well, aren't you sharp tonight," I comment offhand. "I thought for sure you'd start off with a bad pun or joke about centaurs to get the ball rolling with Charlie."

"I'm being sneaky," he says, carefully stashing a long dagger into the lining of his parka. "I'm luring him into a false sense of security with politeness and professionalism, then BAM—I'll hit him with an obscure amount of craziness he'll never see coming."

I throw my head back and laugh. "You're an evil genius."

"Mind you, a selkie *is* missing and a couple of freaks are on the loose. We gotta be actual adults at some point in our lives, right?"

"Well said."

Moments later the garage door of the field office opens and Charlie pulls out in an SUV identical to ours. Hawk steals shotgun and I hop into the second row. We wait for a moment before Melody stalks out of the building and comes to join us. Her blonde curls are in a bit of disarray and her cheeks are flushed. She takes the seat next to me and heaves a sigh.

"Trouble in paradise?" Charlie quips as he shifts the SUV into gear and we roll away from the field office.

"Nessa's promised to sit back for the time being," Melody says and tugs on a pair of black leather gloves. "How long she'll keep that promise is another problem entirely." Her gaze passes over me and she gives me a warm smile despite everything that's going on. It seems like a part of her personality is to make sure everyone around her feels comfortable.

We fall silent as Charlie takes us through the warehouse district and past grain elevators, driving in the direction of the shipping yard. The reality of where we're headed hits me. Someone's missing and we're going to find them either alive or . . . I swallow as I suddenly envision Jefferson's daughter out in the world in some forsaken place. There's a horrible pit in my stomach. Is this what Jefferson feels like all the time? Is this the burden he carries with him everywhere?

"How old are you, Charlie?" Hawk asks, breaking the silence. "I'm just curious when you'll be taking the trials to become a full-fledged agent."

"It's Junior Agent Jaeger. And I'm twenty-one. I'll be taking the trials this summer."

"Oh, you don't say." Hawk glances at me over his shoulder with a wink. "Sounds like we'll be taking them together then."

Charlie shoots him a sharp look. "How old are you?"

"Eighteen."

"And you'll be taking the trials already?" Melody asks beside me, sounding impressed.

"Oh, yeah. We got advanced after the whole Dasc fiasco."

"Huh." Charlie doesn't say anything else and I can't make out his expression from my spot. For people that have been raised in the life, they're usually eligible to take the agent trials when they turn twenty-one. The IMS needs agents badly and are willing to take whoever they can get even at a young age. I can't tell if Hawk managed to impress Charlie or make him more irritated. Not that I care. If Charlie's willing to judge me without even knowing me, then I don't care what he thinks about me or my brother. If we have to work together, then we'll do our jobs. Past that, whatever.

We pull up alongside a fence topped with razor wire and park in the mostly abandoned lot. Across from us sits the blue Mustang. Before we exit the SUV, Melody passes around little headsets and has us link together on a single channel. After a quick comms check, Melody throws a medic bag over her shoulder, and we exit in unison to stalk across the icy lot towards the Mustang.

"Mels," Charlie says—it doesn't get past me that he uses a nickname instead of her last name like he does for me and Hawk—and points to the Mustang's windshield. "No frost."

"Someone's used it since we spotted it," Melody says and lays a gloved hand on the hood. "Not warm, though, so not terribly recent."

We pause as a group and look to the structures surrounding us. Past the razor wire fence is a steel-sided warehouse that rises up next to two slightly less intimidating warehouses with peeling brown paint. There are more warehouses, little shacks, a few commercial office buildings for utility companies, and empty parking lots. Past the first row of buildings are multiple sets of train tracks leading all the way to the harbor.

Charlie reaches the gate in the fence first and jingles the lock sitting open that's supposed to be holding a chain to keep the gate shut.

"Well, someone's definitely been here," he says. "Lock's open."

"Are we sure there's no one else using these warehouses at the moment?" Hawk asks and turns slowly on the spot, scanning the darkened windows up above.

Charlie yanks on the gate and holds it open for us. "Shipping season's on hiatus and won't start back up until March. They keep the warehouses locked for the time being and the workers get a short break. At least for this place, anyway."

The sky's gray and the light is fading fast, turning the warehouses towering above us into cold and daunting behemoths. The shipping yard is an eerie labyrinth as a bitter wind sighs through the spaces between the buildings and creaks some loose metal siding nearby. If I really strain my ears I can make out the sharp crack of ice out on the lake. It's the perfect spot for a monster to camp out.

"We'll go in pairs," Melody says quietly. "Phoenix, you're with me. We'll cover the buildings to the north. Charlie, go with Hawk and cover the south. Stay in touch and call out if you find anything."

Charlie looks none too happy with the group arrangements and I must say I'm nervous myself. I'd like to stick with Hawk if at all possible but Melody is already moving away to hunt for monsters. My brother gives me a quick nod to let me know he's fine so I jog after my partner. As I move away I hear Hawk in my ear through my headset.

"Lead the way," he says to Charlie.

Once I catch up to Melody, I slow my pace and in unison we click on our flashlights as we enter the first of the run-down brown warehouses. There's a huge door with a loading dock for semi-trucks to pull up to but we take a normal door on the far right. Melody gives it a good tug but it's locked. Instead of moving off to find a different entrance, she winks at me and pulls out a pair of lock picks. I hold my light on the knob for her, while keeping my eyes on the area behind us, and her expert fingers open the lock within a matter of seconds. As soon as the door swings open, we slip inside and shut the door behind us.

The beams of our flashlights brush over open crates stacked on top of each other in leaning towers and a dusty floor that opens up into an enormous main room. The light we carry is swallowed up by the sheer vast emptiness of the place stuffed with darkness. Anything could be hiding in the shadows beyond the reach of our flashlights. My heart beats a little faster.

Melody doesn't say a word but gestures with two fingers to a steel door on our right. I nod and follow in her wake as she takes point. Once through the incredibly creaky door, we work our way through a number of dark offices filled with shipping manifests, sprawling maps of the Great Lakes stapled to the walls, silent computers, and paper-lined desks. Past the offices we come to more holding areas with more crates and stacks of who knows what under massive tarps. A fine layer of dust covers everything.

"There's a whole lot of dust here," I whisper but my voice sounds incredibly loud after the lengthy silence. "Doesn't look like anyone's been here in forever."

"It's ore dust," Melody says quietly. "A lot of taconite and limestone gets shipped out of Duluth. The dust gets over everything."

"Oh."

"But you're right. It doesn't look like anyone's been here recently."

We finally circle back to the front of the warehouse and exit the way we came.

Melody presses a finger to her wireless headset. "Boys, you find anything?"

"Nothing yet," Charlie responds.

"We just finished clearing our first building," Hawk adds.

"Same," I say and watch as Melody tries the door at the next brown warehouse. When it swings open, she raises her eyebrows at me. "We just came across an unlocked door, though."

"Congratulations," Charlie says in a monotone. "Would you like a treat?"

"Charlie," Melody says sharply and gives me an apologetic grimace. "Button it up. This might not mean anything so move on to the next building on your side and we'll let you know if we find anything here."

"Roger that," he says.

My face burns and I want to throw some kind of snappy insult at him but I've got nothing. I'm too angry. Clenching my jaw, I storm into the warehouse and take point this time as we sweep through. Melody doesn't say a word but a light touch on my arm lets me know I'm being too noisy. I heave a deep breath and force myself to slow and walk softly. This warehouse is identical to the last so it's easier knowing where we're going.

As we clear through the first couple of offices, I can't keep silent for long. I keep my flashlight up but wrap one hand around the microphone of my headset so the boys can't hear me when I ask Melody, "Can I ask you a question?"

She finishes peering through the small office and clamps a hand around her mic as well. "Sure."

"Why does Charlie hate me so much?" I ask. "I swear, I can't for the life of me get on his good side."

"You mean, when you aren't equally riling him up?"

I fight the urge to roll my eyes. "He jabs, so I jab. But he won't stop throwing punches."

Melody keeps walking and assumes point but continues to hold her microphone to keep our conservation private.

"He's got a sticky past when it comes to werewolves. The way you reacted when your mate Ashley was arrested—well, it triggered that smidge of hatred he always tries to keep buried."

So, he *has* been personally affected by werewolves as I suspected. "What do you mean 'sticky past?'"

"I'm sorry, but that's his business." She raises an eyebrow at me. "If you want to know the details, you'll have to ask him."

Right. Like that's going to happen.

She releases her microphone and it's clear she's done answering my questions.

We shift into a focused silence. This is what each of us has trained for—protecting legendary creatures and taking down monsters. I push aside hostile thoughts of Charlie and keep my eyes peeled for signs of passage through the warehouse.

Melody checks in with the boys once more as we finish our sweep. This time I don't speak lest I get snapped at again for something stupid. Both of our teams move on to the next area and as our shoes crunch in the snow along the way to a massive steel warehouse, I start to doubt if we'll find anything. Maybe our hoodie-guy and scarf-girl ditched the car here and then went somewhere else. They could have easily changed vehicles. They could have killed Gillian and—no. I can't entertain a thought like that. It's our duty to keep looking. We can't give up when there's someone out there that needs our help. If only we could find—

Melody tries the door at the next warehouse. It swings effortlessly open, and through the ore dust is a bare swath like something had been dragged along the floor. We both freeze and follow the path with our flashlights only. There's actually a lot of dust that's been disturbed. In sync, we step forward lightly and draw our bio-mech guns as our lights catch something on the floor not twenty feet in.

It's a bright pink scarf.

"We've got something," Melody says in a breathy whisper over the line. "Pink scarf on the floor. Looks like there might have been a struggle. We're in the last warehouse on the left closest to the parking lot."

"On our way," Charlie says.

I fishtail my flashlight over the floor to see if there's anything else. Dark specks sit in contrast to the gray floor. I inch forward to get a better look. Blood. It looks like there was quite the fight in here. Gillian could have finally come to and faced her attackers. We must be on the right trail after all. My heart picks up its pace again and my fingers itch to grasp the familiar grip of my mother's .45 even though it won't do me a lot of good if we are, in fact, dealing with vampire kidnappers. Vampires can only be killed by a blade to the heart or a beheading. The machete tucked in my parka suddenly feels a hundred pounds heavier.

We keep our eyes sharp until the boys finally sneak in to join us. Charlie avoids eye contact with me and I give him the cold shoulder. Hawk turns his face so the others can't see and then gives me an exaggerated grimace while jabbing his thumb in Charlie's direction. That brings a small smile to the surface but I quickly wipe it away as Melody beckons us to come together.

"We're going to spread out in a line to cover the main floor to see if we can find a trail. Then Charlie will take point and we follow in formation. I'll take the rear. Cover each other." Her eyes flicker over the darkness of the warehouse. "We don't know how many we're dealing with here."

Without further ado, Charlie stalks forward with his flashlight and pulls a blade from his jacket. The rest of us spread out on either side and scan the floor of the massive central area of the warehouse that, for the moment, is completely empty. The trail from the scuffle around the pink scarf becomes muddled with a lot of other fresh footprints and it's difficult to tell where they head in the building. Either there were a lot of people walking here or someone pacing back and forth on end.

We reach the back wall and come to a series of doors set with square windows in the center of each. Shining our flashlights in and peering through, we survey a loading dock area, a storage closet, a utility room filled with pipes and electrical equipment, and a dark hallway leading to a place we can't make out. We try each door but they're all locked.

"Wait a second," Hawk says and holds out an arm to get our attention. "Did you hear that?"

"Hear what?" I ask.

He tilts his head to the side, picking up a noise the rest of us non-werewolves can't hear. He moves silently around us to look down the dark hallway on the other side of the furthest door. Leaning forward until his ear is pressed up against the glass, he nods. "There's someone through here. I can hear them."

Charlie's eyebrows rise but he doesn't look impressed, just skeptical. It's enough for Melody, however. She moves to the door and shines her flashlight into the endless dark of the locked hallway.

"Charlie," is all she says.

"On it." Charlie shrugs past us and stares through the glass. One second he's there leaning forward like he could melt through the door and the next he's gone. Literally. I let out a gasp and nearly drop my flashlight.

"What the—" Hawk says and his breath mists on the glass as his eyes grow wide. He turns to me and points dumbfounded through the glass.

The next second I hear the lock click and door swings open from the other side where Charlie stands rather self-satisfied.

"You coming or what?" he says.

"But you—you were . . ." I look to the empty space beside me and then back to him. "You can teleport?"

He holds the door open wide for us to enter the hallway. Melody doesn't even flinch and strides on like she owns the place. Hawk follows swiftly after and I come grudgingly last. I'm a little peeved Charlie never told us he could teleport. Granted, it's not like we Blessed—which he clearly is—go around telling everyone what we can do. But he can *teleport*? Wow, my powers are so lame right now.

"Can you do that through walls?" Hawk asks with an air of intense curiosity.

"I have to be able to see where I'm going," Charlie whispers then glowers at him and me for good measure. I guess that explains why he needed to look through the window in the door. "Can we talk about this later? Or never? We've got a selkie to find."

Ignoring me once again, Charlie moves light on his feet with his bio-mech gun raised as he moves on. Hawk stands beside me and mouths, *Teleportation? Wow!*

I know, right? I mouth in reply, and then keep at his side as we walk along in an offset group, Melody drifting back to cover the rear.

The hallway eventually opens up into a spacious break room and we come to more offices. It's a lot cleaner back here in the managerial portion of the building so there aren't any footprints to follow. We pause in the expansive room next to a selection of circular tables and listen. When I don't hear anything, I look to Hawk and realize the others do the same. Hawk's eyes are trained on the floor as he tilts his head this way then that trying to locate the sound he heard earlier. Eventually he meets my gaze with a frown and shakes his head.

We team back up on Charlie as he leads into the first of the offices lining the hallway past the break room. There's nothing in it but a worn leather chair, an empty water cooler, and stack of leaflets about taconite shipping. We move through two more offices in similar condition. The place looks normal, harmless, but there's a quality about the emptiness of it all that makes it ghostly. A wind outside rattles something in the vents over our heads and forms whispers under the closed doors.

As we near the end of the hallway I hear a soft sound like someone crying. Charlie holds up a fist, motioning us to halt before we silently group up around the door of the last office. As Hawk and I cover Charlie on either side, Charlie breaches through the door. The rest of us follow swiftly in his wake. Our flashlights rake the room and all come together to form a single spotlight on a girl tied to a chair against the far wall. Her blonde hair hangs in matted curtains around her thin face. Her sequined shirt is torn and splotched with what's sure to be blood. Her arms are bound and her ankles are tied to the legs of the chair.

Her groggy, bloodshot eyes squint at us against our flashlights.

"Help me."

8

Even from a distance I can tell the girl's in bad shape. She's pale, slumped, and doesn't even have the energy to lift her head when Charlie rushes forward to start cutting apart her bonds with his knife. Melody's there a second later, dropping to her knees and slinging the medic pack off her shoulders. She whips around momentarily to point at me.

"Guard the door incase our kidnappers are nearby," she orders.

I do as I'm told and swing the door halfway shut before planting myself as guard in the shadows of the frame. Hawk stands beside me but looks like he desperately wants to help our captured selkie instead.

"Gillian?" Charlie asks and the girl gives two very small nods. "We're going to get you out of here, okay? Just hang on. We'll get you some help."

Charlie gently pulls back Gillian's hair to reveal deep bite marks on her neck. Despite that, there's only a small trail of blood that runs down her arm—a vampire wouldn't have wanted to waste a drop. Melody produces a wad of gauze and starts patching up the bite mark on Gillian's shoulder. Every movement she makes is methodical and controlled, precise and practiced. Gillian's lower lip trembles and her fingers shake. I want to reach out and comfort her but I don't know how. Her skin is so pale and her face sallow, it's a miracle she hasn't gone into shock yet. Her eyes slowly track up to find Charlie's face.

"Can you tell us what happened?" he asks.

She works her jaw a few times and licks her lips. "I can't, umm . . ."

Then she starts crying and Charlie freezes, clearly unsure what to do. I know because I feel the exact same way.

"It's all right," Melody says but her attention is fixed on the wounds and applying bandages.

Hawk strides forward and taps Charlie on the shoulder to get him to move out of the way. The boys exchange places and Hawk takes Gillian's hand. I return my attention to the dark hallway and our only exit.

"Hey, you're safe now," Hawk murmurs with the soothing voice of a parent to a small child. "We're going to get you out of here and to your sister. No one's going to hurt you. I need you to believe that. Can you do that for me, Gillian?"

She nods once and seems to relax a little. He continues to offer her reassurances and lightly strokes the back of her hand. Every expression and gesture he makes is kind and gentle. Sincerity naturally oozes out of him. I've always envied that part of him—I care just as much and wish I could express my feelings the same way he can, but I can never find the right words. My first gut reaction is to act in order to show someone I care, which usually involves beating up someone on their behalf. That's probably not a good thing, but I can paint better pictures with my fists than my words. I don't know a thing about Gillian but I'm ready to pound whoever did this to a pulp. I can't stand to see someone else in pain.

Charlie backtracks to give Hawk more space as if he might catch whatever weepiness Gillian has, until he's shoulder to shoulder with me. His eyes travel over the walls and plain office, a furrow between his eyebrows. "I don't get it. Where did the vampires go?"

"Oh, I didn't realize we were admitting they're vampires now," I say under my breath.

He gives me a sharp look. "There wasn't strong evidence before. Now there is. Those wounds on her neck are textbook vampire bites."

"Well, shouldn't you *teleport* her out of here? You know, before those vampires come back and corner us in here?"

Charlie doesn't even blink. "Teleporting her would do more harm than good."

"Why? Wouldn't it be better than trying to walk out of here?"

"Are you going to sass me the whole time or can you just accept what I tell you about my own abilities?"

I roll my eyes. "Well, considering you've hardly told me anything—"

"I don't know why I even bothered trying to talk to you." He squeezes his eyes shut and pinches the bridge of his nose. He starts to walk away but then stops and spins around, just like he did in the nightclub, to tower over me. "Why is it all you ever do is argue?"

"Hey, I'm not the one that started our working relationship acting as rude as possible."

"Well, you clearly got into the swing of it once we got going."

"Charlie . . ." Melody says behind us with a weary weight like it's a tried and tired old line she's sick of repeating.

"You flaming pile of hydra crap," I snarl, not relinquishing my fury. "Forgive me if I was upset about *my friend being arrested.*"

"Apology not accepted. And for the record, she was arrested with cause. Turning into a werewolf in the middle of Canal Park is *kind of* a big deal."

A small voice from behind interrupts us. "Is she okay? That girl you're talking about."

We both spin around surprised. Gillian stares at us over Hawk's shoulder.

"It went after her," she continues. "The girl in the alley. I tried to help."

"What happened in that alley?" Hawk asks.

Gillian swallows and clenches onto both of Hawk's hands. "I was going to the Blue Comet when I saw him going after that girl, the werewolf. I knew what he was. Filthy vampire." She shudders. "Then the girl changed and ran off. I should have taken the vampire down in an instant but I got hit from behind. There's at least two. I don't know if there are more."

"Can you describe them?"

"Well, vampires obviously," she says and runs the back of her hand under her nose. "Both skinny, pale . . . the boy was always wearing those stupid black pants and hoodie. Blonde, crooked nose. The girl was a brunette and . . . sorry, I never got a good look at her."

"Do you know where they went?"

"No. I never saw the girl after they first brought me here, but I heard the boy yelling at someone somewhere in the building. I couldn't make out the words. Then he just left."

"How long ago was that?"

"A couple of hours maybe? I don't know. I've been stuck here in this blasted chair." She sucks in a sharp breath and it's clear she's fighting back tears. Hawk leans forward and gives her a hug. She basically falls apart in his arms so Charlie and I turn away. Melody stands beside them, tucking her supplies into the med kit, before tossing the keys of the SUV to Charlie.

"I need you two—" She points between the pair of us at the door, "—to get to the SUV and bring it in as far as you can, then carry the stretcher in. I don't want to move Gillian more than I have to."

Charlie and I exchange an uneasy look before we hustle down the hallway, eager to get away from Gillian's sobs. Well, at least I am. Charlie and I move along quickly in a brooding silence to the deepening night outside. While he ports out into the parking lot and revs up the SUV, I open the fence gate and walk back to the loading bay door. The SUV rumbles up and waits as I work at yanking open the enormous metal door to the warehouse. It lets out a horrible screech and gets stuck on its track. I put my muscle into it—managing to not accidentally break anything—and push it open wide enough for Charlie to pull inside.

I wait by the open door and survey the snowy night. There are a couple of floodlights shining like eerie spotlights around some of the warehouses. Otherwise the rest have fallen into darkness and a few even into decay. The snow piles in drifts against the metal sidings and covers piles of things draped with blue tarp. In the distance cars roar on the interstate on the other side of Railroad Street.

It takes me a moment to realize I'm being watched. Just beyond the reach of the floodlights is a slim figure all in black. Whoever it is hasn't moved an inch so I didn't see him until now, tucked alongside the side of the fence opposite me near the edge of the parking lot. He's wearing black pants and a hoodie as Gillian described and like we saw in the surveillance video.

"Hey!" I shout, my first instinct. My second is drawing my bio-mech gun.

The figure starts a mad dash across the parking lot towards the parked Mustang.

"Charlie! He's running!" I shout as loud as I can and take off after what's most likely one of our vampire kidnappers.

The start of my pursuit doesn't exactly go according to plan. I slip on a patch of ice and then nearly trip over a log buried in the deep snow. Once I regain my footing, I drive my feet into the ground and race through the gate in the fence. There are voices yelling in my ear but I can't even make out the words. I'm running as hard as I can, kicking up snow, but he's already slipped into the Mustang and gunning the engine by the time my feet hit the lot.

The Mustang spins its tires and accelerates directly for me. I run sideways and leap for the chain link fence, lifting up my legs. The car glances off the fence but is already turning to escape instead of run me over. The Mustang squeals, fishtailing side to side before it finds traction, and then takes off out of the parking lot and onto Railroad Street.

Rage fills me. The monster that drained and tortured Gillian is *not* getting away. Crazy and idiotic as it may be, I hop off the fence and run after the Mustang's taillights quickly vanishing down the road. My feet pound the salted pavement but there's no way I'll ever catch him on foot.

Just when I'm about to give up, Melody's black SUV skids to a stop a foot away from me. Charlie throws open the passenger door.

"Get in!"

I don't need telling twice. I dash around the front of the vehicle and practically throw myself inside before slamming the door shut. The second I'm in, Charlie floors the gas and we fly down the road.

"There!" I point through the windshield to the taillights shrinking into the distance.

He doesn't say a word but his body language says it all—he stomps on the pedal, wrenches the wheel hard, and there's fury blazing in his eyes. This isn't the sarcastic naysayer anymore. This is a deadly agent on the hunt.

The voices through my headset finally filter into my brain and I hear Melody shouting, "Charlie, you're going to get yourself killed! Phoenix, respond! Guys, talk to me!"

He doesn't respond but makes the SUV go even faster.

"We're okay," I manage to say breathlessly into the headset. "The male vamp is fleeing and we're in pursuit."

"No, you're not!" she shouts, causing reverb through the connection. "We'll track him through surveillance video later. We need to get Gillian out of—"

"Is she stabilized?" Charlie interrupts.

"*Yes*, but—"

"Good."

Then he rips his headset off and chucks it into the well at my feet. Honestly, he's scary at the moment. Fury boils off him and infects me to. Melody keeps shouting at us to turn back and let the vampire go but I stop listening. I take off my own headset and add it to Charlie's on the floor. His eyes flash to me for only a second, a single second where I see the first hint of respect he's ever tossed my way, and then we blaze on.

I'm thankful that the IMS gives us suped-up vehicles. The SUV roars and gains on the Mustang. The vampire must realize it too because he makes a drastic move. He veers off the road to the left and jerks over a set of train tracks before trying to climb the hill into downtown Duluth. Where on earth is he trying to go?

"Hang on," Charlie says and yanks the wheel. We plow through the Mustang's tracks and wrench forward against our seat belts when we hit the train tracks. Charlie manages to keep control of the vehicle and we climb up through the snow until we hit pavement again. One-way signs blur past me and buildings rear up all around us. The Mustang fishtails across a grassy median but manages to even out, nearly hitting a couple of parked cars in its haste to escape. We follow right behind, Charlie expertly weaving around a little coupe in front of us.

An intersection looms ahead with red lights glaring in our direction.

"Look out!"

The Mustang swings through cross traffic and blazes up the road, continuing to ascend the hill. My heart is in my throat as Charlie swerves into the intersection after it. A bus tries to go through on its green light bearing down on us from the left and lurches to a halt not a moment too soon. Our bumper grazes across its grill. Something in the undercarriage screeches as we swing wide on the corner and lose traction for a moment on an ice patch. I instinctively brace both hands against the dash this time.

We crest one block, the streets rising sharply, and I realize this is a really, really bad time for a car chase. There are cars everywhere, not to mention snow and ice and an increasing grade. The Mustang is still fighting for freedom, though. It runs through a four-way stop, slides left, then keeps on until it hits a major roadway going straight up the hill. Charlie manages to stay on it and even gains ground as the Mustang struggles against the steep grade.

I'm trying to breathe normally as we weave in and out of cars moving at the 30 mph speed limit. We're easily breaking sixty here. Memories of my car crash three months ago surface and I swallow back that dread. The road quickly curves and the hill drops away on the right leaving nothing between us and a nasty drop but a guardrail. I see eye to eye with the tops of buildings at this height. I hold onto the door's armrest for dear life and hope beyond hope that Charlie passed all of his pursuit certification tests with flying colors.

The Mustang skims a rusted hatchback in front of us, spinning the car out until it stops, facing us. Our headlights flood over the startled old man clutching onto his steering wheel directly ahead.

"Fracking crap!" Charlie shouts. He white-knuckles a hard turn and slams on the brakes. We jump the curb of the median and fishtail into oncoming traffic on the other side of the roadway to avoid hitting the hatchback.

Of course, to make matters worse, a bunch of cars just cleared from an intersection ahead of us and stream down, honking their horns and jamming their brakes on the slippery road. Charlie guns it again and sends us flying back over the raised median, each of us really testing the durability of our seat belts, and weaves into the right flow of traffic. The Mustang has already cleared the next intersection and slows only enough to cross oncoming traffic and take an even more steeply inclined street, always moving uphill.

The SUV uses all of its horsepower to floor through the green light, slide into the turn lane, and barely avoid getting struck by a truck coming down the hill. My ribs hurt and I don't know if it's from how hard my heart is pounding or from being thrown against the seat belt.

We almost hit a road sign that says Skyline Parkway and Charlie shouts something unintelligible, or he's just primal screaming. I can't tell. I think I lost all of my screams somewhere three roads behind us.

Good news, there's hardly any traffic on this road. Bad news, Skyline Parkway lives up to its name. Once we clear a block or two, the hillside drops sharply a few feet past the edge of the pavement and opens to nothing but sky. At least we're on the right side of the road and have a lane between us and certain death. Oh, and it's not as well treated as the other roads we've been on. We *really* start to slide and the Mustang comes close to driving right off the edge of the world. Twice.

The vampire finally decides that's a good reason to slow down and we come up close on his bumper.

Trying to hit him and spin him out would probably spin us out over the hill too, ending in all of us dying. Our headlights spill into the back of the Mustang and I can clearly make out the back of the vampire's blonde hair. His hood must have fallen off in the middle of driving like a complete maniac.

"Take the wheel!" Charlie shouts.

"*What?*"

The next second he disappears and the SUV immediately begins to slow and drift towards the other lane. I throw myself over the center console, the seat belt trying to hold me back, and grab the wheel with both hands. Driving is a heck of a lot harder when you can't reach the pedals and are trying to stop yourself from running off the road. I can hardly catch my breath as I strain against the seat belt but I manage to get the SUV coasting in a straight line temporarily.

Then I realize the vampire isn't alone in the Mustang anymore, which begins to slow as well. Charlie managed to port himself directly into the passenger seat and has taken hold of the wheel. I'm still trying to keep the SUV in the right lane while Charlie and the vampire struggle inside the Mustang. Punches are thrown, elbows are engaged in combat, and then a gunshot goes off and the passenger side window of the Mustang is blown out.

The SUV starts to lose distance and the Mustang speeds away. I can't tell if Charlie's been shot or not. Fear wraps its shadowy fingers around my throat and I stare wide-eyed. Then, unexpectedly, Charlie is kneeling in the middle of the roadway directly in front of me.

I suddenly find I am very much capable of screaming again. The SUV is mere feet away from plowing Charlie over when he's suddenly back in the driver's seat, my face an inch away from his chest. I let my seat belt jerk me back over into my seat as Charlie takes the wheel, breathing hard.

"ARE YOU INSANE?" I scream at him.

He grimaces and shakes out his right arm. "Yeah, that didn't go as planned."

"You think?!"

The Mustang pulls ahead and Charlie speeds up to catch him again. We're driving a fine line between traction and careening to our deaths. The road twists and curves above what I'm sure would be a spectacular view of the city, but I'm trying my very best not to look in that particular direction right now. I still have no idea why the vampire would flee this way, but it was deliberate enough.

Skyline eventually meets another road, two frozen ponds on either side of us, and we move away from the drop down the hill and into a forested area. The Mustang makes another quick turn into some kind of park.

"This is a dead end," Charlie says under his breath. I don't know if he's talking to me or himself. "What is he playing at?"

Sure enough, we round one last bend at full speed and end in a parking lot surrounded by gardens covered in snow and trees rising up on all sides. We untangle ourselves from our seat belts and jump out of the car, clutching onto our flashlights and bio-mech guns. We come up to the Mustang on either side but it's already empty.

We turn to the landscape around us. Our flashlights flicker over trees and plants wrapped up in burlap sacks to protect them from winter's bite. The snow is a gray, mucky mess disturbed by hundreds of footprints.

We're both breathing hard and look to each other for what to do next.

"If he's packing a gun," I say, "I don't think we should split up."

"It might make him brave enough to come at us if we do. You take point," Charlie says and gestures with his flashlight to the gardens. "I'm going up to the tower—"

"Tower?"

His face goes flat and he points to a massive tower on the very top of the hill. It's a great, dark shadow against the black sky looming over the gardens.

"Enger Tower," Charlie says. "I can be the lookout. See if you can draw him out and I'll port right to you. Element of surprise."

"But he knows you can port now."

"Trust me on this, okay? I know what I'm doing."

Before I can tell him again what a stupid plan this is, he jogs up a set of stone steps leading to the tower. It's an old thing made of thick stone blocks and an impressive steel gate closes off the tower from potential vandals or rampaging teenagers. Charlie shines his light through the bars and then is suddenly on the other side. That's going to take some getting used to.

"Just go!" Charlie whispers. "Keep your flashlight on so I can see you and port to you. We're good, go go."

"You're not the one playing bait," I mumble.

He races up the steps into the tower and I turn around to get a good look at the gardens. The top of the hill is like an enormous bowl with the middle depression being the parking lot. Then the gardens gradually rise up around it to the lip of the hill and a sharp drop past it. There's a pavilion straight across from the tower on the other side of the bowl and another on my left with some kind of bell.

I take a deep breath, rub my sternum that's throbbing after the abuse from the seat belt, and march down more stone steps into the gardens. The beam of my flashlight bounces across the snow, revealing a hundred different footsteps all mushed together. It must be quite the attraction up here. I'm sure it'd really be something to see in the spring. Right now I'd pick finding the vampire over flowers though.

The more I think about it, the more stupid Charlie's plan seems to me. The vampire was running the entire time. He never went after us. Why would he now? I work my way along the paved trail and across some stepping stones towards the pavilion with the bell. Every shadow seems to move around me and I start to feel a little twitchy on the trigger. I don't want to be out here on my own with a vampire packing a gun. Freakin' Charlie. I swear, one of these days I'm going to—

A shadow flickers between the posts of the open pavilion near the bell. I freeze and paint the area with my flashlight. There's no one there but I've got hairs rising on the back of my neck. That's never a good sign. I creep through a Japanese garden until I reach the pavilion.

"She's not here," a voice whispers in the dark. "She left me alone. She's not . . ."

If this guy's going for the creepy factor, I'd say he's nailed it. But the voice gives me a direction and I veer toward it. The vampire slips out of the shadows behind one of the posts and shoves something towards me. A solid wood beam collides with the side of my head and I go down to the loud ringing of the giant bell beside me. I hit the ground hard, light bursts in front of my eyes, and I'm stunned. My flashlight rolls away, broken and useless.

"Mason!" comes Charlie's distant call. Idiot, now he can't help me.

A hand grips my shoulder and starts to half roll me on my side, half haul me up. Hot breath washes over the side of my neck. The vampire doesn't immediately bite, giving me enough time to gather some of my working senses, and then I feel the cold metal of a gun being pressed to my temple.

I fling my head backwards and send my arm up at the same time to drive the barrel away from my head. When the shot goes off just a foot from my ear, I lose most of my hearing but not my reflexes. I elbow the vampire in the face and feel his nose crunch under the force. He howls and falls backwards. I rise partway up and slam my bandaged hand down. He scampers away faster than I think possible and instead of hitting him in the chest, I leave cracks in the cement under my fist.

He scrambles to his feet and opens the distance between us just enough so I can't reach him in time when he aims his gun again. So I quickly roll backwards. The shot passes right over me and I roll far enough that I fall a few feet into a rock garden. That jars my head again and the world starts to spin. I grimace and fumble with my bio-mech gun. I peek over the ledge of rocks I fell from and find the vampire has turned tail and is running into the darkness of the trees.

"Stop!" I shout and rise to fire off a series of pulses.

Unfortunately, I don't get the opportunity to run after

and see if I hit him. Flashing red and blue lights illuminate the garden behind me and men shout at me to get on the ground. I didn't even hear them come up. I guess that's what happens when someone fires a gun twice right next to your head.

Before I do anything else, I activate the safety measures of the bio-mech gun and it morphs into an oval disc in my hand. I slowly turn around, as the eight officers directly behind me are not so politely requesting, and drop to the ground with my face in the snow, knowing I am truly and one-hundred percent screwed.

9

Getting arrested isn't fun in any sense of the word. I find myself with a knee in the middle of my back as my hands are brought behind me and cuffed together. The big brawny officer with a crew cut removes his knee from my back and grabs the collar of my jacket to haul me to my feet.

"Do you have any weapons on you? Anything that's going to stick me if I search you?" he barks at me. I guess our high-speed pursuit really ticked them off. I can't blame them—but I can blame Charlie. Where is my backup now, huh? Probably running into the woods. Thanks, Charlie. You're a big help.

"I've got a machete inside my jacket and a handgun in my waistband, middle of my back. That's it," I say, knowing that lying is only going to make things worse at this point. It's a good thing I already managed to morph the bio-mech gun. It's sitting harmless on the hood of the officer's squad in front of me.

The officer carefully unzips the front of my jacket and pulls out the machete from the inner lining of my jacket. He passes it off to another officer pointing a taser at me. My mother's gun goes next and my chest constricts as I watch it being passed off to a stranger. My wallet and cellphone are taken after that. I hold still to be patted down and obey all their commands. I'm read my Miranda rights, refuse to give a statement, neither confirm nor deny there was anyone with me, and don't respond when they ask who I was shooting at.

"We heard gunshots."

Yeah, but not from me. I keep my mouth shut, though. The officer asks if I want medical attention since I'm bleeding but I decline. The less attention I get the better, even though I'm doing a *fantastic* job so far. The officer starts maneuvering me into a squad car when some of the other officers start shouting and we stop.

"Get on the ground! On the ground now!"

"Easy, fellas!" It's Charlie.

I spot him at the bottom of the stone steps leading up to the tower. His eyes find me and he holds my gaze as he gets down on his knees with his hands on the back of his head. I can't believe he gave himself up. I thought for sure he would run off. The officers surround him and push him all the way onto the ground, giving him the same treatment they gave me. After he's cuffed, they pull him to his feet and haul him over to another squad car near me. He shakes his head to flick snow off his face, the front of his hair smushed up against his forehead and sticking straight up from them pressing his face into the ground.

They start asking him questions but he interrupts and says, "I'm the driver. You got me. She's with me."

He jerks his head in my direction. While they start to pat him down, I'm put into the back of a squad car on an uncomfortable plastic seat. The brawny officer gets into the front along with his partner. They both toss me cursory glances through the wire mesh and glass separating me from them. The squad rumbles to life and we leave the other squads behind. The last I see of Charlie is him shaking his head, pressed up against a squad getting frisked.

Nervous energy replaces my adrenaline and my head throbs where I got whacked by what I think was a bell knocker. My chest burns from all the times I was yanked against the seat belt. All that and the stupid vampire still got away. *Pixies*, what a bad night. At least we managed to find Gillian. That's got to count for something, right?

The squad moves carefully along the ice-slick roads, and we return to the main drag to crest the top of the central hill and travel along a flat stretch surrounded by shops, malls, grocery stores, and other outlets. We take a right into a woodsy area and eventually arrive at a large compound of public service facilities and the county jail. Giant floodlights illuminate the face of the gray building and big glossy words above the doors spell out *St. Louis County Jail*. The squad bypasses the front and moves around to the sally ports. Once we're inside the garage like entrance and the door is sealed, the officers help me out of the squad car. I clench my hands to keep them from shaking.

We pass through a couple of doors that need authorization before we end up in the booking room. They have me stand still against a counter as they undo the handcuffs only to cuff me to a metal railing and have me take a seat in a plastic chair that creaks under my weight. The next ten minutes pass in silence as a sheriff's deputy turns on a video camera and aims it at my face. The arresting officer fills out paperwork at the counter, the only sound the shuffling of pages. My head pounds and the deputy comes over to wipe some blood off my face with gauze and puts a Band-Aid on the side of my forehead where I got smacked. Yeah, I don't think that's going to help much. Ice would be welcome. He mentions getting my head checked quietly to the other officer. There is some whispering and I hope they agree. I would love to get out of here if that means I have to feign a concussion. Actually, I probably *do* have a concussion.

The deputy starts talking to me instead. "Phoenix Mason, you have been arrested for possession of a dangerous weapon—"

Guilty.

"—possession of a firearm while underage and without a permit—"

Guilty. If Jefferson finds out, he'll get mad at me for that one. I'm not supposed to be toting around a handgun until I'm twenty-one, but having my mother's gun makes me feel safer, less vulnerable.

"—and we're looking into reckless discharge of a firearm once your weapon's been tested."

Fantastic.

I'm read my rights again and I acknowledge that I understand each section as the officer reads them off.

"You have the right to an attorney. If you cannot afford one, one will be appointed for you by the state. Do you understand this right?"

"Yes."

"If you wish to speak to an attorney, a phone and

directories will be made available to you. Do you wish to speak with an attorney?"

I try to recall the steps of IMS procedure for getting through this next part. I've kept silent, haven't said anything to indicate myself, and I've gotten rid of any evidence that would point to supernatural affiliations. I need to contact headquarters to let them know I need an assist.

"I'd like to speak with my attorney," I say. "You said you have a phone?"

He nods. The sheriff's deputy comes over to uncuff me and leads me to an old yellowed phone on the wall. I'm in the middle of dialing Jefferson, anxiety knotting in my stomach, when the door at the end of the hallway opens and Charlie is escorted in. The two officers guiding him are stony-faced but, surprisingly, he's smirking. He spots me at the phone and gives a quick shake of his head and mouths, *trees*. What? Trees? Uncertain, I glance to the phone and back to him. He mouths it again as he's pushed up against the counter. Now that he's closer I think I get it. *Trace*, not trees. Any phone call I make from the jail will be traced, probably recorded too. Duh. Well, then I can't call Jefferson. I'm not sure what would be a safe number to call.

I hang up the phone and turn to the deputy keeping a hold on my arm. "I guess I don't actually remember the number."

"Do you want to try a phonebook?" he asks.

Charlie speaks up behind me. "I would love a phone call, thank you."

"Quiet," my officer says sternly.

Charlie smiles in response. "This is all a big misunderstanding. Just let me make a phone call."

"The phone's in use."

I clear my throat and shrug my shoulders. "Sorry, I'm done. I'll pass on the attorney, thanks."

"Are you sure?"

"I'm positive."

"Okay, then keeping your rights in mind, would you like to give a statement now?" the officer asks. Beside him Charlie mouths, *No.*

I sure hope Charlie has a plan. "No, I won't give a statement."

The officer makes a sweeping motion to the deputy clutching onto me and I'm escorted further into the room to something that looks like a copy machine except there's a place for someone to place their hand.

"Give me your right hand," the deputy says in a monotone. I hesitate before holding out my hand and the deputy begins cleaning off my fingertips. *Pixies*, I'm going to get put into the system. Bad, bad, bad—well, I can forget about doing the trials early this summer. Director Knox is going to kill me.

Behind me the other officer reads through the page of rights and Charlie answers immediately that he understands and wants the phone to call his attorney. The officer finally lets him and Charlie rushes the phone as the deputy plants my hand on the scanner.

"Agent Boyd, we've got a situation," Charlie says quickly into the phone's receiver. "Yup. That's exactly where we are. You're as perceptive as usual." He actually laughs. "No, I have not been man handled, but we haven't reached the cellmate introductions yet." The mirth in his voice instantly vanishes after whatever Melody says on the other end of the line. "You wouldn't dare . . . dang it, Melody! Fine. *Fine.* Sure."

I can't help but try to watch the scene over my shoulder as the fingerprint scanner beeps and the deputy has me readjust my hand to get a better scan.

Charlie holds out the phone to the lead officer. "She would like to speak with you, Sergeant."

"Who did you call?"

"Agent Melody Boyd, FBI. She'd like to have a few words with you if you could kindly spare the time."

The sergeant doesn't budge and looks annoyed. I think that's a pretty fair reaction given what Charlie just said. "I don't have time for pranks—"

"It's not a prank."

The officer looks like he wants to roll his eyes but moves around the counter and takes the phone out of Charlie's hand.

"This is Sergeant Miller. To whom am I speaking?"

As the sergeant listens to what sounds like a winded rant that I can almost make out, Charlie leans back so we make eye contact again and he winks. Well, at least he seems to be getting a kick out of the whole being arrested thing. I'm having the worst time trying to make out his character—bitingly sarcastic, then deadly serious, poignantly angry, and now blissfully at ease and even humored in our current situation. I can't pin him down.

"Yes, ma'am," the sergeant finally says. "As soon as you come to the jail and provide proof of that, I'd be happy to listen. For now, these two remain in my custody." More shouting through the line but this time the sergeant chuckles. "No argument here. I'll be waiting at the front desk for you."

He hangs up and moves away from us to have a private conversation with the other two officers that brought Charlie in. After a quick whispered discussion, the two officers exit through a door on the other side of the room.

"Stop processing her for now," Sergeant Miller says.

The deputy had finally managed to get a good scan of my hand but nods, presses a few buttons on the machine, and returns me to the plastic chair. While I'm recuffed to the metal rail, Sergeant Miller brings out another plastic chair a few feet from me and does the same with Charlie. The sergeant returns to paperwork and the deputy turns off the video camera before standing guard, bored and relaxed in the corner with a magazine.

With nothing to do except wait for Melody to show up, my nervous ticks surface. I rub my thumbnails with my fingertips, bite my lip, and flex my toes in my shoes. Charlie sits hunched, his head bowed low, eyes trained on the floor. He never looks up. I can't see his expression from the way he's holding himself but I can see the furrow in his eyebrows and barely make out his lips moving like he's talking to himself in his head. An enigma wrapped inside a riddle and stuffed up a unicorn's butt, that one.

The minutes drag by and I occupy myself by trying to figure out why exactly that vampire made such an effort to get to Enger Tower. He had been muttering something about "she's not here." Was he looking for his female vampire companion for help, hoping to lure us into a trap?

The far door opens and an officer peeks his head in. "She's here."

"Keep an eye on them," the sergeant says to the deputy and rounds the counter.

Before he can make it to the door, however, it flies open and Melody stands there like a five star general commandeering the station. She stands tall, shoulders back, lightning sparking in her livid eyes. Her presence almost reminds me of Draco when he came to find me at the cabin. There's something about the way she holds herself that draws all eyes to her. That, and the fact she starts making demands the second she barges in.

"I want both of them released immediately," she orders, jabbing a finger in our direction. She speaks in a strictly American accent. I haven't known her for long but it still doesn't sound right coming from her. "Any records you made, I want them now and all other copies destroyed. No fingerprints, no file. This all gets erased from the system. Are we clear?"

"Under what authority?" the sergeant challenges. "These two caused three car crashes and seriously endangered the lives of everyone on the road and nearby."

"They sure did! You've no argument from me!" Her eyes fall on Charlie and me—I feel like a cockroach under her glare. "But they are *also* working for me on a classified undercover operation, *which* they have now blown wide open. Trust me, they will be properly dealt with, but this whole fiasco needs to fall through the cracks. I still have a chance of recovering what's left of my operation unless they're charged and this all becomes public."

The sergeant still holds out. "I'm going to need to speak with your supervisor and confirm all this."

"You do that." She whips a business card out of her jacket pocket. "And you tell them I want a new job while you're at it."

He slips out the door. Melody remains where she is, hands clenching and unclenching at her sides. I keep my eyes averted and try not to move or give her any other reason to be mad at us. A couple minutes later the sergeant returns and nods to the deputy. Most of our items are returned to us but they hand the weapons over to Melody. Not long after, the three of us walk out of the jail together. Melody carries a manila folder with everything the police had collected regarding the incident. The rest—as ordered—has been destroyed. Once we reach our vehicle Melody wordlessly passes back our weapons and we climb in. We don't speak a word to each other during the entire drive to the Duluth Field Office. The SUV pulls into the underground garage and we get out in silence.

Melody leads the way through the lower level, heading in the opposite direction from where they had held Ashley, and we enter a rather well-furnished medical suite. There are two hospital beds on opposite sides of the room with curtains able to close them off if needed. Along the walls are metal cabinets, trays of medical instruments, boxes of plastic gloves, rolls of athletic tape, and a fridge with a glass door holding bags of blood inside. Next to it is a flat screen television mounted on the wall with the volume on low and the news on.

Gillian occupies one of the hospital beds—Nessa stands on one side and Hawk on the other. Once we enter the room, Hawk immediately walks over to me, grabs my shoulder to turn me sideways, and inspects the side of my head where I got conked and the deputy slapped a Band-Aid on it.

"What happened?" he asks. "Are you okay?"

"We, uh . . . well . . ."

He steers me to the other bed and pushes me down onto it before getting a cold pack out of the fridge. He tosses it to me and I press it to the side of my head, wincing at the shock of cold and pain.

Melody turns to the television as the news begins a story covering our intense car chase through the city captured by some pedestrians with their cellphones.

"That's what happened," Melody snarls and jabs a finger at the television. Her British accent is back in full swing. "Do you know what that looks like to me?"

"Looks cool from that angle," I say under my breath as I watch our SUV glide beautifully between cars on the road. Just like the movies.

"*Excuse me?*" The look Melody gives me could have cut through ten feet of concrete.

To my surprise, Charlie starts to laugh but then quickly stops and clears his throat when Melody looks like she might murder him. He tucks his head down and leans against the metal cabinets, one hand gripping the top of his right arm.

"*That,*" Melody continues, "looks like two bloody duffers out on a joy ride. You could have gotten yourselves or someone else killed pulling a stunt like that."

Charlie sighs and rubs the back of his neck. "We had a shot to catch the vamp—"

"And did you?"

"Well, no, but—"

"No. No buts. If you saw the vampire and he got in a car, grab the plate number! Get a description! We could have run the vehicle, tracked him through surveillance cameras—"

"And shown up too late to stop him from hurting someone else?" Charlie thunders back, sweeping an arm towards Gillian for emphasis. "By the time it would take us to get the video, comb through it, and maybe trace him somewhere, he could have grabbed someone else!"

"We do this the right way, Charlie!"

"I'm sorry, I'm confused." He pushes off from the cabinet to go toe to toe with Melody. I don't think I've seen him this angry yet, even when he was fighting with me. "Trying to stop a vampire before he snatches another victim is the *wrong* way?"

"Acting rashly only cocks everything up and you know it. You're not your uncle."

The color drains out of his face and he flinches like he's been slapped. "Don't," he says darkly. "Don't you dare do that, Mels."

Her expression and hard edge to her eyes soften. Needless to say, I'm intensely curious what's going on because I have no idea. Clearly something personal. The rest of us in the room glance to each other awkwardly, not sure what to do.

"Did you get anything useful at least?" Melody says with a sigh, no longer hell-bent on chewing us out it seems.

"I overhead him muttering," I say. "The vampire. He fled all the way to—"

I look to Charlie for help and he says, "Enger Tower. Top of the hill."

"When we cornered him there, I heard him saying something about 'she's not here.' Maybe he was talking about his lady friend with the pink scarf? He could have been running to her for help. There could be clues left behind up there."

"If the police haven't tramped all over it looking for clues about us," Charlie says, acknowledging an uncomfortable truth. "And there aren't any surveillance cameras up there. The area's a blind spot."

"It's worth a shot, though, isn't it?" Hawk says, one hand cupping his chin. "I'm a decent tracker. Maybe we can pick up his trail."

"We'll have a run at it," Melody says. "If we can at least track him to a road, we might be able to pick him up on surveillance further out."

"Sounds good." Hawk nods.

"I'll go with," I say.

Melody shakes her head and crosses her arms over her chest. "I don't think so. I have a feeling the bobbies will be keeping an eye out for you. It's best if you stay out of Duluth for a while. Hawk and I can manage on our own."

Anxiety rises in the pit of my stomach. We haven't tried a test of Hawk going solo like this before. If they come across the vampire and get into a fight, Hawk's werewolf instincts could kick in. Any werewolf on the serum could stop from transforming under pressure if they tried, but Hawk's not on the serum. I'm his personal anti-werewolf-lunacy battery. If I leave town, Hawk won't be in range of my powers, and if he transforms things could get ugly real fast. He wouldn't be Hawk sniffing out a crime scene. He'd be a wolf completely.

"Are you sure that's necessary?" I ask, hoping I can convince Melody to change her mind. "We work great as a team."

"I want you out of my city, Phoenix," she says coldly. "We've drawn enough heat as it is. You can come back once they've stopped putting clips of your escapade on the telly."

And to think Melody used to be my favorite person in Duluth. My face burns and I lower my eyes, defeated.

"I'll need backup," Hawk says, trying a different tactic. "We really could use all hands on deck for this if we've got a loose vampire gang out there."

"Oh, I know it," she growls.

"We can help," Nessa offers. "Me and my kin. We all want to put an end to this menace and find out why they took my sister." Her hand tightens on Gillian's shoulder. "Just tell us where to go and we'll follow."

There's something akin to awe in Nessa's voice when speaking to Melody. I don't get it. I thought they didn't get along. Something about Melody threatening one of the selkies? Granted, I punched Nessa and she ended up liking me. Whatever. My head hurts enough as it is without trying to think that one over too. We still haven't fixed the problem of Hawk being out on his own.

"Then what about me?" Charlie speaks up, still clutching at his right arm. Has he been doing that the whole time? "You're kicking Mason out for being a trouble magnet. Does the same apply to me?"

"You either stay locked up in the office with *no* outside privileges, or head to the Moose Lake Field Office for a time if they'll take you."

His eyes narrow. "You want me out, don't you?"

"I don't want you putting your neck out where it's going to get chopped off," she says quietly. "I expected better of you, Charlie."

The open vulnerability in his face is quickly replaced by anger. "Well, then," he says, grabbing a handful of gauze out of the nearest cabinet and moving for the door. "I guess

I better not keep you waiting then."

The next second he's gone, a dark silhouette down the hallway quickly sinking into the shadows of a doorway. An uncomfortable silence follows and no one moves for a long time. Hawk rests a hand on my shoulder. He's steady and doesn't look nervous to me—basically the exact opposite of how I feel.

"Are you good?" I ask quietly. What I'm really asking is if he's going to be able to handle this without me. I don't need to elaborate to know he gets the message.

"I've got it under control," is all he says.

Enough trust exists between us that I don't question it. If this was going to be a problem, he'd give me a sign. If he says he's got it under control, then he's got it under control.

Melody walks over, her demeanor friendly again like the woman I first met. It's almost scary to know what's really underneath that open kindness and British accent.

"Grab Charlie and head out in our SUV. Hawk can drop me off to get my other one in impound, then drive himself home after we try to track this vampire."

I pass the cold pack over and rise to my feet. Hawk holds his hand out at his side and I give him a low five before moving off to find wherever Charlie disappeared to. Under orders to go and with Hawk's assurance he'll be okay, I'm ready to leave as soon as possible. At least it doesn't take me long to find Charlie. The third door on the right is slightly ajar so I knock and push it open to step inside.

No posters or pictures adorn the walls. The space is neat and tidy, bare of most anything except a stack of books on the nightstand. There isn't even a solitary family picture which he can gaze lovingly at when he goes to sleep at night. It's too . . . sterile. He's sitting on the bed, his jacket and scarf laid out neatly beside him. He's unbuttoned his navy blue dress shirt and has pulled his arm out of one of the sleeves, pressing a wad of gauze to the side of his bicep.

"Are you bleeding?" I ask and slip further into the room without waiting for permission.

"Bullet grazes cause that kind of thing to happen," he says without looking up and continues to dab at a shallow graze across his upper arm.

"Why didn't you say anything earlier? Or do this in the med room?"

"Could you hold that in place for a second?" He points to the gauze on his shoulder then reaches for a roll of athletic tape beside him.

I roll my eyes but press my fingers to the gauze to keep it in place. "You're pretty demanding, you know that?"

"And you've been so accommodating." He tosses me a rather insincere smile then focuses on taping the gauze to his arm one-handed.

As I watch him smooth the tape into place, I consider that my day started out interrogating a powerful monster, moved on to rescuing a kidnapped selkie, and ended with—and I might be biased on this last part—a pretty *epic* car chase. I can label it as that now that I'm not in the middle of it hoping I don't die. And here I am, helping a guy I thought I'd sworn to loath. I wouldn't say we exactly get along, there's definitely room for improvement in that department, but I've found there's at least one thing we agree on—getting into reckless situations to save other people.

"Thanks, Doctor Mason medicine woman," he says and offers me a real smile this time. "Now, if you don't mind, I'm going to change into something without my blood on it and I'll meet you in the garage."

10

Jefferson isn't exactly thrilled when I show up with Charlie.

"We're picking up strays now?" he grumbles. "Where are we supposed to put you? And what in the world happened to *you*?" He points to my forehead.

"Oh, it was nothing really," I say casually.

"It was your usual night," Charlie cuts in, slinging his military duffle bag over his shoulder. "Pretty low key. Searched through some buildings, located someone in a warehouse, drove the pursuit vehicle around a bit. I'm sure Agent Boyd will be able to fill in the blanks with a lot of yelling and angry insinuations about our state of mind."

I hide my smile behind my hand and pretend to find something rather interesting on the kitchen counter. Okay, I'll admit it. Charlie *is* kind of funny when he's not being an angry jerk. I'm not going to tell him that though.

"You aren't related to dumb and dumber are you?" Jefferson growls, jabbing his thumb over his shoulder at me.

"You talk just like the wonder twins."

"I don't think my hair's quite red enough to fit in," he says and shrugs. "And I can crash wherever. I'm used to uncomfortable living situations."

"Yeah, and I'm living in one right now," Jefferson mutters under his breath. "You can take the cot in the loft." He turns to raise his eyebrows at me and I get the hint.

"I'll show you," I say and escort Charlie out to the barn.

When I flick on the lights inside he stops to take in his surroundings.

"Wow. Very rustic," he says. "I kind of like it."

"You probably won't like it so much when you wake up shivering." We climb the steps to the loft and I gesture to the cot before taking a seat at my computer.

"I've had worse." He tosses his duffle onto the cot and shrugs out of his overcoat. He's changed into a blue long sleeved shirt. It's simple but he still manages to make everything he wears look fashion forward. I remain tucked inside my parka, pulling it closer around myself before logging into my computer.

"Try sleeping in an igloo up in Canada for a week," he continues. "Hunting a rampaging Jotunn isn't as glamorous as it sounds."

That certainly catches my attention. Part of me wants to be indifferent to Charlie but, dang it, I'm curious.

"You were hunting a frost giant? In Canada?"

He walks around the edge of the room, surveys the boxes on the shelves, runs a hand over the ammo cache, and slowly comes around to the opposite side of my computer.

"Yeah, it had come over from Scandinavia on an ice breaker." He rests a forearm along the top of my monitor, making it wiggle under his weight. "I went along with my uncle to hunt it after it killed a bunch of kids way up north."

We're back to the topic of his uncle and one I'm keenly interested in asking him about. He seemed pretty upset about being compared to his uncle earlier.

"Your uncle?" I ask innocently.

His eyes bore into me. I'm pretty sure my curiosity is blatantly obvious. His cheek presses out as he rolls his tongue around inside his mouth, clearly hesitant to say anymore.

"Look, I don't want to be on bad terms," he says. "If I'm going to be here for a little while I'd rather not have to worry about getting into rows frequently. So, I might as well tell you now that talking about my uncle makes me . . . *testy*."

"Okay . . ." Interesting. "Am I allowed to ask about your parents? Do you have any other family?"

"Why?"

"Why not?"

He sighs and rolls up the sleeves of his shirt even though it's probably only fifty-five degrees in here. In doing so he reveals a leather bracelet on his wrist clasped with a steel link. He walks around the desk and holds out his arm so I can see it properly. The steel link has words etched into it—*Illis quos amo deserviam.*

"It's Latin," he says. "It means—"

"For those I love I will sacrifice."

He slowly withdraws his wrist and crosses his arms over his chest. "Well, let me guess who was teacher's pet in Latin class."

"Old Man Two—a centaur I know in Underground—wouldn't let me work in his restaurant unless I could carry a conversation in Latin with him," I say offhand, my eyes still on the bracelet. "Who gave it to you?"

He spins it absently around his wrist. "My mother gave it to my father before he died. It's the last thing I have of either of them."

"So they're both—"

"Dead." He says it matter-of-factly. I guess I do the same thing, too, when I'm asked the question. It must have happened when he was a kid. You get used to the question being asked so many times and giving the same answer over and over again that it becomes ingrained. It's just a word now, a fact of life, one that still hurts physically inside but there's no point in getting worked up over acknowledging the fact anymore.

"Really, Mason, do you know of any Blessed that has family left?" He squints one eye and looks up at the ceiling in thought. "Well, any family that matters anymore? I don't count my uncle."

"That's a pity."

"No, it's really not." There's that look in his eye again, that dangerous alter ego when he's pressed.

"I've got my brother," I counter.

"Which, in all honesty, is a freak occurrence. Every other Tom, Dick, and Harry I know that's been slapped with a little dragon magic has lost their parents, their guardians, their siblings, their extended family. We're all loners in the end. Loners with superpowers."

He laughs darkly under his breath and moves back to the cot. He spreads out, settles in, and pulls a book out of his duffel bag. To distract myself, I bring up the screen to enter my report for the evening, but my fingers sit unmoving on the keys. I lose my train of thought considering Charlie's words and focus on worrying about Hawk again. He really is the only person I have in my life. Sure, Jefferson's a part of it too but Hawk's my family. I don't know how he's planning on coping up in Duluth trying to sniff out the vampire and its gang. What if he snaps? What if his big secret is revealed and he's arrested by Melody? I'm not there to protect him. The option to run isn't available. I alternate worrying my upper and lower lips and stare at the computer screen, debating sneaking to Duluth to loiter in the shadows to keep Hawk within my bubble of anti-crazy.

"You know," Charlie says over in his corner, eyes still glued to his book, "they haven't upgraded the systems to take your report mentally yet. You actually have to type it in for the words to come up."

"Are you always this snarky?" I growl and strum my fingers on the keyboard.

"Are you always this grumpy?"

I roll my eyes. "I thought you *just* said you didn't want to—" I mime air quotes, "—get into rows frequently."

He lays his book open faced on his chest. "Sorry, force of habit."

"Being a jerk is a habit? How's that working out for you so far?"

Instead of firing back another snappy retort, he sighs and returns to his book, ignoring me. I take that as one point for Phoenix, zero for Charlie, and try to focus on typing up my report. After another few minutes of worrying, I start typing away and force myself to remember the details of everything that happened tonight. Once I'm finished, I scroll through the news feed the IMS puts out to keep its agents informed to keep myself distracted. I come across the article Jefferson mentioned earlier about the suspected leviathan sighting. There's a little update on the bottom asking agents working in the Atlantic Ocean to keep an eye open for suspicious activity due to several ships going missing.

I keep scrolling through articles and I'm halfway through a story about increased vampire activity in Paris when a car engine revs outside and then shuts off. I leap out of my chair and rush down the steps to meet Hawk as he exits the SUV. My first instinct is to check Hawk's eyes but it's impossible in the light—or lack thereof—out here. Does he have yellow rings around his eyes? Would they even appear after so short a time out by himself? Would Melody or the selkies have noticed if they did?

"Hey, how'd it go?" I ask in a rush.

He rubs the back of his neck and blows out a sharp breath. "Okay, I guess." He glances at the barn, then the cabin, and lowers his voice to make sure only I can hear. "I kept it together just fine."

My whole body relaxes and I nod as if I knew that's what he would say the entire time.

"So, did you find anything?" I ask.

"Yes and no," he says. "We found a trail leading away from Enger Tower but lost it on a well-used hiking path. If he stuck to that trail, Melody might be able to catch him on video at a parking lot it goes past."

"So, what are they going to do now?"

"I'll probably head up early tomorrow morning and help her continue the search."

"You're going back?" I ask and automatically grasp his arm. "Hawk, that's a bad idea."

"Why?"

"You know why." I tug him in closer and whisper, "We haven't tried something like this before. You know it's dangerous testing your limits and how long the effects of having me around last."

"We need to test my limits," he argues, his eyes glinting in the glare of the floodlight hanging off the side of the barn. "Otherwise, how are we ever going to know what they are? Look, I handled the first test just fine. I'm okay. Really." He slings his arm around my shoulders and practically drags me over to the cabin. "Besides, the real question we should be asking is whether you've managed to not kill Charlie, and if you can handle being on your own with him while I'm gone."

"Ha-ha, you're hilarious."

We enter the cabin together. Jefferson's door is shut and there's no sign of him so I'm assuming he's holed up for the evening, going over files or something. Hawk combs through the fridge and I lean against the kitchen counter, waiting for my brother to turn around so I can get a good look at his eyes in the well-lit room. When he spins around with a container of leftover venison, his brilliant green eyes lock onto mine for a second before he pushes me aside to reach the stove. There's no yellow taint to their color and I let the matter drop. Maybe Hawk's right. We don't know his limits or mine yet and we need to keep stretching them. If only Jefferson's imaginary expert would get back to us on my blood . . .

Dinner is a mostly silent affair. I think we're both thinking too much and are completely exhausted by the day. Interrogating Dasc again consumes my thoughts. I'll be back at it once his face heals, whenever that is.

I don't sleep well that night. Then again, when do I ever? I dream of Hawk being dragged away by the vampire then gunshots echo in my head and I jerk awake. This would be the moment where I go out to the barn and field strip my mother's gun or one from the armory. I'm halfway out of my bed when I remember Charlie's sleeping in the barn. I silently curse under my breath and I fall back onto my pillows to stare at the dusty ceiling. Now that I'm awake I realize I'm absolutely freezing. My nose and hands are frozen stiff.

There are spare blankets on the dresser and I should go give the furnace a good kick. With another curse under my breath I slip out of the warmth of my blankets and hit the floor with a thud. A soft whine behind me makes me freeze. I slowly spin about on the pads of my feet to find Hawk in his bed, a pair of paws sticking out from under the blankets and a furry wolf head on his pillow. Even as a wolf he drools in his sleep and there's a sticky puddle under his muzzle. He's whining in his sleep and his paws twitch like he's chasing something.

"Hawk, what the crap?" I whisper.

Did he shift on purpose? Pretty sure he's never shifted while dreaming. I hesitate before reaching out and prodding his shoulder. His body shudders and he suddenly wakes with a yelp. I clamp a hand on his muzzle so he doesn't make another startled sound to wake up Jefferson. His eyes are wide and jump all over the place. Then he focuses on my hands, on his paws, and he shakes his head, ears flopping side to side. I let go of his muzzle and he tucks his head back, ears flattening against his head. If I could see his skin, I think he'd be blushing.

I throw my hands up. "What are you doing?" I hiss. "Did you shift in your sleep?"

He shakes his head slowly and pulls one paw up at a time so they're tucked beneath his blanket.

I rub my freezing arms and grab my sweater off the dresser, yanking it over my head while putting my arms through the sleeves. By the time I have it on, Hawk has gripped the edge of the blanket with his teeth and pulled it over his shoulders.

"Piping Pan," I grumble and run a hand down my face. "Did you shift because you were cold?"

He ducks his head so his muzzle is resting on his paws, eyes averted and ears still flattened.

"I'll take that as a yes," I sigh. I turn back to the dresser and rummage for socks. After I pull on a pair, I grab Hawk's closest paw and tuck a sock on. "Well, here you go, you big baby."

He rolls his eyes and tries to pull away but I wrestle with him and manage to put socks on each of his four paws. I can't help but laugh at how he looks—a fierce wolf with stripped socks and one cocked ear. When I'm done I pat him roughly on the head.

"Who's a good boy?"

At that he growls. I wave him off and clamber into my bunkbed toting another blanket. I settle in, tucking myself deep into a cocoon and stare up at the ceiling again. Now that I think about it, I may be the only person on earth that handles having a werewolf sibling as normally as I do. I don't flinch when there's a wolf where a human should be. He's just a big dog, my best friend. Sometimes it's almost like an inside joke. That's probably not a good thing.

"Don't let Jefferson see you like that," I whisper into the darkness. "Or Charlie. I don't think they'll find it as funny as I do."

His tail thumps once in agreement.

In the morning Hawk wakes me up as his normal self, his red hair plastered to one side of his face. I glance at the clock on my phone and find it's 5:00 a.m. My brother's already dressed and zipping up his jacket.

"You're actually up early?" I say and rub at my eyes.

He points sluggishly to a steaming mug on top of the dresser before finger combing his hair. "There's this magical brew called coffee that's like catnip for sleepy werewolves. There's a pot on if you want some." He gives me a good slap on the shoulder. "I gotta meet Melody."

"This early?" I'm met with a surge of anxiety.

He grabs his mug and starts heading out the door. He vanishes then reappears a second later, sticking his head through the opening.

"Oh, and I told the principal you were out yesterday because you came down with a bad case of diarrhea."

"*What?*"

He laughs and dashes away before I can even chuck a pillow at his head. Well, that's not completely embarrassing or anything. If I'm lucky, no one else overheard Hawk's excuse for my absence. I'd much rather tell the school I was off on business for a secret government agency interrogating a highly dangerous criminal under a dragon's supervision.

By the time I change into my running clothes and head into the kitchen, Jefferson is already there pouring himself a cup of coffee. We make eye contact for only a second before each of us looks away. I guess we're still in that awkward phase of "we sort of had a fight and don't know how to talk to each other unless the other one starts a conversation first." So, I don't say anything at all and slip past him to the door.

It's dark out and frigid. I clip a flashing button to the front of my jacket, turn on my MP3 player, and start a steady jog down the driveway to warm up. It feels good to be moving again. I run a couple of miles out on the salted pavement in the quiet darkness of the winter morning before heading back.

Charlie is outside with a cup of a coffee by the time I reach the cabin. He takes a long sip and watches me over the rim of his cup as I slow to a walk and pace in front of the cabin to cool down, doing my best to ignore him.

"Isn't it a little cold to be out for a run?" he asks.

My eyes rake over him. His shoulders are hitched up and he's trying to hide his chin in the collar of his jacket. I turn my head to hide my smile.

"I'm sorry, is it too cold for you?" I ask and continue to pace.

"Nah, I'm great. Peachy, even." A shiver runs down his arms and he almost spills some of his coffee. "Just not quite used to Minnesota yet."

"Didn't you say you were in Canada before? This has got to be a walk in the park compared to that."

"Only for a week. I was actually in Nevada last. Area 51. I'm used to heat." He smiles and laughs quietly to himself. "Probably the longest I've ever stayed in any one place."

I stop my pacing. "You got to stay in Area 51?"

"Those are indeed the words that came out of my mouth."

"Did you get to see the gryphon armada?" I say in a rush, unable to stop myself before I remember I'm not supposed to care about anything Charlie says or does, but Area 51—Dreamland—has all the cool stuff happening. I've read up on the gryphon training camps housed in enormous underground bunkers fifty stories deep. They're the legendary world's version of the military. The gryphons hardly operate anymore but the stories I've heard are incredible. I'd kill to see them in action.

His smile widens. "I had a front row seat to their maneuvers. My uncle had a case in the state so I got to stay there for—I think it was three years?"

"Wait, your uncle had a case that took three years?" I ask, then realize we're back on the subject of his uncle. It's surprising how often that's happened considering what he said last night about *not* wanting to talk about his uncle.

"Funny you ask." He takes a long sip of his coffee and then rotates the cup several times in his hands before responding, his eyes down. "He went missing during his mission and was presumed dead for almost a year. I didn't have any other guardian and the boys at Dreamland didn't know what to do with me so I just kind of stuck around, learned the ropes, watched the action, and all that. They eventually found my uncle. I guess he had faked his death so he could do some undercover work to locate a shapeshifter ring trying to raise a hydra out in the desert. Yeah. That was a hoot when he finally came back."

There is no possible response I can give after hearing that story. I can't even imagine living through something like that—thinking your family is dead and you're left all alone. Then the fact that Charlie's uncle did it on purpose makes it that much worse. I can see why the subject of his uncle is a touchy one.

"So, you see being a jerk is actually working out really well for me," he says, responding to my jab from last evening. "The less people I have to care about, the less I have to worry about them dying or doing something monumentally stupid. You might want to keep that in mind."

On that cheerful note he takes his cup with him into the barn and disappears. At least that explains some of Charlie's personality and hostility towards me. He got so mad when I defended Ashley because I didn't consider who she might have hurt. It's pretty obvious Charlie's still hurting from what his uncle did. There's more than that, though. As I recall, Melody mentioned he has some sort of beef with werewolves in particular, but I guess that's a story for another time.

Revelations aside, after a quick shower I get dressed, throw on my backpack, and rush outside to drive myself to school only to remember that Hawk took our SUV. Only Jefferson's 442 and Charlie's car are here now. I don't like the thought of asking either of them for a ride considering my current relationship with them both, but I'll be late if I try to walk all the way there.

The big doors to the barn creak open and Jefferson waves me over.

"Come on," he says gruffly. "I'll give you a lift."

I swallow and hustle over without a word. He pulls out the Green Monster, a sparkling emerald against the snow, and I shut the barn doors behind him before getting into the passenger seat. The first couple of minutes make for an extremely awkward ride. I stare out the window and catch glimpses of Jefferson's scowl out of the corner of my eye.

He finally breaks the silence once we reach town. "I heard the story of what happened in Duluth last night."

Oh, no. Here it comes. He must be furious.

"You did good, kid." He gives a solemn nod.

I stare and clutch my backpack in my arms. "Who are you and what have you done with Jefferson?"

He shrugs and raps his fingers on the steering wheel. "You took initiative. Sure, it could have turned out better but it could've been worse, too. You found the girl, you went after a monster, and then you took the right steps when all hell broke loose. I know you don't do things for show." He gives me a sideways look. "You do things because you care. Honestly, I think we could use more of that in the IMS."

I bite my lower lip but can't stop a smile from spreading on my face. The panic and dread of Jefferson hating me for bailing on the Dasc interrogation lifts from my shoulders.

"You have no idea how glad I am to hear you say that."

His scowl deepens. "Don't go crying on me or asking for hugs."

"No hugs or tears. I promise."

"Good. Then tighten your belt and get your head on straight because when Dasc wakes up for round two of interrogations, you need to be ready. And I'm not letting you go in there alone again. I'll be coming with."

I'm surprised even though I should have expected it. "But Director Knox said—"

"I don't care what he said or what he thinks he knows," he growls. "You aren't going to do this alone. We're a team, right?"

My smile widens and I duck my head. "Right."

The Green Monster rumbles to a stop in front of the steps of the high school. Jefferson pulls out a crumpled piece of paper and starts writing out an excuse for me. He hesitates and points his pen at me.

"What were you out for this time?" he asks.

I clear my throat and mumble, "Diarrhea."

"Excuse me?"

"You heard me."

"That brother of yours . . ." He writes in slow strokes, saying the words out loud as he puts them to paper. "*Out with the runs.*" He pushes the note into my hand and shoos me out the door. "Don't get into any fights."

"Make good choices!" I shout back and hustle up the icy steps into the school.

The familiar tangle of students, foot odor, body spray, and lemon cleaner surround me. Everyone's pulling off their winter jackets and tracking trails of slush through the hallways. I navigate between the quickly moving flow and enter the office on my right. Two other boys are in line ahead of me turning in their own parent notes. I recognize both of them as werewolves. Joe and Nick. The secretary, in a disturbingly bright purple sweater today, scowls at each of us. The two boys brush past me on the way out, nodding in my direction.

"Note?" the secretary asks without preamble when I step up to the counter, and then does a double take to stare at my face. I did my best to cover up my black eye, lacerations, and bruising with makeup this morning but my skills must be lacking.

To redirect her attention to something that isn't my

battered face, I slide over the rumpled note and she looks at it with disdain. To my horror, she calls Principal Tippy over. His long limbs precede him like spider legs as he exits his office and walks over to the counter, adjusting his hairpiece with two fingers. He looks thinner than usual and that's saying something. Must be because half the student population is werewolves. He takes the note from the secretary with skeletal fingers and lets out an oozing stream of baritone discontent like a gas leak.

"How many absences has this been, Ms. Mason?" he asks and clears his throat loudly. "The runs was it? Bit of bad seafood perhaps?"

I press my lips into a thin line and need a second to collect myself. I'm going to strangle Hawk.

"Bad shrimp," I say as unsarcastically as possible, which doesn't really work.

"Last week it was a toothache."

"I had to get a filling replaced. Came loose apparently."

"The week before that it was scarlet fever."

"I got it from my uncle."

Principal Tippy starts snapping his fingers together and his face screws up tight in thought. "And the week before that it was . . . it was . . ."

"Taking care of your dying uncle," the secretary chimes in unhelpfully.

"That's right," I say, taking it in stride. "That was when *he* had scarlet fever."

"Oh, that's right," the principal says and snaps his fingers loudly in my face. "And what else was there, Doris?"

The secretary holds up a hand and starts counting off fingers. "Your pet rabbit died and you had to give it a proper funeral, you had to bail your uncle out of jail, you sprained your ankle, your house caught fire, and—this is my favorite—you were hit by a semi!"

Out of all the ridiculous excuses, the one they find hard to believe is the only one that's actually true?

"I lead a difficult and danger-ridden life," I say without flinching. It's certainly true, and yet they are more likely to believe scarlet fever and bailing "Uncle" Jefferson out of jail than chasing after a fresh werewolf, breaking up wolf fights, or tracking down a vampire.

Principal Tippy clears his throat again. "I've made a call to the truancy officer. You'll meet with him in a couple of days to explain this difficult life of yours. Your brother as well."

"Sounds swell."

"I do hope your brother is here today."

"Oh, no." I hold a hand over my heart. "I'm afraid he's come down with a case of the runs as well."

"I thought you said it was from bad shrimp."

"Yeah, he ate the leftovers last night. Now, is it okay if I head to class? I can't wait to discuss *Hamlet* in first period." I give them a big encouraging smile but they aren't having any of it.

Thankfully, Ashley flies into the office at that very moment to come to my rescue. She trots in through the glass door in a bright red t-shirt boasting a slew of comic book characters and pushes a bottle of something dark purple into my hands.

"Phoenix, oh thank goodness!" she squeals in true Ashley fashion, her blonde ponytail bouncing in her excited motions. "Are you okay? I got you some prune juice. That's supposed to help right? I'm so glad you're feeling better. We should get moving before we're late for English. Oh!" She spins about to face the principal as if she's just noticed him for the first time. "Good morning, Principal Tippy! How are you today?"

"I'm fine," he says, a crease between his eyebrows. "And you?"

"Fantastic! Well, we better get going. I'll see you during third period to copy those reports, okay? Great, thanks, bye!"

She roughly grabs my shoulder to turn me around and push me through the glass doors. We hustle down the hallway and pause in front of my locker. Ashley is grinning from ear to ear.

"Thanks for that," I say and stuff my backpack into my locker.

"Oh, that was exciting," she whispers. "Like an undercover mission to break you out of jail."

I laugh. "Throw on a hood and cloak and you're a regular ol' vigilante."

"I know, right?" She bounces on the balls of her feet and shakes her hands in excitement. "Hawk told me you were out on business and I needed to help cover for you."

"Well, that was thoughtful of you two. And, uh, you can have your prune juice back. You realize it's used to ease constipation not diarrhea, right?"

"Oh, actually this is grape juice." She takes the bottle from me, cracks it open and takes a sip. I slam my locker shut and we walk together to first period English. "But, on a side note, did you—" She glances both ways down the hallway. "Did you guys find anything on that vampire?"

I give a single humorless laugh and make a circle motion about my face. "Courtesy of sir jerk vampire." Her eyes go wide and her jaw drops open. "He's on the run but we'll catch him. Don't worry."

"Are you okay?" she breathes and shies away from the wounds on my face as if they might start spurting blood at any second.

"Simply fantastic." I roll my shoulders and release a sigh.

Ashley puckers her lips and glances around the hallway awkwardly like she's searching for a change of subject in the yellow lockers around us. Eventually she asks, "How's Hawk doing?"

"Hawk's fine. He's out on business today."

She scrunches her face up and twists the bottle of juice between her hands. "So, he's okay?"

"Yeah. He didn't have the pleasure of getting beat in the face like I did."

"No, I mean—well, I mean after yesterday . . ."

My face tucks into a frown. "What are you talking about?"

She tosses up her hands as if it's obvious. "He was acting defensive all day yesterday and then got into a big fight with Matt. I'm pretty sure he got detention. He didn't tell you?"

11

I'm a heartbeat away from texting Hawk when the bell rings. Ashley and I rush into English at the same moment and practically dive into our seats. Our teacher scowls at us but doesn't call us tardy. She moves to the front and starts up a discussion about *Hamlet* but I tune out. I try passing a slip of paper to Ashley to figure out what happened with Hawk yesterday but I'm caught the second I reach out. The teacher clicks her tongue at me, shakes her head, and keeps an eye on me the rest of class, forcing me to wait for information on my brother.

Why wouldn't Hawk mention he got into a fight? We tell each other everything. The few times I've tried to keep a secret from my brother, he found out the same day anyway. Secrets between us are pointless. Maybe he didn't tell me because it had something to do with his wolf half. I hadn't been around to keep that part of him at bay. He doesn't have the benefit of the serum like every other werewolf in town. They can all go about their lives as normally as they please. Not for the first time, I question why Hawk so adamantly refuses to take the serum. I know he has his reasons but he's never told me the whole story.

Huh. I guess there is one secret that's always been kept between us after all.

I tap my foot and rap my fingers anxiously throughout the class and the second the bell rings, I pull Ashley to the side.

"What happened with Hawk?" I ask in an undertone. "He was being defensive how?"

She shrugs and fiddles with the corner of her notebook. "He seemed stressed out, and I heard Matt kept making comments."

"What kind of comments?"

"Oh, you know Matt. He's always a jerk. He was just being rude in general. Some gripe about the soccer game and how Hawk's a big shot and needs to be knocked down a peg. Then at lunch Matt said something to Hawk and he snapped. He tossed his tray and went after Matt. Some of his friends held him back so Matt didn't get his butt kicked, but still."

"Do you know what Matt said to him?"

"No, I was sitting at a different table." She bounces on her feet again, nervous this time. "Then he just kind of kept to himself and didn't want to talk to anyone after that."

A pit forms in my stomach. I wasn't here for my brother when I should have been. I glance around the hallway looking for Matt.

"When I find that punk—"

Ashley grabs my sleeve and scowls. "You're in enough hot water with the principal. Don't go picking a fight, Phoenix."

I roll my eyes. "I don't care about school, Ash. They can do whatever they want."

"Well, I care!"

"And I appreciate that."

She sniffs haughtily and holds up her chin. "Come on. We have to get to our next class."

We retreat to our separate lockers to exchange our textbooks then head together to second period. Sociology is a lot different than it used to be. Mr. Webster is gone and sitting in a penitent cell in Underground for his part in Dasc's scheme. In his place is thin, narrow-faced Mrs. Leech who, incidentally, sucks the fun out of everything.

I sort of nap through class and then perk up for third period. Ashley and I part ways as I head for biology, a class I share with Matt Jones—my target today. On my way into the classroom, I bump into Peter. He readjusts his glasses and gets a better hold on his textbook which is hiding a comic book sticking out between the pages.

"Peter, hey," I say and tap him on the shoulder before he moves away. We had gotten off to a bumpy start when I first came to town, but after he found out I work for a secret government agency, he's been more than happy to be my personal snitch for any werewolf not toeing the line.

"Hey!" he says. "You were gone yesterday. Are you okay? You look like you took a beating."

I lean in closer, look both ways, and say under my breath, "I was out on business."

His face lights up like a fire sprite burning down a house. "What were you—"

"You know the rules."

"Oh, right. It's classified."

"That's right."

His face falls but he quietly asks, "What can I do for you, Agent?"

"What do you have on Matt Jones?"

Our heads automatically swing to where Matt is sitting in the middle of the room, playing around with a microscope, and accidentally breaks a glass slide. He pushes the broken slide towards his friend and points to his buddy when our teacher looks over. Peter and I both roll our eyes and focus on each other again.

"I'm ashamed to call him one of us," Peter says under his breath.

I pat him on the shoulder. "I hear you, buddy. Now, what do you have for me?"

"Just the usual. He's been picking on everybody and everything. Although, he did get into a fight with your brother the other day." He wiggles his eyebrows at me.

"What do you know about it?"

"From what I gather, it was sort of an alpha challenge. That's a werewolf thing, right?" He scrunches his nose in thought as if he doesn't know. Of course he knows. He's a werewolf. When the disease is strong, it makes werewolves long for some kind of pack order, but with the serum that doesn't happen. At least, it *shouldn't*, but throw all those werewolves together in high school and what looks like forming a pack is really the same system of teenagers forming groups of friends or cliques—there's just a lot more fur.

"So Matt wants to play alpha?" I ask.

"Yeah. Like Mr. Krushnic."

All curiosity runs out of my veins to be replaced by something much more powerful—survival instincts and a rush of anger. Anybody trying to replace Dasc a/k/a "James Krushnic" is on a very dangerous course and one I can't allow. Talk about adding to my plate. Worrying about Hawk, vampires, selkies, and Dasc himself is starting to wear me out.

"Well, what started the fight exactly?" I ask.

"Jason."

I blink. "Jason?"

Peter nods. "Matt's been picking on him a lot lately when you guys aren't around. I mentioned this to Hawk a while back. He didn't tell you?"

No, he didn't. I try to keep the frown off my face as I say, "We've been busy, and we'll work independently on jobs sometimes." It's not true but I can't instill distrust in the werewolves around town. They need to believe we're hard-working, trustworthy IMS agents.

"Anyway," Peter continues. "Matt was really going off on Jason—"

"Why?" And why does Jason's name always pop up when things go wrong? "Why is he so set on bullying Jason?"

Peter shrugs. "I'm not sure. Matt was saying Jason's going crazy and he's bananas and he needs to lay off the crazy juice because he's got mad eyes and—"

"Yeah, I get the picture."

"So, Hawk was there and he intervened. Punched Matt in the jaw and everything."

And that's the surprising part. Hawk's good at winning fights with words. He doesn't get physical—well, unless someone's seriously trying to hurt me. He only acts out when he's *really* angry, meaning it's something deeply personal. *I* am the one that goes around punching people on a whim. But this is Jason we're talking about. Hawk wouldn't attack someone to defend the kid that bite me, the one that went on a rampage at the school dance, the one that captured me and Ben and brought us to Dasc to be killed.

Yet this isn't the first time Hawk's stood up for Jason now that I think about it. He always volunteers to do Jason's probation scans, to talk to him when there's an issue, and to pass Jason a friendly greeting when no one else will. I always figured Hawk did it for my sake so I wouldn't have to. Is there more going on here that Hawk isn't telling me? That worries me more than Matt being a jerk.

"Thanks, Peter," I say at last to cover my overly long pause. "I owe you."

His face brightens again and he moves for his seat with a skip in his step. Instead of taking a seat myself, I move very purposefully up to the teacher's desk, which is in clear view of Matt and his friend. I plant both hands on the desktop and lean in towards my balding biology teacher.

"Mr. Koop?"

He looks up from a paper he's grading and gives me a wide smile. "Well, Ms. Mason! I'm glad to see you're back with us. No more trouble I hope?"

He raises his eyebrows and I know he means more than my health. Mr. Koop was one of those turned during Dasc's uprising. Mr. Koop was pretty cool even before he was a werewolf. Now he lets me and Hawk do whatever we want because he knows who and what we are. He's easily my favorite teacher.

"Actually, is it okay if I step out for a while? I need to go check up on someone."

He looks confused but says, "Yes, of course. You'll need a hall pass. Just a second."

"Thanks."

As he fills out a little pass slip, I turn and glare in Matt's direction. He notices and gives me a cocky smile for a second before it melts off his face and he swallows as if he's afraid. Good. He *should* be afraid of me.

Mr. Koop hands over the pass and I try to keep my stride at a normal pace as I walk out of the classroom. I dump my book back at my locker and head for the rear of the building where I know Jason will be. I really only know his schedule so I can avoid him—wow, it's gotten bad, hasn't it? Knowing his schedule in order to adjust mine. It's not like he's Dasc. My footsteps falter for a moment before I pick up speed again.

Near the back of the school is a series of classrooms where the "rowdy" students go. I swear Principal Tippy would love to throw me back here one of these days since I'm so "disruptive." Apparently the school finds it best to wrangle them all together and try to help them through their issues away from the normal students so they don't interrupt their studies. After the whole werewolf fiasco with Dasc, Jason got a one-way ticket to these special classes.

I slow and pause fifteen feet down the hallway from the closed classroom door and lean against the wall to watch the class through the paneled window in the door. I spot Jason sitting by himself at the back of the room. The rest of the class must be doing some kind of team exercises because everyone else is sitting in groups, but not him. No, he's always been the loner. I watch for a few minutes, studying the back of his dark shaggy hair, when the teacher sits down beside him to have a private conversation. It looks like she's trying to coax him to join the others but he shakes his head.

I'm not sure what I'm expecting to see or gather from this little bit of spying. It's not like I'm going to solve the riddle of who and what Jason is by staring at the back of his head. My heartbeat picks up as I remember that night when Dasc revealed himself and tried to kill me. Jason was the one that caught Ben and me in the forest. He claims he was under Dasc's sway at the time but I have my doubts.

As soon as I get the chance, I need to corner Hawk and figure out what's been going on with him. But for the moment, I'm content to keep an eye on Jason from a distance.

The teacher eventually leaves Jason alone at his solitary table. After another minute or so, he slowly raises his head and swivels towards the window where he spots me leaning against the wall with my arms crossed. He stiffens and one hand grips the back of the chair like he's ready to launch himself out of it and start running. I let him soak in that terror and all the horrible possibilities of why I'm watching him—oh yes, I want him to know I have my eye on him—before I push off the wall and go back the way I had come.

When I return to my biology class, several heads turn in my direction but I ignore them and sit silently in the back of the room, contemplating the enigma that is Jason.

I'm in a bad mood through third and fourth period and certainly not ready for bumping into Ben when I enter the cafeteria for lunch. His face instantly turns red and he gives me an over the top goofy smile. For a split second I don't understand why he's acting odd, before I remember he tried asking me out at the soccer game. Oh, someone shoot me.

"Heeeyyyyy, Phoenix," he says, once again over the top. I have a feeling it's his instinctual defense for dealing with awkward encounters. "You're back."

"Yup. I'm back." I enter the shuffle of students holding trays for today's meal. Unfortunately, Ben follows right behind me and tries to keep up a conversation.

"Everything's good with you?" he asks. "Wow, your face—"

"I'm fine. I'm a unicorn on a rainbow."

He laughs louder than necessary. He doesn't know that I actually mean I'm in a really bad mood but that's sort of the point. He had to go and make everything awkward. Our friendship was perfectly fine with me. I can't waste any brain power trying to worry about having a boyfriend. There's no time for that and I don't need it.

Food is plopped onto my tray, I pay my lunch fee, and hunt for a table that's mostly full so Ben can't join me. He must be especially determined to ask me out again because he's still dogging me.

"There's a couple of open spots over there," he says and points to a table on the opposite end of the hallway. "Hey, are you busy this weekend?"

"I don't know yet," I say. For all I know there could be another hunt for the vampires in Duluth or interrogations with Dasc.

"Well, if you're free, the senior class is putting together a black out night in the school."

"A what?"

The fact that I asked makes his smile widen. "We spend the night in the school and play laser tag, watch movies, basically just hang out and mess around."

"Seriously? The school lets you do that?"

"Oh, yeah! There'll be a few teachers around to supervise, obviously, but it'll be fun. You should come."

I nod and reluctantly sit next to him at the far table. "I'll think about it, but like I said, I don't know what's on my schedule."

"Too busy saving the world?" He nudges me with his elbow.

A voice says loudly behind me, "Are you kidding? She's doing it single handedly."

I spin around on the bench so fast I almost knock my tray of food to the floor. Charlie stands over me in his tailored peacoat, a gray scarf trailing down between the lapels, and black dress pants. Does he ever *not* dress like he's a high fashion model? He winks at me and starts to wiggle between me and Ben, pushing Ben to the side to sit backwards on the bench.

"Pardon me," Charlie says and leans back with both elbows on the table top. His face is less than a foot away from mine but I don't move. I'm still recovering from the shock of Charlie appearing in the middle of lunch.

"What on earth are you doing here?" I hiss.

"You think I'd miss out on seeing you in your natural environment?" His smile is cocky. It makes me want to punch him in the face. He inspects the trays of food over his shoulder and other students around us. "Look at this place. The badly cooked meal, the smell of body odor, the prevalence of acne, the suffocating air of judgmental stereotypes. How can you stand it here?"

I can't formulate words to express the train of anger and surprise in my head. "What—you—can I talk to you privately?"

"Excuse me," Ben interrupts. "Who are you?"

Charlie's crooked smile lands on him next. "Oh, I'm sorry. Mason here's never mentioned me?"

I have a bad feeling this is going to end in a train wreck. I sling an arm in front of Charlie to pin him against the tabletop so I have a clear line of sight to Ben.

"This is Charlie. He's a . . . an acquaintance."

"Companion," Charlie interjects.

"*Colleague.*"

"Oh, don't be modest." He shrugs his arm out from under mine and holds a hand towards Ben. "I'm her boyfriend."

The entire table has fallen silent by this point, mostly from everyone being curious of this bizarre newcomer, but when he drops that false bombshell, I can see the hormonal instinct to gossip light up in the eyes of everyone around me. Ben's face has frozen in shock and he doesn't move to take Charlie's hand at all. It takes me three whole seconds before I can compose myself. I grab the lapels of Charlie's jacket and yank him up.

"I need to talk to you," I snap and drag him away from the table of gawkers.

"Of course, honey," Charlie says loud enough for all of them to hear.

My face is on fire and I speed up to a jog still dragging Charlie along behind me, until we turn down a hallway and are out of sight of the lunchroom. The second we stop Charlie yanks away from me and smooths out his lapels.

"Geez, Mason," he says. "I think you almost ruined my jacket."

"What in the name of the six majestics are you doing?" I say, nearly popping a vein in my forehead trying not to shout.

He shrugs and doesn't appear the least bit concerned. "Anyone could see that kid was bugging you. Was he hitting on you?"

"For the love of—" I clamp a hand to my forehead and pace away then back again. "And that was your grand plan to intervene? Say you're my *boyfriend*?"

"Are you . . ." He steps closer and points at me, humor dancing in his eyes. "Are you embarrassed?"

"Of course I'm embarrassed!" I actually do shout this time. When a door starts to open further down the hall, I take Charlie roughly by the arm and march him away to another empty hallway. "What could possibly compel you to say something like that?"

"Imagining your reaction for one. By the way, you really delivered on that."

When I slug him in the shoulder he flinches and scowls.

"Well, aren't you a hard hitter."

I glare at him. "I was holding back. I could have broken a bone if I wanted to."

"I'm touched. You didn't want to hurt me."

I jab my finger in his face. "Shut up. Is there a reason you're here?"

"Of course there is," he says and rubs his shoulder, angling himself away from me defensively in case I decide to strike again. I certainly haven't ruled it out. "Melody and your brother uploaded surveillance video to the server. While they're out collecting evidence they want us to keep an eye on the feeds."

"You couldn't have called? Or have Jefferson come get me?"

He holds up his hands in innocence. "I texted but you didn't respond, and Agent Barnes is off doing something."

"Doing what?"

"You think he told me? He just drove off."

"Weird," I say under my breath. Maybe Jefferson got an emergency call? He usually lets me know, though. I shake my head. "I can't up and leave."

"Why not? I hate to break it to you, but I'm pretty sure the school can run itself while you're gone. This is important."

"School is also my cover. I've been gone enough as it is."

He throws his hands up and slaps them back down against his sides. "Okay, then come up with an excuse."

"To leave in the middle of the day? I've already used every excuse in the book and then some. In fact, I've got to talk to a truancy officer in a couple of days."

"Ha!" He holds a hand over his mouth to cover up the rest of his laughter and then heaves a sigh. "Well, I could kidnap you."

"You could *try*," I growl. This is getting us nowhere. He's right though. Checking those surveillance feeds is more important than babysitting the werewolves who are clearly doing fine. Moose Lake runs smoothly most days. I don't need to be here. I don't *want* to be here. I want to find that vampire.

"Okay," I grumble. "I think I can do food poisoning again."

He cocks his head. "Again?"

"I had bad shrimp the other day for my excuse. Come on." I grab his arm again but this time I pull it around my waist and then sling my arm over his shoulders. "I'll need your help to sell this."

For the first time he looks startled. "What? What are we doing?"

"Just follow my lead. You may have to carry me."

"Excuse me?"

We walk back into the cafeteria arm in arm. I cover my mouth with my free hand then hunch over and making groaning sounds. Heads turn in our direction and I keep us moving on through towards the hallway that'll take us to the exit.

"I said you shouldn't have eaten anything after that shrimp!" Charlie says in a mock condescending tone. "The food here's going to kill you!"

"Over-actor," I mumble.

One of the paraprofessionals starts heading in our direction but Ashley appears out of nowhere and misdirects the adult before we're intercepted. We make it to the doors just as Ashley jogs over to help escort us out. Once we're out of the cafeteria I start to straighten but Ashley pushes me back down into a hunch.

"You might run into some other teachers." Her eyes slide to Charlie and she clenches her jaw.

"Oh, hey," Charlie says. "It's you. What's your name again?"

I swivel my head to level a glare at him. "You can't remember the name of the person you arrested two days ago?"

"Meh, I'm terrible with names."

We make it down the hallway without incident and stop beside my locker. I quickly grab my jacket and backpack. Charlie—still pretending to be a gentleman and my boyfriend—helps me into my jacket and slings my backpack onto his shoulder.

Ashley pats me once on the back. "I'll let the office know. You should go before Principal Tippy wants to have you checked out. You're going to need a doctor's note to convince him this time, I think."

"Thanks, Ash," I say. "I'll see you tomorrow, okay?"

Charlie and I hustle out of the school together and, after making sure the coast is clear, jog over to Charlie's SUV. The tires spin a bit on the ice before they find traction and we move slowly through town towards the cabin. I heave a sigh once we're free.

"I'm so getting kicked out of school," I say under my breath.

"So what?" Charlie responds. "I don't know why you guys didn't go with a home school cover or no school cover at all. This really binds you up."

The truth is I need to stick close to the werewolves in case some of Dasc's influence has lingered. Obviously, I can't tell Charlie the truth. My abilities are a secret and I plan on keeping it that way for the time being.

"It's how we discovered Dasc," I say. "We can't just drop the act now."

"I guess."

When we reach the cabin, I hurry inside to drop off my things, grab something to eat since I didn't even touch my food at lunch, and meet Charlie in the barn. He's already logged himself into Jefferson's computer. I sit at my own computer and log into the IMS servers as I scarf down a sandwich. A new message pops up from Melody and allows me access to old surveillance video and live feeds.

"One of us should comb through the old stuff and the other should watch the live feeds," I suggest. "Rock, paper, scissors for the old footage?"

There's no argument from Charlie, which is a relief. I thought for sure he would think I'm being unprofessional or something. Of course, he hasn't been very professional himself—just uptight. My paper beats his rock so I open the log of dated video and scroll through. I open file after file until I find the closest view of the warehouse. It overlooks the parking lot that I chased the vampire from. Skipping ahead to that night, I watch myself run after the vampire as he hops into his car and then tries to run me over. Moments later, Charlie slides to a stop in the SUV beside me and we take off together.

"It was kind of cool though, wasn't it?" I say aloud. "Being in a car chase."

Charlie doesn't say anything but looks like he's fighting a smile.

Once I've got an idea of the timeframe I'm looking at, I start rolling backwards through the videos to try to retrace the vampires' steps. While I do that, I notice Charlie has some other document up on his screen apart from the live feeds of downtown Duluth. I lean over and can make out the top of a medical report.

Charlie notices and gestures to the file. "Gillian's physical examination."

"Anything useful?"

"One thing. She had track marks on the inside of her elbow."

"Track marks?" I lean forward in my chair. It's not completely uncommon for magical individuals to use drugs like your average smoking Joe, but it's not what I'm expecting. Needles don't just inject things though—they take, too. "So, either Gillian likes hard drugs, they were injecting her with something, or taking her blood. Did she have anything to say about that?"

"Says she couldn't remember." He rubs his chin in thought. "The selkies can be a little wild but I doubt Gillian would be using drugs, especially with Nessa as her sister. It would deteriorate her ability to be a guardian. And I can't imagine they'd inject her with anything except a sedative. Taking blood would make more sense. Vampires have hit up blood donor vans before. If they liked the high of the magic in her blood, they probably wanted to store some for later."

"I don't know," I say and frown at my computer screens. I've frozen the image on the vampire in the hoodie running out to his car. "Something feels off about that. Vampires go wild over fresh blood. Why bag it up when they've already got her captive? Any other vampire would just bleed her out then and there, not bag her blood. I've never heard a vampire do that before. They're sharks. They don't stop once they start feeding."

"Well, there's no denying it was a vampire. The rest is conjecture."

"Okay, fine. Then let's find some hard evidence."

"Let's."

We return to silence as I backtrack through the video until I reach the point where the Mustang pulls into the empty lot. Our hoodie vampire gets out of the driver's seat and the girl with the pink scarf emerges from the passenger side. Together, the two captors pull Gillian out of the backseat and sling her across the male vamp's shoulders to carry her into the warehouse. A tremor goes down my spine. This isn't like watching a movie. This is real. This happened.

There's no movement for a while so I fast forward through the video until something catches my eye. A third figure stalks across the lot in long strides but I can't tell if it's a man or a woman beneath their heavy winter jacket with the hood up and a scarf wrapped around their face. Whoever it is marches straight up to the warehouse where the vampires are hiding and enters.

"Charlie," I say without taking my eyes off the screen.

"It's Junior Agent Jaeger."

"Whatever. I've got someone new here."

He wheels over and we both watch the screen.

I point to the warehouse door as I speed forward until there's movement again. "There. We have a third person—or vampire."

"Well, we figured there could be others."

The mystery figure emerges first and walks over to the Mustang. Following behind comes hoodie-vampire with a girl draped over his shoulders in a fireman's carry. For a second I think it's Gillian but the hair and clothing are all wrong.

"Wait, that's our pink scarf vampire," I say. "What are they . . ."

The girl is dumped unceremoniously into the trunk before the other two get into the car and drive off. There's no struggle, no wrestling her into the car. She's either unconscious or—

"Can you pick them up on another feed?" Charlie asks, leaning into my personal space.

I click through the videos, eyes dancing over the footage until I manage to pick them up again moving into the city. Unfortunately, that also takes them out of view from what surveillance feeds Hawk and Melody were able to acquire.

"I lost them," I grumble. "But our male vampire comes back at some point, we know that."

"Then speed up until the Mustang comes back."

I give him a sharp sideways look. "What do you think I'm doing?"

Holding up his hands and rolling his eyes, he gives me some space as I angrily click the mouse button and fast forward again. Eventually the Mustang does return hours later. Once it reaches the lot, I start to backtrack the video to see where he came from. Maybe that'll point us in the right direction as to where he is now. The Mustang zooms backwards further into the warehouses, past grain elevators, and along train tracks until it finally stops at the very edge of my surveillance feeds right next to the edge of the frozen harbor. I zip back to the point the Mustang first shows up there and then stop to watch.

The vampire gets out of his car and opens the trunk. When he pulls out a big, lumpy black bag, my stomach knots.

"Charlie . . ."

I can't look away as the vampire drags the bag over to the edge of the frozen inlet from the lake, then hops onto the ice and breaks open a hole. Charlie rolls closer again to look over my shoulder as the vampire shoves the bag into the hole and it disappears beneath the surface. The vampire glances around then gets into his Mustang to drive to the warehouse.

I look to Charlie and his expression is grim. "You don't think that was . . ."

"Keep rewinding," he says.

He scoots closer so we can both watch as I push the video back further and we track the Mustang's path. It drives into the docks from the interstate but we lose sight of it continuing to go back in time. We spend another fifteen minutes searching but without luck. Charlie claps a hand on my shoulder.

"Keep looking," he says. "I'm going to call Melody and have her find out what our vampire dumped in the lake."

He pulls out his cellphone and returns to Jefferson's desk with the phone to his ear. Out of the corner of my eye I see him pull up a live feed of the same area of the lake where the vampire disposed of the bag. I try to focus on finding the Mustang in the old footage but can't help dreading what Melody and Hawk might find. Charlie has a quick chat with Melody and then we wait. Twenty minutes pass before Charlie snaps his fingers and points to the live feed.

"They just arrived," he says for my benefit.

I roll over in my chair and we both watch the long pixelated view of Melody, Hawk, and a woman I assume is Nessa get out of their SUV to walk the perimeter of the frozen inlet. Charlie calls Melody again and directs them to the right spot. There's silence for a long time as they work at breaking up the fresh ice to see what's underneath the surface. We watch Melody jog to the SUV and grab a shovel at one point. I'm almost holding my breath as they manage to find the black bag and haul it out of the water.

Charlie turns the phone on speaker and we wait, listening to the rustle of the bag and the labored breathing on the other end of the line. The suspense is killing me. All three of our teammates freeze on the surveillance feed as Melody opens the bag.

"What is it?" I ask, unable to restrain myself. "What's inside?"

Silence echoes for three seconds before Melody responds. "As far as I can tell, it's a body."

Despite expecting the confirmation, a shock goes through my body. Charlie glances to me with a frown and leans in towards the phone. "What do you mean, as far as you can tell?"

"Well, to put it more accurately, there are parts of a body. Lots of parts."

12

There's a hollow ringing in my ears and a part of me goes numb. I've seen movies before where the poor victim's body is mutilated, or the cops find a foot by itself in a river, or you watch the actor's reaction to finding parts of a body but the camera never shows it. Knowing someone's been dismembered into so many pieces that you can't tell if it's more than one body or not, and knowing it's *real*, is something on a completely different level.

Charlie and I watch the team in Duluth haul the bag into the back of the SUV then search the area for any clues or other bags the vampire might have dropped there. We keep the phone line open and listen to commentary from Melody through the speaker.

"We aren't finding anything else," she says. She's vanished from the angle of the live feed. "We'll take the body back to the office and see what we can work out. I need you two to comb through the old footage and see if you can find anything else. There may be more victims we're not aware of."

"You got it, Mels," Charlie responds.

"And keep it light, okay? Take a breather if you need one. This is grisly but we've got jobs to do. I'll send you more footage once we get it and pictures from the autopsy after I get Dr. Malkebar here."

Charlie's eyes flicker to me for a second before he leans in towards the phone. "If you need more hands on deck up there, we'd be more than happy to—"

"*No*," Melody says sharply. "You have your job, so get to it."

The line clicks and the conversation's over. Charlie rather savagely shoves the phone into his pocket and rubs the back of his neck, eyes downcast. My gut continues to twist over the fact that somebody was chopped up and dumped in the lake. More than likely it's the pink-scarf vampire but why would they kill her? What on earth is going on here? This isn't normal vampire behavior. They never go to the trouble of chopping up their victims. They bleed them dry, leave them, and move on. They're always looking for the next source of fresh blood, not messing over their leftovers. And Hawk's up there right now with that psycho on the loose.

"Let's get to work," I say and dive into the old footage.

Charlie doesn't respond but drags his chair to my side so we can go over the videos together. I let the footage play from when the hoodie-vampire dumped the bag in the lake just in case anything else happened between the time he returned to the warehouse to when we showed up. He pulls into the parking lot and exits the Mustang carrying some kind of box with a handle.

"Is that a cooler?" Charlie asks.

I nudge him with my elbow. "Blood needs to be kept refrigerated. Maybe our wild conjecture isn't that far off."

Not long after the vampire enters the building he leaves again with the cooler in tow. Instead of driving off again, he sets the cooler on the backseat of the Mustang and then walks off between the buildings. It looks like he's meandering until he stops against the side of one of the warehouses, braces his hands against the wall, and his shoulders start to shake.

"Wait, is he . . . crying?" I ask and squint at the pixelated image. "Do vampires even cry?"

Charlie's eyes narrow as we both study the bizarre behavior. Nothing in this case has been making sense, this more than anything. The vampire stands there for a long time before he wanders between the buildings and disappears near the lake. Eventually our SUV pulls into the lot and I watch as we check the Mustang, then split off into teams.

"There," Charlie says and points to the dark side of the warehouse where our vampire is barely visible. He stands there and watches as we move between the warehouses and eventually all enter the one where Gillian is being kept. He doesn't run off like a vampire ought to when the IMS prowls around. He doesn't find a weapon and come after us either. He waits and waits and when Charlie and I exit the building to bring the SUV in, he actually shuffles forward a bit so he's visible against the fence next to the parking lot.

"What the—he wanted us to know he was there," I say. "He waited until I spotted him before taking off. He wanted us to follow him. Why?"

"Now *that* is an excellent question."

"I think we should—"

"Start from the beginning," we say in unison. Charlie leans into his chair like he's shocked we're on the same wavelength. I roll my eyes and dig through the list of feeds until I find the ones that cover Canal Park. Once I find one looking down the main drag in front of the Blue Comet, I blow it up and let it play. Charlie reclines in his chair as we watch the night progress.

It takes some time for the players in this whole mess to appear. Ashley walks along the street, moving from one shop to the other at a leisurely pace. Several steps behind we spot pink-scarf-girl and hoodie-guy following in her wake, each sporting sunglasses even though it's twilight. Once they come into view, both Charlie and I lean forward on the edge of our seats, eyebrows knit together in matching frowns. Ashley is all but oblivious to the two vampires stalking her, following her every move. I'm so focused on them that I don't even notice the group of selkies making for the Blue Comet until Charlie points them out.

The selkies walk towards the nightclub, and on the opposite side of the street Ashley's two stalkers give them only a brief glance before remaining glued to Ashley moving into the Chocolate Factory. A while later she exits, hesitates on the sidewalk, then chooses to walk into the alley next to the Blue Comet. The girl dashes across the street and disappears behind another building, probably to head Ashley off, while hoodie-guy walks into the alley.

"They were following Ashley the entire time," I murmur. "They wanted *her*. I think they only took Gillian because she got in the way."

"But why?" Charlie asks. "If they wanted a meal, there were plenty of normal people walking around and in those alleys that they could have taken. Why would a couple of vampires pick out the one werewolf in the crowd?"

Those are all excellent points and each make me incredibly uneasy. A thought suddenly occurs to me. "What if they're still after her? Ashley could be in danger. That hoodie-loving vampire is still out there along with whomever our third mystery person is that checked into that warehouse and probably helped kill scarf-girl." I'm already buttoning up my jacket. "I need to get to the school and warn her."

"I'm coming with," Charlie says which surprises me.

"You think I'm right?" I ask, turning to the weapon rack to grab a bio-mech gun and machete. The blade slides into a sheath inside my parka and the gun I tuck into a front pocket—my mother's gun is already hidden in the holster on my belt.

He shrugs into the sleeves of his jacket and starts trotting down the stairs. "I think we're on to a possible lead and someone could be in danger. That's enough for me."

We hop into the SUV and Charlie floors it to the school. My pulse quickens and I glance at the car's clock every few seconds. We've spent enough time going through surveillance video that there's only half an hour of school left. Ashley will be inside and that offers some protection. A vampire wouldn't walk into the middle of a crowded school and pull her out. No, he would be waiting outside if he's here at all. I need to keep my head on straight and do my due diligence. I call Hawk but it goes to voicemail so I leave a quick message letting him know what we discovered and what we're doing now. As soon as I hang up, Charlie swings into a parking spot and turns off the vehicle.

"You clear right and I'll clear left?" he says. I nod. "Okay, and make sure no one sees you. You're supposed to be out sick puking your guts into a toilet."

"Roger that."

We bail out at the same time, closing the car doors in sync. I can't help but notice that we work well together when we're focusing on the job and not on each other. That's something I guess. He starts to edge through the parking lot, hands tucked into his pockets and glancing into vehicles. I walk in the opposite direction sticking to the outer edge of the lot which should be far enough away from the school's windows so no one will recognize me. As I take careful footsteps across the icy pavement, I send a quick text to Ashley telling her to stay inside the building once school gets out and wait until we come get her. Hopefully she won't freak out too much. I didn't come right out and say there may be a vampire on her tail but there's enough of a warning in my message that she could get worked up.

I check through frosted windows and brush away snow here and there to make sure there aren't any creepers lurking out here. A neighbor shoveling off his porch stops his work to watch me and I realize I must look like I'm trying to break into cars. Stopping to give him a friendly wave and dissuade his attention, I notice I've got a shadow coming up behind me and fast. My hand instinctively goes for the handle of the bio-mech gun in the pocket of my jacket and I spin around.

Jefferson grabs my arm to keep me from pulling the gun out. He's wearing his usual scowl.

"What on earth are you doing?" he growls under his breath, his eyes flickering to the guy shoveling who's paused again to watch our interaction. We both crack smiles and then Jefferson slings an arm around my shoulders to forcibly walk me towards the Green Monster parked on the far side of the lot.

"I could ask you the same thing," I say once we're far enough away from the curious onlooker. "Where did you go? We tried to call you."

He shrugs. "I had to take care of an emergency call that came in."

My eyes narrow. "Why didn't you say something? You always let me or Hawk know before you run off so we can cover the office."

"Well, it's a good thing I came back when I did," he says, completely sidestepping my question. "I passed you and the boy wonder driving this way when you're supposed to already be in school. Why are you prowling the lot?"

I quickly fill him in on what we saw on the surveillance video and our suspicions that hoodie-vampire could be following Ashley. He scratches at his beard and we pause next to the Green Monster to scan the area.

"If this vampire wanted to go after Ashley," he says, "he's already had plenty of time to do it. I don't think he'd be waiting outside the school to grab her now."

I roll my lips and look away, shaking my head. "I really thought you'd be with me on this one."

"Oh?"

"I figured you'd be tired of trying to protect people after the fact," I say bitterly. "I know I am."

"Phoenix—"

"So what if I'm wrong?" I say and throw up my hands. "Better safe than sorry, right? No one else is going to get hurt under my watch, you got it? I'm not letting anyone down like that again."

I try to storm away but he grabs my arm and pulls me back. It'd be easy to throw him off but I don't. Instead, I refuse to look at him and stare angrily at the ice covered bricks of the school. I don't want to talk about this. I had enough therapy sessions after shooting Dasc.

"What is this all about?" he asks and tries to turn me so I have to meet his critical gaze but I don't budge. "Might as well get that stick out of your butt before it starts to ache."

"Gross."

"This is about Dasc isn't it?" he continues. I press my mouth into a thin line. He's not going to let this go, is he? "Who do you think you let down, hmm? I'd be dead and your brother would be a brainwashed attack-zoid if it wasn't for you. Half this town might be missing and turning the rest of the state if you hadn't stopped Dasc."

"But I didn't stop him, did I?" I finally meet Jefferson's gaze. "I just got there in time to stop something worse from happening but he had already won. How many people did he turn? How many people are still missing? We can't change any of it, Jefferson. He gets to sit in that stupid little cell and gloat about it because we can't change the past. We were too late. We're always too late."

For a second I fear I've said too much. He holds his jaw rigid, his eyes dark, and I realize I probably touched a nerve. After all, without even meaning to, I alluded to Jefferson's own past mistakes and what he wasn't able to stop—like my parents' murder, his wife's murder, and his daughter's disappearance. My face goes red and I quickly look away.

"You can't stop every bad thing from happening," he says gruffly. "Stop trying to blame yourself for things that were never your fault in the first place. You blasted kids are going to give me a coronary. And don't you dare correct me calling you kids because right now you're acting like a child."

That makes me angry again and I glare at him.

He points a blunt finger in my face. "See? There it is again."

"I'm *not* acting like—"

"But you also have a point," he says, cutting me off. "There's enough evidence that we ought to be cautious. These vampires of yours are acting odd and there's no telling what they're up to. Now, then." He grabs my arm again and steers me into the passenger seat of the Green Monster. "You're going to stay out of sight of any teachers and I'll finish checking the area with Jaeger."

"I'm supposed to meet Ashley inside," I protest but he just waves me down.

"I'll make sure she gets out safely. You just sit here." He closes the door on me but then leans in against the window and says loudly through it, "Don't. Move."

He stalks away and I slump in the seat with my arms crossed. I hate being stuck on the sidelines, but I respect Jefferson so I do as he says. Every couple of seconds I check my watch for the time. Charlie eventually passes by and gives me the okay sign with his fingers, letting me know the coast is clear of danger. I nod and he strides back to his SUV before taking off. I give a little sigh of relief but don't let my guard down. Just because we didn't find anyone right this moment doesn't mean there isn't someone close by or coming.

Eventually I hear the faint ringing of the school bell. Students emerge in a flood heading for the buses neatly parked in front of the entrance or for their cars out in the lot. I slide down lower in the seat and flip up the hood of my parka to hide my face. I don't need anyone pointing out my reappearance lest the teachers catch wind of it. I wait another good ten minutes before the buses pull out and take away most of the crowd with them. Once the parking lot thins out and only a few stragglers are left, Jefferson emerges from the school with Ashley by his side. They hurry over to the Green Monster, each of them glancing this way and that. I slip out of the car once they're close.

Ashley hurries forward to clutch my arm. "What's going on? I thought you left with that other agent for an emergency. You weren't coming back until tomorrow. Now *he's* coming to pick me up—" She jerks her head in Jefferson's direction, "—and your message really freaked me out. I'm not in trouble, am I? I swear I've been taking my doses and filling out my logs and I already talked to that counselor about my little incident in Duluth and—"

I grab her by the shoulders and give her a small shake. "Ashley, calm down. It's okay. You're not in trouble."

"I'm not?" Her face twists up in confusion.

"No. It's . . . uh, some new information came to light after I left." My eyes flicker to Jefferson and he raises an eyebrow at me as he goes to stand at the driver's side door and rest his forearms across the hood of the Green Monster. His eyes stay glued to me, clearly waiting for me to continue with my explanation. "You haven't noticed anyone following you have you?"

Her whole body tenses. "What?"

"Is that a no?"

"I don't know!" she shrieks. "I haven't exactly been checking to see if I'm being *stalked*. What's going on? Am I in danger?"

Her voice carries across the lot so I smile to try and make her relax. I wish Hawk was here. He's better at this.

"How about we talk in private?" I say and start guiding her over to her old, brown Buick Century on the other side of the lot. I look to Jefferson over my shoulder and say, "We'll meet you at the cabin."

"Roger that," he says and slides into the Green Monster.

I walk Ashley to her car and then take the keys from her since her hands are shaking. Oops. She's freaking out already and I haven't even mentioned vampires yet. This is going to be a long afternoon.

The second we close the doors and I turn on the engine, Ashley swivels in the passenger seat to face me.

"Tell me what's going on," she demands.

The Buick rumbles out of the lot and I navigate the icy roads through Moose Lake. I roll my lips together, considering how much I ought to tell Ashley and what she shouldn't know.

"Well, last night we found the vampire that attacked you in Duluth. To summarize, he ran, we chased him, he got away, we were arrested. Good times." I shrug and decide not to mention finding Gillan tied up in a warehouse after having been tortured. "Anyway, we've been scouring video to figure out where he went and I watched the night he went after you in the alley.”

“Okay, yeah,” Ashley says, clearly impatient. Her leg is bouncing fast and she’s starting to bite her thumbnail. “So, what happened?”

I give her a sideways look before returning my eyes to the road. “Have you ever seen that guy before?”

“No. Why?”

“He was following you, Ash. He ignored plenty of other *better* targets and went after you. I don’t know why and it’s possible he’s still after you.”

Silence fills the old sedan as Ashley takes that bit of information in. We don’t speak again until we come to a stop next to the black SUV in front of the cabin. Jefferson is closing the doors to the barn after having parked the Green Monster and meets us outside.

“So, what’s the plan?” Ashley asks and hugs her arms to herself.

Jefferson turns to me. “Yes, what’s next, Phoenix?”

Startled, I stare at him. I thought he was going to be the one coming up with the plan. He’s the lead agent after all. I shrug and he gives me a hard look.

“Okay . . .” I wring my hands together and nod slowly to myself trying to think of what a full-fledged IMS agent would do. “Ashley should stay where it’s safe until we know for sure whether there is or isn’t a threat.”

“Good,” Jefferson says. “What else?”

“What else? Sorry, that’s as far as my plan goes.”

He rolls his eyes. “You need to pay better attention to the details.”

“I don’t plan ahead, Jefferson. I just roll with the punches.”

"I've noticed." He rests a hand on Ashley's shoulder. "Safest place for you right now is here."

She shakes her head. "I need to tell my parents. Oh my gosh, what about my parents? Do you think they'd be in danger too?"

That's a scary thought and one I haven't considered to be honest. It would also be sort of awkward trying to explain the situation to them since they don't even know Ashley is a werewolf. She wanted to keep it a secret—as is her right—because, as she put it, her mother is "the biggest gossip to have ever walked the earth." That, and her father has heart issues. She didn't want to scare him into a heart attack.

"Okay, new plan," I say. "We'll say we're having a sleep over and I'll stay the night at your place. Then you're safe, your parents are safe, everyone's happy."

"Except my parents," Ashley says in an undertone. When I give her a sharp look, she shrugs and says sheepishly, "They don't think you're a good influence."

"And rightly so," Jefferson says under his breath which earns him a glare. He ignores the gesture and continues, "Well, that sounds fair enough to me. I'm sure you can handle things on your own. I'll stay here with Junior Agent Jaeger and keep going through the surveillance feeds. Keep in touch, Phoenix."

"Right. And you'll keep me updated?"

"Sure thing."

He moves off to the barn and I playfully punch Ashley in the shoulder to try to lighten the mood. The scowl she gives me would have impressed a centaur.

"Wait here a second," I say and hurry inside. Jogging into the cabin, it takes me only a second to grab what I need. I've got a "go bag" under my bunkbed with two sets of clothes, a flashlight, a revolver and tranquilizer gun plus ammo, as well as a few personal care item essentials like toothpaste and deodorant. Jefferson was impressed when he discovered I had a go bag—although, it's really more of an "escape bag." Ever since Hawk stopped taking the serum and our first attempt at running away was unsuccessful, I've kept a bag handy in case we need to flee on a moment's notice.

There's an odd plastic crunch when I sling it over my shoulder. I set it on the floor and check the outer lining pocket to find several candy bars stuffed inside with a note written on the largest in black permanent marker.

Just in case. —The Better Looking Twin

Hawk's note and surprise present make me smile. Thanks, Brother. I needed that right now. Picking the bag back up, I meet Ashley outside and we take her car to her family's quaint two-story house at the end of a rutted and slushy gravel driveway. The engine falls silent at the twist of the key and we both remain seated staring out at the bay window of the house where soft yellow light ebbs out.

"So, what do I tell them?" Ashley asks in a small voice.

"Sleepover," I say. "That's it. Nothing crazy. It's all good. This is only a precaution and me being paranoid. I'm sure there's nothing to worry about."

"You really think so?"

No, but I'm not about to tell her that. Instead, I nod with a smile and step out of the Buick. When we enter the house, her parents' reaction to my presence is about what I expect. Her mother is a small plump woman with a mop of curly brown hair and is rather unassuming except for the intense scowl she gives me when I wave at them both as I walk in the door. She's organizing a bookshelf and Ashley's dad, in his plaid flannel shirt, is sitting in a recliner reading a newspaper. Their scowls match perfectly.

"She's spending the night," Ashley says in a rush and points to me as if they can't figure it out for themselves who she's referring to. "That's okay, right?"

Her mother crosses her arms over her chest. "That's short notice."

"We have a paper due tomorrow," I say, stepping in. "We've got a lot of work to do so we figured we'd make a night of it. It's nice to see you again, Mrs. Nelson." Then I give her dad a nod. "Mr. Nelson."

He makes a sound like "harrumph" and turns back to his paper. Ashley grabs my arm in a fierce grip and drags me up the stairs to her bedroom. On the upstairs landing we're met by Ashley's golden lab, Duke, that follows her around like a puppy. He comes over to me once to lick my hand before sticking to Ashley like glue. I guess he's discovered his alpha of the Nelson family. We move down the hallway and when we reach Ashley's room, she shuts the door behind us and lets out a heavy breath.

"That was awkward," she says.

"I've had worse," I say and absently gaze around at her walls that are plastered with posters of comic book heroes, action movie stars, and an enormous collage of pages torn out from some celebrity magazine. "I once farted in front of a whole line of centaurs. Then Hawk was there which made it worse."

When silence follows I turn around and find Ashley fixing me with a look like I'm insane. Right. I guess she wouldn't understand centaurs don't laugh or find humor in much of anything. They're all very uptight and stern so it was an incredibly awkward silence for about five seconds before Hawk started laughing hysterically. Mind you, everyone else was dead silent at the time and all the centaurs gave us the look of death.

"Never mind," I say and wave my hand dismissively.

"So . . ." Ashley sets her backpack at the foot of her dresser and slums onto her bed. "What now?"

"Well, if you have any homework, now would be a good time to do it."

She plays with a lock of her blonde hair and twists it round and round to the point I fear she might pull it out. Of course she's nervous. I just told her a vampire might be stalking her. I know I should comfort her but first things first. I go to her window and check the surroundings outside. The sun is already starting to set and twilight is moving in. There's a small backyard directly below overshadowed by the forest that borders the edge of the property. The trees would provide great cover if there is someone out there watching the house. I keep that thought in mind. At least the snow seems undisturbed except for dog prints.

When I turn back Ashley is mindlessly petting Duke and by all appearances is miserable and close to tears. So, trying to do what Hawk would do, I take a seat next to her on the bed and cross my legs beneath me. I lightly punch her in the shoulder to get her attention. She gives me another cold scowl. I guess I should stop punching her. That tactic isn't exactly producing the desired effect.

"Hey, is there anything you want to talk about?" I ask.

She shrugs noncommittally. "I don't know."

The only thing I can think of to get her mind off the current situation is to offer up the game Hawk and I play when I'm trying to distract him from his own problems.

"Who do you think would look better in a wig?" I ask. "A three-headed dog or a hydra?"

My random, supposedly hilarious question gets me a very severe look from Ashley. That abruptly ends my attempt at humor. I'm trying to lighten the mood, not make it worse.

"I don't know," she says sharply and rolls her eyes. "I swear you're so weird sometimes."

"Oh, gee, thanks," I mumble and try petting Duke but he shuffles closer to Ashley. Wow, I really feel out of place here. Where's Hawk when you need him? Oh right, he's investigating a body shredded to pieces, the same fate I'm trying to protect Ashley from, who now of all times decides to become hostile. I remove myself from the bed to stand guard at the window. It feels like a good move to make. Ashley clearly doesn't want to talk and truthfully I don't either. I want to do my job.

"What's with you and Ben?" Ashley asks out of the blue.

I don't bother taking my eyes off the peaceful scenery outside. "There's nothing going on with me and Ben."

"Okay, then what about you and Charlie?"

This time I can't help but roll my eyes. "I don't have a *thing* for or with anybody."

"Why not?"

The absurdity of her insistence makes me spin around. "Why do I have to?"

She pouts and Duke puts his head in her lap. "Ben would totally go out with you if you'd say yes."

"But I don't want to say yes. I'm a little preoccupied with, you know, a whole town of—" I glance to the door before whispering, "werewolves. I don't need a boyfriend. That's a whole messy swamp of awkward I don't want to deal with on top of everything else."

That's mostly the truth, anyway. There are werewolves and vampires to worry about but my biggest concern is always going to be my brother. Who has time to fuss over a romantic relationship when I've got family to worry about going dark side when I'm not around? Sure, I've seen the movies about falling in love and the action flicks with a side of romance, but I haven't given it much thought myself. Those are other people's stories. Maybe someday that will be me, but for the moment I'm fine with my life the way it is.

"You and Hawk seem to handle it all better than the rest of us," Ashley says quietly. "Having a werewolf in the family and all that. You make it look easy."

"It's experience, that's all," I say and muse over the fact that this is the second time someone has commented on us being well adjusted with the werewolf disease. I didn't realize we're such prize specimens. "Hawk and I have been dealing with it since we were kids. It's a part of our lives. You'll get there."

"Did you know I got grounded?" she continues in that soft voice as if I hadn't said a thing. "That night I was bitten and had to stay at that werewolf farm? My parents flipped out because I was missing that whole night and didn't call. But I couldn't tell them the truth, Phoenix. My dad, his heart's been bad for a while and I . . ."

We're getting close to teary-eyed territory. Ashley quickly looks away and dabs at her eyes while I stand there awkwardly, unsure of what to say. I've never really dealt with this part of the werewolf problem before. When we lived in Underground everyone knew who and what we were. I've never had to hide from the people I care about. Then at school there wasn't anyone we cared about enough to feel guilty keeping a secret from. I have no words of comfort for Ashley. Being a werewolf is going to be tough for her. If only I had acted faster at the high school and stopped her from being bitten.

I turn to the window and stare out into the deepening twilight to brood. Movement beneath the trees catches my eye. A slim figure wearing a dark hoodie steps out from the shadows.

13

The figure's face, obscured beneath the hood, tilts to look directly at me in the window. My heart thunders in my chest and I freeze. We have a staring contest for a solid ten seconds before Ashley speaks up from her spot on the bed.

"Phoenix?"

Without taking my eyes off the figure below, I ask, "Where's the backdoor?"

"At the end of the hallway just past the bottom of the stairs," she says rapidly in a high voice, her breathing starting to hitch. I guess she's figured out something's wrong from the way I've frozen at the window.

"Call Jefferson and stay here," I warn, then lunge for the door. I've already got my machete in the lining of my jacket and the bio-mech gun in my pocket. The second my fingers close around the gun, I fling open the bedroom door, fly down the stairs, and launch myself out the backdoor.

I take great bounding leaps through the thigh-high snow

and move around the corner of the house to where I last spotted the mysterious figure. He's gone but I can hear him crashing through the trees. Despite there being hardly any light to guide me, and having forgotten my flashlight in my bag, I plunge in after the noise and activate the bio-mech gun so it fits to the curve of my hand. A shadow darts between the trees and I race after between the pines and bare birches. Whoever it is zig-zags so much that I can't get a clear shot. That doesn't stop me from letting a few pulses fly. The shots hit trees, causing them to sway precariously and shower me with snow, bits of bark, and pine needles. I have to shield my face after one particularly bad shot lets loose a cascade of debris that nearly gets me in the eyes.

Eventually the figure trips on something hidden beneath the snow, allowing me to catch up, get a solid beam on him, and shoot him square in the back as he tries to regain his footing. His back arches from the strength of the pulse and he falls face first into the snow. I inch forward keeping my gun trained on him while taking great gulps of frigid air, and extricate the machete from the lining of my jacket.

He should be out cold, or at least stunned, but I nudge him with the toe of my boot before flipping him over to see who I managed to tag. Snow clings to his jacket as I roll him over and lift back his hoodie to reveal his face. In the darkness it's hard to be certain, but I swear the face I'm looking at isn't a vampire.

"Jason? What on earth . . ."

He's out cold, his eyes closed. A thousand scenarios for why he's creeping around outside Ashley's house flash through my mind, and none of them are good. I still have the scar that proves he can be a monster. Jason may not recall the act but I certainly remember being bitten. In my mind, I can't see him as anything but an enemy, the werewolf that tried to kill or turn me. I don't care if Dasc had a grip on Jason at that point. He's a threat and for some reason he decided to sneak around outside Ashley's house. There's no explanation that's going to satisfy my distrust.

I tuck the machete back into my jacket and dig in my pocket for my phone. Just as I manage to tug it out, I hear something crash through the brush behind me. My bio-mech gun is up and extended before I even fully turn around to face whatever is coming up fast behind me.

A big golden blob runs through the trees and almost runs me over. Duke starts licking my hands the second he reaches me. Ashley appears a moment later.

"Phoenix!"

Pixies. "Ash, I told you to stay in the house."

She ignores me and walks forward with her eyes glued to Jason lying unconscious on the ground. Suddenly she clasps her hands over her mouth like she's about to scream.

"He's fine," I say quickly and stretch out an arm to keep her from coming any closer. "Just stunned. I thought he was our vampire."

"He said he was going to come see me," Ashley says, eyes wide. "I thought he was going to go to the front door."

"A little warning would have been nice."

Ashley spins about on me. "Well, I wasn't expecting you to go flying after him like a maniac."

Oh, you've got to be kidding me. I gesture widely with my arms to Jason unconscious in the snow. "I thought he was a vampire trying to kidnap you or worse! It's dark out, he comes out of the woods, what was I supposed to think? A friend was coming over for a late night chat?"

She huffs, crosses her arms over her chest, and looks pointedly away from me.

"You know what?" I say. "Fine. Be angry. I'm just trying to do my job." I tuck my bio-mech gun into my pocket before kneeling beside Jason and carefully lifting him into a fireman carry across my shoulders. "Did you at least call Jefferson like I asked?"

"*Yes*," she snaps. "I didn't know what to tell him except you ran off into the woods."

"Well, hopefully that means he'll be heading in this direction then." Wrapping my arm across Jason's left foot and arm, I hold him steady as I dial Jefferson and press my phone to my ear.

He picks up on the second ring. "Phoenix?"

"Hey."

"Thank God," he says, audibly relieved. "Ms. Rainbows-and-Sunshine called me in a panic. Did your vampire show up?"

"No, it's Jason. I think we have a situation."

He sighs. "Good, you found him."

My chain of thought derails. "You were looking for him?"

"We got an alert that he ditched his probation ring. I called his folks but he was already gone."

"Well, it sounds like he was planning on meeting up with Ashley tonight," I say slowly, knowing Jefferson will get my meaning. If Jason ditched his probation ring before coming to find Ashley, his intentions seem even more unsavory. "I've got him in the bag in the woods behind the Nelsons' place. I'll walk him out to the road west of the house."

"I'll meet you there," he says and hangs up.

I begin to trudge through the dark woods with Jason slung over my shoulders. Duke and Ashley stay at my heels—the latter makes it a point to voice her disgruntlement.

"What are you doing with Jason?" she asks shrilly. "He wasn't doing anything wrong, he was just coming to see me! You have no right to knock him out and then haul him off like—like a—"

"Like I'm doing my job?" I retort. "Ashley, you should have stayed in the house. Your parents are going to start wondering where you are." She scoffs at me. "Whatever. You better stick with me since you're out here. I'm not leaving you alone."

She grumbles something unintelligible and continues to follow in the trail I'm breaking through the snow. Duke hops around us, stopping to sniff at things every so often before jogging to keep up. Well, I certainly wasn't expecting tonight to end up like this. It's possible a vampire is still out there, though, and watching from a distance. At that thought, I pause to get a good look at my surroundings to make sure we're alone before moving on. Ashley goes on a tirade about how I have no right to haul Jason around like a sack of potatoes. I really wish she'd realize the danger she could have been in if I hadn't been here. I need Jason to wake up and explain himself.

We finally make it out of the woods, climb up a steep ditch, and find Jefferson waiting a few yards down the road beside our SUV. My pants and shoes are completely soaked through by the time I reach the vehicle and Jefferson opens the side passenger door so I can dump Jason inside.

"What are you going to do with him?" Ashley squeaks.

Jefferson grabs Ashley's arm before she can climb into the car after her boyfriend and then he gives me the evil eye. I shrug. It's not like I had a lot of options for stopping Ashley from following me short of shooting her.

"Ashley, you should've stayed in the house," Jefferson says sternly. "Wandering around outside was *not* the plan to keep you safe."

She sticks her chin up and remains stubborn. "Tell me what's going to happen to him."

Instead of rolling his eyes or grumbling something like he usually does, he draws back his shoulders, straightens to his full height, and towers over Ashley with a menacing gleam in his eye. He's actually pretty threatening when he wants to be.

"Are you saying you'd rather interfere with an official investigation?"

"What investigation?" Ashley cows a bit in her stance and shrinks away from him.

"Your boy here took off his probation ring." He swings an arm up to point at Jason for emphasis without taking his eyes off of her. "He deliberately took off the only device we could use to track him and his next step was to find you. Now I don't know what you think you know, but in my experience, when a werewolf goes off the rails like that, they aren't looking for a friendly chat. Whatever his intentions were of coming here, they weren't good. If Phoenix hadn't been here to save your butt, there's no telling what he would have done."

She wrings her hands together and curls them in under her chin. "He wouldn't hurt me," she says in a small voice.

I feel a little guilty for Jefferson using this particular

tactic but it's the only thing that's finally getting through to her. She's got to understand.

"You don't know that for certain," Jefferson says more gently this time. "And I know you've heard what some of the others around here have done when they broke probation."

I lean against the side of the SUV and rub my frozen hands together as Ashley drops her head. Yeah, we know what happened to a group from school that decided they'd rather fight the law. About a month back a few boys ditched their probation rings, stopped taking the serum, and went on an animal killing spree. It's the only major incident we've had since we took Dasc out of the picture. They didn't want to be controlled so they flew off the handle and killed a slew of cows, chickens, sheep, and even a few family pets after they gave in to their inner animal. A couple of people were almost attacked as well. Jefferson said it when I first came here and I saw it those few days—some people get a high off the hunt. Hawk was the one that tracked them to Mr. Wick's back fields. We sprung a trap for the three idiots and they got shipped off to Underground to sit in the penitent cells. They still haven't come back.

My fingers are frozen stiff, I can hardly feel my toes or nose, and my teeth are chattering, but I want to stay outside to handle the situation with Ashley. Unfortunately, Jefferson takes notice and he jabs a thumb at the front passenger door.

"Phoenix, get in and warm up before you lose a few toes or fingers," he says. The tone of his voice makes it clear there's no room for argument.

I slip between them and enter the warmth of the running SUV with the heaters on full blast. I curl up around the air vents and stick my wet feet directly beneath the ones in the footwell. Behind me Jason starts to stir so I shift slightly to be able to keep an eye on him. Outside, muffled through the closed doors, Jefferson continues to give Ashley reasons not to interfere. From her hunkered stance, I can tell he's near victory when Jason suddenly jerks awake and slams a foot against the door, drawing everyone's attention.

Stupid me, I don't think about pulling my bio-mech gun out until now. I have trouble extracting it from my pocket with my clumsy, stiff fingers. Jason bolts upright and launches for the door in a panic.

"Ease up!" I shout at him. On the other side Jefferson throws his shoulder against the door to keep Jason from flinging it open. I finally get my gun up and lean back against the dash of the vehicle to gain what little distance I can from the psycho werewolf before aiming my gun. I hit the locks before he can try anything else.

"Let me out!" he yells and starts banging his fists on the window. He's wide-eyed and hyperventilating. I don't think I've ever seen anyone freak out like this before. Through the glass I see Jefferson push Ashley back and raise his own bio-mech gun, one hand braced against the door handle to keep Jason inside. He looks to me and I nod. I've got this.

"Jason!" I shout and he hardly even gives me a passing glance before leaping for the door on the other side to escape. "I already hit the locks. Don't try it." He ignores me completely and keeps trying to claw his way out of the vehicle. "JASON!"

This time he whips his head in my direction. His eyes are bloodshot and his face haggard. Was he always like this? I guess I haven't been paying as close attention to Jason as I should have. That was a mistake.

"Do you want me to shoot you again or are you going to calm down?" I ask and motion with the gun in my hands for emphasis. His eyes follow the barrel and he pushes back against the seat as far as he can go, tucking in on himself as if he might be able to disappear into the leather upholstery. He's a trapped animal—and trapped animals are dangerous.

"Are you going to listen to me?" I ask as sternly as possible. He nods. "Okay, then I want you to belt yourself in so you're at least a little restrained." He shifts over into the far seat and clicks the seat belt into place over himself. "Good. Now, you want to explain what on earth you were doing tonight?"

Jason stares at me, dark shadows under his wide eyes and his hair in complete disarray. Everything about him is disheveled and he clutches onto the seat belt for dear life. He's always had his issues but this is new. When I first met him he was already under Dasc's sway but once that compulsion was gone he remained a loner in the background. He keeps to himself except for when Ashley drags him out to hang with friends. He always seems distant and on more than one occasion I suspected he might be using drugs. Is that what this is? Some reaction to drugs he's taking? Does Hawk know Jason's been like this?

He pushes his lips around and keeps silent, refusing to answer my question. Jefferson waves to get my attention so I unlock the door for him. He eases open the passenger door on the opposite side of Jason so we can all talk. Jefferson keeps his own bio-mech gun at the ready in his hand, a glint of steel in his eyes.

"Why did you take your probation ring off, Jason?" he asks gruffly.

Jason's eyes water and I'm struck stupid when he starts to cry. This isn't what I'm expecting, not by a long shot. Jefferson and I glance at each other. Is this some ploy? Is he trying to gain sympathy to get out of charges?

"Calm down," Jefferson says. "Talk. This is your chance to have your side of the story heard."

"It hurts," Jason says hoarsely and so softly I think I've heard him wrong.

"You mean when I shot you?" I ask, uncertain.

He shakes his head and cries some more. I catch a glimpse of Ashley past Jefferson's shoulder and she's on the verge of tears too.

"Being *alive*," he says and grabs at his hair with both hands. "It hurts. This curse inside me. It hurts so much I think I'm going mad."

Jefferson's eyebrows rise until they're lost in his shaggy gray hair. "You have to explain better than that, Jason. Answer my question. Why'd you take off your probation—"

Jason suddenly tries to launch out of his seat directly for Jefferson but is wrenched back by the seat belt. There's nothing of the crying boy in his face anymore. There's a monster in his eyes, in his bared teeth, in the hands reaching out like claws ready to rip and shred. Is the werewolf disease truly distorting Jason's mind? I've never heard such a thing before. It terrifies me. Could the same thing happen to my brother?

He doesn't even flinch at the two bio-mech guns raised with acute accuracy at his chest.

"Jason!" Jefferson thunders, the sound filling up the SUV.

The next second the beast is gone again and Jason slumps

in his seat, panting hard. "I'm sorry," he wheezes. "I'm so sorry. Sorry, sorry, sorry—"

"Look at me," I say. Jason tilts his head to the side to fix me with those despairing eyes. "Tell us what's going on so we can help you. I want to help you."

He slumps further into his seat and I'm completely bewildered. First he panics, then he cries, then he tries to attack, and now he sits almost catatonic, staring dead-eyed at nothing in particular.

"Every day," he breathes in a monotone. "It hurts. I've got fire in my veins. Each time I take the serum injection it gets worse. I can't do this anymore. I'm done."

I can see it in his eyes, too. He's given up. Whatever this pain is, it's too much for him. But I'm stuck on the fact that he's saying the *serum* is making him feel this way. The serum, the only thing that lets a werewolf keep their mind when they shift, that takes away the instinctual urges, that keeps them human. The serum that's turning Jason into a patient eligible for a psych ward. Piping Pan, is this why Hawk always refused to take the serum?

"That's why you took off the ring," I say. It's not a question. I know exactly what Jason was planning because Hawk and I made the same plans before. "You were going to run."

He nods mutely, defeated. Then silent tears start to fall again.

"Why come here?" Jefferson asks.

I don't even look at Jefferson when I answer for Jason, the reason obvious. "He didn't want to be alone. He was going to take Ashley with him."

When Jason nods again, Jefferson swears under his breath

and half turns in the open door so he's facing the road behind us. He lifts his face to the sky, closing his eyes. I watch him closely, wondering what this news means to him and what we're going to do about it. Either way, Jason seems resigned. He hasn't moved an inch since he slumped down. The way his eyes almost look sunken in, he could be a corpse on that seat. It's like the serum's hollowed him out. How many other people experience this sort of reaction to the serum?

"I'm sorry," Jefferson says at last and faces Jason again, one hand hanging on to the roof of the SUV as he leans in through the doorway. "You still broke probation and it's a serious offense. I'll take you home and we'll sort it out with your parents, but I'll have to take you to Underground to be treated and kept under supervision until . . ." His eyes flash to me. "Before we can sort your symptoms out."

Meaning, there's not going to be any peace for Jason until a cure can be made from my blood. And we don't have a clue how long it'll be before my blood has "incubated" but it's going to be too long. Jason needs help now—all the werewolves do.

Jason doesn't even react to the news. He just sits there. Ashley on the other hand, reacts enough for the pair of them.

"You can't haul him off!" she shouts. It's a good thing there's no one else in the area as her voice goes up in pitch and a few birds fly off from nearby trees. "He needs help! Look at him!"

Jefferson turns around to deal with Ashley but I'm glued to the wretched boy. His eyes find me again, pleading.

"I just want it to end," he whispers. My chest aches. I hate feeling this useless. I should be able to help him but I can't. "*Please.*"

There's not much I can do, but I can at least give him peace from his agony for a short while. I dig into the glove compartment and pull out a tranquilizer gun. I remove a dart and hold it up for him to see.

"This will knock you out for a couple of hours. I'm sorry but that's all I can offer you right now," I say.

He nods and I lean forward to stick the needle into his thigh. He gives a sharp intake of breath then eases back into his seat and closes his eyes.

Once he's out, I rest my hand on his shoulder. I think of Hawk, of that horrible pain I fear he's experienced from the serum before, and let it fuel me. Heat rolls off my skin and I will the magic that's in me to fix Jason somehow. I'm pouring out everything I've got. A little bit of color returns to his face. Come on, just a little more. I can cure him. I have to.

My arm starts to shake but not from the cold. A tingling crawls up my spine and heat blossoms around me. Even though there's no sign to tell me otherwise, I know it's not enough. I need more. I need more power, more energy, more something. Chills start to race over me. How hard can I push myself? How far can I go? I dig deeper and I feel warmth in my nose as a trickle of blood runs down to my lip. It's too much.

Jefferson is still arguing with Ashley outside and doesn't notice. Good. He'd probably yell at me if he knew that I'm pushing myself over the edge. I can feel it. This isn't like before in school, all those months ago, when I was just trying to calm werewolves. I'm trying to burn the disease clean out of Jason and wash away the serum poisoning his body. I don't want to stop, but eventually something gives out deep in my chest and my hand falls from Jason's shoulder and I collapse in my seat breathing hard.

I try to catch my breath and curl in on myself as fever chills wrack me while Ashley and Jefferson continue to duke it out. Even though there's no way of knowing for sure, I know I've failed. I'm not strong enough for the disease, and I don't know how to beat it.

Jefferson eventually leans into the vehicle and I hastily run my gloved hand under my nose to wipe away the blood evidence that would clue Jefferson in to what I tried to do. He stares at Jason's unconscious form then raises his eyebrows at me.

"Tranquilizer," I say. "He wanted it."

He sighs and gestures with one hand for me to get out. I slide out of the SUV and hug my arms around myself. My feet are freezing and my shakes are worse than ever. I need to eat something and soon.

"Walk Ashley back to her house," Jefferson says as he climbs into the driver's seat. "I'll take care of Jason. Keep an eye on her, will you? And watch out for yourself."

"Jefferson."

He stares straight ahead through the windshield and doesn't look at me. "Yeah?"

I lean in through the passenger door. "Are we going to talk about what just happened? Have you ever heard of anyone reacting like that before to the serum?"

He swallows and moves his thumbs in circles on the wheel. "I've heard rumors, but I've never seen it firsthand." His gaze is distant and the weight of his years settles on him, each weary wrinkle prominent. "Set it aside for later, Phoenix. You've got a job to do."

I roll my eyes and slam the door of the SUV, staggering back from the force of doing so. Jefferson peels out a second later, leaving Ashley and me alone on the salted road. Ashley glares at me but doesn't say a word before she starts marching back to the house. I follow in her wake through the trail I had made earlier. Duke races around us and whines occasionally when he tries to lick Ashley's hands.

When we reach the house, Ashley's mother yells at us both for running off and how we need to be more responsible. We just take it and then hide in Ashley's room. I strip off my wet shoes and socks immediately, throwing on a fresh pair of socks from my bag, and dry the ends of my jeans in front of a portable heater at the foot of her bed. I'm not going to bother changing into pajamas in case I need to run outside again. I take up my perch by the window once more, chowing down the candy bars Hawk stuck in my bag, and Ashley ignores me completely. Well, there's another burned bridge.

"I'm sorry," I say at last when she's tucked herself into bed and turned away from me, Duke curled up along her back. Ashley doesn't respond even though I know she's still awake. Feeling miserable about everything, I pull the portable heater over, prop my feet up against the window sill, and try to make myself comfortable on a chair I pull over from her computer desk.

I text Hawk a few times to let him know where I am and asking when he'll be back from Duluth. He doesn't respond. I need to talk to him and I hate waiting. The light from the kitchen below turns off and I hear the Nelsons move up the creaky stairs to their bedroom. Night closes in and breathes in silence but I can't fall asleep. I keep thinking of Jason's desperate plea. *I just want it to end. Please.*

The light of my phone nearly blinds me in the darkness as I flip through pictures of me and my brother to pass the time. A smile slowly creeps on my face at each memory—there's one of Hawk half-buried in a snow bank (I had pushed him into it), the pair of us wearing stupid 2010 glasses during the New Year, Hawk way up in a tree after he insisted on climbing it. If what Jason said was true, none of this would have happened if Hawk had been on the serum. That thought gnaws away at me.

My phone buzzes in my hand with a new text from my bother. *I'm outside.*

Quietly as I can, I tip toe out of Ashley's room and to the front door. Our SUV is parked out on the road with the lights on. I slip out of the house and hurry down to it. Hawk exits when I get close and meets me at the end of the driveway. It's too dark to see, but with what little light comes from the SUV I can make out Hawk's hunched shoulders and bowed head. He looks about as good as I feel.

"Hey," he says, the word heavy as it passes his lips.

Without a second thought, I wrap my brother in a hug and rest my chin on his shoulder. We stay that way for a long while with no teasing or joking this time. I've had a very bad day and I can't even imagine what Hawk went through up in Duluth with that body chopped into pieces.

"Are you okay?" I ask.

He lets out a shuddering breath. "It was horrible."

"Do you want to talk about it?"

"Not really." He steps back and pulls a hand down his face. "But the body wasn't human. It was a vampire."

I blink. "So it *was* the pink-scarf girl?"

"We think so. Melody's still . . . trying to piece the body

back together with the doc." He swallows and shakes his head. "Why would anyone, or any*thing*, do that to someone?"

"I don't know and I really don't want to think about it to be honest."

"Well, we'll have to if we want to figure out what the heck these vampires are doing. This is *not* normal for them."

"I know."

We fall silent and gaze up at the stars in the velvety night sky. I need to get the truth from Hawk but he's never wanted to talk about those days when he was forced to take the serum in Underground. We even ran away so he wouldn't have to take it anymore. I did it without question back then. I trusted my brother. I still do, but I need to know.

"Hawk, why did you stop taking the serum?" I ask quietly.

Even though it's dark, I can feel his eyes lock on me. "You've never asked before."

"I'm asking now."

He lets out a sharp breath. "I don't want to talk about it."

"Why not?"

"Because I don't," he snaps.

Taken aback, I lean away from him. "Hawk, it's me, remember? You can tell me anything."

"Why is this such a big deal?" he growls.

"Are you kidding me?" I throw up my hands. "Why is this a big deal? Really? How about because not taking the serum is a serious offense? How about because we just arrested Jason for taking off his probation ring? He said the serum was hurting him. It was driving him mad. Is that what happened to you when—"

"You arrested Jason?" he asks sharply.

"Jefferson took him off for treatment and to be monitored, but yeah. He took off his ring, and according to the protocol—"

"Screw the protocol," he snarls and spins around to slam a fist into the side of the SUV. He's breathing fast, raking his hands through his hair, and starting to freak me out. I don't know if his fit is because he's been away from my bubble of anti-crazy the whole day or because how much this topic affects him.

"Hawk, what's been going on with you?" I ask.

His response is a little too fast. "Nothing's going on."

"Well, I hear you got into a fight with Matt because he was ragging on Jason. Was that nothing too?"

He turns around and his eyes glint in the darkness. "You think I'm cracking, don't you?"

"Are you?" I say, voicing my true fear.

"I don't need to be a psychotic werewolf to get angry when some low life picks on someone constantly," he throws at me. "So maybe I've been a little on edge. Maybe I'd like to kick Matt's butt and send him packing. I'll admit it. I've wanted to hit something for a while."

"That's not it, is it?" I draw away as I put together the clues I've been trying to ignore, the ones I don't want to be true. "You knew, didn't you? You knew Jason was having problems with the serum." Now that I say it, it all makes sense. "That's why you always volunteer to do his probation checks. Have you been altering his data? Has he even been taking the serum, Hawk?"

The color drains out of his face and his hands clench into fists at his sides. "Do you honestly think I would do that? Put everyone at risk by covering up for a loose cannon?"

"Hawk, what do you think *we* do every day?" I gesture angrily between the pair of us. My insides become a twisted mess. "It's not much of a stretch to think you'd try doing the same for someone else!"

"Not for him!" He throws his arms out wide and we're both trying to hold in our shouts. "Not for the guy that almost got you killed! Twice!"

"Then why always volunteer to help him out? Defend him against Matt? Be his buddy and—"

"Because I didn't want him to end up like me!" He's blue in the face and when the words leave his mouth we both lean back like neither of us can believe what he just said. He runs his hands through his hair while I try to think of something to say but my thoughts bleed dry as I wrap my head around Hawk thinking he's a person to be ashamed of.

"I thought if I was nice to him, gave him some moral support, was his friend, that he—somehow he could, I don't know—" He heaves a shaky breath. "The only reason I kept sane during the time I took the serum as a kid was because I had you. I had a friend I could lean on even if I couldn't tell you that the . . ." Another deep breath. "I thought if he had a friend, he could get through it. You don't know what the serum's like, and now you've shipped Jason off to the hole where the people like me go and never come back. This was personal, Phoenix. Jason was me without you. *That's* what's been going on."

He stalks around the SUV, gets into the driver's seat, slams the door shut, and floors it down the road. I'm left in the empty darkness with a crushing weight settling on my shoulders, making me feel more alone than I've ever been in my entire life.

14

I hardly sleep that night. Hawk's words repeat over and over again in my head. We don't fight often and it bugs me to no end whenever we do. So, I lay spread out on Ashley's floor and stare up at the ceiling listening to Duke whine as he chases something in his sleep. The morning can't come fast enough and I'm pacing out on the porch by the time Ashley is ready to go to school. I buzz Jefferson to check up on Jason and learn what the plan is for the day. He lets me know Jason has already been picked up by another agent and is currently in Underground getting looked over.

"I'm heading up today to help out Agent Boyd," Jefferson says. "You and Hawk have already missed so much school that it's getting noticed. Just keep your head down and get through your classes without threatening anybody."

I grimace. "I don't *threaten* people."

"Uh-huh. Keep 'em in line," he says. "Just don't over do it, maverick."

"Are you approving of my threats of bodily harm, Jefferson? It's hard to tell."

"Make good choices," is his response and he ends the call.

When Ashley hurries outside, she brushes right past me as if she doesn't even see me. That hurts. I jog after her and slide into the passenger seat of her old beater with my go bag before she can pull away without me. She turns on the radio and cranks it up so loud that the bass makes my teeth vibrate. There's no chance I can even try to apologize again over the music. Then the second we reach the school, she flies out of the car and leaves me in the dust. I sit there for a minute and take measured breaths in and out through my nose, willing myself not to punch a hole through anything. Everything just had to go to crap. Wonderful.

I don't want to get out of the car. Leaving its safety means a day of going over material I've already learned, enduring high school stigmas, and interacting with people I want to punch in the face. I'm in a mood and seriously consider ditching despite Jefferson's warning.

Someone knocks on the window and I jerk away from the sound. Hawk peers in from the outside and his breath fogs the glass.

"You taking a nap in there or what?" he says, his voice muffled through the closed door.

I roll my eyes and climb out, hauling my go bag over my shoulder. Hawk takes it off my hands and exchanges it for my backpack. He's acting normal, though maybe a little tired. There are shadows under his eyes.

"Are we talking again?" I ask, feeling rather irritable. "Or should I punch a car and drive off in a grand huff?"

His eyes narrow. "How about we not fight and you don't

patronize me?"

"Maybe I'm in a mood so I don't give a crap? I've already ruined one friendship. Why not a familial one next to keep it interesting?"

He rolls his eyes and heaves a sigh. "You didn't get a lot of sleep, did you?"

"I never get a lot of sleep," I mutter and sling my backpack onto my shoulder before ripping my go bag out of Hawk's hands. "Where did you park?"

"Why should I tell you?" he says. "I thought you were ruining our familial relationship. For all I know, you'll go punch a hole through it to spite me."

"Well, that'd be stupid. The SUV isn't yours."

"Oh, good point. In that case," He jabs a thumb over his shoulder. "I parked it on the west corner."

"Thank you."

He presses a hand over his heart. "Pleasantries now? I don't think you understand how this whole 'ruining relationships' thing works."

"Oh, shut up," I say and shove past him to march to the SUV. After I dump my go bag in the back for safe keeping and slip my machete out of my jacket to tuck it under the passenger seat, I walk towards the school. Hawk falls into step beside me.

"I'm not going to apologize, you know," he says.

"Great. Then neither will I."

"Status quo. I like it." He bumps me with his shoulder. "I did miss your snoring last night, though."

I throw him a dirty look. "*I* snore? I'm surprised you can even hear me over the train engine coming from your bed every night."

He hoists his chin and sniffs indignantly. Drama queen. "That train's a one way trip to dreamland where I get to pet raptors and poop rainbows. You're not invited."

I bark out a laugh despite myself. Then I catch Hawk's eye and keep on laughing, the sound booming out of me. He grins and throws an arm around my shoulders.

"You can't burn this bridge, sorry," he says. "This bridge is made of pure awesome."

"Well, then I guess I better stop trying." I nudge him in the ribs with my elbow and he leaps out of reach.

The crushing weight in my chest floats away and I take a deep breath. Hawk's still holding out on me but maybe he's got a good reason to. I shouldn't push him to open up about what the serum does to him. He'll tell me when he's ready. I don't want to be at odds with my twin.

We part ways as he makes for the office to explain his absence. I watch from a distance and laugh to myself when he glares at me over his shoulder through the glass door. I guess he doesn't like saying he has diarrhea as an excuse either. Once he comes back with the cheery announcement that he, too, will be meeting with the truancy officer, we head to English together.

The school day goes by like any other. We get assigned lots of homework neither of us wants to do, there's gossip about who's dating who, the werewolves nod their acknowledgment in our direction when we pass by, and at least two girls flirt with Hawk. Whenever that happens, I tend to move away as quickly as possible. We espy Matt in biology and each give him death glares. Lunch rolls around and we sit amongst a group of werewolves. Ashley is still avoiding me and I guess her attitude has passed on to her friends because they give me dirty looks. I've been shunned in school before so I know the feeling well. Doesn't mean I like it, though.

Hawk acts like his normal self with no violent outbursts or grimaces of pain. He tells me about pestering Charlie when he got home the other night and interrupting him when he was trying to read a book. Apparently Charlie ended up locking himself in the bathroom for a while to get away from him and finish his book. We laugh and joke with the others around us. And yet, there's a feeling like we're in the eye of a storm waiting out the calm until all hell breaks loose again.

We don't hear from Jefferson until the end of the school day. He sends us a text letting us know they don't have any new leads but they did find something interesting on the chopped up body. The vampire had track marks on the inside of her elbow. They almost missed it because the body had been mutilated as if to cover up the evidence. Hawk and I share a significant look after we read his message. What's with the track marks? I might understand a vampire stocking up on selkie blood, but why would they take some from their own? It doesn't make any sense.

The final bell of the day rings and we hurry to escape the halls of the high school. As soon as we're in the SUV and the doors are shut, Hawk throws up his hands in irritation.

"Does anything about this case make sense to you?" he asks and shifts the SUV into gear.

I shrug and prop my elbow up on the door. "Monsters are crazy?" I suggest. "Maybe their logic is different than ours."

He shakes his head and takes us home. By the time we set down our backpacks in the cabin, we get another text from Jefferson reminding us to go through our combat exercises. There's a P.S. from Melody asking us to include Charlie. We both groan. Ignoring our homework for the moment—not that we care to actually do it—we change into our exercise gear. Together we trek across the icy path to the barn and hear the snap of wood on wood inside. We stand outside the door for a moment listening before Hawk leads the way in.

Charlie's in his own training gear—black, sleek, and fashionable as always—and working with nunchucks against one of the dummies. The hard hits reverberate through the barn and shudder through the soles of my feet. He doesn't even pause as he attacks and attacks again, each hit precise and lightning fast. Impressive.

"Enjoying the show?" he asks through his fast breathing.

"Oh, definitely," I say. His next attack hits way off center and the nunchuck flies from his hand. His cheeks, already flushed, turn an even brighter shade of red and he doesn't look at either of us as he goes to retrieve the nunchuck in the corner of the barn. I laugh under my breath but my brother shakes his head.

"So!" Hawk says loudly and claps his hands once. "We're supposed to train together. Orders from the top."

Charlie stalks back to the dummy, his eyes flashing between us. "What do you have in mind?"

I give him a wicked grin. "Hand-to-hand combat."

He smirks as if amused. "Are you sure you can handle that?"

"How about my fists ask your face?" I snarl and crack

my knuckles. I've got a lot of steam to burn off and Charlie's been bugging me since the moment we met. It's about time we duked it out. Hawk steps off to the side so he's an equal distance between me and Charlie, then sits on a bench and props his chin in his hand like he's enjoying a show.

Charlie and I meet in the center of the spacious barn floor to circle each other. There's sweat on his forehead already from the workout we interrupted and his hair's damp.

"You'll never even make contact, Mason," he taunts. His green eyes are bright with challenge, and that ghost of a smile never leaves his face.

"Them are fighting words, Nix!" Hawk says through cupped hands around his mouth.

"And you'll never know what hit you, *Charlie*."

That forces his face into a frown. "It's Junior Agent—"

"Jaeger. Yeah, I got that the first fifty times you said it. What's with you and last names anyway? You call Agent Boyd by her first name, but not us."

Before he can respond, Hawk says from the sidelines, "I don't think we've breached the friend barrier yet."

Charlie gives him a sharp look before returning his focus to me. "And you never will."

"Pessimist."

"Beserker."

Then he vanishes. The next second there's a hard blow to my ribs from behind that knocks the air out of my lungs. I sidestep to gain distance but Charlie isn't your average opponent. He's already vanished again.

"Cheater!" I shout. This time I get a kick to the backside of my leg and I go down on one knee. My hands span out in front of me to brace myself against the floor and I rear up to kick behind me with my other leg. Charlie's not even there anymore. *Piping Pan*, he's fast. Freakin' teleporter. I glance to my brother but he's wide-eyed and his mouth drops open as he watches the fight.

I rise to my feet and spin about only to find a fist racing to meet the side of my face. I throw up my arm just in time to block but then Charlie's gone again and I'm getting my legs swept out from under me. I fall backwards, my pride vanishing as fast as Charlie moves, and hit the ground hard. In an instant he's on top of me with a knee digging into my sternum and his forearm across my throat.

"I'm sorry, my face hasn't heard a question from your fists yet," he says with a smile.

"Oh, you're *so* dead," I manage to grind out despite his weight squeezing the air out of my chest.

He's made the mistake of staying in one place for too long. Before he can zap away again I grab his shoulder and fling him to the side off me. Hawk cheers on the sidelines as I flip over like a cat, grab Charlie again before he can vanish, and raise a fist to smash in his stupid shiny, white teeth. His eyes flick up and he's gone. *Again.*

"What the—" I swivel around before he can reappear behind me but he's not there. He's not anywhere. Hawk shrugs a second before Charlie falls on top of me from above, slamming me face first into the ground. I blow out what little air there's left in my chest to expel the hay from my mouth. I'm pretty sure I taste blood too.

"Should've checked the rafters!" he says with a laugh that's quickly cut off as I jab my elbow up behind me and feel it connect with something hard, hopefully his jaw.

I fling my body to the side and effectively throw Charlie off in the process. I push up into a crouch and lunge as Charlie rolls to avoid me. Energy courses down my arm as I slam my fist into the ground a hairs breadth shy of Charlie's shoulder. A shudder ripples through the ground and a cloud of dust and hay rises at the impact. A cloud so thick that I squint against it. A cloud that should momentarily blind Charlie as well. He said before he needs to see where he's going. So what if he can't see?

Even though the dust forces my eyelids down to slits, I know where Charlie was last. I lurch forward and my open hand meets a body. I grab the fabric under my fingers and wrench it towards me. I pull the same move Charlie did earlier and pin him with a knee to his sternum, one forearm pressed against his throat, and my fist hovering over his face.

He blinks a few times as the dust slowly settles and silence echoes in the barn, the only sound our ragged breathing. I wait for Charlie to vanish again but he stays where he is, hands held palm up in surrender. The boiling in my blood is washed away with something much more satisfying—victory.

"What question would you like my fist to ask now, *Jaeger*?"

"How about, can I breathe again?" he wheezes. "What obsession do you have with crappy fist jokes?"

I ease my knee off his chest and rise to my feet. He sits up rather stunned, and we both look to the crater in the middle of the floor. Hawk stands off to the side with his jaw hanging open and eyes wide.

"That was . . . well, wow," Charlie says. "You weren't aiming for my head just then, were you?"

The crater is a good two feet down through solid, frozen earth, and there's a ring of dirt spread so far it reaches the walls on all sides. I freeze and the only thing that races through my head is it's a good thing Jefferson's Green Monster isn't in here. Jefferson would have killed me if I damaged his car—although he's probably going to kill me for putting a *crater* in the middle of the barn.

"Umm . . . oops?" I say and shrug half-heartedly.

"Okay, how about we not spar?" Charlie says as he gets to his feet and brushes himself off. His black outfit is completely covered in brown dirt. "Because I very much like my life."

"I didn't mean to—" A horrible thought strikes me. "Sweet unicorns, I really could have killed you."

"So you *were* aiming for me?" Charlie asks, indignant and a hand held to his chest.

"Uh . . . near you."

He glowers. "Right."

I've never caused damage like this before. I didn't even know I *could*. Holy crap. I clench and unclench my fist, studying my fingers in horror. I know I have strength. I didn't realize this much.

"I think you've always held back," Hawk says and is suddenly standing beside me. "Always the shield, never the sword, right?"

My eyes lock on his as he echoes back Jefferson's words. He studies me as I study him. I can tell he's wondering what I'm thinking but I don't even know what to think. What does this mean for me? Does this show progress in the strength of my blood or is my magic attuning to something different than anti-werewolf?

Hawk breaks the connection and claps Charlie on the shoulder with a big smile. "Congratulations! You ticked her off enough to want to turn your head into a crater! That's quite the achievement!"

"Hawk." I give him a cold look and stalk away from them to the ring of dirt and debris pushed out to the sides of the barn. Well, isn't this fantastic. I keep my back turned and hope they get the message that I don't want to chat. At least Hawk gets my clue and starts chatting up Charlie instead.

"You've got to show me how you do it," Hawk says. "It's impressive."

"Maybe not as impressive as other things," Charlie says quietly and I can feel his eyes on my back.

"So you have to have a direct line of sight to port where you want to go?" Hawk presses and they start talking shop about Charlie's ability. I listen to their conversation as I study the hand I had punched into the earth. The skin across my knuckles is cracked and stings now that my adrenaline is burning off. Blood slowly wells beneath the abrasions. At least I'm not indestructible. I think I would have been more freaked out if I was.

"Yeah, I have to physically be able to see where I'm going," Charlie explains behind me. "Why do you want to know?"

"I'm not going to spill your secrets to the monsters, don't worry," Hawk says. "I'm just curious. What does it feel like?"

I scan along the wall until I find a shovel and scoop up a pile of loose dirt to dump into the crater I made.

"It feels . . . I don't know. Tight, I suppose. Like I'm squeezing in on myself and shooting out the other side of where I'm trying to go. I've heard it hurts like a harpy for the people I bring with me."

"You can port other people with you?" Hawk oozes with awe.

I don't chance a look at Charlie but I can tell he's soaking it in. "Of course I can."

"Could you port me?" Of course Hawk would want to try it.

"Look, Mason, I'm not kidding when I say it'll hurt. *Bad.* Even worse for people with magic."

I keep dumping the loose dirt back into the center of the crater and try to smooth things out. It's not going well. My hands are shaking a little.

"What do I have to do?" Hawk asks. "Do we need to hold hands or something?"

"You seriously want to do this?"

Hawk nods fervently. "Yeah! Let's do this. Come on."

I stop what I'm doing to watch. Charlie sighs and puts a hand on Hawk's shoulder.

"You sure?" he asks.

Hawk smiles wide. "Stop stalling. Let's do—"

They vanish and reappear across the room to the loud cry of pain from Hawk followed by a string of curses. My heart leaps into my throat and I toss the shovel aside to rush for my brother. He drops to his knees and pants hard. Charlie stands over him nonchalantly with his arms crossed.

"Don't say I didn't warn you," he says.

I slide to a stop in front of my brother and grab his shoulder. He's breathing hard and grimacing but waves a hand at me to let me know he's okay.

"Holy *crap*," he pants. "You really weren't kidding."

"You okay, you big idiot?" I ask.

He gets to his feet, rolls his shoulders, and gives me a goofy smile. "Well, that was something else." He turns to Charlie who's sporting a smirk. "You don't feel that pain at all? Only the people you take with you?"

"Yup. Well, people with magic anyway. It still hurts for normal people but nowhere near as much."

"Magic fights magic," I say under my breath and move back to my shovel where I had dropped it.

The boys chat some more and start to spar themselves. They seem to be getting along fine now that Hawk has passed Charlie's pain test. Boys. I shake my head and keep cleaning up my mess. By the time I finish, my hands and legs are covered in dirt and I can't get the floor to smooth out to my satisfaction. Guess it'll be fun trying to explain to Jefferson why there's a weird hole in the middle of his floor. Once I'm done and brush myself off, I don't offer to spar with the others but go through the motions against one of the training dummies. It jostles under my blows but nothing snaps off, thank goodness.

A tremor passes through me when Charlie says, "We should hit up your gun range."

"Yeah, sure thing," Hawk says and claps him on the back, already becoming a fast friend by the looks of it. "I'll show you where we keep our armory."

"Let's be honest, Mason," Charlie says and cocks his head, "It's not much of an armory."

"Don't need to hate, Jaeger." Hawk's use of Charlie's last name sounds more like a nickname than a formality. I'm not sure if Charlie notices or not.

I keep silent as the three of us trek up into the loft and pull guns off the weapon rack. The boys lead the way to the gun range but I hang back and focus on loading my magazine. I really don't want to practice in front of either of them. I've done my best to make excuses and not let my brother see how my hands shake, and I don't want to know what Charlie will say when he sees it.

They reel out a target and Charlie takes to it first. The second his gun goes off the shakes are back in my hands and I can't stop it. He's precise and deadly, as expected. His shots are in a tight grouping in the center. He tosses a big grin at us, clearly impressed with himself.

"Oh, I think that's a challenge," Hawk says. "Don't you think, Phoenix? Let's show him up."

I smile weakly but don't say anything. I'm trying desperately to think of some excuse that will allow me to walk away without drawing their suspicion. Could I call myself to make my phone ring and then pretend it's Jefferson?

Hawk reels out another target and steps up to the marker in the snow to line up his sights. Each shot is flawless, even when he draws fast and drops to one knee. The bullseye is blown out in a clean circle. Just like everything else he does, Hawk has taken to shooting like a selkie to water. He's a natural.

"You've got to be kidding me," Charlie says and gapes at the target when it's reeled in. "You're an expert marksman. That's dead on."

"You can teleport. Phoenix punches holes in the ground. I can snipe you from hundreds of yards away." He shrugs like it's no big deal.

I can almost smell the testosterone in the air. Hawk reels out the next target and then steps aside for me. My feet don't move. Sweat gathers on my forehead and my hands shake holding the gun. My breathing turns shallow and I can't believe I'm freezing up. I'm terrified and embarrassed and they're both looking at me like I'm losing my marbles.

"Phoenix?" my brother prods. He takes a step towards me with a hand extended but I don't want to be patronized.

I can do this, I tell myself. It's just target practice. It's just a sheet of paper hanging on a wire. No one's getting hurt here. I step up, rack the slide to put a bullet in the chamber, line up my sights, and flick off the safety. My hands shake so much I can't pin the bullseye. There's no way I'm going to hit the target. Practice is fine when I start out by myself and can empty a clip before the shakes really get to me. Having to wait for the other two to finish first hasn't helped in the slightest.

The boys don't say anything as I fire shot after shot, all of them missing wide and taking chunks out of the fence. There's a deadened silence when I'm done and my face is on fire. My brother puts a hand on my arm but I shrug him off and walk away from the source of my shame before they can say anything that will only scar me further. This stupid thing is all Dasc's fault. Ever since I shot him, I've been broken and can't be fixed. I've been trying to wrap my head around it without any progress.

I hurry into the barn and take the steps up to the loft three at a time. After slapping the gun onto the table, I pace across the open space between the computers and the cot. Hawk slips up the stairs and pauses at the landing. I can't even look at him.

"You hid it well enough," he says quietly. "Why didn't you tell me?"

I bite my lower lip and fight the burn behind my eyes. "Why do you think?"

"I don't know. That's why I'm asking. You trust me, don't you?"

"Of course I trust you!" I stop and glare at him. "That's not it."

He takes a step closer and keeps a hand on the railing, rapping it lightly with his fingers. "Okay, then what is it? Are you embarrassed? You have nothing to be embarrassed—"

"Don't. Don't do that." I hold up a hand then continue pacing. "I should be able to hit that target consistently. I *used* to. I *can* when I first start but then I—look, I don't want pity. I just want to fix whatever this is. And I don't want you to . . . to think that I regret what I did. I'd do it again in a heartbeat. You know that, right?"

"Is that what you're worried about?" He shakes his head. "You think I'll hate you because you're experiencing some form of PTSD for saving my life? For saving everyone? *Piping Pan*, Phoenix. If anything it makes me feel guilty. You were forced into that position and you did the only thing you could in shooting Dasc. There's no shame in that."

I fight the raw emotion building in my throat and grimace. "Then why do my hands shake!" I yell. "Why can't my stupid brain figure out that I did what I had to and get over it!"

"We'll figure it out."

"I'll never be an agent, Hawk. Not like this. I—I need some air."

I shrug past him, race out of the barn, and keep running. My feet carry me down the driveway but I stop halfway once I'm immersed in the pine trees. My chest is tight and something ugly rears its head inside me. I need to calm down and even out my breathing. I close my eyes and let the cold winter air wrap its icy fingers around me.

Dasc's voice echoes in my head. *Phoenix Mason, the girl who tried to kill me.*

My brain buzzes in a whirl. I'm a killer. My fists can break the earth. What kind of power is that good for except destruction? There's a reason such reckless strength is my power.

I'm a killer.

My phone buzzes in my pocket and I ignore it. There's no one I want to talk to in the heat of this moment. The ringing stops for a moment only to start up again. Whoever is calling is insistent. I open my eyes and pull my phone out of my pocket.

Minneapolis Division displays on the screen.

Dread coiling in my gut, I pick up. "Hello?"

"Mason." There's no mistaking that voice. It's Draco. "We're ready for you to try again."

15

I'm not able to sleep. It's nothing new but I'm exhausted. I'll be facing Dasc in the morning and that keeps me awake. Not to mention going over what happened yesterday afternoon over and over and over again in my head. Hawk and Charlie were giving me funny looks after I came back from running off. Hawk kept trying to be close to me as if to give me a hug or rousing speech but I didn't want any of it. I don't want to be coddled. I want to be fixed. Charlie, on the other hand, watched me like a scientist examining a rather peculiar specimen. I have no idea what to make of him.

Rolling onto my side, I stare out the window and wait for my brain and body to finally shut down and give me what little rest I can before I have to face the monster of my nightmares again.

Sometime during the night I fall unconscious but am jolted awake when I fire my mother's gun into Dasc's chest, just like every other night. This is really getting ridiculous. It's been months now. Heck, the counselor in Underground even cleared me after the shooting. I kept going on about how relieved I was that Hawk was alive and the others were safe. That was good enough for them. Why can't it be enough for me?

I roll out of bed and dress as quietly as I can so as not to wake up Hawk. He's lying face down into his pillow and I know there's going to be more dried drool there in the morning. After I grab my phone and throw on my parka, I walk outside with no real purpose in mind. The moon's out in full tonight and bathes the snow in light. It's freezing and my nose goes numb as I stare up at the stars. I knew becoming an agent wouldn't be easy but I thought it'd be eas*ier*.

The sounds of a wintery Minnesota night surround me. There's a general hush but then an owl hoots in the distance and a car's engine growls far away. A deadly cold breeze brushes over the snow with a sound like feathers falling. When a creaking groan breaks the calm, I jump and my heart is instantly pounding in my chest. I spin about, hand already reaching for my mother's gun tucked in the pocket of my parka, only to find Charlie standing in the open doorway of the barn. The light behind him turns him into a towering silhouette.

"I'm sorry," he says.

I shrug as if it's nothing and exhale sharply before turning away, my face lifted to the black velvet sky. The adrenaline in my veins is making me shaky. I don't want him to see me like this *again*. The crunch of footsteps lets me know he's coming up beside me but I still don't look his way.

"Can I talk to you?" he asks. His tone is so much gentler than it's ever been. So much that I look to him in surprise. Surely, this is some kind of trick. I can hardly see his face and only his eyes glint in what little light can find him.

"Please," is all he has to say and I'm following him into the barn.

We walk up to the loft and he gestures for me to take a seat on the small table beside the cot. Dreading what he's going to say, I slump onto the table as he sits opposite me on the cot. His hair's ruffled and he's wearing a worn hoodie underneath his tailored peacoat. It's the most relaxed and underdressed I've ever seen him. He rests his forearms on his thighs and clasps his hands in front of him.

He chews slowly on his lower lip before he speaks. "About four years ago, I went out on my first mission with my uncle. We were tracking a pair of wendigos over in Wisconsin. They had been attacking and eating hikers. You know wendigos, yeah?"

I nod mutely. They're grotesque humanoid monsters that feast on the flesh of humans. They usually stick to the woods and hunt alone or in pairs.

"Mind you, this was back when I was inexperienced and absorbed with the heroism of fighting monsters. I'm sure you know what that's like." He raises his eyebrows at me and I'm not sure if it's supposed to be an insult. "Anyway, we tracked the wendigos to an abandoned cabin out in the woods along the northern border near Michigan. There was a heap of body parts inside."

He swallows and I clench my jaw. This story isn't heading in a happy direction.

"I knew we were up against something evil, something

unnaturally wrong." He shakes his head and his eyes are distant like he's back in that cabin witnessing the macabre. "We waited for the wendigos to return but they were already there watching us from a distance. We fell right into their trap. I won't bore you with the details but I ended up facing one of them on my own. I fought tooth and nail for my life. I managed to stab it with a silver blade right through the heart.

"Movies and books make it seem so easy to get past. You kill something evil and you move on. But going through something like that leaves a mark." He cocks his head to the side. "I couldn't go anywhere without a blade after that."

I clench my hands together and avert my eyes. He tugs out a sharp eight-inch blade from inside his peacoat. He twirls it expertly in his hands. "Still can't, actually. My point is, when you go through something like that everything changes but it's nothing to be ashamed of. It happens. You're the one that shot that werewolf leader, aren't you?"

"I didn't actually kill him," I mumble.

"But it was still a life or death situation, right?"

"Yeah."

"Then it's the same thing. Mason, it takes time to sort something like this out. The rest of the world stays the same but you change, and other people just don't get it. Their eyes haven't been opened to the true darkness of reality." He tucks the blade away and appraises me. "We hunt monsters, Mason. Killing stuff comes with the territory. You've got to accept what happened. You shot a monster. You saved a town. *You* did that. It's done. It's in the past. You can't change it. All you can do is accept it."

It can't be that simple. I've already accepted what I'd

done. I know I can't change it. In fact, I wouldn't want to change it. If I hadn't done what I did, Jefferson would be dead and Hawk enslaved. Why would I want to change that? I tilt my head as if looking at it all through a different angle.

"I don't want to change what happened."

He points at me. "Now *that's* acceptance. But it's only the first step."

"Then what's the next?"

"Retraining your brain to how you react to that event. You've got to dig deep into what that memory triggers. Why do your hands shake when you hold a gun?"

"I don't know!" I say angrily. "That's the whole point!"

He shakes his head, those green eyes of his boring into mine. "I don't think that's it. I think you're afraid. The question is, what are you afraid of?"

"I'm not afraid! I—" The words surface but I almost choke on them as I realize the truth. My courage wanes and I almost keep my mouth shut. Charlie's still practically a stranger to me. These things are something I'm not ready to share. But Charlie might also be the only one who'll understand. He's already shared his story with me. The least I can do is reciprocate.

"Every time I hear a gunshot I'm back at that night. I wanted to kill him. Sure, I hesitated, but there was a part of me that wanted him to suffer. He killed my parents." I pause to wet my lips as Charlie waits patiently for me to continue. "He's a murderer and in that moment I almost was to. I was a monster, just like him."

"I think that sounds like someone saving lives," he says. "Look, when I showed up—in case you forgot, I *did* show up with the code black squads—your only concern was making sure your brother was okay. And everyone was so grateful you were there to save them. That doesn't sound like a monster to me."

When I don't say anything, he reaches into the pocket of my parka and pulls out my mother's gun. He spins it around and offers the handle to me.

"You drew this when you had to," he says and takes my hand to press the grip of the gun into my palm. "It doesn't fire unless you want it to. You are in control. It's just a tool. If someone came after your brother tonight and using this was your only way to stop them from killing him, what would you do?"

"I'd save my brother," I whisper.

"Darn right, you would."

I stare at the weapon in my hand. It doesn't move to bite me, it sits cold and steady in my hand. I am in control. Charlie rests his hand on top of mine and waits for me to look at him again.

"It takes time," he says quietly. "But you've already been facing your fears every time you go out to that range. You've been fighting it all along. You're a fighter. You'll beat this, too. Now, you tell yourself that every time you draw that gun and sight in on a target, all right? You're in control and that gun won't fire until you want it to. We only do what we have to, Phoenix."

The warmth of his hand leaves mine and he draws back to give me space to breathe. Something happened in the last few minutes and the burden on my shoulders doesn't feel so heavy anymore. Charlie beat this before. So can I. Someone else let me in that knows exactly how it feels to fear yourself and what you're capable of.

"Did you just call me Phoenix?" I ask.

He puffs out his cheeks and slowly shakes his head. "Nope. Definitely not."

"Liar."

When I smile, he smiles back. He clears his throat and gestures to the stairs. "Well, you should, you know, sleep and stuff."

"Yeah, sleep. And you should sleep, too. I don't even know why you're still awake." His eyes dart to the side and I spot a book lying open-faced on the cot beside him. "Or you could keep reading. Whichever sounds better."

He laughs under his breath. "Reading always sounds better."

"Well, then." I tuck the gun back into my pocket and rise to my feet. At the top of the stairs I stop to say, "Thanks, Charlie."

His eyes widen a little like he's surprised I would actually be thankful. "You're welcome."

I return to the cabin holding back a smile and curl up in my bed with a heavy sigh that lets loose the tension in my shoulders.

~

Despite having gone through this once before, I can't help but feel even more nervous than the first time. I have some small idea of what to expect but that doesn't actually calm my nerves—in fact, it makes them worse. I keep telling myself that I'm in control, I'll be the one asking the questions this time, Dasc's got nothing on me. Then the other half of my brain starts telling me that he's got all the cards—he knows where the missing people are, he's the one harboring all the secrets about the stupid war he mentioned, and he knows more about everything than I do. I emptied a full clip of wolfsbane bullets into his chest and he still hasn't gone down. Nothing I do can stop him.

"Phoenix, you've got to relax," Jefferson reminds me for the umpteenth time. He glances at me from the driver's seat with a scowl. "Working yourself up isn't going to help anything."

"How am I *not* supposed to get worked up?" I shoot back. "And I still don't understand why you think it's a good idea for us to get there early so we can sit around and I can work myself up *more*."

He shifts his weight around in his seat before settling. "I just think it's a good idea."

"Okay . . ."

We sit in silence for the rest of the ride until we pull up to the cement bunker containing the secret entrance to Underground. Together we check in with the topside guards then stand side by side on one of the big black lifts by ourselves. It feels so odd coming here with Jefferson. It's the past and present crashing together. I wring my hands over and over again, gnaw on my lower lip, and bounce on the balls of my feet. Once we reach the bottom and move past Bernie the guard, I'm about to ask Jefferson what his brilliant plan is. The words never make it out of my mouth because when we pass through the doors into Underground, a familiar face is waiting with a brilliant smile.

"Oh, my sweet Phoenix!" Celina the faun, my surrogate mother, rushes forward and wraps me in a hug. I'm so shocked it takes me a moment to hug her back. She's in a bright green silk drape with flowers stitched in intricate designs across the fabric. The smell of her, of cool grass and roses, makes me think of home and comfort. I didn't realize I missed her this much until right now and it hits me hard in the chest.

"It's so good to see you," I say and she draws back to look me over like I imagine a concerned mother would.

"I swear you've grown over the months since I last saw you," she says. She takes my face in both hands and her deer-like ears twitch back and forth. "Your eyes have aged."

"Living with this old grouch will do that to a person," I say and glance at Jefferson who's hanging off to the side. His smirk vanishes and he glowers at me.

Celina laughs and the sound is light and merry. *Pixies*, I needed this reprieve. She slips her arm through mine and starts to walk me into the center of the market. Jefferson waves us on.

"We've got time," he says. "I'll catch up to you later."

The market comes alive as the shopkeepers open their doors, food begins to cook, and goods for sale are set out in bins for the few customers wandering in. We take our time walking arm and arm down the long row. Each building is familiar, each marble column, cement wall, and red tiled roof. The gargoyles sit still as stone on the rooftops but one or two shuffle their wings when we walk past below. No matter how long I've been away, this will always be home to me.

"Dear, you look like you haven't slept in ages," Celina coos. "You must tell me everything. Not a detail left to the void!"

I haven't wanted to talk in a while but here, wrapped in the aroma of Old Man Two's soup and under the dazzling lights of the sprites dancing through the air in the upper rafters, I feel a coil unwrapping around my chest. No prompting is necessary for the story of the past three months to spill out. Celina guides us to a table at the centaur's restaurant and we sit and chat for what feels like hours. The market starts to thrive around us and customers come and go. I'm so engrossed in letting it all out that it takes me an hour to realize Jefferson is sitting at a table on the opposite side of the open restaurant keeping an eye on us.

Celina follows my gaze then gives me a warm smile. "I'm glad you two finally met."

"What? Do you—do you know Jefferson?"

She nods and sips at her soup. "We're very old acquaintances. Back when he was a young agent working in the field, he saved my life. I owed him a debt, and he collected about . . . well, fourteen years ago, give or take."

I blink. "What did you say?"

Her eyes sparkle and she reaches across the table to lay a hand on mine. "Dear one, Jefferson was the one who asked me to look after you and your brother when you first came here."

Heat flushes my face and I can't help but lock onto Jefferson at his solitary table. He glances over now and then trying to act casual.

"He did?" I manage to say.

"Oh, yes. He felt terrible, oh so terrible, about what happened. He never said it but I could see the shadow of guilt in his eyes. Shortly after Draco left the pair of you in the care of IMS agents, Jefferson came down himself and asked me to watch over you." She takes my hand with both of hers. "He wanted to make sure you both had someone. He didn't want you to be alone."

I swallow and fight back something bubbling in my chest. It isn't ugly or horrible—it's beautiful and warm and yet so, so heavy.

"He's been looking out for us all this time," I murmur. "I didn't know."

"He didn't want you to, dear," Celina says. "I think the guilt he carries forced him to step back from the pair of you."

Jefferson had mentioned as much before, back when Hawk and I learned the truth of what happened to our parents. He didn't want to face the children he felt he had failed. The truth is he never really failed us at all.

"Don't tell him I said anything," Celina continues in her bubbly voice. "I promised never to tell."

"Cross my heart, knock my hooves, paint my antlers, the whole schebang," I say.

She starts to tell me how things have been in Underground while I've been away and it takes effort to focus on the conversation. Not much has changed but she has spotted Draco a few times. Apparently I'm not the only one that finds him intimidating. Celina's sharp mind also noticed there are fewer werewolves in the city. I know Director Knox is the cause but I can't say anything. It's need to know only when it comes to Dasc. She's in the middle of telling me rumors she's heard of leviathans and other ancient monsters being spotted when Jefferson comes over and knocks twice on our tabletop.

"Time to go, Phoenix," he announces. "Good to see you again, Celina."

"Likewise."

We say our goodbyes and I follow Jefferson through the market. I steal glances at him as we walk to the penitent cells.

A part of me suspects he knows Celina just confessed what he did for me and my brother. He always seems to know. I'm dying to say something even though I told Celina I wouldn't. I'll have to tell Hawk about it once I return to Moose Lake. Maybe we could do something for Jefferson to show our appreciation. Celina had been a gift to us and one we couldn't have lived without. We owe him.

The door to the penitent cells is in sight when Jefferson says, "I've got an idea for how we might get an advantage over Dasc."

"Oh?"

"I want to talk to the shapeshifters and Mr. Webster first. They probably won't tell us anything but everyone's got tells. If there's anything we can use from them to make Dasc talk . . ."

"I like it," I say. "Let's do it."

"As long as Director Knox gives us the okay. He could say no."

"We'll persuade him," I say darkly.

Jefferson gives me a long sideways look. "You're scary sometimes, you know." He bobs his head to the side. "It's good."

I laugh under my breath and we push through the door together. As before, a unicorn, centaur, and two gargoyles guard the way in. After we clear their checkpoint, we pass through the large door protected by the dragon's barrier and find Director Knox waiting on the opposite side. He's in a crisp navy blue suit and has his hands clasped behind his back. He stands with impeccable posture and I instantly straighten under his commanding gaze.

"How's the hand?" he asks.

I glance at the bruises fading on my knuckles. "Healing."

His gaze passes to Jefferson next and his face shows no change in expression. "Agent Barnes. I thought I told you to stay out of Underground."

"I need him," I say before another word can be spoken to kick Jefferson out. "I can't do it without him. I won't." I meet Jefferson's beady eyes. "We're a team."

The skin around the director's eyes tightens a fraction. "He doesn't go in the room with you. He stays in the observation room with me."

"Deal. Oh, and we want to talk to the shapeshifter we captured in Moose Lake and the ones from Werevine Pharmaceutical. And Mr. Webster."

"They aren't speaking either. I'm not sure what you think you'll gain by trying to talk to them."

"People can give away information without ever saying a word," Jefferson says and stands over my shoulder like a bodyguard, always protecting me it seems. "And if anyone can help us get a rise out of them, it's Phoenix. She's beaten them all and her presence will work them up. I'll walk her through what needs to be said. If there's a chance we can get something out of them that will give us an advantage, isn't it worth it?"

If I didn't know any better, I'd say there's something of a smile on the director's face. He almost looks . . . glad.

"You always were a good agent, Barnes," he says and motions for us to follow him.

Jefferson and I walk side by side behind Director Knox through the maze of hallways going deeper and deeper into the penitent cells. He takes us to the same room where I first met Draco and Major Lynch. It's empty at the moment except for the black table that takes up most of the space like an ominous void ready to devour the room.

"Wait here," the director says. "I'll get the shapeshifters and Mr. Webster lined up for you."

He closes the door, leaving us alone. Jefferson walks absently around the table and runs a hand along its surface.

"What was the procedure the last time you came here?" he asks.

"Well, they told me I needed to talk to him, get information on the people missing and his plans, and then they basically threw me into the wolf's den. I had an earpiece but Dasc refused to talk when I had it in."

Jefferson shakes his head. "Okay, first things first. Put your hair down."

I blink. "What?"

"You always have it up in a ponytail and that makes it obvious if you've got a piece or not," he grumbles. "So, put your hair down. You look more like a young girl then too."

I frown as I tug off the ponytail holder and comb my fingers through my hair. "And that's a good thing?"

"It'll make them underestimate you," he says.

"Well, each of them has already faced me before."

"That was on a different playing field." His squinty eyes inspect me as I hold out my arms to show I'm ready to go. "You want to look relaxed but not arrogant. Don't make any show of emotion for anything they do or do not tell you. Pretend to be mildly interested the whole time you're in the box. You've got to act like you've got all the cards. You're in control."

"Am I?" I mutter and he grasps my shoulder.

"If you act like that in there, you won't be," he growls. "It's a game, Phoenix. It's chess. You gotta play to win."

"Right." I suck at chess. It's probably best not to mention that.

"I'll walk you through the earpiece but you're the one that has to sell it. You can do this. Use that charm of yours."

"Well, now I know you're definitely joking. Charm? Me?"

"Or sass," he says gruffly. "Whatever works."

"I can do sass."

"You don't have to tell me that."

A smile spreads on my face. This is what family feels like.

He rolls his eyes. "Wipe that grin off your face. You look ridiculous. And before we get started, there are a few things you should know."

For the next ten minutes Jefferson gives me a crash course on interrogations, physical indicators, and psychological reasoning. It's clear he knows his stuff from all the fancy terms he throws at me. The door opens and Witty peers in from his wheelchair. He looks a little terrified when he spots me. I guess I scared the crap out of him the last time I was here.

"Hey, Witty. We ready to rumble?" I say to show I'm not psychotic this time around.

"Yeah. Yup. Umm, hi." He dips his head in Jefferson's direction. "Agent Barnes."

Jefferson points at Witty but looks to me. "This is the kid on the phone?"

"The one and only."

Witty's face turns bright red and he starts to wheel away. We follow him out the door and down two different hallways before we stop in front of a barred door. I take a deep breath—so far my jitters haven't gotten the best of me like the last time around. It helps having Jefferson here. There's a confidence in me I didn't have before.

"This is the shapeshifter from Werevine," Witty says as he waves at the door. "We still don't even have a name."

He passes an earpiece to me and beckons Jefferson over to the next door down. Before he moves away, Jefferson whispers his instructions to me and has me acknowledge I understand before he wishes me luck and the dragon's barrier drops. I push the door open and shut it behind me before turning about to meet my chess opponent.

He wears a face I hardly recognize. The first time I met him he was in the form of a pudgy little man pretending to be the CEO of Werevine. Now he's stick thin, spindly, and in dire need of a shave. His eyes are cold and I feel like I'm falling down a dark well looking into them—they narrow the second he recognizes me. Despite his gaunt and raggedy appearance, he has a formidable air about him.

I take the seat across from him and fold my hands together on the tabletop separating us. He doesn't move and I allow a small, pitying smile to slide into place on my face.

"I wanted to say thank you," I say. His eyes narrow even more. "Capturing you made my career. Who would have thought such a random assignment would have turned into such a goldmine?"

The shapeshifter doesn't move, doesn't speak, doesn't give any sort of reaction at all.

Jefferson's gruff voice speaks quietly in my ear. "Good. Now, make your next move."

"Between you and me," I say quietly and lean in, "I'm not actually supposed to be in here. I sort of know a friend of a friend and . . . like I said, I wanted to say thank you for making my first mission so easy."

He freezes in his chair, an indicator in itself. He's holding himself rigid on purpose, trying not to make a move to show I've hit a nerve.

"I mean, your berserker friend was terrifying but, then again, she wasn't very hard to take down either." I laugh and lean back in my chair.

"Tick him off," Jefferson whispers through the earpiece. "Twist a strand of your hair. Look like an airhead."

I take a chunk of hair between my fingers, twirl it around my fingers, and give the shapeshifter a wrinkle-nosed smile. A smoldering rage passes through those dark eyes of his.

"This job is boring though," I say and blow a few stray hairs out of my face. "I mean, a couple of shapeshifters here, a few werewolves there. I don't even know why you guys were trying to find that idiot. Werewolf, who-cares-wolf. Why even bother? They went down easy enough."

The shapeshifter is still trying to keep it together but a muscle twitches in his jaw. I'm getting close. I can taste it. We know the shapeshifters were combing through the werewolf records like they were searching for one in particular. I've been careful not to drop a pronoun that'll hint male or female. We want the shapeshifter to do that for us. Snap his ego and maybe he'll rise to defend it.

"Punch his pride again," Jefferson instructs.

I rise from the chair and turn around so I can see my reflection in the one-way mirror in order to fix my hair. Play-acting is difficult and I rack my brain for another jab.

"We appreciate the tip," I say in a high, chirpy tone. "Looks like we did your job for you."

The shapeshifter speaks at last. "You didn't."

"Sorry, what?" I face him with a wide smile.

"I don't believe you." Oh, come on. Let a hint slip, just this once.

Jefferson whispers, "Help's coming. Play the caught troublemaker."

There are several loud knocks on the glass from the other side and a muffled voice shouts, "What are you doing in there?" It's Director Knox. He must be my help.

My eyes go wide and I frantically move towards the door.

"Oops! Crap." I bite my lip and readjust my hair.

"You can't be in there! Get out!"

The shapeshifter starts laughing as the door flies open and Director Knox marches in to grab me by the arm. I blink several times and try to force my eyes to water like I'm about to cry. As we're leaving I stutter an excuse to the director, and the shapeshifter yells at me from his seat.

"I knew you couldn't have taken him down, you pathetic little wench!"

The door slams shut and I give the director a wicked grin. He let's go of me, stunned. Jefferson walks out of the observation room with the biggest smile I've ever seen him wear and we give each other a high five.

"And now we know a gender and that he's a single person."

16

Knowing the shapeshifters were looking for a male individual doesn't seem like much but it's enough to use on the berserker next. Jefferson whispers to me again before I enter the woman's interrogation room. We won't go for a pride-and-ego down again. This time Jefferson wants me to make the berserker mad. It's a good thing Director Knox doesn't know that or he probably wouldn't let me walk in. Pixies, I don't know if *I* want to go in with this sort of plan but I trust Jefferson. He must know what he's doing.

When I shut the door behind me the female berserker lifts her face to see who's come in. She instantly goes red in the face. For a second I think she's going to puff up and rage out but she remains composed in her chair with two guards flanking her, their bio-mech guns trained on her back. Surprisingly, she doesn't look much different than the woman she had impersonated at Werevine. Still severe, still dark haired, but her nose is much less pointed and her eyes are mere pinpricks in her face.

I take the chair across from her, lean forward on the table, and smile like I did for the other shapeshifter. "*Pixies*, you're even uglier than before."

Not a twitch or grimace from my remark. In fact, she's ignoring me as she gazes at a corner of the ceiling like she's disgusted by some hidden stain or spider web I can't see.

"I guess there's no point exchanging pleasantries then?" I say and settle in my chair with my arms crossed. "I don't know why they even bothered putting me in here. They thought I could elicit a reaction from you since I'm the one that took you down." I laugh once and pretend I'm bored myself, gazing around the room with no real interest, even though my heart is hammering in my chest. I still remember what it was like being stalked by her on the executive floor of the Werevine building. She was terrifying.

"Get mean," Jefferson says in my ear. "Make a fool of her. Bring up her buddy."

"What's the point?" I grumble and inspect something under my nails. "We already broke the other guy days ago."

Her head snaps in my direction. I give her a mocking expression of surprise.

"Oh, so you *do* care? Big scary monster has a heart after all it seems."

"He means nothing," she spits at me.

"You know, denying it only really confirms the opposite. And yet you let him get taken down like a sack of potatoes!" I slam my hands on the tabletop and lean in with a sneer. "You two are *pathetic*."

The berserker gives me a smile that could curdle milk and I involuntarily swallow. "You'll have to try better than that."

Static pops in my ear. "Take control again," Jefferson says. "Bring up our mystery man. Pretend we have him."

"Your friend should have tried better, too," I shoot back. "We know you were looking for *him*."

That gets her attention and her cruel smile loses some of its edge.

"Well, you're too late!" I rise slowly from my chair with my hands planted on the table in an attempt to tower over her. It would work better if she wasn't so tall. "Thanks to the mess you made at Werevine, you managed to get yourself caught *and* lead us right to him."

"He's been captured? You have him?"

"What do you think I just said?" I roll my eyes for emphasis and hope she doesn't snap and try to break my neck. "Now the director just wants to know who you're working for and then we can all go home. Unless . . . unless you think *he* can give us a name instead?" I stand and gesture to the two guards in the room. "Let's pack this up. Once he knows we've got her here, I'm sure we can get a—"

She expands faster than I think a berserker has a right to. Both her arms fling back, breaking the chains from her wrists—the cuffs themselves still manage to hold with the dragon's barriers intact—and she hits both guards in the chest before they have a chance to fire. In the blink of an eye her fist flies at my face. But I'm in control. Energy shoots through my arm and I grab her fist with my bare hand, holding back that powerful blow. Her fist and my hand lock in position above the table. If it's even possible, her face turns a more brilliant shade of red as she tries to push me back. When she can't, she punches with her other fist but I grab that too. Sweat breaks out on my forehead as I hold her in place. My bruised knuckles protest at the strain.

"Not so fast," I pant.

"Your prison can't hold the first," she hisses. "He will flee and she will come for us for our failure."

"What on earth is that supposed to mean?"

"You're all going to die!" she shouts, spittle landing everywhere including my face.

My hands shake from holding her powerful fists. *Pixies*, she's strong. She must be trying too hard though, because the red starts to recede from her hands and up her arms. It's only been a couple of seconds but it's forever until the door finally opens with backup. Shots fire and I feel the breeze as the bio-mech pulses rush past me and hit the berserker. She screams before a barrage of pulses knocks her down and she falls unconscious to the floor. Guards flood inside the room and I'm shuffled to the wall. Jefferson pushes past them to grasp my shoulders and hunches to my eye level.

"Are you okay?"

I exhale sharply and wiggle my fingers. "Everything's intact anyway." I sway a little and Jefferson's grip tightens. "You wouldn't happen to have a candy bar or something on you, would you?"

He throws an arm around my shoulders and walks me out. "Yeah, you're fine."

"No, seriously. A little food would go a long way right now."

"I'm sure we can scrounge something up for you." He gives me a little shake. "You did great, kid."

"I did? Sorry, I'm a little distracted by the fact I almost got my face punched in or my hands ripped off. Are those guards okay?"

He glances over his shoulder as we continue to walk away. "They'll be fine."

We eventually stop and Director Knox walks at a fast clip to meet us at an intersection with another hallway.

"You heard her?" the director asks once he reaches us. "The first."

Jefferson nods but I flex my aching fingers as I process this information. The shapeshifters were looking through werewolf records trying to find "the first." There's only one werewolf I know that fits that bill.

"I guess we weren't actually lying when we said we had him," Jefferson muses.

"They were looking for Dasc the whole time?" I say and the cogs in my mind start to speed up. "We always assumed they were working *with* him. We've been looking at it all backwards. Dasc said there was a war coming."

"I think we just found the opposing side," the director says, his expression serious as always.

"Monsters fighting monsters," Jefferson grumbles. "Is there even a point to that? You'd think they'd team up against the IMS, not each other. We're the ones picking them off."

"They've been known to squabble over territory before," Director Knox points out.

A frown pulls at my face. "I don't know."

"Something you want to add, Phoenix?" Jefferson removes his arm from around my shoulders and looks down his nose at me.

"It's just something Dasc said before. *There are bigger monsters than me.* I don't think he meant literally—because, obviously. I think he meant worse. And he's the first of his kind, someone who's murdered and turned and butchered people for hundreds of years. What kind of monster like that thinks there is another one that's *worse*?"

"Perhaps we ought to ask him," the director says. "And see what he knows about this 'she' the berserker referred to."

Before we move on to Dasc, we decide to try this new information on the shapeshifter that had been working alongside Dasc and then Mr. Webster. Both of them are surprised to see me—Mr. Webster actually looks better now that he doesn't have access to hideous sweaters—but they each clam up the second I mention anything about a female opposing Dasc. My lucky streak with the interrogations hits a dead end and all too soon it's time to work Dasc himself.

Anxiety creeps up on me again and Jefferson must see it too. We stand together outside the shielded door and talk in hushed voices.

"Just lead with some simple questions," Jefferson advises, one hand resting on my shoulder while he gestures with his other. "He's a slippery little devil and even though he says he'll talk, he's not going to open up for the big questions. Not until he thinks he has something more on us."

"You think so?"

"I've been studying his interrogations," he says. How could I forget? "He's actually managed to break some of the agents they sent in to question him. If he wants to talk, let him. It may be lies, it may be deceptions, but at least he'll be talking and maybe we can catch him slipping up."

I gnaw on my lower lip and twist my hands together. "What about the missing people? When should I try bringing that up?"

Jefferson seems to recede in on himself and I know it must physically hurt him to think of all the horrible possibilities of what's happened to his missing daughter. He's desperate for answers and I'm just as desperate to help him the way he helped me.

"We wait," he says through clenched teeth like it's painful even to say it. "That's his biggest card and he's not going to show it. Small fish first."

"Okay."

"You can face him. I'm here. You're not alone."

He gives my shoulder one good squeeze and I nod, ready. He goes to the next door down and disappears inside before the barrier drops before me and I step inside.

Dasc sits chained to the table, posed as usual. His black hair is untidy and he's got a terrible purple bruise that runs along his entire jaw and partway up his face. His skin's a little puffy and though I see him trying to work a taunting smile, he can't manage it.

"He looks like a steak left out in the sun too long," Jefferson says in my ear. I crack a smile and take sure steps to the open chair across from the monster haunting my dreams.

"Wow, what happened to you?" I say sarcastically and fold my hands together on the table. The other interrogations have warmed me up for this encounter. I *am* ready. "Did you get hit by a bus? Or did karma feel like giving you a good right-hook to the jaw?"

"And how is karma's hand doing?" he says tightly

through lips that don't move much. He must be in a lot of pain. Good.

"Healing well." I flex my fingers. "So are you ready to deal or are you going to do something stupid again?"

"Who says I've ever done anything stupid?"

My eyes narrow. "That mark on your jaw is pretty clear evidence."

"Sometimes you have to sacrifice pieces in order to play the game." He leans forward and sets his shackled wrists on the table.

"Is that what you consider the people you turn?" I ask. He's closer than I'm comfortable with but I fear moving back will make him think he has the upper hand.

"Those people are my people. They belong to me."

"They don't *belong* to you," I snap.

Jefferson whispers in my ear, "He's trying to rile you up. Don't let him."

Dasc manages a faint smile. "And how are my people doing? How is Moose Lake faring?"

It seems like a harmless enough question but he's got to have some ulterior motive in asking. He doesn't really care what happens to the people whose lives he's ruined and changed forever.

"They're great actually," I say and rein in my anger. "Better without you around in fact."

"Are they now? Oh, I do love to hear they've found their independence." He tilts his head—always the curious dog.

"Well, better apart from the fact a vampire tried attacking one of them."

Dasc's reaction is instant. His coy little smile and arrogant demeanor vanish and his bright blue eyes pierce me as if he can pull me apart piece by piece to find what's underneath. He doesn't say anything and it's clear he wants me to keep talking.

"No vampire has been seen in Minnesota for over fifty years, or so I hear," I say. "The state is werewolf territory. Of course, you already knew that, didn't you? So, why would they come back now, I wonder?"

He sits like a statue. "How many vampires?"

"We're onto something here," Jefferson says. "Tell him."

"At least two that we know of," I say.

There's another shift in Dasc's demeanor and he shifts his gaze to the side as his eyes flicker, clearly thinking fast. He must come to some sort of conclusion or plan because he stares me down again.

"Vampires wouldn't dare come into Minnesota," he says.

"And why not?"

"Because *I* told them not to," he growls. "They don't touch this state. It's *mine*." He bares his teeth, his inner monster showing through, before he seems to realize what he's doing and straightens in his chair. "They must be making a play since I haven't been actively present. I've been *here*. If the vampires are not checked, if I do not make a display of force, they will sweep through."

I shake my head. "What would be the point?"

"Because they hate me, and because I limited their territory to only certain areas. "

That's a surprise. "The vampires actually listen to you?"

He laughs. It's a chilling sound. "Vampires don't listen to anyone, but they fear me enough to know that I will kill every last one of them if they turn against me."

"If they're so afraid of you, then why would they even

try antagonizing you? It wouldn't have anything to do with the coming war you mentioned, would it?"

His face falls into shadow as he bows his head. "You better pray that war isn't upon us already."

"How about you enlighten me on this war instead of making cryptic chitchat that makes me want to rip your head off?" I snarl. This is getting old really fast. Energy surges down my arms and some horribly violent part of me wants to reach across the table and rip out his tongue.

"You have to go to the vampires," he says, and his face lights up as if he's come up with a brilliant idea. I don't like it one bit.

"Excuse me?"

"Or would you rather have them seek out my werewolves and tear them apart one by one?" he says darkly. "Because that's what will happen if you don't."

"What exactly are you asking? That we stroll up to the vampires and tell them to stop it? Slap their wrist, maybe?"

He extends his hands like he wants to touch mine. I instantly recoil with disgust.

"There is a place where my people and the vampires meet when we have occasion to . . . sort out our differences. You go in my stead as my representative, follow my instructions, and warn them what will happen if the vampires do not leave immediately."

I lean back as far as possible and cross my arms over my chest. "So we're supposed to go handing out your threats for you?"

"*Listen* to me," he says and his voice rises for the first time. "If those vampires cross the border, there will be blood."

"I thought you liked spilling blood."

This time he snarls and it's not a human sound. It's a wolf growling at me. "If any of my werewolves are harmed because of you, there's no place you can hide, nowhere you can run, that I won't find you and rip your throat out."

If I didn't know any better, I'd think he actually cares. He's certainly putting on enough of a show to try to convince me.

"And it won't just be my werewolves that are attacked," he continues. "Your innocent bystanders will become blood bags bled dry for the benefit, and amusement, of the vampires. I've kept them on a leash. If they think they're free, it'll be a massacre. And I know that heroic virtue you cling to so desperately won't let you allow that to happen. Or will you, Phoenix?"

He's breathing hard and straining against the shackles holding him in check. It's all a trick somehow, some ploy. He's not convincing me. He's not. Is he?

"Come on out," Jefferson says in my ear. "We need to talk."

I shove away from the table and make for the door.

"Your brother's going to end up with his head on a stick if you don't listen to me!" he shouts at my back.

The barrier drops, I wrench the door open, and slam it behind me. Jefferson and Director Knox come around the corner but I hold up a hand letting them know I need a second to calm down. I'm trembling again and clench my fists against the shakes. Seconds later a third person exits the observation room and Draco walks into our midst, a tall commanding presence. I didn't even know he was here today. I guess he didn't care for the other interrogations, just Dasc's.

"As much as I hate to admit it," the director says. "I don't think we can ignore this potential threat."

"Are we really believing this pile of crap?" Jefferson says and gestures widely to the door behind which my parents' murderer sits. "Are we accepting he's been keeping the vampires in check?"

Draco's frosty gaze passes over all of us and rests on Jefferson. "You underestimate his influence. If Dasc believed the vampires would be a threat to his territory and plans, there is nothing he would not do to keep them in check. Incidents with vampires have grown considerably less since Dasc resurfaced. This intelligence may be genuine."

Despite Draco confirming something rather horrible to contemplate, he sounds merely bored at the prospect of vampires and werewolves under the heel of a psychopath and the possibility of vampires slaughtering everyone in the state. He's cold.

"We have something he desperately wants," Jefferson says. "We can bargain. If we do this meeting with the vampires, he gives us our missing people. This is the best shot we've had so far."

There's hope in his voice and fevered excitement, but I worry it's misplaced.

"He won't do that," I say quietly, daring to speak. "He knows we won't let a threat like this pass. We'd take care of it anyway."

"We've got to try and use this regardless," the director says. "If you can get him to bargain then we'll settle the terms, but you have to convince him first. Are you up for this?"

"It's not like I have much of a choice." I draw back my shoulders and nod. "But I'll do what I can."

"Then make sure you get him to agree to terms. I have faith in you, Junior Agent Mason."

It's the most glowing compliment—or compliment of any kind—I've ever received from the director. My focus shifts to Jefferson. Even though he tries to hide it, I can see the dark swirl of emotions beneath his stern expression. If I can pull this off, we have a shot at getting his daughter back. If I don't . . .

Before I can work myself up about it too much, I walk into the interrogation room. Dasc peers up at me and I ease myself into the empty seat. He doesn't say anything but his hands tighten on the chains leading to his shackles.

"We're going to make a bargain," I say.

"Are we now? And what, exactly, is there to exchange?"

"I want the locations of all the people missing from Moose Lake and anywhere else you've taken people from." I feel calm even though my hands are trembling as I clench them together on top of the table. "Then we'll play messenger to your vampire friends. And I'll keep coming here, just like you want. I won't try to fight you. I'll answer your damn questions."

His eyes spark. "That's a nice try."

"You said you would answer my questions if I answered yours," I growl. "You knew exactly what I wanted to know when I first came here but you said you'd answer anyway. Or were you lying from the start?"

"You never answered my first question, though. You aren't exactly playing along." He leans towards me so slowly it's almost imperceptible. "Answer my question, and I may be willing to bargain."

"He's playing you," Jefferson sighs through my earpiece. "Don't answer that—"

I tuck my hand into my hair with the pretense that I'm thinking it over and tug the earpiece out. Without a second voice in my head trying to change my mind, I plow right ahead into dangerous waters.

"You want to know what I thought of Draco's timing in coming to my rescue?" I ask. Dasc nods. "He couldn't have known what was going to happen. Even if he did, why would he wait? He's been hunting you for who knows how long. He wouldn't have waited. He would have caught you."

A smile flickers across his face. "Was that so hard?"

"Was there even a point to that question?"

He smooths out the collar of his white prison garb like he's adjusting a suit. "Time stretches on into an infinity that mortal minds cannot comprehend. It distorts reality. Logic to you might not be the same logic to someone who's lived a thousand of your lives."

"Meaning?"

"Patience, Phoenix." He licks his lips and brings his head low so he can comb his fingers through his hair. What, is he preparing for a date? "Scotland."

My breath catches in my throat. "Excuse me?"

"You wanted a location, didn't you?"

"That's an entire country."

"And it's a big world. Now I've narrowed your search to a fraction of that. If you want the specifics, then there's something else I want from you." He works past the pain in his jaw to give me a mischievous smile. "I want you to promise me two things apart from bringing the vampires into check. Promise, and I'll lead you straight to your missing townsfolk. Including, I might add, a certain Genevieve Barnes."

"She's alive?" I breathe, unable to believe my ears. He nods.

The confirmation is all I need to know I'll do whatever it takes to bring Jefferson's daughter home. My chest hurts from my thundering heart.

"I'll promise," I say, jumping in blindly. "What do you want?"

His smile spreads. "So accommodating. First, I know that Director Knox will want to send in a squad of his code black agents to handle the vampire meet. I want you to go instead."

"Why?"

"Because you're the only one that can convince them. You have a werewolf brother. These vampires will rip him apart. You'll make sure they back off. I know you will."

I swallow my fear and ask, "And the second thing?"

"I want you to owe me a life debt for all the lives I'm returning to you," he says. Like it's so simple. Like it's easy. "The next time you have a reason to kill me or someone else is trying to kill me—which will happen, trust me—you have to pay that debt."

A muffled voice shouts behind the one-way mirror. "Phoenix, don't!"

"You shake on it," Dasc says as if there is no interruption at all and extends his hand. "A life debt for the return of all those people."

Someone pounds on the mirror and yells at me again to stop, that I don't know what I'm doing. I would owe Dasc a life debt. I would owe the man who killed my parents a debt to save his life the next time he's in danger. The next time I might very well be the one trying to kill him. The potential possibilities for damage are endless. What might Dasc do with such a sworn promise?

Genevieve Barnes. He will take us straight to Jefferson's daughter who's been missing for over fourteen years. That alone is worth it, isn't it?

"Shake on it now," Dasc commands. "Or you'll never see any of your missing people ever again."

My heartbeat rises into my throat. "One condition. You never hurt or go after my brother again."

He smiles. "Deal."

The door to the room flies open and Draco shouts at me to stop.

I grasp Dasc's hand and give it one firm shake. What I'm not expecting is a biting heat to wrap around our hands like a red-hot net binding our hands together. I gasp but can't pull away. Dasc just continues to smile until the heat vanishes and I jerk away from him.

Even though nobody speaks a word, I know without being told that my promise somehow became permanent and bound in magic.

A promise I can't break even if I want to.

I bounce on an uncomfortable bench seat in the back of the van as it heads for the meeting with the vampires. Jefferson sits across from me on the opposite bench with his head bowed and hands restlessly twisting together. Beside us are three other agents and a fourth drives us to our destination. They're all quiet and don't seem particularly inclined to start a conversation. That's okay. I'm too distracted.

My ears are still ringing from Draco chewing me out. It was truly terrifying to be pressed against a wall and shouted at by a dragon wearing a man's skin with the capability of bringing the whole of Underground down. I had invoked an ancient magic, apparently, that I didn't even know existed by making a devil's bargain with Dasc. Swearing a life debt to an enemy triggers that sort of thing to happen it seems. Honestly, it would have been a good idea to teach that in my lessons during junior agent training. How was I supposed to know that magically binding contracts are a real thing?

Director Knox tried changing the plans so I wouldn't be going to meet the vampires myself, but then Dasc refused to tell anyone but me what the secret code words were to verify I am indeed his representative. Once Dasc told me, I refused to tell the director and risk jeopardizing my agreement with Dasc. *That* ticked off the director. But that was the deal I struck so I'm going to go through with it.

Jefferson's been quiet ever since. I want him to reassure me that I'm making the right call but I worry he'll say the opposite. Maybe his silence is preferable after all.

The van rumbles along as I pull my phone out of my pocket and dial Hawk. It rings a few times before he picks up.

"Hey, everything okay?" he says.

"There's been a change of plans." I heave a sigh. "We got some new information on the vampires and we're going to check it out. We won't be back until tonight at least." I don't need to say anymore to know he gets the message. My anti-werewolf won't be around for the rest of the day.

"Okay. I'm good, I promise," he says without a hint of hesitation. "Well, Charlie returned to Duluth this morning after you left. I guess things have cooled down enough that Melody wants his help again. Oh, and Deputy Graham is putting together a capture the flag game tonight. If I'm not at the cabin when you get home that's where I'll be. Otherwise, it's all quiet here. No more movement on the vampire front in Duluth."

"Hawk, that game—" If he plans on shifting for capture the flag, things are going to get ugly fast. I still remember the way he had acted when he came home from Duluth after spending an entire day without me. And that didn't include any shifting.

"I'm just refereeing," he says quickly. "No need to panic. If things get . . . touchy, I'll leave or take the serum."

That's surprising. "You will?"

"I know what I am, Nix. I don't want to be trouble any more than you do."

"As long as you're sure."

"Where exactly are you heading?" he says and it doesn't slip past me the quick change in subject.

I glance to the other agents in the vehicle. "A city in central Wisconsin. That's why we won't be back until late. I'll keep you posted."

"This is something dangerous, isn't it?" His voice is wary.

"Oh, it's nothing." A lie. "It's just a lead on why there are vampires in Duluth in the first place. I'll call you later, okay?"

"You better."

I hang up and tuck the phone into my pants pocket. When I look up again I find Jefferson staring at me.

"You didn't have to make a bargain like that," he says quietly.

"Yes, I did." The rest of the words sit on the tip of my tongue but I don't speak them—the words that say I owe him. I owe it to him to find his daughter for all that time he watched over me and my brother. I owe it to the people of Moose Lake, to Deputy Graham, to everyone who's lost someone because of Dasc. It was my choice and one I'll live with if it means repairing even a little of that horrific loss.

"He'll eventually use that debt against you, you know," he says, his voice dropping even lower.

I avert my eyes. "I know."

The rest of the ride is carried out in silence for the duration of the two and a half hour drive. One of the agents cracks open a book and reads beside me. It reminds me of Charlie. Then another takes a nap with his head tipped back against the wall of the van and the woman next to Jefferson reads something on a laptop balanced in her lap. They're all dressed casually in jeans and winter jackets. They'll blend into the crowds and watch me from the shadows when I go in. Jefferson insisted on coming along as my second—which Dasc said is normal for this kind of meeting—but Director Knox refused, said I needed a young, spritely agent to watch over me against a pack of vampires. Yeah, Jefferson just loved that. So, instead I'll have the man sitting beside me come into the meeting as my bodyguard. I don't know him and that makes me nervous. I would rather have someone I trust being my backup.

He had introduced himself as Agent Oliver Brooke in Underground before we left. He's quiet but nice enough, and he's relatively young like the director wanted. I would guess he's in his late twenties, early thirties. His strawberry blonde hair is short and he sports a handsome amount of stubble. His pale blue eyes focus intently on the pages of his book but every once in a while he glances my way with a sneaking smile as if to reassure me. It's better than going in with a grump I suppose, and Director Knox assured me Agent Brooke is one of the best swordsman in the business which is pretty paramount considering you either have to stab a vampire through the heart or behead it to kill one.

Thinking about having to do either, I swallow and pat where I've got each of my weapons for the thousandth time to make sure they're still there. I've got a machete in the lining of my jacket, a bio-mech gun in my back pocket, and two retractable blades tucked into my belt hidden beneath my winter jacket. If things go south, I'll need to defend myself.

Bored and nervous, I read Agent Brooke's book over his shoulder. It's some science fiction story about aliens being discovered through a black hole. I try to stay engrossed in it and not let my anxiety get to my head. It works . . . sort of.

All too soon, the agent at the front announces, "ETA five minutes to La Crosse. Get ready. I'll drop the first couple of you at the end of the bridge heading into Wisconsin."

There's some shuffling and Agent Brooke tucks his book into a bag at his feet. The others straighten. The woman hits the guy snoozing and he jerks awake to roll his head around his shoulders.

Jefferson reaches across the space to touch a few fingers to my knee. "Are you going to be okay?"

"I'll be fine. I've got Mr. Brawny with me." I jerk a thumb in Agent Brooke's direction, who crosses his well-built arms over his chest and smiles faintly. "And you won't be far away. It'll be fine."

"The second there's trouble," he warns, "you call us in."

"Let's not blow the operation open too early," Agent Brooke says. "We'll do what we have to, Agent Barnes. We can handle a little trouble."

The agent's response makes Jefferson look grouchier than ever, but he doesn't reply. The van glides to a stop and Jefferson and the woman hop out. I briefly catch sight of cement dividers and slush before the doors close and the van moves along again. Shortly after, we stop again and Agent Brooke shuffles to the back and holds the door open for me. I follow him out and go to stand on a cement sidewalk lining the massive bridge I find myself on before the van continues on with the remaining two agents who will stay on patrol further in the city.

The Mississippi River surges beneath the steel and cement bridge that marks the divide between Minnesota and Wisconsin. I lean over the railing and watch my misty breath drift away like the rushing current far below.

"Let's do this," Agent Brooke says.

At his word, I tug a red ribbon out of my pocket and tie it to the frozen steel railing. It flaps in a chilly breeze but holds. Agent Brooke and I walk down the bridge towards the Wisconsin side. Traffic rushes by us as we amble along and eventually stop fifty yards away from the ribbon I tied to the railing. I tuck my hands into my pockets and alternate between watching the roadway and the dark river. Agent Brooke leans against the railing and surveys the scene like he's simply out enjoying the weather.

"Remember the plan?" he asks casually.

"Yup."

"Good."

We're silent after that. The wind knocks us about until I can't feel my face and I start to shiver, but we continue to wait. Eventually, when I look back at our red ribbon I spot a black one next to it.

"There's our signal," I say. A vampire must have slipped over when we weren't looking and tied it to the railing next to ours. According to Dasc, that means they'll be at the meeting point at the time and place we specified with the red ribbon.

"Time to move," Agent Brooke says and I follow him off the bridge.

It's a twenty-minute walk to the meeting location. Our breath mists before us and salt and slush cover our shoes. Turning right after we reach the first intersection, we keep moving into a section of La Crosse that's mostly brick office buildings and warehouses along the river. Daylight is already starting to fade in the short winter day. We come to a set of train tracks like Dasc said we would and turn left into an old gray building surrounded by a clump of silos. We each slow our pace and keep our eyes peeled. We pass under an enclosed walkway and enter through an unlocked backdoor into the building.

"We're here," Agent Brooke whispers for the benefit of the rest of our team listening in.

"We're in position," Jefferson responds. "Going radio silent."

We're early by about an hour but that's the plan in order to clear through the building beforehand and make sure there aren't any traps waiting for us. The place is quiet and our footsteps are muffled by a layer of sawdust covering everything. The sheet metal walls are dirty, boxes of wood sit around every corner, and the stale air smells of oil and wood chips. It's a large warehouse and we hasten our footsteps to cover the entire place before it's time for the meet. What is it with vampires and warehouses anyway? Agent Brooke leads the way with a machete drawn and I flick open my retractable sword to sneak along in his footsteps. There are two floors that appear mainly disused. A walkway on the second floor circles and looks down on the main level, supported by massive steel beams thrust into the floor. The catwalk's rusted metal railings creak as we pass.

"Looks like we're good to go," Agent Brooke says once

we complete our sweep and then hang out near a wall on the main floor. He pulls back his sleeve to look at his watch. "Time to sit tight."

I retract the blade of my sword and tuck it loosely into the band of my pants so I can pull it out quickly if needed—hopefully it won't come to that. My breathing is a little unsteady and there's too much time to think. There's still at least one vampire loose in Duluth and its buddy was torn into little pieces. Are those the kind of monsters I'm about to face with only one person beside me? I clench and unclench my hands, and repeat what Charlie told me last night. I'm in control. I have power and it's mine to wield.

All too soon I hear a door creak open and shut on the opposite side of the building. Agent Brooke pushes off from the wall where he had been leaning and comes to stand over my shoulder. We share a nod and then walk to the center of the room. I do my best to look intimidating but it's hard when all I can think about is if we're going to get out in one piece. I stand with my arms loose at my sides with my weapons within easy reach.

From out of the gloom on the other side of the room two figures emerge. They both wear hoodies that are pulled up to hide their faces from the light of the fluorescents overhead. There's nothing human about the way they walk. They stalk forward like predators because that's really what they are in the end. Once we're standing fifteen feet apart, they lower their hoods in sync, remove their sunglasses, and I stare into the bloodshot eyes of two vampires. We all size up each other and Agent Brooke moves subtly behind my shoulder, angling himself more towards me defensively.

The two male vampires are pale as death and their white

skin glows oddly under the flickering lights. The first smiles and his elongated canines sit on his bottom lip. The other doesn't move from his rigid stance except to cross his arms over his chest. Since he stands behind the other's shoulder like Agent Brooke does for me, I assume he's the bodyguard. The one in front with shaggy black hair that only accentuates the paleness of his skin drops his smile.

"Is red the color of war?" the lead vamp asks.

"It's the color of the blood I'll shed in victory," I respond as Dasc instructed.

It's enough for the vampire. "Why are we here?"

Good. Let's get right to it. "The better question is, why are some of your degenerates in Minnesota?"

His eyes narrow. "We haven't crossed the border. The truce is still intact."

"Lie to me again," I snarl and take one menacing step forward, hands clenched into fists at my sides. I need to threaten and be cold. I'm Dasc's representative despite how much I hate the thought of it. "I'll rip your throat out with my teeth."

His bodyguard shows his fangs and hisses but remains where he is.

"I'm surprised Dasc doesn't have the balls to come here and deliver his threats himself," the vampire says and shares a look with his bodyguard as though unimpressed. "I didn't realize he'd send one of his Whispers."

A Whisper? Dasc never mentioned anything of the like. Typical. I keep my expression the same and don't allow myself to show my confusion.

"A threat is still a threat, no matter who it comes from," I say.

"Well, I want to hear it from Dasc, or is he otherwise occupied?"

That's just great. "He sent me. That's all you need to know."

The vampire's hands twitch at his sides. "So you spoke with him personally, then?"

He's reaching for information on Dasc, that much is obvious. Are they searching for him like the shapeshifters from Werevine were? I've got a really bad feeling about this.

"I said *that's all you need to know*. You've royally ticked him off." I take another step closer. "You're going to remove your vampires from Minnesotan soil or we'll send them back to you in *pieces*. You don't *touch* any of ours. The next move you make on us will be your last."

The vampire laughs. *Pixies*, this is not going the way I had been hoping.

"If Dasc was really threatening us, he'd have done that already and brought their heads here as evidence. He would have come out by now. So where is he?"

This is more than just reaching. They want him. They want Dasc. A pit forms in my stomach. The puzzle pieces come together in my head. Dasc wasn't faking when he reacted about vampires going after Ashley. He would have gone and ripped them apart if he wasn't currently sitting in a cell. These vampires know it too.

Oh, sweet piping Pan. They sent the vampires into Minnesota to lure Dasc out.

This is a trap.

I bring my hands up to my waist, getting them close to my hidden weapons.

"Why do you want him so bad?" I ask.

He snaps his teeth together. His fangs stick out and the ruddiness in his eyes brightens with a fresh shot of red. There's a subtle creak above us and I know there's someone on the metal walkway overhead.

"Do you ever get lipstick on those fangs?" I say loudly. Hopefully Jefferson caught our panic word of "lipstick" and will be breaching the doors at any second.

"Just your blood," the lead vampire growls.

There's another creak above us and I glance upwards. Beyond the glare of the fluorescents I spot at least four bodies. The explosive sound of a gunshot blasts through the expanse of the warehouse. The next second I'm shoved roughly to the side as Agent Brooke moves me out of the path of gunfire. I trip over my own feet by the force of his push and he grunts in pain as I stumble away, trying to regain my feet while getting out of the middle of the death trap.

Turning about, I bring up my bio-mech gun to cover Agent Brooke so he can escape as well—only I find myself being bull-rushed by the vampire bodyguard. He's on me before I can let off a single shot and catches me around the middle. I squeeze the trigger instinctively as the breath is knocked out of me and the pulse goes high, hitting the catwalk overhead. The vampire and I hit the ground hard, me taking the brunt of the blow on my back. His hands quickly wrap around either side of my head and yank me hard to the side, exposing the flesh of my neck so he can snap forward like a snake and bite down.

I let out a cry of pain as his teeth rip into my skin. I manage to bring my arms up beneath his hold and shove as hard as I can. His head jerks back and his hands release my face. Warm blood coats my neck and runs into my jacket as I grab him by the collar and force us to roll, losing my bio-mech gun somewhere in the process.

Another gunshot echoes and the sound scrambles my hearing. The vampire I roll with shudders and then there's dark blood flecking the side of my face. I'm pretty sure the idiots accidentally shot their own vampire and his blood spurts out the back of his jacket as I force us to roll over once more to seek cover behind one of the huge metal supports. Sawdust covers my arms and face, sticking to my blood and getting in my eyes. Blinking fast, I clear my vision just as the bodyguard tries to bite my neck again but my forearm across his chest keeps him at bay. There's nothing human in that face. Only a monster.

My fist meets his face when he extends his fangs towards me for another go of it. My knuckles throb and split as the bones in his face crumple inwards. He gurgles, not able to even yell properly, and slumps to the side off of me. More shots sound and bits of the ground fly up around me at their lousy aim. I scramble to crouch in the shadow of the support beam and avoid the reckless fire. In the chaos, I have a split second to wonder where the heck Agent Brooke is. Crap, I hope he hasn't been shot. Maybe he engaged the lead vampire. I need to find him and get out of here.

I press a finger to my earpiece only to find it's missing. Well, that's just great. Where is the rest of the team? We could really use them right now. Since this is a trap, I guess they could have been jumped outside. Crap. Crap, crap, *crap*. One thing's certain, though. I can't stay here. If I don't move, I'm going to be pinned down and swarmed.

My eyes latch onto my bio-mech gun on the ground not

ten feet away in the middle of the dusty floor. As I wait for some kind of lull in the firing, a sharp whistle grabs my attention. Agent Brooke stands tucked in the safety of the hallway entrance to the room and waves a hand urgently to get my attention and beckon me over to him. He's back far enough that the vampires up top can't get a bead on him but his sharp whistle drew their attention and they fire in his direction anyway. Their focus is momentarily off me. Now's my chance.

Leaping forward and tucking into a roll, I grab the bio-mech gun and in two seconds have it aimed up at the dingy light bulbs. Two well-aimed pulses send a hail of glass shards raining down and throws the room into darkness to cover my escape. As soon as the lights are out, I run blindly through the darkness in the direction of the entrance. There are a couple of thuds behind me and before I get very far, angry claws for hands grab me from behind, trying to tear my arms out of my sockets. My right arm is twisted so hard that my fingers can't retain their grip and the bio-mech gun slips from my hand for the second time tonight. Panic surges up my throat as another set of hands in front of me find my neck in the dark. Sharp nails dig into my skin and start to choke the air out of me. I plant my feet and throw my body to the right. The grip on my arm from behind loosens, so I ram my elbow backwards into the gut of my attacker then punch forward into the ribs of the one in front of me. My knuckles throb against the hard curves of the vampire's ribs that crack under my blow. He screeches and his hands drop away.

The second I'm free I dart sideways and scrabble for the retractable blade in my belt. The grip is warm in my hand as

I flick the blade fully open and sweep a wide arc in front of me. The tip meets resistance and there's a sharp hiss from the vampire I managed to slice. There's no time to hunt for the bio-mech gun that I dropped as I hear more footsteps thunder my way. I can't let them surround me again.

I do the only thing I know how. I stretch up on my toes, pull my fist back, and use the full force of my body to slam my fist into the ground. The entire building shakes as soil and chunks of wood explode outwards from my point of impact. I squeeze my eyes shut against the debris and listen to the yells and heavy thuds of the vampires sent tumbling away. I cough against the cloud of dust in the air, shake out my throbbing hand, and run towards the faint light that I think is the entrance now that my eyes have adjusted.

The darkness fills with shouting, more shots, and cries of pain. I can only hope my team has finally arrived and is inflicting the pain and not the other way around. Every now and then I can hear a bullet ricocheting off a wall nearby or hit the ground at my feet. In my haste to get to cover, I nearly run straight into a wall and clip my shoulder on the corner. Grimacing from the impact, I feel my way along the wall until I see a glowing red exit sign above the outside door. There's a breath of movement to my left so I extract the machete from inside my jacket to wield both of my blades. It comes out sticky with my own blood still running into my jacket from my neck.

I need to find Agent Brooke and get out of here. Unfortunately, my act to blind the vampires also made it impossible to find my teammate. I can thank my idiotic self for not planning ahead.

Adrenaline—my dear old friend—keeps the pain in my

neck from slowing me down but I wince as I look this way and that trying to find my partner. I give a low whistle and a sharp one answers in reply on my left before it's cut off with a grunt.

Light coming in from a window high up paints a stripe on the floor in front of me where a battle takes place. Agent Brooke fights three vampires at once, his sword a flashing specter when it catches the faint light, but his other arm dangles at his side useless and dark blood flicks off his fingertips. One of the vampires stumbles out of the fray to fumble for a gun on the ground. Before I can take two steps, the vampire levels the gun at Agent Brooke and fires.

He stumbles backwards and collapses to the floor, sending up a cloud of sawdust.

I rush forward before the vampires realize I'm there and stab my machete through the chest of the closest one from behind. I've got a gun at my head the next second and duck immediately. It goes off inches above my head and I wobble as ringing fills my ears. I send an elbow into the gut of that vamp, then wrench free the machete and swing right as hard as I can. Its edge rips across the vampire's throat and dark blood sprays over my side. Despite the damage, the vampire remains standing.

While the one grabs at his throat gurgling blood, I send a kick into the last one still fighting and send him onto his back. I don't think. I just move. Using my momentum as I spin around, I slash the thick machete and finish off the one clutching at the blood running from his throat. The vampire's head topples away. There are more coming. I feel the force of their footsteps through the soles of my feet but can't hear a freakin' thing.

The last of the trio jumps up from where I kicked him down only to find my machete waiting for him. He impales himself on the blade in my hand. He grabs onto the front of my jacket as the last of his blood pumps out of his heart and runs down my arm. I watch as he dies hanging onto me, the light in his eyes a mere flicker then gone. He falls backwards and the blade pulls free from of his chest.

The footsteps of a dozen angry vampires pound the floor and reverberate up my legs. I need to move but I can't. I'm frozen to the spot. Move, Phoenix. I just killed three people. Move, move, move. They're monsters but they're still . . . *MOVE.*

The world moves too fast and too slow at the same time as I turn to help Agent Brooke only to find him struggling to his feet already. He's bleeding heavily from somewhere but the light's too dim to see where. Without a second to lose, I tuck his good arm around my shoulder and force him to jog with me towards the exit door. When we reach it, I slam my free shoulder into it, blasting it right off its hinges.

Agent Brooke says something but I don't catch the words. Once outside under a couple of floodlights, I can see a bullet must have torn right through his shoulder and his leg's bleeding just as bad. We've got to get out of here.

"Can't hear!" I know I've said the words even if I can't hear myself. "Run!"

I spin around to the door to bar it with my blade but find I accidentally busted the hinges on my way out and the whole thing hangs crooked. There's no stopping the vampires that way. I reach for my back pocket only to remember my bio-mech gun is gone, lost somewhere inside. If they come out shooting, we're goners. There's no cover here and the edge of the building is too far away for Agent Brooke to make it, but if I carry him, then we'll both be completely exposed.

"Just run!" I shout and press up against the wall beside the doorway with machete and sword at the ready.

My ears are still ringing so I don't have the advantage of hearing my enemy before seeing them. That's okay, though. Even though my head is starting to spin, probably from blood loss, I need to hold the line until Agent Brooke can get to cover and the others arrive. This is my fault. I got us here. I shot out the stupid lights. This is on me.

The barrel of a gun peeks out from the ruined doorway. I sweep up my sword, cleaving through flesh. The vampire's hand drops to the ground as he screams in agony. I pivot on my toes, slice with my machete, and his head hits the ground before his body does. His comrades come next with guns raised. This is really an unfair fight—they know they can kill us from a distance but we have to be up close to get them.

I'm too far away to reach them. Their fingers are on the trigger.

I'm going to die.

Someone shouts and the vampires halt. Enough of my hearing has returned for me to realize someone behind the three vampires is shouting. I can't make out the words but the vampires part and a fourth marches up behind them drawing a gun and not just any gun. It's the bio-mech gun I had dropped earlier. Before I can dive out of the way, a pulse ripples the air. A force like a giant sending its fist through my body hits me in the chest and I fly backwards onto the ground.

Darkness touches the edges of my vision and I can't move. I can't even think. I don't know how much time passes until I blink away the haze over everything and find the barrel of a gun digging into my shoulder. Four leering vampires stand over me. My machete and sword lie useless on the ground five feet behind them.

"Go find the man," the vampire holding the gun orders. Two peel off from the pack to race after Agent Brooke. I can only hope my distraction was long enough for him to find the others.

"And *you*," he snarls, digging the gun in until it hurts. "You're going to tell me exactly where we can find Dasc. If we go back empty handed, they'll wipe us off the map."

I laugh weakly and even manage to gather up a glob of spit to launch at his face. The vampire flinches and his eyes stretch wide, his lips curled in a terrifying snarl.

"You can forget it," I wheeze out.

The gunshot is deafening in my ears.

18

Blood splatters across my shoulder and the side of my face but it's not my blood. The vampire gasps and tips to the side, a bullet hole torn clean through his shoulder. The other vampire spins about and hisses like an angry cat before a bullet goes straight through his forehead. Out of the broken doorway Jefferson strides with a gun raised in his hand. He's got flecks of blood on his face but otherwise he doesn't look harmed. No, not harmed at all—furious. The woman agent marches along behind him.

With the two vampires distracted, I wrench the gun out of the vampire's hand and clock him in the side of the head with it. He falls to the ground and I roll away from him before he can grab me. Completing the full turn to end up on my back again takes a lot out of me.

Jefferson and the woman are on the vampires in a second. A couple of deft strokes with their own blades and the area is neutralized. I let my body go limp on the ground and lie there in the freezing snow.

Jefferson's at my side in an instant.

I raise a shaky hand and point in the direction the other vampires went. "Two went after Brooke."

"The rest of the team already picked him up," Jefferson assures me as his eyes go from the ragged teeth marks in my neck to the blood covering my torso and arms. "We gotta get you out of here."

He takes me by the elbows and hauls me up. I groan and wince against the pain. I wish my adrenaline would come back. The numbness has faded and everything hurts. He slings my good arm over his shoulders and we walk slowly away from the carnage.

"You need to tell me, Phoenix. Is it just the bite on your neck?" Jefferson asks. "There's too much blood on you. I can't tell if you're injured anywhere else."

"Just my pride," I say hoarsely. My throat burns with each breath. Getting strangled does that. I gaze down at myself and realize I am *really* covered in blood. It makes me queasy.

"Did you ingest any of their blood?"

The only way to turn into a vampire is by ingesting their blood, so I understand his concern. I kept my mouth closed for as much of the fight as I could, though.

"I'm good."

His sigh of relief rattles through his arms as he helps me along. We round the corner of the building and find the van waiting for us. The other two agents already have Agent Brooke in the back and are getting him patched up.

"But where did you all go?" I ask once they're within range.

"We were jumped outside," the woman responds on behalf of everyone. "Right after you gave the distress signal. This whole meeting was a setup."

Jefferson gives me a hand up into the van and I collapse onto the bench opposite Agent Brooke. He nods weakly to me. The others pile in and the driver makes a call to one of the IMS cleanup teams as sirens grow louder in the distance. The van lurches forward and we hurry out of La Crosse. As we rattle across the bridge, I do my best to sit still as Jefferson dabs at the nasty bite on my neck with alcohol. It burns horribly and I accidentally rip out part of the stuffing of the seat beneath me as I clutch onto it. Once he secures a bandage to the side of my neck and gives me some pain meds, I feel like I can finally breathe again.

"They were after Dasc," I say hoarsely and accept a bottle of water from the female agent. "The trap was for him, but since he didn't show, I'm pretty sure they were going to torture me until I told them where he is."

Everyone's silent for a long while. Jefferson passes me a damp towel and I focus on wiping the insane amount of blood off my hands, face, and jacket. My hands are shaking so badly that eventually Jefferson takes the towel to dab at my hands and face himself. His own face is hollow. I can take a guess why. Getting the vampires to back off was part of my deal with Dasc. I imagine they'll retaliate after this fiasco. If I just screwed up the agreement and Dasc decides not to give us the location of Genevieve Barnes . . .

I'll never be able to live with myself.

After some work, Agent Brooke is stabilized and given a

bag of his own blood. I didn't realize they even had a store of blood for each agent on this trip. He must be feeling well enough after the infusion because he asks for his book and reads it one-handed as we race to Underground.

The female agent sets me up with my own IV bag—since I didn't know a bag of my blood was a travel necessity—and I drift in and out of sleep. When I wake, I find Jefferson's arm around me and my head on his shoulder.

"We're nearly there," the driver announces from the front.

My attention drifts to the rear window and I watch the skyscrapers and mingling traffic of Minneapolis flash by under yellow streetlamps. A light snow falls and the city is peaceful at the moment. I wonder how much longer that will last after the massive can of pixies we just opened.

No one says a word as we enter a hidden parking ramp into Underground where a medical team is waiting for us. Agent Brooke is wheeled away and they try to force me onto a stretcher too but I refuse. Instead, I follow the med staff down the dark, sloping tunnels until we reach black lifts that are miniature versions of the ones at the main entrance. We ride them to the lowest level and enter the medical unit of Underground. I'm directed to a bed and cordoned off with a white curtain as they peel back the bandage on my neck and give me a thorough once over.

They ask me questions about other injuries so I give them short answers. I don't want to talk. I'm waiting for the hammer to drop. Things went to crap and it could spell big trouble in the near future. For all I know, the vampires could be amassing at this very moment for an attack.

I've still got vampire blood in the creases of my skin, all

over my clothes, and even in my hair. A nurse guides me to a large shower area and leaves fresh clothes by the door. Vampire blood is dangerous. They need to get rid of it before they can be certain I'm not infected.

The hot water runs over my face and washes away the grime covering me. My hands shake as I comb my fingers through my hair. I should eat something. That'll make me feel better. I think. Once I dry off, I shrug into the clothes they left for me—a junior agent uniform—and walk out of the showers to find Director Knox speaking with Jefferson. They both spot me at the same time and quickly stop talking. Lucky for me, a nurse grabs me again so they can slap on fresh bandages. They deliver a tray of food at my request and then leave me alone behind that white curtain.

I slowly eat my way through a turkey sandwich and chips. Shallow thoughts skim the surface of my mind but I'm exhausted. I've little energy left to put much thought into anything. Unfortunately, Director Knox decides it's time to talk and there's no avoiding it.

"Agent Barnes has filled me in," he says. I can see Jefferson's shadow hanging around on the other side of the curtain. "There's nothing else you can do today. We'll have you speak with Dasc tomorrow after we have a better idea if we can expect vampire retaliation of any sort like he suspects. We'll be in touch."

And just like that I'm dismissed. Jefferson reappears and we walk out of Underground together. He lets me know Agent Brooke should be fine, and passes along the agent's thanks for saving his life. It only makes me feel worse somehow. We get in the SUV and Jefferson takes us out of the power park.

"Do you want to talk about it?" Jefferson asks.

He's worried about me? He should be worrying about his daughter, about the fact that I screwed up everything. If I had been more threatening with the vampires, maybe I could have prevented this from happening. Maybe I shouldn't feel guilty, but this had become my plan. I made the agreement with Dasc.

"I want to go home," I say quietly and stare out the side window.

Silence accompanies us on the interstate for the long drive through the dark. A light snow continues to fall and flashes by like pieces of ash. My neck throbs and I clutch the little bottle of pain medication the nurse gave me before I left. It feels like forever before we reach the cabin. The floodlight is on but Hawk isn't there when we go inside. The lack of his presence hits me hard. I need to see my brother. I sling on my mother's worn bomber jacket and head towards the door.

"Hawk's at capture the flag," I say and hold out my hand for the keys to the SUV. "I'm gonna head out there."

Jefferson shakes his head. "Phoenix, you've been through hell today. I don't think you should—"

"I *need* to see my brother, okay? I just do."

Something like pain crosses his face and he drops the keys in the palm of my hand. "Don't be out long. You need to get some rest."

"Yeah. Sure thing." I certainly plan on sleeping like the dead tonight. I'll probably get some sleeping pills on the way home in fact. The kind of dreams I'll have otherwise . . .

I take the SUV back out and work my way to Mr. Wick's farm where we usually hold our werewolf games.

Sure enough, when I pull into the driveway there's a slew of cars parked wherever they can fit. I spot a Carlton County Sheriff's squad car parked near the end of the driveway. I guess Deputy Graham is here. Should I tell him that his sister might be alive and in Scotland? He deserves to know.

No, I can't. Need to know only. Plus, the plan to get specifics on the location of the missing people might be a lost cause at this point.

Flipping up the collar of the bomber jacket, I grab a flashlight from the glove box and step out into the cold. I stop at the house first to say hello to Mr. Wick and find out where on his property the game is taking place. He directs me into the west woods and I follow the trodden path through the snow behind his house.

The snow magnifies the light I carry but it's still dark. Dark just like that building in La Crosse. I involuntarily shudder and quickly scan the woods around me but I'm alone. No vampires here . . . yet. The farther out I go, the closer the sounds of barking and howling become. I spot another light in the distance and hear laughter. My heavy footsteps announce my presence and I find a flashlight beam pointed directly at my face. I lift a hand and blink against the light.

"It's me, Deputy," I call.

The beam falls and he waves a hand. "Hey! I didn't think you'd make it. We could use another referee out here. They're being a little rowdier than usual."

I halt beside him and he slouches from his towering view at six feet and some inches to peer at me.

"Hey, are you okay?" he asks. "You look terrible."

"It's been a long day. Where's my brother? He's supposed

to be here."

"Yeah, he was helping me out until about half an hour ago."

I squint at him against the harsh lights we hold. "What do you mean 'had been'?"

Deputy Graham points through the trees to the west. "A couple of knuckleheads split off from the game that way, outside the perimeter we set. He ran after to haul them back and I haven't seen him since. Do you mind—hey, where are you going?"

I'm already running through the snow in the direction he pointed. Hawk's been out here by himself, without my anti-werewolf ability, in the middle of a game full of wolves. He ran off and hasn't been seen? Nightmare scenarios race through my mind. Hawk promised he would take the serum if he needed to but a small voice in the back of my head knows he wouldn't. Hawk swore ages ago he'd never take it again. If he couldn't fight a compulsion tonight without me here—oh, sweet majestics. Hawk.

The snow is thicker here between the trees where it hasn't been disturbed in a while or melted by the sun. It rises and falls in enormous drifts that I struggle through since I'm already so drained. I stop and swivel about to locate some kind of trail indicating where he might have gone. Who had he gone after? Where were *they* going? The anxiety crawling under my skin gets worse the more I think about it.

My flashlight flickers across a deep path cut through the snow. I jog over, breathing hard already as I have to lift my feet way up and down to get through the thick stuff. I stop and inspect the trail. It's a mess but I can clearly make out paw prints here and there. A group of werewolves must have broken off. In the middle are some clean boot tracks. Those must be Hawk running after them. I pick up my feet and run.

He's been gone a half-hour. Why didn't the deputy go look for him? Why didn't he help him? A lot could have happened in that span of time. The trail continues on and I'm not sure if I'm even on Mr. Wick's property anymore. If I leave the trail I'm on, I'll be lost. I pause to catch my breath and lightly touch the bandage at my neck. There's already blood seeping through. Crap.

Noise up ahead has me drawing my bio-mech gun and flashlight together. Figures emerge from the shadows and into the light—three boys, none of them my brother. Their muted laughter stops the instant they realize they're in a beam. None of them speak. Matt Jones spearheads the small group of his friends and holds up a hand to shield his eyes.

"Hey, man. Sorry," he says. He must not be able to see who I am. "We got lost out here. Could you point us towards a road?"

I storm forward, tuck the gun into my pocket, and grab Matt by the collar of his jacket. My hand aches but in the moment I feed off that pain. Matt's eyes go wide.

"Where's my brother?" I shout in his face.

"Woah, woah, woah. Phoenix?"

I lower the flashlight so it's pointed at the ground instead of their faces. The other two back up a step. "I asked you a question," I snarl.

"Oh, Hawk?"

"No, my other brother. Of course I mean Hawk!" I shake him and even though I mean to do it lightly, I end up over doing it. His hair flops back and forth from the force of my grip. "Why did you run off? He followed you."

He looks to his friends who turn sheepish. Guilt. That's what I'm seeing. Guilt at getting caught in the act. My hand tightens on Matt's jacket and the fabric tears beneath my fingers.

"You lured him out here on purpose, didn't you?" I say, my voice dark and deadly. "What did you do?"

Matt's starting to turn purple in the face and he gasps for air. His friends don't even bother trying to help him as I begin to suffocate him. I blink and realize what I'm doing. Who's the monster now? I let him go and shove him back a pace.

"Phoenix, we didn't mean to—"

"WHERE IS HE?" I scream in his face. They have no idea what I've been through today and what nightmares I have imagined happening to my brother in this moment. I beheaded people today. If they knew that, maybe they'd speak a little faster.

The three try to talk over each other in a jumble so I raise a hand and point to Matt alone. They quiet and Matt says in a strained voice, "Last we saw, he was running off that way." He points to the area they just came from. "Towards the Nelsons'."

I'm sick to my stomach and sway on the spot. "Did he shift?"

"I think so."

It's like I don't even see the three boys anymore. I push past them in a daze, throwing Matt bodily to the ground, and run head long into the trees continuing to follow the trail.

With a shaking hand I pull out my bio-mech gun again.

I get dizzy from the light in my hand bobbing across the

uneven ground. The trail turns into a right mess before I find a single trail leading out instead of four. It continues on through the woods, weaving away from the sound of a road nearby and deeper into the wilderness. I cross a frozen stream and a few tears I don't even realize I'm shedding splatter the jacket of my arm as I cut through the air.

Not Hawk. Not my brother. Oh, please, not my brother.

Please, don't let that monster inside him get the better of him.

We should have run. We should have left ages ago. We knew this was dangerous and yet we stayed. We played werewolf games and ignored the monsters hiding underneath. We dismissed the serum because we thought we were stronger.

Please don't let anyone pay for our mistake.

The light hits something dark and I stumble to a stop. I flick my flashlight up and down until I spot it again. Blood. Droplets of blood in the middle of a messy trodden patch of snow. Breathing hard and dreading what I'll see, I move forward slowly along a wider path dotted with more red. The tracks are swept away in a wide swath where it looks like something had been dragged.

A threatening growl ahead makes me raise the bio-mech gun next to my flashlight. Taking one cautious step in front of the other, I soon reach a furry body crouched low in the snow. Green eyes tinted gold reflect the light like a demon, bright and terrifying in the cold face of a wolf. Red fur encases the top of its head and there's no mistaking who it is.

"Hawk," I breathe.

He snarls and saliva drips from his mouth. Not just saliva but blood. There's no trace of my brother in those vicious snarls, raised hackles, and flattened ears.

"It's me. Hawk, please don't make me shoot you," I choke out. Heat rushes up my back and down my arms. I shiver against the power shifting inside and making me sway as it takes too much out of me.

The wolf shell of my brother takes two fast steps forward and pauses again.

"Hawk, please."

Warmth radiates from me in waves and my hands shake. His snarls begin to quiet. He shakes his head and scratches his muzzle with his paw. Then he tucks in his tail and a keen howl escapes him. The fur recedes or falls away into nothingness. Before long the wolf is gone and Hawk is on all fours in the snow breathing hard. I don't move as he turns to the side and wretches into the blanket of snow. He does so again and a third time before he finally falls back on his knees and makes a horrible, anguished sound.

Slowly he brings up his trembling hands before him. They're spotted with blood. Tears streak his cheeks and run through the drying blood around his mouth.

I don't know what to do. What am I supposed to do? I take a step forward and he quickly scampers back from me holding up a hand.

"No, stop!" he cries. "Don't come any closer. Don't . . ."

Something ugly is climbing up my throat, burning my eyes, and drowning out the rest of the world. I take another step closer and Hawk hangs his head, still keeping one hand up telling me to stay away. His body heaves with his panicked breathing and he keeps making that wretched, hopeless sound.

No words form on my lips. I'm petrified. What do I say?

How am I supposed to make *this* better?

I kneel in the snow in front of my brother and hold the flashlight down so I don't blind either of us. I reach for him but he shies away. With only a couple feet between us, I can see the streaks of blood on his neck and staining the top of his shirt and jacket.

His tortured green eyes meet mine at last.

"Help me." It's the plea of a little boy, not my joking, confident twin. "I don't know what I've done, Phoenix. I don't know what I've done. I don't remember."

He finally lets me put a hand on his upper arm and I give him a reassuring squeeze. I have to be strong. That's the true reason for my strength. It's so I can be strong for him. Who cares what happened earlier today? My brother is in pain.

"Then we figure it out," I say evenly. "Just you and me. Okay?"

He sucks down air. "Okay."

"Come on."

I help him to his feet. When he staggers, I let him lean on me for support until he manages to even himself out. I force myself to look at our surroundings calmly despite the panic I'm battling inside.

"I came from that direction." I indicate with the flashlight, then turn in the opposite direction to paint another trail with the light. "So that must be where you came from. We'll go together. We take this one step at a time."

He nods and brushes the back of his hand across his mouth. The second he sees the blood smeared onto his hand, he grabs a handful of snow to scrub at his face and neck. Each movement is desperate and panicked. I'm tearing apart at the seams.

I take the first few steps and he hesitates before following. Our pace is slow. Neither of us wants to know what's at the other end of this trail. More blood droplets line the tracks, more signs of struggle. Tuffs of fur catch my eye here and there. I'm not sure if they're from Hawk or from some other animal. What if he only attacked some random creature out in the wild? That could be it. If he went after a deer or a bobcat or something, we'll be okay. Wolves hunt other animals. It'll be fine.

The trail expands into a sprawling trodden patch stretched between the trees. This must be it. Whatever Hawk did when he wolfed out happened here. Please, let it be a deer. An old deer ready to die. A deer that would have fallen during hunting season anyway.

I halt and Hawk falls to his knees in the snow again. The beam of light wavers at the force of my shakes.

Lifeless and cold in the snow lies a golden lump, blood matted in its once glossy fur.

It's Ashley's dog.

It's Duke.

19

A hollow ringing fills my ears. The body in front of me isn't some random cow, a piece of livestock that can be easily replaced. I know . . . knew Duke. Ashley loves this dog, this beautiful, happy dog that's dead at my feet.

"We did this," I whisper to the darkness and let it consume my words.

We always knew the risks and yet we pushed our boundaries. I should have seen this coming and stopped Hawk, but we thought we were stronger than the disease. What fools we've been.

"It was me," Hawk says weakly beside me. "This is on me. I killed—oh, pixies—"

He vomits to the side again but there's little left in him.

How can I ever explain this to Ashley? If she found out what Hawk did, they'd haul him away just like Jason. He'd be held like a prisoner and forced to take the serum. He'd go mad. I might not ever see him again if the stories are true of the other werewolves that have disappeared. I can't let that happen.

A dangerous plan forms in my mind and it makes me sick to my stomach.

"No one can know," I say quietly. "Not a soul."

Hawk's lifeless eyes stare up at me as a grimace lingers on his face. "Phoenix . . ."

"I'm going to bury Duke." I swallow past the horrible taste in my mouth. Ashley is going to be frantic looking for her dog and I'm going to have to lie straight to her face. I am a monster. "I'll bury him out here beneath the snow so no one finds him. Then we're going to sneak back to the car. We're going to clean you up."

"And what happens the next time I can't control myself?" Hawk retorts.

"I'm not leaving you again," I say sharply. Shadows fall under his eyes and he doesn't argue. "We're going to clean you up and pretend like this never happened. We can't—" What I suggest next hurts even more. "We can't tell Jefferson. He can't know."

"What if he finds out?"

"He won't unless we tell him. You got that? You keep your mouth shut, Hawk."

I don't know who this person is that's speaking with my mouth and walking around in my skin. I don't recognize myself, this person that would lie to her friends and hide such a dangerous truth. But I can't let them take Hawk. The cure is in my blood. I can still make this right.

The brutal work begins and I force Hawk to sit off to the side as I snap a branch off a nearby tree and use it to clear away the snow and break open the frozen ground. The branch splinters under the force I put into it and I have to grab branch after branch to dig open the ground, occasionally punching the earth to break it apart more easily, but I'm so, so tired. Every other minute I have to stop to catch my breath. Dirt covers me and I can hardly breathe as I lift Duke's stiff body and lay him gently into the grave. I rest a hand on his foreleg.

"You were a good boy," I murmur and fight the burn behind my eyes. "Ashley loved you but I think you already knew that. You'll be missed, big guy."

I give him one last pat to send the faithful dog on his way and then rise to give him a blanket of soil for his long sleep. No stone or makeshift marker is left to draw attention to where he lies. And to my everlasting shame, I push the snow over the grave until no one passing through could possibly know what lies beneath.

It's a long walk back through the woods. No words pass between us. Shivers wrack me and my shoes are completely sodden. I'm in real danger of frostbite at this point. Yet that somehow feels justified.

We've been out so long that the sounds of capture the flag have vanished. Everyone must have left already. Even so, I have Hawk wait in the shelter of the trees as I jog to our SUV parked outside the farmhouse. Nearly all of the cars are gone but to my horror, Deputy Graham is still there and sitting in his squad car with the door open on a phone call. He notices me before I can decide if running is a good option and he instantly gets out of his car to meet me.

"I've been worried about you," he says. "You and Hawk never came back. I've got Jefferson on the line right now."

He holds up the cell phone in his hand for emphasis.

I can't muster the courage to talk to Jefferson in this

moment, so I say, "Let him know we're fine. Hawk got stuck out in the woods but I found him."

The deputy looks around past my shoulder. "Where is he?"

He *has* to be observant. "Behind the house. He's picking up a few of his things before we leave."

"I can go help him."

Without warning he starts to walk around me so I throw out an arm. Despite his size and how frail I am right now, my arm acts like a steel railing and forcefully stops him. He squints down his pointed nose at me.

"Everything okay, Phoenix?"

"Everything's great, Jared. It's just been a really, *really* long day."

His stern expression lets me know he's not buying it but he eventually gives a short bob of his head with a murmured "Have a goodnight," and heads to his squad car. Once he's gone I start the SUV to get the heaters going and jog back to find Hawk sitting against the barn. One of the horses inside keeps blowing its nostrils in his direction, clearly agitated. It could be the blood that covers him—or it senses what lies beneath that hollow expression. Hawk's a shadow of himself.

"Time to go," I say.

He stands and follows me to the SUV but it's like he's going through the motions. There's no thought to what he's doing. This whole thing didn't rattle him—it broke him. All this time I've been worrying about vampires and Dasc and becoming a lousy shot when I really should have been focused on my brother.

We sit in the growing warmth of the SUV for a time

before I put it into gear. I don't take us to Jefferson's. We're not ready for that confrontation yet. Instead I make for town and stop at one of the lesser-travelled gas stations. Hawk stays in the car as I go in, pay for a tourist sweatshirt that says "Got Moose?" and get the key to the bathrooms outside. After making sure the coast is clear, I grab the first aid kit and pull my brother into the bathroom to clean up.

The mirror reflects two really awful looking teenagers. I've still got a cut healing that trails up into my hairline, a black eye, and a big sodden bandage on my neck. My face, hands, jacket, and pants are splattered with muck. Beside me, Hawk is a gaunt ghost, pale and smeared with blood. When he freezes in front of the dirty bathroom mirror and doesn't move, I have to direct him to pull off his jacket and offer him a wet pad of gauze to clean himself with. He does so with robotic motions.

Once most of the evidence of our secret in the woods is gone, I pass Hawk the sweatshirt, and gather up all the dirty bandages and Hawk's filthy jacket. We climb back into the SUV and I glance at the clock. It's nearing midnight. I check my phone and see a slew of missed calls and texts from Jefferson wondering where we are. I shoot him a single text confessing that I need some time alone with my brother after what happened today. I can only hope he buys it.

We pull out of the parking lot and I don't know where to go. Hawk's still too far gone to face Jefferson. I just start driving and wander through Moose Lake. Without realizing where I'm heading, within ten minutes we're pulling up the driveway of our parents' old house. It's eerie with no lights in the middle of the night. Hawk shows his first sign of life by looking to me in confusion.

"I don't know where else to go," I say quietly and step outside.

Hawk follows me like a silent shadow as I gather up all the used bandages and ruined jacket and carry them towards the house. I unlock the deadbolt with my key and let my brother inside. He stands in the dark for nearly half a minute before turning on his flashlight. I move around him through the living room and to the kitchen that I know by heart to dump the load in my arms into the rusted sink. No evidence should be left behind to be discovered. So, I grab one of the cabinet doors, rip it off its hinges, and start snapping it into pieces. Once I have enough kindling, I array the pieces in the sink around the dirty bandages.

"Do we have a lighter in the car?" I ask.

My brother nods and walks off only to return a minute later with one in hand. He passes it over and I work on getting the bandages to burn. After coaxing the flames to life, we watch our little fire burn in the pit of the sink. I soak up the warmth and hover over its radiant light, its cleansing flames.

"You unlocked the front door," Hawk says. A spark of life returns to his eyes. He hasn't shutdown on me completely. "It didn't have a lock before."

"I guess this is my little secret," I murmur. "I couldn't let this place go. I've been coming back for months. I put locks on the doors, swept up a little."

"Why?"

I shrug. "I don't really know. I guess . . . it's the only bit we have left of Mom and Dad. I didn't want it to rot."

He's quiet again and the firelight reflects in his eyes.

"I hate this house," he whispers. "To me, it's not where

Mom and Dad lived or where they raised us. It's a ruined monument to their deaths. It's a reminder of the monster I've become."

"You're not a monster."

"Yes, I am. Don't tell me that I'm wrong." He turns away and wanders into the living room with arms crossed over his chest and chin tucked down. Eventually he sits beneath the boarded up bay windows and watches the flames from a safe distance.

A wall has been raised around him and I want to break it down. Shutting me out isn't going to help either of us. I walk over and sit beside him. The flames in the sink lick up over the sides in a sporadic dance.

"Talk to me," I say and hold my hands in close to my chest for warmth.

He leans his head back against the dusty boards. "I didn't take the serum. I said I would but I didn't." He closes his eyes as if pained. "You have no idea what it feels like, Phoenix. When I took it as a kid at the beginning of all this, I felt like it was scooping out my insides and replacing them with acid. It was a constant pain and it ate away at me. I couldn't sleep. I couldn't eat. And I knew it wouldn't go away. They forced me to keep taking that serum and they never listened when I tried to tell them it hurt. No one seemed to have the same problem so they dismissed my complaints as a little boy wanting attention."

I'm biting my lower lip so hard I'm pretty sure I'm going to start bleeding. I remember parts of that—I remember he wouldn't touch his food, kept to himself in his room, and never wanted to play. Our caretakers told me he was sad—probably depressed but I wouldn't have known what that was as a child—and he would get over it soon. I was there the whole time but he never confided in me and never showed a trace of that pain.

"Why didn't you tell me?" I whisper.

"Because you've always been the strong one. I was a little kid. I didn't want you to think I was weak like everyone else apparently did."

"And when we grew up? Why not then?"

"By then it didn't matter anymore. I wasn't taking the serum so why bring it up? Even now I—" He heaves a sigh and runs a hand through his hair. "I still feel like I'm the culprit. I'm the reason the serum did what it did. It was *my* fault. I'm too much of a monster so instead of giving me peace of mind, it tried to destroy me. I didn't want you to think the same of me."

I want to reach out and hug him but he might think I'm patronizing or pitying him. The words to comfort him don't come. I never had the same gift for that as he does. I can't mend wounds with pretty sentences. My way of caring has always been to act.

"And this house reminds you of that?" I ask.

He nods mutely.

"I'm sorry. I shouldn't have brought us here."

"I'd burn it to the ground if I could." He fiddles with the strings of his sweatshirt.

The gnawing ache in my chest becomes even more painful. My brother and I have almost always been on the same page about everything since we were kids. Now it's like we're on opposite sides of a divide. Hawk's so ready and yearning to destroy the one place we have left of our parents but I desperately want to keep on stitching this house back together. I tilt my head and stare up at the decayed ceiling, the water damage stains and flaking bits of paint, the cobwebs and dust.

This place is ugly. It's revolting. Why am I trying so hard to hold on to this place? So what if I manage to fix the holes in the walls? Redo the paint? Patch the roof? Replace the floors? It'll never matter how much effort and hard work I put into this house. I'll never be able to fix the one thing I'm truly trying to repair.

It'll never be enough to bring back our parents.

Time to be reckless. "Then let's do it."

His head turns sharply towards me. "What?"

"Let's burn this piece of crap to the ground."

"But you—"

"Anything that hurts you, hurts me," I say firmly. "If this broken house makes you think you're a monster, then I'm sending it off to high heaven in flames. And by rights it's ours anyway. I'll do whatever I want with it. There's enough snow packed around the house to keep the fire here and the closest trees are too far away. It'll be fine."

He considers me for a long moment. "And if someone sees us? We'll be arrested for arson."

"Then we give ourselves a good head start before the cops and firefighters show up. Besides, it belongs to us. It's ours to burn." I get to my feet and hold out my hand. Without any hesitation, he takes it and I haul him up.

Together we walk to our little sink fire and I break apart another cabinet door. I pass him one stick for a torch and we hold the ends in the flames until they catch fire.

"Are you ready?" I ask.

"I've been ready to do this for a long time," he says darkly.

I grab hold of the sink, wrench it onto its side, and let the burning debris spill across the floor. The rotten boards catch quickly and we move to the other side of the house to set fire to the peeling wallpaper and toss our sticks up the stairs to get the upper level going. Like shadows we slip out of the house and stand together next to the tire swing as the inside of the house glows brighter by the second, until flames lick through the windows and door. Minutes tick by and smoke rises above like a signal to the world. The old house, filled with memories forgotten and lost, turns into a blazing inferno of hot rage, purging the bloodstains and broken promises of a brighter future.

Hawk holds my hand and we watch as our past goes up in a firestorm.

~

Jefferson gives us space when we finally return to the cabin. I hope he takes our vacant expressions as worry about the vampires or something. We both collapse in our bunks and I'm asleep almost instantly. I must be so exhausted, either from the day itself or the constant use of my magic, that my sleep is devoid of dreams. It's one small mercy.

When I wake I have a plan ready but it's so hard to get out of bed. Grimacing against the pain in my neck, I slide down to the floor. Hawk is in bed but he's not actually sleeping. He stares at the top bunk mindless again. I don't disturb him but slip off to the bathroom to get ready. After I take a shower and put a new bandage on my neck, I creep out into the kitchen area. There's a pot of coffee brewing and bread warming in the toaster. Jefferson's bedroom door is open so I move to stand in the doorway.

Jefferson looks up from where he sits on the edge of his mattress, a picture frame clutched in his hands. It's the only photo I've ever seen of his daughter. She's on a pink bike wearing overalls and her black hair flies behind her in a pair of long braids. I'd say she's maybe seven in the picture. From what little Jefferson has told me, it was taken only a month before Moose Lake became a hot spot and his daughter vanished along with Dasc.

"How are you feeling?" he asks gently.

My hand automatically touches the bandage on my neck. "I'll live."

He nods and his focus shifts back to the picture in his hands. Cautiously, I walk into the room and take a seat beside him. This is the first time he hasn't told me to get out of his private space immediately. I wait for it but I think he might actually want company.

"She'll be twenty-one now," he continues in that gentle voice I rarely hear him use. It makes my chest ache. "I got that bike for her birthday that year. She loved that thing. Rode it round and round. Almost ran over a cat, silly girl."

He smiles faintly, sniffs once, and then runs a hand over his mouth.

"I've missed fourteen years of her life, Phoenix. Fourteen years during which only God knows what that monster did to her. She won't be my little girl anymore. She won't even know who I am."

I wrap my hand around his and we just sit there staring at the memory of who Jefferson's daughter used to be. Genna Barnes. The clock ticks out the slow, painful seconds.

"We're going to make things right," is all I can say.

"When we find her," he says and faces me, "I hope she's someone like you."

My lower lip trembles and I swallow a few times. Jefferson isn't just my mentor anymore. He's not just my comrade. He's family. And I don't deserve him. I think of that unmarked grave in the woods, of the way I lied to Jefferson when we got home, of the smoldering ruin of my parents' house.

I hope Genna Barnes isn't like me at all.

I slip my hand out of Jefferson's and rise. In unison we clear our throats and avert our eyes. I guess neither of us are good at this part.

"Hawk and I better get to school," I say.

"You can take the day off. Heck, take three. You have my permission after the mess you went through yesterday."

I let a faint smile touch my lips. "A little normalcy will be good for me."

"Only if you're sure and you take it easy. There's a bit of breakfast for you in the kitchen."

"Thanks, Jefferson. For everything."

I move out to rouse Hawk and eat the toast waiting for me. It takes visible effort for Hawk to offer Jefferson a normal "good morning." I keep him moving and we climb into the SUV.

"I don't know if I can do this today," Hawk says from the passenger seat.

"Then I guess it's a good thing we're not really going to school." I turn the wheel as we reach the intersection into town and head in the opposite direction from the route we usually take.

"Where are we going?" he asks.

"To get answers."

We go up the main road before making a left onto a one-way street and stop in the parking lot for the Moose Lake Public Library. When I try the glass doors to the building I find they're locked and see a note listing the business hours. It'll be another hour before it's open.

"Come on," I say and usher my brother over to Java Jitters up the block. After ordering a pair of espressos, we sit in silence at a small table tucked in the corner by the windows. For a whole hour, I contemplate everything that happened the day before with the vampires and Hawk. I've been so caught up with everything around me that I've hardly had time to give my own blood much consideration. I've been through enough life changing experiences lately that maybe what power is in me has enhanced or matured. I need it to. I need it so desperately.

The second I see a pair of women through the window unlocking the doors to the library, I hop out of my seat and beckon my brother along. Hawk gives me a long sideways look as if I'm crazy but keeps quiet. He follows me out of the café, across the street, and into the library. I walk straight up to the front counter without preamble. We've wasted enough time. I came here twice before with Jefferson and the same stick-thin librarian waits on us at the desk. Her mousy hair is pulled back into a pristine bun and everything about her face is sharp—cheekbones, nose, eyes, chin.

"I'm looking for the first edition of *Apollodorus*," I say. I'm glad I'm able to remember the title of the book for Jefferson's dead drop to communicate with his hidden "expert."

The woman's razor eyes narrow as if testing me, but then she takes long elegant strides into the backroom.

Hawk hovers at my ear and says under his breath, "Okay, so what's going on?"

"I'll show you in a second."

The librarian reappears without making a sound and slides *Apollodorus* across the counter. Its brown leather cover almost sticks to the glossy countertop when I pick it up and the yellowed pages crinkle as I shrug it into the crook of my elbow.

"Thanks," I say and steer Hawk towards a computer cubicle out of sight from a couple of newcomers walking in. Glancing over my shoulder to make sure no one is watching us, I flip open the book to reveal the hole cut out in the center of the pages. I grab a piece of scrap paper lying nearby and a pencil to hastily write a note.

"What on earth?" Hawk breathes and runs his hands along the false book.

"This is how Jefferson sent my blood to his expert," I whisper and keep writing. "I think it's about time we met this expert, don't you?"

"How do we know they'll even respond to us?"

I finish my note stating in urgent terms that we have to meet immediately as a matter of life or death. I close the book and meet Hawk's uncertain gaze.

"We don't have any other options," I say and return to the counter.

The librarian tugs the book from me with a scowl and returns it to the backroom. Before she returns, we quickly exit and go sit in the SUV. Instead of pulling away, I lie in wait at an angle so I can see if anyone goes up to the counter to ask for *Apollodorus*. I have no idea how this expert is even supposed to know when there's a message waiting or if they check it at regular intervals like clockwork. I'm determined to sit here and find out. I'm sick of waiting for my blood to incubate or whatever the crap they want to call it. I need that cure yesterday.

"You never told me what happened the other day with your vampire lead," Hawk says and sounds guilty. "I was a little preoccupied with . . . you know . . ."

I keep my focus on the counter. A man is waiting at the front with a stack of books to check out but the librarian isn't back yet. "Yeah, I know."

"You got hurt."

"Yeah, psycho vampires will do that to a person." I give him the short version of my interrogations with the shapeshifters and Dasc, then the battle in La Crosse. I consider leaving out the bit about owing Dasc a life debt but then think better of it. We aren't keeping secrets anymore and I don't want to start that up again.

The guy at the counter looks furious there's no one to check out his books and a line forms behind him. A younger girl moves up to man the counter but the main librarian still hasn't come back.

"As if things weren't bad enough," Hawk mutters. "Why can't these monsters go live in Antarctica and not bother anyone?"

"That can be our plan B," I say. "Ship everyone to Antartica if this blows up in our faces."

"Us or them?"

I shrug. "Maybe Australia instead. Isn't that what people used to do?"

He laughs under his breath and it's a good sound. I had been afraid he'd never laugh again after the way he looked last night.

I catch movement in the corner of my eye and spin around in my seat as the rear passenger door opens. Hawk jerks back and without warning the librarian that helped us earlier slides into the seat and shuts the door behind her.

"Well, you two aren't exactly stealthy," she says and gives us a sharp, appraising once over. "You make your business sound so dire and then you squat in the parking lot. Don't you realize you're blocking other people from parking here to get their library books?"

Her tone is indignant and I'm completely baffled. My mouth opens and closes a few times but I'm drawing a blank.

Hawk manages to speak up for the pair of us. "What—I—I'm sorry, who are you?"

She heaves a sigh and smooths out her pencil skirt. "I certainly hope you can at least remember a face you saw only a couple of minutes ago."

"I know who you're *supposed* to be," he says. "What are you doing in here?"

"You said it was urgent," she says like it's so blatantly obvious. "I'm taking you to your expert. So, are we going to waste more time or are we going to get moving? Phoenix, dear, you really shouldn't leave your mouth hanging open like that. A pixie might rip out your tongue."

I close my mouth but still can't get my brain to function. The librarian makes a little circle motion with her forefinger indicating I ought to turn around in my seat and get us out of here. Hawk is wide-eyed and shrugs. This is what we wanted, isn't it?

Allowing myself to be bossed around by a stranger, I rev the engine and pull out of the lot.

"Where am I going?" I ask and watch her in the rearview mirror.

"Eyes on the road, Phoenix." She clucks like a hen. "Make for I-35 if you'd please."

"North or south?"

"South. Go on, now. Traffic is waiting for you."

I share an annoyed frown with Hawk and pull out onto the one-way street. The librarian is quiet only for a short while as I navigate to the interstate. We merge with the traffic going south and when I ask for the next set of directions, she waves her hand at me.

"I'll notify you when the turn approaches," she says dismissively. "I certainly hope you slept well enough last night to keep sharp while driving. It was quite an eventful evening for our fiery redheads, wasn't it? Burning down your parents' home was quite the statement."

I almost swerve off the road.

"Clearly, *not* enough sleep then," she says and clicks her tongue. "Eyes sharp, dear."

Repeatedly calling me dear makes me think of Celina but this woman is so much different than my surrogate mother.

"What do you know about it?" Hawk asks and turns about in his seat to talk directly with the librarian. I'm glad my seat belt is keeping my heart securely in my chest. It feels like it's trying to jump out and run for the hills.

"I know you two can be rather rash. Brave and loyal, but rash. One day you may regret stomping on the bones of your past, but I assume this urgency and the deliberate arson of last night are related."

"Just get us to the expert," I growl.

A devious smile grows on her face. It's animalistic. "Next turn up ahead, dear."

She must know we're desperate and her subtle threats are cluing me in that if we make the wrong move, she can tear us apart with what she knows. I try to push that happy little thought out of my mind and take the off ramp to Sturgeon Lake. The librarian directs us across the overpass, down a forested road, and between a couple of lakes until we're deep in the woods.

"Turn right up ahead and mind the gate."

I do as she says and pull onto a paved driveway guarded by a massive wrought iron gate designed with intricate swirls and whorls. As if they know who we are, the gates unlock all by themselves and allow us through. Curious. Massive pines line the driveway in orderly rows and the paved road seems to go on forever, deeper and deeper into the forest. At last we come to a turnaround in front of the nicest house I've ever seen. No, not a house. A mansion.

A leafless gnarled oak sits in the middle of the roundabout and tastefully spaced trees decorate the expansive flat land that encircles the building. Enormous windows face the driveway and sunlight passes through revealing massive couches, tables, and benches inside. I bring the SUV to a stop between the marble pillars that hold up an awning over the walkway to the double oak front doors.

"The expert lives here?" I ask and crane my neck to survey the marvel of a house through the windshield.

The librarian sniffs in disdain. "Where else should she live? The depths of her knowledge has afforded her a comfortable living. Come along."

We unbuckle and step out to gaze in awe at the house. The librarian ushers us inside to a grand foyer laced in marble and some kind of red wood. The entrance is spacious and leads to a massive circular room in the center of the house with a ceiling two stories high.

The librarian pauses fifteen feet ahead of us in the middle of that room, rolls back her shoulders, and lets out a relieved sigh as her skin seems to drape off her body, expanding out like a cloak behind her. Her clothes melt together with her skin, lengthening and changing color to a vibrant green. She stands taller—no, she physically *becomes* taller—foot by foot until she's a good eight feet by my estimate. The deep green cloak about her shifts as if in a breeze and from beneath a tail uncoils. A row of spikes expand along the top of the tail and climb up her back as her legs and arms change shape.

In less than thirty seconds, the human that had been before us is now a scaled, slender lizard of shifting hues of vibrant green and florescent blue accents. The shape of her is almost like a greyhound but the size of a horse. She curls around to face us, tail coiling around her ankles, claws clicking on the marble floor tiles, and looks down her elongated snout at us. Short blue frill frames her face and falls in layers down the sides of her neck, which puffs out briefly before lying flat against her scaly skin.

The librarian is a dragon.

"Well," she says in that same clipped tone but with a bit of a growl. "Here I am. What can I do for you?"

20

The dragon waits politely for us to overcome our shock. *The dragon.* I've never even seen one in real life, only in pictures during my studies. Sure, I've been hanging around Draco a lot lately but I've never witnessed his true form.

"Your mouth is open again, dear," she says and holds up a forefoot to inspect her deadly, shining claws.

I close my mouth and reach blindly to the side for my brother. He does the same and we grasp each other's arm.

The dragon-librarian tilts her head and the frill along her jaw expands briefly. The irises of her eyes have transformed into reptilian slits but they still have the same sharp intelligence about them.

"It's charming the way you two seek comfort in each other," she says and lowers her forefoot to the floor. Her claws click on the marble surface. "Two sides of the same coin, ever bound."

"You're a dragon," I manage to breathe.

"Yes, you're quite astute."

"And you've been here this whole time?"

Her long, thin tail flicks once like a cat studying prey. "*This whole time* is a rather general span of measurement, wouldn't you say? But as I assume you mean since you came back to Moose Lake in October, then yes, I have, and a little longer. But never mind that. You had urgent business."

I let go of Hawk and take a step forward. "You were around when Dasc attacked. You could have helped. Why didn't you?"

"I was unaware when he struck, and my reasons are my own."

"That's not good enough," I snap, completely forgetting her head is a good two feet over mine and she could probably tear me in half if she wanted to.

She brings that elongated face down to my height, eyes narrowing. "Do not judge so harshly when your own rash actions have caused a ripple effect throughout the legendary community."

"What?"

"Do you think your capture of Dasc and battle with the vampires has gone unnoticed? You're on a path where mere mention of your name will elicit a reaction. Be careful where you tread. In your current state, anonymity may be a wiser stratagem."

My current state. Right. "Look, we came to you because we need a cure."

She recoils and sits posed like a statue. "Your blood is not strong enough to purge the werewolf contagion."

"We can't wait any longer," I argue and step closer. Hawk

is right on my heels. "Please, there must be something you can do."

"Has your patience run out? Or has something happened?"

Hawk puts a hand on my shoulder to keep me back as he steps forward. "It's because of me."

"Hawk, no," I warn but he doesn't stop talking.

"I did something horrible last night, and I know what my options are at this point." He sounds resigned but I won't have any of it. "I've lied about it now and we've covered it up. I haven't taken the serum for years and I . . . I killed a friend's pet last night while Phoenix was away. I can't keep doing this. I can't keep lying but I can't take the serum either. And if I can't handle those options, then I know eventually I'll be dragged into one of the werewolf rehabilitation centers and I'll never leave. If there's nothing you can do, please just tell me now and save me the trouble of hoping there's a normal future for me."

I bow my head and study the marble beneath my feet. It sounds like waiting for my blood to be ready isn't even in the cards for him. It's gotten this bad and I hadn't even realized. The foyer falls silent except for the deep breaths of the dragon. This is it for us, isn't it? The hope in me starts to drain away.

"Follow me."

Well, that's not a no. I'll take it. The dragon turns and walks deeper into the house. Together we jog after her long strides, through the circular room in the center, make a right, and trot down a large stairwell to the level below.

"What do we call you?" Hawk asks.

"What to call me indeed," she says. We make it to the bottom and enter a long hallway lined with glass walls that reveal a massive laboratory. "I've had my share of names but I seem particular fond of . . . *Scholar*."

"Isn't that more like a title? Or a description?" I say offhand and gaze at the rows of medical equipment, metal tables, and huge monitors displaying information I can't wrap my head around.

"Yes, it describes me perfectly, I must say. It also makes me sound rather mysterious, which I do enjoy."

She trots to a large open doorway and we follow her to a glass case full of an assortment of trinkets and jewelry next to a large map of star constellations. Scholar has a little bit of everything down here in her sanctuary—her superhero spy lab. Hawk peers in through the glass of the display.

"What are these?" he asks and I join him in examining the rows upon rows of gold medallions, necklaces shaped into symbols of an ancient language, rings stamped with seals, and branded bracelets. Squinting at them, I realize they're the same symbols that cover the black arch in the middle of IMS headquarters. Dragon script.

Scholar walks around to the other side and rests a clawed forefoot lovingly on the edge of the glass to gaze inside. "Heirlooms and little babbles I've made over the centuries."

Centuries? How old is this Scholar? Not all dragons are immortal—only the six majestics. Then there's the noble class of dragons who can fly and live for hundreds of years. Below them are the regals, a smaller breed with a shorter life span but they can still fly. Next come the terrenes, those dragons without wings with significantly shorter life spans. I'd say Scholar fits in the last category but a terrene usually only lives to be about a hundred and twenty.

"Scholar, what class of—or, excuse me, who are you?" I ask, doing my best not to affront the dragon two feet away from my face.

Her frill rustles. "Clever girl. Kept up with your studies, have you? I'm clearly not majestic enough, or noble, or even very regal. Apparently, all I can be is *earthbound*. Those classification systems were always pointless and rather indelicate, if you ask me. They could have at least titled us poor *wingless* individuals as grand, or splendid. I would even be amenable to stately, I suppose. Either way, I am a separate entity to their classification system as my abilities and lifespan do not scale to their ratings."

Her indignation at the affront and her cool response make me start to like her.

"But we've gotten off topic, dear," she says and raps a sharp claw on the glass. "Each of these items has very specific properties, ones that are particularly conducive to the binding of magic. My magic in particular. Hawk, please choose one which is most desirable to your tastes."

His head snaps up. "You want me to have one of these?"

"I want to fill one with some of your sister's blood and have you wear it, yes. Goodness knows we could use a decent field test at this point." She waves her paw over the case. "A little binding magic from me and it will be near indestructible and near impossible to detect."

That shrinking bubble of hope in my chest suddenly swells. If Scholar is saying what I think she is, then Hawk will have a little bit of me with him wherever he goes and that piece will contain my magic to keep the werewolf disease at bay.

For such a monumental and significant item, Hawk takes

his time perusing the trinkets. Scholar starts to pace beside the case like a cat until she decides to sit several feet away to watch. Curiosity draws me over to her.

"Does Jefferson know you're a dragon?" I ask.

"Oh, yes." The dragon keeps her eyes trained on Hawk and her tail twitches back and forth, clearly interested in which of her handcrafted pieces he'll choose. "Jefferson and I have been friends for many years."

"So, do you work for the IMS?" I ask which earns me a low growl. I hold up my hands. "I'm just trying to figure out where you fit into everything."

"The majestics' original intentions for the International Monster Slayers may have been good, but the six always like to overextend their reach."

"You don't agree with the organization? But it sounds like you've been helping Jefferson to analyze my blood."

Her tail slithers near me then flicks away to curl around her forelegs. "The difference between the organization itself as a whole and the people who work for it is the difference between arrogance and wisdom."

"I don't—"

"It means blindingly following orders from those with unknown intentions and boasting a greater cause is not the same as understanding the need of the important work being done." She lifts her snout to the ceiling and gives her spine a long stretch before resuming her previous posture. "Jefferson understands why he does what he does. Admittedly, he struggled to see the difference between evil and those affected by evil after what happened to his family but . . . I think you're bringing him around. I've been watching you."

Oh, that's comforting. "Since when?"

"Since I tested a vial of strange blood sent to me by Jefferson and observed the profound effect it had on a disease once thought to be incurable."

If that's the case, she most certainly could have helped against Dasc. If I'm so special, why didn't she show up when Jefferson, Hawk, and I were all in his grasp about to die? Does her intense dislike for the IMS have anything to do with it?

Another thought strikes me, about how she knew Hawk and I had burned our old house to the ground. "I found tracks around my parents' house before. That was you, wasn't it?"

There's a glimmer in her eye and what I think is the start of a smile but it's hard to tell whether she's simply baring her teeth. "Yes, I have watched you patch up your former home like putting bandages on an old, festering wound. I found your actions to be most telling of your character."

A hot flush goes up my neck. "And what, exactly, does that say about me?"

"You don't let go," she says in a singsong voice that's almost cheery but her words hit me in the gut. Then she leans in closer and those sharp eyes cut through me. "And you don't give up."

For some reason, the way she says it doesn't make it sound like a compliment. I swallow and alternate between worrying my upper and lower lip. Scholar seems to have everything figured out, doesn't she? Maybe she can answer another question that's been on my mind.

"Jefferson warned me not to tell the IMS what I'm capable of," I say. Hawk appears to be deciding between three pendants and is oblivious to what's going on behind him. "He's never told me why."

"Probably because he didn't want you to lose faith in the only family you've ever known apart from your brother."

I purse my lips. "Can no one ever give me a straight answer?"

A thin hiss escapes between her bared teeth. "So impatient."

"I should go announce my gifts to the director right now," I shoot back. "Draco might still be around. He ought to know, too."

"Foolish, stubborn girl," she growls. Her head swivels on me less than a foot away. "Where do you think the power for the serum comes from, or the bio-mech guns for that matter?"

I lean back and shrug. "It's dragon technology."

"It's blood." A low growl emanates from her throat. "Consider that for a moment before you take any hasty actions."

She gets up and stalks away from me to peer over Hawk's shoulder at the pieces he's picked out. Blood. Whose blood? Jefferson has been warning me that I'd be locked up in a lab the rest of my life if they knew. Is this what he meant? Are there other people being held at this very moment, their blood being used to produce the serum and bio-mech guns? A shiver runs down my spine. That can't be true. The IMS wouldn't hold someone against their will like that. Would they?

"This one," Hawk announces and holds aloft a small, bronze pendant in the shape of a coin. As long as this works, I'm not going to think about the rest right now.

Scholar leads us to one of the medical stations and has me sit in a chair as she shrinks into her human form in order to take a fresh sample of my blood. After two vials, she takes the pendant Hawk selected and with a press of her finger it pops open. We both watch with fascination as she adds several droplets of my blood into a minuscule compartment hidden inside. Ever so gently, she closes the pendant again and clutches it tight in her palm before handing it over to Hawk. The faint glimmer of a dragon barrier fades into the metal and it becomes an ordinary pendant once again. Hawk pulls it over his head and tucks it under his clothes.

"And that's it?" I ask.

"If my theory is correct—and mine usually are—the blood in that pendant will react any time Hawk is affected by the werewolf disease. It'll be as if you're there with him. It's still not a cure, but it's enough to buy us time until there is one. And it'll need to be refreshed with new samples every so often."

Hope reflects in Hawk's face again and he smiles. "Thank you."

"Thank your sister," she says.

"It feels warm," he murmurs.

Scholar clicks her tongue at him. "And if you go over the edge, that little pendant will burn rather painfully and should snap you back to your senses. The more powerful the disease, the more powerful the reaction." She puts her hands on our backs to guide us out of the lower level and to the front door. "You must tell no one of that pendant or from whom you received it. I haven't lived here all this time for the country's rustic charm. No one must know where I am. No one. Not the IMS, not your friends, not a soul. If anyone catches my scent, they will all come for me. It was difficult enough not letting Dasc find me."

"You're that valuable?" I ask.

She straightens to her full human height with a dignified air. "Yes. Now go on." She holds the door open for us and we move out into bright sunlight. "Before you go, know this. The vampires are hardly ever this organized. This is an anomaly."

For a shut in, she certainly seems to know a lot. "How do you know about—"

"The vampires are cowards. They won't go to war unless something, or someone, forces them to. Normally, I would say the only ones capable of doing such a thing would be Dasc or their own alpha, but considering Dasc is in custody and their alpha's been dead for centuries . . ."

"Dasc said a war is coming," I say.

"Then I guess he knows something the rest of us do not." She closes the door so there's no chance of asking her anything further.

We stand together on the doorstep and Hawk puts a hand to the pendant hidden under his shirt. I hope Scholar is as clever as she thinks she is. That pendant is our best hope of giving Hawk security against the beast inside him, and so what happened to Duke never happens again. Another silent moment passes beneath the awning as the sun climbs higher before disappearing completely behind a row of heavy storm clouds. A bitter wind blows in and brings a dusting of snow with it.

I lead the way to the SUV and climb in. I consider where we ought to go next when my phone buzzes in my pocket.

Hawk frowns when his buzzes at the exact same time. Curious, I pull out my phone to find a single text from Jefferson.

Emergency with Duluth team. Need you back ASAP.

"Did you get it too?" I ask.

Hawk holds up his phone so I can see. "That doesn't sound good."

"Let's get moving."

I drive the SUV through the turnaround and head full steam down the driveway. The iron gate swings open upon approach and we make our way to the interstate. An emergency with the Duluth team—that could be anything, but after what happened in Wisconsin, I've got a bad feeling.

"It can only be one thing, right?" I say. "The vampires."

"*Pixies.* The hits don't stop coming do they?"

The snow flurry quickly increases, faster than I thought it could, and I slow as visibility reduces within minutes. A storm *had* to come today. The exit to Moose Lake appears through the snow flurry and we make slow time. I heave an audible sigh when we finally pull up in front of the cabin. Jefferson waves us over to the barn and we march through the snow blowing around our feet to shelter inside.

"I've got Agent Boyd on video chat," Jefferson says and we jog up the flight of stairs to huddle around a video he already has open on his screen. Agent Boyd's face fills the screen. Her curly blonde hair is frazzled and she looks furious.

"Agents," she says curtly. "This morning another one of the selkies went missing and we suspect the vampire took her. Using surveillance video we tracked the Mustang to the University of Minnesota Duluth. Charlie and I, assisted by some of the selkies, started combing the area. Charlie reported he found something suspicious on the campus but his call was cut off. He and the selkie who went with him are now missing as well."

Oh, pixies. *Charlie.*

"I need all hands on deck," she says, her voice strained. "I'm going to continue my search but we have an agent and two selkies missing. My other agents are heading down from the Boundary Waters to assist but they're hours away."

"You can count on us," Jefferson says. "We're heading out now."

"We'll meet you at the main campus of the college. And hurry."

The live chat closes and Jefferson immediately begins to grab retractable blades, machetes, and bio-mech guns off the walls. "Gear up. We're leaving immediately."

Hawk takes the offered weapons and passes along a few to me. I quickly tuck them into my belt and lining of my jacket.

"What about the people here in town?" Hawk asks. "With the threat of a vampire attack incoming, someone needs to stay behind and man the office."

"Maybe we should call in a code black," I suggest. "Get some extra manpower up here."

Jefferson frowns at the machete he holds in his hands. "We can't."

"Why not?"

"Because about forty-five minutes ago a leviathan was spotted off the coast of New York." He gestures to the computer and I hunch over the back of the chair to see the emergency response message in the upper corner of the screen. You've got to be kidding.

"It was *real*?" I ask in disbelief. "All those sightings were true?"

He nods, a dark frown on his face. "Most of the code black squads are headed that way to back up Draco before that thing wipes New York off the map. There are a couple of squads still in the area but they're watching the Wisconsin border because of the vampires."

"A leviathan? Seriously?" Hawk peers over my shoulder. "A leviathan hasn't been seen in over a hundred years."

"Well, a lot of crazy crap has been going on lately," Jefferson grumbles. "Get in the car. I already contacted Deputy Graham before you two got here and he's going to man the office temporarily. And I sent out a werewolf wide alert so they all know to keep indoors somewhere safe. Now, we've got people missing. Let's go bring 'em home."

His beady eyes are livid and I know what he's thinking of—missing people reminds him of what he's already lost. We're not going to lose anyone else today. I race after him and we pile into the SUV. Jefferson spins the tires as he guns the engine and we fly out of Moose Lake. The snow is incessant and getting heavier by the minute. Jefferson curses under his breath several times as the roads quickly worsen. Snow plows come out of their dens but the snow is falling faster than they can remove it. I turn on the radio and listen to the weather forecast. It's a massive storm and is supposed to last for a couple of days. The estimated snowfall is at least a foot. Fantastic.

And Charlie's missing. How on earth can anyone even get the jump on him? Can't he just port away to safety? This is really, really bad.

The hour-long drive tests all of our patience. Melody

calls Jefferson when we're halfway there to let us know they still haven't found Charlie or the selkies yet.

But what could get Charlie? Vampires are fast but . . . there have been hints everywhere that something else is driving the vampires. A mysterious "she" mentioned by the shapeshifters, the vampire in La Crosse saying their failure meant getting wiped off the map, and that vampire at Enger Tower mentioned something about a "she" not being there. What if the big bad we're looking for isn't a vampire at all? Something with influence on the level of Dasc and the long dead alpha vampire. What kind of monster are we really hunting? The fact that a leviathan is alive and attacking pops into my head. If something like that has resurfaced, maybe another one of the ancient monsters has come back to spearhead this . . . whatever this is.

At long last we reach the top of the hill and although I know Duluth is directly below us, I can't see it through the gusting wind, wall of snow, and low cloud cover. The SUV is buffeted as we make our descent and Jefferson expertly avoids cars that skid out on the road ahead of us. We follow the interstate deep into the heart of the city and eventually work our way up the hillside through residential neighborhoods. These streets are even less taken care of and slow us to a snail's pace.

How long has Charlie been missing now? *Pixies*, I hate this.

"We're here," Jefferson says and I crane my neck to look up through the windshield. The buildings of a college campus rise around us several stories tall plastered with snow, and we pass beneath a windowed walkway. I can't see much else of the campus through the blizzard ravaging the place. A line of cars is trying to escape in the opposite direction and students flee to their vehicles.

"They must be closing the campus because of the storm," Jefferson mutters. Past a bus stop and beneath another walkway, we come to a parking lot where Melody stands braced against the frigid wind. The second Jefferson parks, we all bail out.

Melody waves us over and we're almost shouting to each other to be heard over the wind trying to tear my hair out of my head.

"I tried pinging his cell but it must be off or broken," Melody shouts. "We've already gone through the main building, and Nessa has some of her other mates combing the streets. If he's not here, we don't have any other leads."

So, either we find him here or we don't at all. I swallow.

"We go in pairs," she continues. "The selkies have agreed to help us out. I'll keep going round with Nessa."

"We stick together," I shout and point between me and Hawk. I'm not letting my brother out of my sight. Melody looks to Jefferson for confirmation and he shrugs as if to say "whatever."

"Okay, then Barnes, you can go with her." Melody points to a tall brunette standing against the side of the building out of the wind. "Keep on the line. Call out the second you find anything."

We all patch our cells into a single line and go our separate ways, quickly disappearing into the gusts of the storm. Hawk and I head southeast towards the section of medical buildings. Melody texts each of us a picture of Charlie so we can stop people to ask if they've seen him. Hawk and I enter the closest building and ask a couple of students on their way out if they've seen him. They just shake their heads and move off like the building's on fire. We pass more students and ask a few professors as we make our way through to another parking lot on the other side of the structure. No one's seen Charlie.

A group of students hurry past in their parkas with scarfs wrapped tightly about their faces. They're all wearing sunglasses.

"Are you kidding me?" Hawk grouses to me. "Who wears sunglasses inside? And the sun isn't exactly shining outside."

I come to a halt and hold out an arm to stop him. "You know who I *have* seen wear sunglasses inside? Vampires."

I pivot on my toes as the four students pause in the doorway to the lower parking lot. One even gives me a small smile to display a set of elongated fangs before hiding his face in his scarf again.

"Hawk."

"I see 'em."

The group vanishes outside into the storm but we're hot on their tails. At least, I think we are until we get outside. It's a complete whiteout. The most I can see is ten feet in front of me, if that. I knock a fist against Hawk's shoulder and we both draw our bio-mech guns.

I hit the alert sound on my cell to notify everyone else on the channel, and then lift it to my ear, "We're onto something just east of the medical suite."

"Come again, Phoenix!" Melody shouts through the line but is hard to hear over the wind. "I didn't read your last."

"Medical suite!" I shout. "Four vamps. Wearing sunglasses."

"Phoenix, over here!" Hawk shouts and rushes forward. He vanishes into the storm.

"Wait!" I run after him and nearly slip sideways into a car. I slow down with the bio-mech gun raised in one hand and my phone to my ear in the other. The snow comes and goes and it turns me around. Then a figure appears directly ahead of me between the cars. "Hawk! Don't run off like . . ."

The person stands facing away from me and doesn't move. Wait a second . . . Hawk's hat didn't have that gray strip along the edge before. The figure turns around to look directly at me. Not Hawk. Not even remotely like Hawk. A woman. Even through the blur of the snow I can tell there's nothing human about those eyes. They're serpentine slits.

I fire the bio-mech gun as adrenaline surges through me in a flood. The snow billows out in a cloud around the pulse but the figure is gone. She doesn't jump behind a car or run off. She's just gone. It's the same way Charlie gets around. If it's the same way then—behind me!

A hiss slithers in my ear and a pair of rough hands shove me onto the ground. Strength rallies in my muscles and I throw back my shoulders to knock her away. Then there are more hands before I can turn around to face her. The group with the sunglasses surround me and I thrash against them, knocking one of their sunglasses off to reveal the bloodshot eyes of a vampire. But what the crap is the other thing that ported behind me?

Arms wrap around me from every direction and they tear at the collar of my jacket to expose the skin of my neck.

"No!" I shout. "Hawk! Jefferson!"

Brutal fangs bite into my exposed flesh and I let out a cry of pain. My head swims and this isn't like the bite of a vampire. Whatever that thing with the slit eyes is, it's worse. It's so much worse. My knees buckle beneath me and my vision blurs as whatever venom is in its bite takes me under into darkness.

21

I don't know how much time has passed by the time I come to again. I keep my eyes shut and do my best not to grimace against the pain in my neck—both sides in two days. That must be some kind of record. But that other . . . *thing*. What is it?

I realize I'm in a sitting position with my hands tied to the sides of a chair. The sharp iron taste of blood is in the air. It could be mine, could be more than just me. The air is hot and muggy, kind of like that club where the selkies hang out. There's also a smell of smoke. Something hisses and I almost shudder thinking it's that thing again, but it sounds more like a gas leak, or steam. Steam would make more sense for the heat and humidity. Where the heck am I?

There is no sound of footsteps but the hairs on the back of my neck rise and I realize there's someone behind me.

"We should kill the other two," someone whispers close

by. I remain motionless to let them think I'm still out of it so they continue to talk. "This is definitely the girl."

Me? Why do they want me? And the *other two* . . .

I crack my eyelids open to slits and see a pair of sneakers directly in front of me. I recognize those shoes—they belong to Hawk. So they did get him. Crap. My eyes shift sideways and I can make out another pair of legs before a chair to my left but I don't dare move anymore to see who is it is, though if I had to guess, I would say it's Charlie. Those shoes are too immaculate and fashionable to belong to anyone else.

The voices talk more softly so I almost can't hear.

"Check that one again," a woman says and her voice makes me want to shiver. It's cold and there's a barely audible hiss when she speaks. "I sensed something odd about him."

"He's just a werewolf," a boy says and terror reeks in every word that comes out of his mouth.

"I said *check him*," the woman says slowly, forcefully, the hiss rising.

A boy—I'm assuming a vampire—shuffles around me and I ease my eyes shut as he moves over to Hawk. Please, don't let them hurt my brother. I swear if they harm a hair on his head, I'll rip them all to pieces. Fabric shuffles, someone breathes in rasps, and then I get that sense of movement again without actually hearing footsteps.

"*Pathetic vampire wretch*," the woman snarls. There is a panic-inducing shrill cry, the tearing of flesh, and the unmistakable crack of bones. My hands shake and I can't keep my breathing even anymore. What will my eyes meet when they open again?

"You just wasted a perfectly good meal, Zeta," another woman's voice says directly beside me. "All that blood is getting filthy on the floor."

"He was a fool," the one called Zeta snaps. "And I rather like this strength, although something about it is setting my chest on fire."

"I told you not to drink from the girl," the other sighs.

I struggle to string together the clues and run through the list of all the monsters I know. I have a theory, one that's so outrageous that it can't possibly be true, but I need to see. I need to confirm my theory and try to find a way out of this nightmare. If they are what I think they are, then they should have patches of snake scales on their skin. I crack my eyelids open and find a pair of slit eyes only a couple inches away.

"I knew you were awake," she hisses.

I jerk away and strain against the thick chains wrapped around my chest. She laughs and straightens to her full height, those deadly poison-green eyes watching my every move. Even wrapped in a winter jacket, scarf, and thick boots, I can tell she's lithe. Her bare hands show the edge of scales peeking out beneath the sleeve of her jacket, confirming my fears. Her dark hair hangs straight to her waist and she'd be absolutely stunning if not for those freakish eyes, shark-like teeth, and a pair of even longer fangs. Everything about her screams deadly.

Like a key sliding into a lock, all the little clues come together and open the mystery of what these creatures are. It's a good thing I had that refresher in history class with Dasc or I might not have remembered all of the Greek mythology. The serpentine eyes, the fangs, the knockout venom, biting people and taking their magical abilities for their own—these are lamia. I thought they were all supposed to be dead. Back in the day they wreaked havoc with the ability to drink the blood of magic wielders and temporarily gain their power. They feed off magic. If Zeta is the one that bit me, then the strength she just used to kill the vampire is *my* strength. That must be why she could teleport—she drank Charlie's blood too.

There's a good chance none of us are getting out of here alive. Back when the lamia were still active, they were considered level 4 monsters. Some even wanted them reclassified as level 5, the highest rating on the deadly monster scale.

It's hard to look away from the menace towering over me as if I'm her next meal—which I very well could be— and survey the area around me. Straight across from me Hawk is strapped to a chair and unconscious as a similar blonde woman, Zeta, pats him down. To my left Charlie sits slumped in his chair with his chin resting on his chest. There's a needle in his arm and his blood drains out into a bag. A couple of other bags are already full and stacked beside him. He's much too pale with bruise-like shadows under his eyes and he's either unconscious from lamia poison or blood loss. I guess that explains the needle marks on the selkie and the vampire we found. The lamia were collecting blood to feed themselves. If they had simply bitten their victims, the bite marks would have given them away.

Thick pipes crisscross overhead in the dark room and more border our little section of space. We must be in some kind of heating facility and the hiss I heard earlier was steam in the pipes. Are we still on the college campus?

On the floor, even though I'd rather not see, is the body of the boy vampire. His head sits face first on the floor, physically ripped from the rest of his body. I fight back bile in my throat and a wave of dizziness sweeps over me.

"Epsilon," Zeta calls and tugs at the chain around Hawk's neck to pull out the coin pendant that Scholar gave him.

Oh no.

Zeta tries to grab the pendant but the skin of her fingers sizzles as the metal burns her. She hisses and quickly drops it against Hawk's chest.

"It's the demon!" she shrieks and Epsilon stalks over to bend close and inspect the pendant.

Demon? Pixies, do they recognize Scholar's work? Scholar had said if anyone knew where she was, they would all come for her. What did Scholar do to earn that much hatred in the twisted expressions of the lamia as they study the pendant from a safe distance?

The two monsters back away and talk to each other as if I'm not even there.

"Surely, this is more important than Lycaon?" Zeta says. "If the demon is here—"

"Then we kill them both. Our mission is the wolf first."

Their conversation confirms my suspicions at least—they had been attacking the werewolves, using the vampires to carry out their dirty work, to lure Dasc out. So, why do they want me?

"You." Epsilon snaps her fingers at me. "You know where he is, don't you? First you come to this city racing after our vampire and then you reappear in La Crosse using a code only Dasc would know. The little ginger girl gets around. We knew you were bound to come running to help your rather tasty friend here if he found himself . . . missing."

I swallow back the fear roiling in my chest. They captured Charlie to get to me. This is my fault.

Epsilon steps closer. "You know where Dasc is hiding or being held."

As much as I would like to leave Dasc for the crows, he's in a place that isn't even supposed to exist and he's my only hope for finding Jefferson's daughter. I don't speak a word. I brace myself for what comes next, because for monsters like them there's only the next logical step to take with an unwilling prisoner. I clench my hands and strain against the chains. My skin is sure to be bruising underneath as the restraints cut into me but they give a little.

The two lamia watch me, amused.

"Do you want to feel the power of your own strength?" Zeta purrs and flicks her hand open to reveal razor sharp claws where fingernails ought to be.

My breathing quickens and I clench my jaw. I just need to outlast them until Jefferson and Melody show up. They've got to find us soon, right? They'll come for us. I keep my eyes focused on my brother as Zeta stalks over to me and pushes her pointer finger into my shoulder.

"Where's Dasc?" she asks.

When I don't respond, she pushes that claw right through my jacket and pierces my skin. I cry out and struggle against the chains, kicking my feet uselessly. She pulls her finger out, painted in my blood, and gives it a lick.

"That's disgusting," I pant. "And probably . . . not very hygienic. You don't know where that blood's been."

"Oh, a comedian?" Zeta smiles at me and Epsilon stands behind her with arms crossed over her chest. "Tell me another joke. I love jokes."

My shoulder screams in pain and I grimace as the pair of lamia soak up my agony. Then Zeta's expression flickers and she gives a grimace of pain of her own, pressing one hand to her chest. What's wrong with her? Whatever it is, I hope it hurts like the devil.

"You should take a TUMs for that heartburn," I say. "I guess my blood doesn't agree with you."

Epsilon's eyes snap to the back of Zeta's head. The next second her hand flashes out and her claws rake across the side of my face, eliciting yet another cry of pain. Oh, for the love of—this *sucks*. My face stings from the scratches across my cheek, and the rest of my body pulses with fresh pain. And I thought vampires had bad tempers.

At least my cry manages to do one thing. Hawk stirs across from me and looks up in horror to the scene before him.

"You really ought to file your nails," I gasp, continuing to taunt the two women—that can literally rip my guts out—even though I'm terrified. "You might accidentally cut yourself."

That earns me fingers digging into the fresh bite wound at my neck. I fight the hold and a cry rips out of me. Warm blood runs down my neck which the lamia licks up like it's syrup, freaking me out even more. I think I'm really going to vomit this time. But Zeta makes that expression again and clutches at her stomach. I slouch over breathing hard and my own blood stains my jacket. Again.

"Leave her alone!" Hawk shouts.

"Hawk, no," I wheeze. Why did he have to draw attention to himself? He was supposed to wake up and figure out a way out of his chair while I distracted them.

Epsilon struts over to my brother. "Finally awake, are you?"

"Let her go."

"No." She takes one of her bloody claws and lifts his chin with it. He winces. "Don't worry. It'll be your turn once this one tells me what I want to know."

"Tells you what?" he manages to say without moving his jaw too much.

"Dasc's location. And then you can tell me where you got that pretty little necklace."

His wide eyes move to me slouched in my chair. I shake my head ever so slightly. Zeta rests her hand on my shoulder and starts to squeeze. I clench my jaw and strain the muscles in my face trying not to make a sound.

"Stop it!" he shouts.

"You don't like that, do you?" Epsilon says softly by his ear as she leans over him. "Protective? The family resemblance is obvious. Your sister. Ever heard her scream before?"

Panic flushes his face. "If I tell you what you want to know, will you let her go?"

"Hawk, you can't—" I begin to protest but am cut off by Zeta clutching at my throat.

"I'll think on it," Epsilon says like she's bored. "If you actually have useful information."

"I can take you right to both of them," Hawk says quickly. "I'll take you all the way—as long as you let my sister live."

There is no good way out of this situation and we both know it. No matter what we do or say, they'll kill us both. But maybe, just maybe, if we can split them up and get them moving into the open, we might have a chance of fighting back. Hawk levels his gaze at me and I know that's exactly what he's trying to do. Give us a fighting chance.

"She'll remain alive as long as you deliver that dragon and werewolf," Epsilon says. "Tell us where they are."

He shakes his head. "I'll show you. That's the deal."

"What if I don't like the deal?"

"Then you'll never find them."

The lamia rolls her eyes and flicks a hand at Zeta. "So dramatic. Let's move. I don't have time for this nonsense. Bring the bags."

Zeta scoops up the blood bags filled with Charlie's blood, wincing as she does, and slings a full duffle bag over her shoulder. Is that all blood? That couldn't have all come from Charlie or he'd already be dead. There's just *so much* blood in that duffle bag.

Oh, no. The missing selkies. That much blood could only mean . . .

Zeta slips out of the room with her haul. Epsilon whistles sharply and three vampires creep into the room from behind the pipes surrounding us. I recognize one of them as the hoodie vampire that dumped his comrade's body in the lake.

"Keep an eye on those two," she commands and yanks Hawk to his feet to bind his hands together. When she spins Hawk away and his back is turned, she mouths to the vampires. *Bleed them out.*

So much for the lamia's promise. This is it. I have to

fight my way out or die. Hawk manages to swivel his head to see me before he's shoved out by the lamia. They're going to kill him once they find Scholar and realize where Dasc is. They're going to kill my brother. It feels like my bones catch fire. It doesn't numb the pain in my neck and shoulder but makes it negligible. Something is coming worse than agony or death.

I'll make them pay if they hurt him. They'll all pay.

The lamia disappear with my brother, and the group of vampires come in with their fanged smiles, needles, hollow tubes, and bags for blood. If they take another drop from Charlie, he's going to die. I can't let that happen either. If that lamia became strong enough to rip a vampire's head clean off, then I can do the same. That strength is *mine*. It belongs to *me*.

I wait for one of the vampires to stick a needle in my arm and get close enough. While he's adjusting the blood bag, I slam my forehead into his with a painful crunch. As he staggers back, I throw my wrists and torso forward against the chains and end up crashing onto the floor, splintering the sides of the chair apart in the process. The vampires shout and I roll across the floor with the broken segments of the chair. The first vampire that comes close enough gets a solid kick to the chin that splits his jaw. The other two, stunned as their comrade falls backwards with a heavy thud, don't come after me at once and give me enough time to shrug out of the chains and roll to my feet.

Their focus switches to Charlie motionless in his chair and I see their wicked chain of thought. They want to use him against me and they're closer to him than I am. The pair rush towards him so I send a fist into the ground. The whole building shakes from the force. Pieces of tiled floor, wood, and cement burst into the air from the impact and I have to close my eyes against the debris. I run forward blindly and blink away the dust to find the two vampires struggling to their feet.

Running out of time, I give them both a sharp jab to the ribs to get them out of my way, then a few more feet and I'm in front of Charlie. I can't fight the vampires with him in the room. The chances of him becoming a casualty are too high. I don't bother trying to remove the restraints on him. I grab the back of the chair and drag the whole thing behind me as I sprint down the first hallway I come to. The slapping footsteps of the vampires give chase as I enter the maze of pipes pulling Charlie along. The chair tips awkwardly as I try to round a corner and he almost goes down. We balance out against the hot pipes that nearly singe my skin and I keep running.

I end up running right into a supply closet. The door's a thick steel make and it's the best protection I'm going to have for Charlie at the moment. Commercial cleaners, rags, mop buckets, and tools line the shelves of the cramped space around me. The lamia took my weapons so I don't have many options. I'll need to improvise and fast, just like Jefferson's been teaching me these last few months. If you don't have the tools, then you make do with what you've got. The first thing that catches my eye is a soot covered shovel. The vampires round the corner and are almost at the door. Before they can breach the safety of the closet, I jump outside, slam the door shut, and give the knob a good kick to break it off. That should slow them down at least if they try to get inside. Charlie's temporarily out of the fight.

Having to take the time to do that, though, exposes my back. My face slams into the same steel door as a vampire leaps onto my back. Another one grabs a handful of my hair and keeps slamming my head into that stupid door. With the shovel braced in my hands I use it to push away from the supply closet and we stumble backwards into the steam pipes lining the hall. The vampire on my back howls when he meets the hot pipes but doesn't loosen his grip. The second runs at me with hands extended and the third, oozing blood from his chin and mouth, stumbles in the second's wake. Freakin' vampires!

I manage to swing the shovel in front of me to keep the other two at a distance while the stupid monkey on my back sinks his teeth into my already open and bleeding wound. With a shout of fury, I push off with my feet and slam him into the pipes again. This time he lets go, and I dart away between the three of them to stand further down the hall so they aren't surrounding me anymore, then spin around with the shovel at the ready.

They're looking pretty battered but I'm sure I look worse at this point. I've got blood running down my face from somewhere and my neck is hurting like mad. Even in my current ragged state, the vampires don't seem anxious to meet the end of the shovel when held in my hands. My previous displays of strength are making them more cautious.

"That it?" I say and spit out a bloody glob at their feet. "Suck on that, you ticks."

A classic Minnesotan insult prime for driving vampires crazy. The three charge at the same time. Good thing this shovel's long. I lunge at the one in the middle, holding the shovel like a rapier, and catch her right in the throat. She chokes on her own blood and draws back as the other two try a pincer move on me. I swing the shovel left and kick right, managing to hit both. They crash into the pipes and cement wall. All three momentarily stunned, I close in on the one that insisted on getting a piggy back ride from me and smash the shovel into the side of his face. He hits the ground hard, leaving his neck completely exposed.

I swing the steel shovel plate down before I can hesitate, before I can think about how much blood there is already and how much more there's about to be. The solid end of the shovel holds as it severs the vampire's head from its body but the handle breaks from the force I throw into it. I've got a splintered chunk of wood left in my hands when the female lunges at me from the right. I pivot on my feet and hold out the improvised stake. That's all there is to it and she impales herself right through the heart.

One left. Clever this one—he pulls my feet out from under me and I almost fall face first into the decapitated vampire's bloody mess but I catch myself. The shovel plate. It's right in front of me. The vampire claws at my feet dragging me towards him. I reach out and my fingers brush the edge of the shovel. He keeps pulling. I flail my feet and manage to hit him in the shoulder. The small opening is all I need to grab the edge of the shovel. He yanks me backwards but I've got a weapon again. Getting one hand under me, I manage to flip myself onto my back and use both feet to kick him backwards into the wall.

I'm on my feet before he manages to step a foot away from that flat expanse of cement and I drive the edge of the shovel into his throat. It's really close and personal this time as the edge of the shovel digs into my palms and I push against flesh and bone. I close my mouth and turn my head as blood spurts over me. His body drops to the ground but his head remains held up by the edge of the shovel against the wall. I quickly let it drop and the head rolls away behind the pipes.

Sucking down air and breathing in the foul aroma of blood and vampire decay, I brace a hand against the wall and vomit all over the floor. Absolutely shaking, I empty my stomach again before spitting out what's left in my mouth—unable to use the back of my hand covered in blood to clear my lips—and stumble to the supply closet.

For a moment I simply stand there with knees knocking together and blood dripping off my clothes. Then I give the door a good kick and the steel screeches as it's forced inward off its frame. Luckily the door only clips the edge of Charlie's chair and doesn't hit him.

He's partially awake and trying to focus on me through half-lidded eyes. He looks awful. I wipe my filthy hands on my pants and kneel to pry the ropes off of him—I guess he wasn't considered strong enough for the addition of chains.

"I've got you," I say in that encouraging way Hawk used for Gillian when we rescued her. "You're going to be okay."

"Mason . . ." His reply is weak and breathy. His eyes start to flutter shut again.

"Stay awake, Charlie!" I shout in his face to wake him up. He blinks fast and is clearly working hard at staying conscious. "You don't want me to slap you, trust me."

I grab his arm to throw it around my shoulders and haul him to his feet. His toes catch on the ground and we stumble together through the hallways. I manage to get us lost a few times before we come full circle to where we had been held. A half-full bag of his blood still sits on the floor. I stoop to pick it up.

"We're definitely going to need this," I mutter.

Charlie's in bad shape, and when I say bad shape, I mean he looks like death. It's clear he can't walk any further so I tuck the bag of blood into the front of my jacket for safe keeping and then readjust him so he's in a fireman's carry on my back. The wounds around my neck strain and I choke back a cry.

"Okay, which way's out?" I say to myself through gritted teeth.

If it wasn't so ridiculously dark in here . . .

The lamia took Hawk down the path to the right. That must be the way out. I walk along it, panting hard, and make a few wrong turns again before I find myself in a pitch-black room. My hand hunts along the wall until I find a light switch and flick it on. I give a sigh of relief when the light illuminates a large garage door on the far wall. The next second I almost stagger backwards aghast at the sight in front of me.

Two women lay face down on the ground unmoving, their skin deathly pale. Next to them lie two charred piles of a fleshy substance I can only assume were their seal skins. Easing Charlie down against the wall, I hurry to check both of the selkies. Tremors shake my hands when I can't find a pulse. The lamias bled them out and burned their skins. They're dead and we failed them. I fight back bile again and a terrible burning behind my eyes.

If I don't keep moving, Hawk is going to end up just like them.

Feeling wretched and like the worst person on the planet, I remove the jacket from the closest selkie with a silent apology and wrap it around Charlie so he's doubly insulated for where we have to go next. He's on dangerous ground and going out into the cold is probably the worst possible thing for him in his condition, but I'm not leaving him behind.

I move to the door and grasp the cold metal handle that bites into my skin. With a grunt I pull on it only to find it locked. Letting out a primal scream, I give it a good yank. The lock begins to break apart and after another good tug, I get the door free.

A blistering wind slams into me from outside.

"And a storm. Because why not? How can we make this day worse?" I mutter, continuing to talk to myself to keep myself distracted. Returning to Charlie, I ease him onto my shoulders once again and step carefully past the women I force myself to look away from. "*Pixies.* Charlie, I'm sorry, but we're heading out there together. Just hang in there. I'm gonna get you help even if I have to walk through a freakin' blizzard."

He mumbles something but I can't hear over the roar of the wind. Icy snowflakes stab at my face but the cold wraps around my cheek and neck, blissfully numbing the surface pain. Blinking against the blinding snow, I search for a sign of civilization or life but there's nothing but pavement ten feet in front of me, the limit of my vision.

One step after another, I march out into the snow without a clue where I am, and no idea how to save myself, Charlie, or my brother.

22

I almost cry with relief when I see a sign appear out of the whiteout that says *UMD Parking*. We're somewhere on the college campus. I stomp through snowdrifts across the barren parking lot, wobbling as I'm buffeted by the wind. Every now and then I think I hear people calling but can never tell what direction it's coming from. Instead I move until I hit the curb of the parking lot and follow along its edge until a building looms up out of the snow flurry in front of me.

"Look, Charlie," I pant. "A doorway. And what's behind door number one?" I put one foot in front of the other towards that beckoning door-double entry. "Let's tell 'em what they won. Why it's a crabby old agent who loves venison and shouting at kids in the rain. *Pixies*, I seriously hope Jefferson is through here."

I reach the door and find it locked. Why does everything have to be locked! Adjusting my balance with Charlie on my shoulders, I give the door a good kick and the lock and part of the frame breaks apart to let me in. Warmth hits me like a tidal wave and I pause to soak in its embrace. Well, we're out of the storm but we need to get out of here. Hawk's out there on his own. My overactive imagination starts to entertain all of the horrible possibilities that could happen to him. They could bleed him out like those two selkies we couldn't save—

"Can't think about that," I scold myself. "Just keep moving, Phoenix."

I glance up at the skylights overhead in the two-story entryway I've broken into. Nothing can be seen outside the windows, only white. There's a scattering of comfy chairs for students to lounge in so I drip blood across the floor on my way to the closest one and carefully ease Charlie into it. His half-lidded eyes struggle to reach mine and he pools in that chair like there's not a single ounce of energy left in him.

"Well, at least you're still awake," I say and survey the area around me. "There's got to be a phone around here. Don't move."

I pull up the collar of my jacket and press it against the wound bleeding freely at my neck. Oh, *pixies*, that hurts. Grimacing as I keep pressure on it, I jog to what looks like a help desk. Maneuvering around the counter, I find a phone waiting on the desk. My movements are purposeful and direct as I dial Jefferson's cell.

It rings. Then it rings some more. Come on, come on.

"Who is this?" he growls.

"Oh, thank my lucky stars," I say in a relieved rush. "Jefferson, it's me."

"Phoenix!" Now it's his turn for a big relieved sigh. "Where are you? We've been looking all over."

"I'm not sure. I'm on the campus somewhere. There are skylights here, not sure if that helps. But, Jefferson, the vampires weren't working alone. Two lamia nabbed Charlie, Hawk, and me. I managed to get away with Charlie but . . ." I work a muscle in my jaw, fighting back a sob of panic, and press the phone to my forehead before bringing it back to my ear. "They killed the selkies and took Hawk. He's taking them to Scholar and Dasc on the promise they'd let me live."

"You—what? How do you know about Scholar?"

"That's not important. We have to go after them but Charlie's in bad shape. Real bad shape." I glance over my shoulder where Charlie's slouched in that cushioned chair. "If he doesn't get help soon, he's not going to make it."

Wind whistles through the connection. "You've got to give me more on where you are. Are there any signs around you that say what building it is? They've all got names."

"I'll check but it's somewhere near the campus heating building or whatever. That's where we were being held. Hold on." I set the receiver on the desk and jog back to the double doors, gazing around for any kind of sign. I push outside, get slammed by the wind, and turn around to scan the outside of the building. There's something on the right but it's completely covered by snow. Using my sleeve, I brush it off to uncover the letters then rush to the phone inside. "Solon Campus Center."

"We're coming."

"Call in a code black," I say.

"We already did," he says a little out of breath, presumably as he starts to run. "The closest team is three hours away and can't get here much faster with this blizzard. Hang in there. We'll find Hawk."

I'm not sure if I believe him. "Yeah," I say anyway as dread wraps around me. "Course we will."

Then I hang up before he notices how very unsure I sound. Pixies, I can't think like that. I can't let this fear consume me. Hawk's out there and I have to find him. One step at a time. I can do this.

I find a nearby bathroom and grab a fistful of wet paper towels. When I get back to the main room, Charlie looks like he's napping.

"Hey, hey, hey!" I shout at him. "I told you I don't want to have to slap you awake." I give him a few soft pats on the side of his face and his eyelids flicker open again. "It's a miracle you haven't gone into shock already. But don't worry. I kept a little of you close to my heart."

I yank out the blood bag to show him and hope my teasing irritates him enough that it forces him to stay awake. I don't have a lot of tactics but I can pull that one off easily. Using the paper towels, I clean the blood off my face and hands, not sure what's mine and what's vampire.

"I'm surprised you let those lamia get the jump on you," I say and peel back the edge of his jacket to find a lamia bite on his neck too. At least it looks like his tailored peacoat acted as a bandage. He flinches when I dab at the blood on his neck and press the towels to his bleeding wound. He's lost so much blood . . .

"With you so out of it you can't respond with those witty combacks of yours," I say, hoping to prompt him to speak up and show a little more life. He's scaring me. "Come on, tell me how insufferable I am."

He works his lips but no sound comes out.

"I really wish I could hear a snappy retort from you right now," I say more subdued. What's taking Jefferson so long?

As if in response to my silent plea, footsteps echo down the hall and Jefferson rounds the corner on the other side of the lounge area. Melody and Nessa are hot on his heels. They fly through the lounge and then Jefferson has an arm around me and is asking where I'm injured. Melody has Charlie's face in her hands and acts like a mother frantic over her son. I point out the bag of blood they need to give Charlie and Melody offers me a silent thank you. Nessa clenches her jaw and swings around a backpack she's carrying to reveal it's full of bandages, athletic tape, rubbing alcohol, water, and a machete.

While the selkie passes over gauze to Jefferson and Melody, she asks in a tight voice, "Any sign of Ailsa? Or Coira?"

"I'm so sorry," I say hopelessly. "They didn't make it. The lamia killed them both. They're back at the building we were being held in."

"And you just left them there?" Nessa hisses at me. "For the crows to feast off their bodies?"

"What was she supposed to do? Carry three people on her back?" Jefferson snaps. Bless him for sticking up for me. I have no idea how to even respond to Nessa's anger. "We'll go find them and bring them back. I know the general direction of the heating plant. Phoenix, stay with Agent Boyd."

"What about Hawk?" I ask. "We have to go after him!"

"Then bring the SUV around so we can get Charlie out of here and to the Duluth Field Office," he says sharply. He must deem me medically fit to be running off by myself again. I'll admit, I do feel better having a bandage on my neck—both sides—now. "The faster we get moving, the sooner we can save your brother." He tosses over the keys.

Melody gives me a once over. "Look at her. She shouldn't be—"

"I'll do it," I say and start jogging the way they had come.

I weave through the hallways and stop at a map of the campus affixed to the wall to get my bearings. Once I know the location of the parking lot where we parked the SUV, I run down the dark hallways and pass a security guard that shouts at me to stop. My blood's pumping and I wince against the strain in my neck and shoulders.

Too much time has passed. Would Hawk have actually gone where he said he would? Or would he go somewhere else as a diversion? How do we find him? The only plan I can form is to make for Scholar's mansion first and make sure they haven't stopped there. If they have, maybe we can head them off. Scholar's got to be able to handle herself, even against a couple of lamia. They called her "the demon." They must have for a reason.

The wind rocks me backwards when I exit out the other side of the building near the skywalks. I hold a hand up against the wind to shield my eyes and walk bent against the force billowing into me. Movement on my right catches my eye and I freeze. A flag ripples through the wind, having been ripped free from wherever it had been. I clutch a hand to my chest, willing my aching heart to stop pounding, and keep moving.

The SUV magically appears out of the whiteout but it's

completely covered. With a growl, I fumble with the keys and get the stupid thing open. A gust blows in a cloud of white so the seats are dusted when I climb in and grab the snowbrush out of the footwell behind the driver's seat. It'll take too long to clear it all, I realize, and do something stupid as I usually do. I shove against the side of the car to shake the thick snow off. A majority of it falls and I brush off the rest before throwing myself back into the vehicle and pulling out.

It's a good thing the SUV is all-wheel drive. Still, I have a hard time on the road that hasn't been plowed yet. I guess they decided not to do anything for the campus since it's closed. The SUV slides and lurches back and forth as it fights through snowdrifts. There's no way we're going to get to Scholar before the lamia, but hopefully, the lamia won't be able to get there so fast either. I finally make it to the main road and skid across an ice patch.

"Seriously!" I shout and turn the wheel, steering the tires into the skid before managing to regain control as the all-wheel drive regains traction. This is ridiculous.

A huge, orange snowplow comes up in the opposite lane, a cloud of snow rolling off the metal scoop. An idea strikes me, the sort that could get me in big trouble, but I'm up for anything to get to Hawk. I yank up a box underneath the passenger seat and sift through the emergency supplies. Once I find what I need, I step out of the SUV, blink against the snow, and light the flare in my hand. The snowplow has already passed so I aim at the front near the scoop, raise the flare, and hurl it.

The flare tumbles in an arc through the snow but the wind catches it so it ends up landing on the hood of the truck. The massive vehicle comes to an abrupt halt and I run up behind it through the trail it made and jump onto the step next to the driver's side door to bang my fist on the window, careful not to shatter the glass.

"I need help! Open up!" I shout.

A stout, heavy-set woman stares wide-eyed at me under a bomber hat and wrapped in enough layers its like she's hiding in a comforter.

"Just look at me!" I shout again and gesture to the bloodstains all over my jacket. Unfortunately, I don't have a badge I can flash at her to make her comply.

She gestures at me to back up. Hoping it's not so she can just pull away, I step down so she has enough room to open the door. Luckily for me, she does.

"Did you throw a *flare* at me?" she says as she leans out the door.

"I had to get your attention," I shout over the rumble of the truck and roar of the wind. "We've got people injured at the southeastern end of the college campus, but we can't get out with this storm. Please, you have to help us." She glances over her plow, undecided, so I say with all the desperation I'm feeling, "You're our only hope, or they could die."

With a sharp jerk of her head, she says, "What can I do for you?"

"Thank you," I say and rest a hand on her arm. "They're at the Solon Campus Center. If you can plow me a way, I can follow in my SUV."

"The college is supposed to be closed," she says and hunches down so her chin is hidden in the layers of the jacket.

I shrug and wince at the pain in my neck. "I know I might not look like it, but I'm with the FBI. We were chasing several suspects that took another agent hostage."

"Then where's your badge?"

Non-existent. "Lost it in a struggle. The agent in charge can explain once we get there. I promise."

Her pudgy hand reaches for something on the side of her seat that I can't see. Probably a gun or pepper spray, who knows. As long as she drives and doesn't try to shoot me, I'm good. She studies me for a terse ten seconds before her hands go back to the wheel and she nods. I jump off the step and hurry to my SUV as she turns around in the intersection up ahead and blasts back down through the snow. The SUV follows easily in her wake and, just as she promised, she plows a way through the storm right to the front of the center. She comes to a halt outside the doors, and I throw the SUV into park before racing outside.

Climbing back onto the step, I knock on the window and she cracks open the door for me.

"Wait here," I say. "I'll have Agent Boyd badge you in a second and then we need to get one of our agents out of here so he can be treated."

The driver looks bewildered but at least she doesn't leave when I run into the building. Melody's waiting for me inside the doors.

"What on earth is a plow doing here?" she says and raises a hand to the big orange beast, its hazard lights flashing through the snow.

"We need to get out of here and having a plow is our best option." I jerk my thumb over my shoulder. "I told her we're FBI. It'll be fine."

"Protocol dictates that we don't involve civilians," she argues.

"Then protocol's going to kill Charlie and Hawk," I snap. "So screw protocol. Let's get him out of here."

I march past her to Charlie slumped in his chair. At least he's more alert. I guess that little bag of blood helped.

"What's going on?" he asks weakly.

I grab his arm to wrap around my shoulders and pull him to his feet. "They took Hawk and I'm going after them."

"Took him? Why?"

I avert my eyes. "They're looking for someone else. A couple someones actually."

Despite Melody's protests, she holds the door open as I help Charlie out and guide him to the second row seats of the SUV. Melody heads over to the snow plow and flashes her FBI badge at the driver. Once Charlie's buckled in, she stalks back only to draw her bio-mech gun and aim over the hood of the SUV at something I can't see. I stiffen and reach for the machete hidden under the seat where Charlie sits.

"It's us!" Jefferson calls.

I hustle around the vehicle to find him and Nessa each carrying one of the fallen selkies across their shoulders. Nessa practically shoves me out of the way to ease her deceased comrade into the SUV next to Charlie. After Jefferson settles the other in on the opposite side, I take Jefferson by the arm and pull him away out of earshot of the others.

"Do we tell them about Scholar?" I ask.

"I'm pretty sure that's the whole reason they're here," Jefferson says and throws a hand out towards Nessa. "They came here to protect her but Scholar didn't want them to, so she made them stay out of Moose Lake and Sturgeon Lake to make sure they didn't draw attention to the area."

"Well, that seems pointless now," I mutter and run a hand over my hair to draw the whipping strands out of my face.

Melody comes up behind us. "Before we go anywhere else, we're heading to the Duluth Field Office to pick up Charlie's blood supply. I can drive the SUV."

"I'll drive the snow plow," Jefferson volunteers. "We can't bring a civilian anywhere near this. Phoenix, you're with me."

We hustle to our assigned spots. Jefferson leaps up into the cab of the snowplow and I fumble my way in after him. The woman—whose name I never thought to ask—sits like a turtle hiding in the bundle of her clothes. Only her head peeks out.

Jefferson takes the middle spot next to her. "I'm sorry but this is your stop. It's too dangerous where we're headed." And classified. "We've already called for a squad to come pick you up and take you home. We're taking the plow."

She starts to protest but Jefferson very kindly escorts her out of the vehicle and then assumes her spot in the driver's seat.

"Just like riding a bike," he mutters as he inspects the controls uneasily.

He takes stock of every button and shifter in front of him before putting the massive rig into gear and then, finally, we're moving. Jefferson guides the snowplow with precision out of the narrow campus roads and into the surrounding neighborhoods.

The snow flies around us illuminated by the emergency lights mounted on each corner of the enormous snowplow. I allow myself to lie back in the seat and catch my breath. My body aches from everything that's happened not only today but over the last week. Everything has to happen all at once, doesn't it?

My eyes are half lidded and I'm ready to take a fast nap when Jefferson pushes something crinkly into my hand. It's a small bag of beef jerky.

"Where'd this come from?" I ask.

He pats his pocket before putting both hands on the wheel. "I always carry some around. Just in case. You probably should start the habit."

"Yeah. Thanks." I rip into the bag and stuff the jerky into my mouth. Using my magic and having my blood drained has sucked away my energy and I'm going to need every last ounce when we go up against those lamia.

It takes forever to get to the bottom of the hill. We maneuver around a few idiots that thought they could make it through the storm and got themselves stuck. Emergency responders and police squads are all over the place towing cars and helping at accidents. We plow—literally—right through and make for the docks. We eventually come to a stop in front of the red Duluth Field Office.

"Now what?" I ask.

"Now you're going to wait here," Jefferson says and hops out, leaving me alone with nothing but the growl of the engine to keep me company as the wind tries to break through the windshield.

Minutes tick by until Jefferson climbs back in. A shock of cold washes over me before he shuts the door.

"Where do you think your brother would have gone?" Jefferson asks.

"I don't know. He wouldn't have wanted to put anyone else in danger but if he really thought he had a chance of saving me . . ." I let out a shaky breath. "Our best bet is to head to Scholar's home first to make sure she's okay. Is there any way we can warn her?"

"She doesn't believe in phones," he grumbles. "She thinks they're too easy to trace."

"Then I guess this will be a surprise visit. If they didn't go there, then we figure out our next step."

"Good."

"What about the others?" I ask. "Is it just us?"

"Melody's coming the second she's got Charlie hooked up to his blood supply. Nessa's going to rally together her selkies to avenge their fallen. I'll let them know where to go."

"Charlie's going to be okay?"

He nods. There's that at least. Seconds later Melody hops in, passes out a set of machetes, retractable blades, and bio-mech guns, then settles in beside me. Jefferson shifts the plow into gear and we blast back down the road, the snow a billowing cloud off the side of the scoop. This is it. We're finally going after Hawk—hopefully not a second too late.

Jefferson expertly steers the plow through the blizzard but the trip to Sturgeon Lake takes an eternity. I run a gloved hand over the blade of the machete and imagine every time I've killed a vampire. They're very weak offshoots of the lamia so killing a lamia is similar. Although, you can't hope to kill a lamia by stabbing it through the heart. The only way is a clean beheading—if you can get close enough and not die in the process. Whenever we catch up to Hawk and the lamia it's going to be a brutal fight and there's no doubt in my mind that they will try to use my brother against us.

I start to hyperventilate with too much time to think about it. My hands shake and I tuck my head down to my knees. I try to remember what Charlie told me. I'm in control. I am the weapon. I can do this. Jefferson gives me a single pat on the back.

"Don't give in to panic now," he says. "You've been doing great so far. You can do this."

After a long deep breath, I raise my head and stare out the windshield, gathering all my wits and focusing them into the machete clutched in my hand.

"I know," I say.

The rest of the journey is silent but my blood is boiling. Melody shifts several times beside me, restless. Jefferson clenches and unclenches his hands in a rhythm. These are two experienced agents prepping themselves for battle. Focusing on my blade, I run my hand over the length of it again and again as if my fingers could sharpen it.

Melody never asks where we're going or who the lamia are after. Did Jefferson tell her already? Or does she not even care?

Moose Lake passes us by. It won't be long now.

"They took Charlie's blood," I say into the roaring silence as we take the ramp off the interstate to Sturgeon Lake. "They'll be able to teleport."

"His ability requires line of sight," Melody says calmly as if we're driving to the store. "At least with the blizzard they can't see far. Use your flashlights to blind them if you can."

Then we're turning and the iron gates sit undisturbed in front of us. There aren't any tire tracks but the blizzard could have easily swept them away. Jefferson hesitates momentarily before he drives forward. The gates swing open to allow entry and we take the long driveway. The mansion blinks into view between the snow flurries. In the distance I hear a resounding clang.

"What was that?" I ask.

"The gate," Jefferson says and he sounds worried. "It doesn't do that unless there's an intruder."

We hustle out of the plow to the sound of an alarm every few seconds announcing some imminent danger. A rumble echoes from the mansion and the next second a faint blue light pulses at the top of the mansion through the snow.

"The defenses have activated," Jefferson says. "Son of a—"

The blue light spreads like paint sliding over a ball and descends rather quickly over the entire house. When it reaches the ground, it shifts into a shiny see-through bubble around the mansion. There's no sign of Scholar yet.

"Dragon's barrier," I say to no one in particular. I reach out a hand to the shimmering wall. It doesn't hurt me but resists against the pressure, pushing my hand away. "So, Scholar's safe inside and we're stuck out here."

"For the time being," Jefferson says. "Eyes sharp. They're here somewhere."

As if in response, a menacing laugh comes to us on the biting wind. It's a woman's laugh. The lamia are here. Thunder drums in my ears and I lift the machete in my hand at the ready, my other hand flicking open the retractable blade. Melody lifts her flashlight and her sword as well.

Jefferson aims his bio-mech gun at the swirling snow—it won't be able to take a lamia down but it might slow it enough for us to chop its head off.

"You think you're so clever," the female says through the wind. I think it's Epsilon. The three of us form up side by side with our backs to the dragon's barrier. I can't see a thing.

"Your brother tried to lead us astray," she says, still a ghost somewhere in the whiteout. "But I knew you'd come for him eventually. You've led us right to the demon's doorstep. Well done."

The pit of my stomach drops into the soles of my feet.

"No." The word comes out of me like a desperate plea as if I could go back and fix what I've done.

I led them right to Scholar.

That laughter taunts me again. "Oh, yes. Dasc will be next once the demon is dead. As for you . . ."

As if on cue, figures materialize through the snow all around us. They come in on all sides, dark silhouettes and ghosts, disappearing and reappearing closer to box us in against the barrier. Where did they all come from?

Then out of the storm comes Epsilon and Zeta, Hawk tied between them. Epsilon smiles and her gaze passes over us to the mansion beyond.

They vanish.

I pivot on my toes as I realize where they've gone. The lamia smile over their shoulders at us as they drag Hawk into the house.

They teleported past the barrier. And we're trapped outside.

23

They took my brother. They got past us like it was nothing. The dark figures surround us and start to move in one creeping, cautious inch at a time.

"We've got to get through that barrier," I snarl. "I don't care what it takes."

"It won't go down while a threat exists," Jefferson says.

"Then let's take out the threat."

The figures sneak closer, and from the outside lights mounted on the awning of the mansion, I see that they're vampires come at last for their revenge at the bidding of the lamia. I twirl the machete in my hand. Melody tucks her flashlight away in order to draw her bio-mech gun.

"What are you waiting for?" I shout.

Jefferson fires and hits the closest in the chest to knock it to the ground. I sweep into the mass of bodies and the machete in my hand sings as it slashes upwards. The vampire doesn't even have a chance to scream before his head rolls.

My sword lashes out and cuts across torsos, hands, and arms. Vampire hisses fill my ears and then the inevitable blast of a gun firing a bullet, not the pulse of a bio-mech gun. Figures. I tuck down and roll to rise at the back of the first row of attackers only to realize there's a heck of a lot more out here.

It's three against dozens if not more.

I spin about to find one with a gun aiming at my head. My sword drives through his throat and I lean forward in the same movement as the gun fires. Ringing fills my ears but the bullet misses over my shoulder. I jerk the sword to the side and it tears out the side of the vampire's neck. A quick pivot on my feet and I come back for a finishing chop with the machete. Two down.

Bio-mech pulses blast through the swarm of vampires and send them to the ground in clumped groups. The stronger ones get up quickly and charge headlong. Those focused on Jefferson and Melody find my blade stabbing through their chest from behind and they crumple to join the rest of their dead.

Melody moves like a storm unto herself, locked in a graceful dance of blood and death against those coming too close to Jefferson. As she holds the front, Jefferson keeps the vampires incapacitated, and I sweep in through the back. Every now and then a pulse comes too close to hitting me but I manage to dodge or duck out of the way. More gunshots echo and some ricochet off the dragon's barrier. I make my way to a gun on the ground dropped by a decapitated vampire and kick it across the ground to Melody. The second it reaches her feet, she picks it up and lets off a series of deadly shots. They don't kill the vampires but slow them down.

Distracted for a split second, a vampire rushes me from the side and knocks us both to the ground. Not this again. My elbow slams into its face and he falls into the snow where my machete finds his chest to impale him to the ground. Jefferson shoots over my head to keep another one from jumping on my back. I rise to my feet and slip through the vampires to rejoin Jefferson and Melody.

We're all panting from exhaustion. Even if we manage to kill all the vampires and get inside, we're not going to have enough strength left to take on the lamia. A loud crash echoes behind me from inside. I risk a glance over my shoulder and see a lamp roll across the entry hall but there's nothing else. Our only hope is that Scholar can hold out by herself for a while.

"There's too many!" Jefferson shouts.

I bump against the barrier as Jefferson steps back into me when a vampire launches at him. I jab out my machete from around his back and stab it through its chest, spraying us both with blood. Melody's dispatching another on the other side so we're left exposed a moment too long. Two more swarm in and pin us up against the barrier. We're a tangle of limbs and fangs and punches. One grabs the bandage on my neck and I let out a cry of pain. Jefferson manages to bring his bio-mech gun around and shoots the vampire off me. Once I'm free, I help him by throwing off a vampire trying to bite his neck. Somewhere in the melee, Jefferson is wounded and blood trickles from his gray hairline. The vampires don't give us a moment to breathe before we're fighting for our lives again.

More crashes and shouts come from behind. Hawk. Please let Hawk be unharmed. It distracts me and leaves me open for another vampire to try ripping the flesh from my neck. Melody comes to my rescue this time but we're moving a little slower. This battle's gone on too long already.

Lights appear through the snow and grow steadily brighter, illuminating the vampires still hiding deeper in the blizzard. Headlights. An engine roars and a black SUV floors it through the vampires, sliding across the ice until it comes to an abrupt halt against the dragon's barrier. The doors fly open and tall, beautiful women wrapped in tight black armor stream out of the SUV. A second vehicle races up, a truck with a plow that scatters the vampires on the other side. More selkies emerge and whip out their vicious blades.

Nessa turns her dark eyes on us. "We've got this." Then runs head first into the swarm of vampires.

And stumbling out of the SUV last comes Charlie, ripping a needle out of his arm and tossing aside an empty blood bag. Melody and I rush for him as the selkies create a barrier of bodies between us and the vampires.

"You tried to leave me behind?" Charlie asks, exasperated. He's still too pale and shadows paint the underside of his eyes, but at least he doesn't look like death any more. They must have given him a lot of blood.

"You idiot!" Melody snaps and drags him to the dragon's barrier away from the fighting. "What are you doing here?"

"The selkies told me about the barrier defense." His green eyes, made even more brilliant by the darkness around them, inspect the barrier behind us. "I can get us through."

"If you try to make a jump in your current state it'll kill you."

"I can do it," he argues. "Just one jump. I can do that."

"You're *not* going in there by yourself," Melody argues. "And I *know* it takes more energy to bring people with you when you teleport."

"I can take one person," he says, panting. It must be taking him too much energy to simply stand but if he can do it, if he can get someone across the barrier . . .

"Take me," I say without hesitation.

Jefferson's hand plants itself on my shoulder. "Phoenix, no."

"My brother's in there," I snarl. "Look at me. Tell me if you think I won't do everything I can to save Hawk and Scholar."

He blinks and lets his hand drop. Melody's eyes are wide and furious. I ignore her, moving to wrap an arm around Charlie's waist and face the barrier.

"You can do this?" I ask.

"You are *not* going in there without more help!" Melody argues, a tendril of panic in her voice.

"I can't bring any more people with," Charlie says and slings an arm around my shoulders—I'm not sure if it's to pull me along or steady himself, maybe both. There's something dark and deadly in those eyes. He nods just once.

"Charlie, no!" Melody shouts and reaches for us.

"Get me in there," I say quickly and hold on tight.

I remember when he ported Hawk. My brother nearly collapsed from the pain of it. I brace for that same horrible pain. We're going to be trapped together in a building with lamia. I can't afford to be vulnerable for even a second.

We vanish before Melody can grab us.

The air tightens in my chest and the snow disappears to be replaced by the marble floors and columns of the grand entry. My skins burns but it's a dull pain. The only real problem is a bit of disorientation. My feet don't realize they're standing somewhere else and my legs feel like jelly. Charlie slumps against my side. It's a good thing my arm is around his waist otherwise he would have fallen to the floor.

"Charlie?" I whisper at his ear.

He's unconscious but alive.

The noise of everything outside is muted and every sound I make, like breathing, is too loud. I remain motionless where I am but my eyes dart around the room for danger. Once I think we're clear, I drag Charlie over to a closest and hide him amongst the coats hanging inside. If the lamia don't know he's here, then they won't go after him. I shut the door noiselessly behind him and creep into the house at a crouch.

Signs of destruction and chaos mark a trail through the center of the house. Upended tables, broken lamps, claw marks on the walls, and something white and powdery spread over the floor. A bag of flour sits slashed around the next corner and a faint cloud of it still hangs in the air, leading me past the center room and to a massive kitchen beyond. Steel tabletops are dusted with more flour, powdered sugar, and splatters of what looks like blood. What happened in here? A confection massacre?

Footprints and signs of a struggle run through the powder in the kitchen evidencing some fight I missed while preoccupied with the vampires outside. Where did everyone go?

A tremor passes through my feet and the hanging fixtures rattle above me like some kind of earthquake. It vanishes as quickly as it came until there's another aftershock that sends a painting on a nearby wall to the floor.

A crash in the basement lets me know where the source of the destruction is coming from. I pause at the top of the landing and try to think things through before barging downstairs head first. If these lamia are using Charlie's power, then I need to remember his weakness. He needs to be able to see where he wants to port to. My best bet is to find a way to blind them, even if for a brief moment. They won't be able to use that power indefinitely. Eventually it'll run out, unless they're carrying around bags of his blood and taking sips the whole time. Crap.

I inch down the staircase and the sounds of battle grow louder with each step. Glass shatters somewhere close by. I force myself to keep moving until I'm on the bottom step. Peering carefully around the corner, I'm met by a scene of destruction. Glass shards cover the floor from the demolished dividers that had separated the hallway from Scholar's labs. Metal tables are bent and twisted, televisions and computer monitors spark where they lie in smoking piles on the floor, and there are dents in all of the walls.

Another crash gets me moving in the right direction towards the end of the hallway. I run at a crouch and stop at each steel support to hide and get my bearings before continuing on. This place is ridiculously big.

Growls, hisses, and the occasional grunt of pain wrap around me. In the very last section of the lab the lamias and Scholar are set in a vicious dance of limbs and blades around a cadaver table. Scholar seems to have shifted partway between her human and dragon forms. She's humanoid but with scaly green skin on her hands and arms and a tail lashing out like a whip as she fights the lamia off with a broadsword. The lamia hiss their fury as she cuts across their hands, their legs, anywhere she can reach. Black blood drips from their bodies and they're every bit the monsters I saw a glimpse of in those horrible eyes.

When Scholar pushes out an empty hand at Zeta, a shockwave ripples out before her and blasts the lamia back. Another tremor passes through the house and I realize Scholar is the source. She's the earthquake. Despite the power Scholar holds, the lamia are quick to recover and renew their attack. Zeta rolls to her feet from where she fell, ignoring the shards of glass imbedded in her arms, and lashes out again.

But where's Hawk? It takes me a moment to spot him. He's picking himself slowly off the floor a few feet behind Scholar. He's bleeding from his scalp and there's a sour grimace on his face but he's alive. Scholar must have been able to separate him from the lamia. A wave of relief rushes through me.

I jog as quietly as I can to the next pillar behind the lamia where they have Scholar and Hawk cornered. Another powerful blast pushes through the air almost like the pulse of a bio-mech gun but its shockwave sends cracks through the floor. Glancing around the support beam where I hide, I watch the lamia push themselves off the floor as Scholar leaps in. They're both focused on stopping her from chopping their heads off and lose a few fingers instead. Now's my chance.

I pivot around the steel beam, feet crunching on broken

glass, and in the same motion send my sword swinging for Epsilon's head. An inch away from her neck, her hand snaps up and grasps the blade with her bare hand. While Zeta tries to bite Scholar's arm, Epsilon spins about on me, fangs dripping with blood and serpentine eyes promising my death. She clenches her hand and the sword cracks in her grip. I swing with the machete but she grabs that too. We struggle with the blades between us and I push as hard as I can against her. Her feet slide across the floor from the force.

Then she redirects my arms to the left as she lets go and spins right to send her elbow into my ribs. I stumble back and fall heavily when her backhand comes at me next. Glass presses against my face and pierces my skin. My hands grab at the splintered floor and I hurry to push myself up before I'm beset upon again.

"Phoenix!" Hawk cries as Epsilon grabs the back of my hair and wrenches me up to bring a sharpened claw to the front of my throat.

"Her blood is on your hands, demon!" Epsilon screeches.

Out of the corner of my eye, Scholar's eyes go wide as she dodges Zeta yet again. I grab Epsilon's hand and fight against her trying to cut open my throat. She's strong. Maybe she kept a little of my blood. My impending death distracts Scholar long enough so she leaves herself open. As the dragon raises her hand to blast Epsilon away from me, Zeta launches at her middle and they fall into a heap behind the cadaver table.

In a desperate move, I twist Epsilon's wrist at an awkward angle and manage to wrench her to the side. She drags me down with her by the hand still in my hair so we're both on our backs. She's hissing and spitting like an angry cat and removes her hand from my hair to wrap around my neck. I tug at her arm as it gets harder and harder to breathe and flail my body to try to throw her off. My toe catches something in the struggle and I realize it's the machete I had dropped.

Past the table I catch Hawk's eyes as he scuttles forward, favoring one of his legs. I kick the machete across the floor towards him. He picks it up easily and rushes at the lamia, but doesn't get a chance to end the fight. Epsilon lets go, shoves me away from her, and rolls across the glass shards to put ten feet between us. Hawk limps to my side with the machete in hand and we face off against Epsilon.

She smiles. From out of her jacket she pulls a bag of blood—Charlie's blood. She brings it up to her lips. Hawk hurls the machete end over end and it embeds itself in her chest above her heart, tearing through the bag of blood in the process. It sloshes over the floor and she screams. The hair on the back of my neck rises at the hideous sound. But there's still some of his blood on her fingers.

She licks it off and vanishes from sight.

Claws drive into my back from behind and I scream. Her fingers dig into my flesh around my spine like she intends on ripping it right out of my body. Hawk snarls and turns around to grab her but the agony in my back dissipates as she reappears a foot in front of me. I send a jab to her face but she's gone again.

"Back to back!" Hawk shouts and angles about so his back is pressed against mine.

She grabs my arm on the left and moves to throw me. Remembering my fight with Charlie, I grab her arm and refuse to let go even as she rips those vicious claws across the back of my hand and tries to sweep out my legs. Hawk spins around behind her and locks her head in a vice to get her claws off me. The machete is still sticking out of her chest like part of a zombie costume. Black blood runs from the wound, a dark sludge. I grab the machete and rip it free. She doesn't even flinch but reaches over her shoulder trying to gouge out Hawk's eyes.

I grab her left arm, raise the machete, and chop off part of her hand. The claws twitch just once as three fingers roll across the floor. At least I've partially disarmed her—literally. She doesn't scream or cry out in pain. In fact, it hardly seems to faze her at all. She kicks out and hits me in the gut. Hawk wrestles with her and their struggle sends them into the cadaver table.

Scholar continues to dance around Zeta and manages to blast her off her feet. Once the lamia is prone on the ground, Scholar slides forward in order to deliver the killing blow. Epsilon shoves Hawk around so she gets a good look at the fight going on behind them. I lift the machete ready to take one of her hands when she vanishes again and takes Hawk with her. The pair reappear directly behind Scholar as she's in mid swing and Epsilon lurches forward to bite at the dragon's neck. Scholar seems to anticipate it and sends her elbow into Epsilon's face, but it throws off her swing. The sword makes a divot in the floor and Zeta grabs Scholar's arm to hold her in place—long enough for Epsilon's fangs to puncture Scholar's shoulder.

"No!" I shout and rush forward as the lamia gets a taste of that powerful blood.

A shockwave explodes in all directions from Epsilon. The cabinets around us burst into splinters, the remaining glass shatters in a deadly rain, the table blasts off its legs, and everyone apart from Epsilon is sent flying. I tumble like a doll through the air and bodily hit one of the metal support beams that manages to stay upright. Hardly able to breathe, I grab the edge of the beam and drag myself across the ground to shelter behind it as wave after wave blasts apart Scholar's basement labs.

"Hawk!" I scream through the sound of metal wrenching apart and wood splintering. I don't know where he is. I try to peek around the beam but am forced back by glass pelting my skin.

There's got to be something I can do. Think, Phoenix. Shielding the back of my head with my hands against the debris getting blown past, I scan everything in front of me for something I can use to take Epsilon down. Where does Scholar keep her weapons? Shouldn't she have weapons somewhere? I see Medical supplies, gauze, broken computers, busted bits of furniture, upended tables, and a glass case tipped on its side spilling out a collection of jewelry.

Scholar's artifacts—the same make as Hawk's pendant that burned the lamia when they touched it.

I try to time the waves. There are only seconds at best between them and in that gaping silence I can hear Epsilon laughing. Sucking in a breath, I lunge forward during those precious seconds and slide across the floor with both hands reaching out. My fingers grasp chains and tokens when the next wave hits. I ram my fist into the floor and create a handhold so I'm not blasted further into the room. The ripple of the wave rolls off my skin painfully and lifts my whole body for an instant before I fall back to the ground.

In the next seconds I secure my grip on the trinkets and create another hold in the floor as I make for Epsilon. I move forward three times and when I look up to gage the remaining distance, Epsilon's eyes lock onto me full of hatred. Zeta has managed to rise to her feet and stands in Epsilon's shadow, enduring the shockwaves behind her comrade's back. Scholar crouches behind another pillar holding her hands out in either direction in fierce concentration like she's trying to stop the building from collapsing—which is probably exactly what she's doing—and Hawk is pinned by the top of the cadaver table near the wall. One of his legs is trapped but he's protected from the worst of the waves by that steel block.

The closer I get, the more painful the waves become. It travels through my bones and boils my blood. It breaks me apart from the inside. What *is* this power?

I can't keep going. This is too much. I'm dying and I know it.

Epsilon keeps on laughing and I'm starting to think that's going to be the last sound I ever hear. Then I'm close enough that I can't breathe during the waves and I just lay there in the dust and debris catching my breath before the next wave comes.

"You thought you could defeat us?" Epsilon shouts between blasts. "We will sweep over your pathetic world. Your agents will be the corpses we feed upon, your homes our bonfires, your death our ecstasy. What clever quip will you say when we feast upon the bones of your brother?"

She's talked so long it's given me time to regain my breath and say, "Catch."

I hurl the trinkets at the pair of lamia and the metal hisses as it hits their skin. They screech and bat the little pendants and rings off themselves. While distracted, I grab a jagged piece of table leg still bolted to the floor, and yank it free of its screws. I get my feet under me and leap forward to stick its sharpened end through Zeta's chest. The metal goes right through and pins her against the wall. Spittle flies as the lamia hisses and wrenches this way and that trying to extricate herself.

Unfortunately, that's about as far as my plan goes. I duck beneath Epsilon's blow and try to pick up the fallen talismans for weapons but a single powerful shockwave rips through my chest. I fall on my back again, the wind knocked clean out of me. I expect her to stomp on my head or rip it clean from my body next but she stalks away—right for Hawk pushing the tabletop off his leg.

"Hawk!" I scream.

He looks up to realize the lamia is almost on top of him. Epsilon clutches my machete in her hand from wherever it had fallen. I'm struggling upright when she reaches him. He's fast and dodges her first and second blows but she manages to get her bloody mess of a hand around his throat and drives him to his knees.

The machete rises in her hand.

In that moment the world stands still, hanging on the precipice before a long dark drop into a void as I realize what my life will become if she drives that blade home. If Hawk dies, I will become the monster. It breathes under my skin. I've always known it's been there biding its time.

I reach for them as if I could stretch across the room and stop that blow—that world-ending blow. Something dangerous comes alive inside me and swells, breaking through my skin as I scream for my brother.

A visible bubble-like pulse bursts from me and the air becomes much too hot. As if a vent opens up beneath my feet, wind gusts where I stand. Or is it wind at all? It feels solid and real and moves like a thick, deadly cloud away from me, expanding to fill every crevice.

The lamia seem paralyzed by whatever power I'm channeling and the machete drops from Epsilon's hand as her entire body shakes. Zeta chokes on words or cries, I don't know. All I know is that whatever is pouring out of me is making them grimace and fold in on themselves despite trying to fight it.

But this hurts. It hurts deep in my bones. The blood across the floor—*my* blood, I realize—sizzles.

Hawk, my brave brother, grabs the fallen machete off the floor, rises, and with an almighty sweep cleaves at Epsilon. There's just enough vitality in her that she manages to dodge the blow and lick at the drying blood on her fingertips, the remnants of what she took from Charlie. The next second she vanishes. I wait for claws to dig into my back or rip at my throat but there's nothing but falling darkness. Hawk glances frantically around the room letting me know that Epsilon has fled this fight.

I'm crumpling in on myself with my hand still outstretched to will the last lamia not to break free of where I pinned her, for her to simply end.

Scholar appears from the other side of the room wielding that broadsword of hers and ends Zeta for good. The head of the lamia rolls until it halts against the twisted metal of the table.

I let go of the energy rushing out of me and it comes crashing back, pulling me in with it into darkness.

24

In the darkness I hear Scholar whisper my name. She'll come back for me she says, but right now she has to run. That's the only thing I remember until I wake up and don't know where I am.

I feel older somehow, as if I've been asleep for years. Deep in my core I'm different.

Stronger.

Apart from that, all of me hurts.

My eyelids fight to open while a monitor somewhere on my left beeps a continuous two-beat rhythm. The smell of antiseptics and cleaner remind me of a hospital but there's something more underneath that's so familiar. It's warm, and every now and again I catch the odd breathy snort of a deer.

"I think she's starting to wake up." Hawk. He's nearby.

"You sure?" There's Charlie's skeptical voice. They both talk gently and each is a little hoarse. "Nah, she's not waking up."

"I'll bet your pudding," Hawk says.

"You already ate half of my fries. You're not touching my pudding."

"Hey, you were moving so slow on that food I was just helping out."

Well, they both sound fine and if Hawk's sneaking other people's food, he's definitely okay.

There's shuffling and a slapping of hands. "Hands off, Hawk!" Charlie protests.

My brother's laughter fills the room. The sound revives me and I open my eyes.

I'm propped up on a hospital bed in a room with cement walls painted green. A heart monitor beeps beside me and an IV hangs next to it, feeding fluids into the back of my hand. On my other side asleep in a chair is Celina the faun. Her head is tilted back and she snorts softly in her sleep. Directly across from me on another hospital bed lies Charlie with Hawk perched in a chair between our beds. They're each wearing pale green patient scrubs. Both boys smile when I focus my bleary eyes on them. With Celina here and the green painted walls, I know we must be in Underground's medical unit.

Hawk swipes a plastic cup of pudding off Charlie's bedside table and hops away with it in his hands. "Winner!"

Charlie rolls his eyes and stays where he is. He looks tons better but still has faint shadows under his eyes. There's a pile of books on his food table and around his bedside. One even has a balloon tied to it wishing him to "get well soon" with a handwritten note in permanent marker beneath that says "you bloody idiot."

My brother hurries over to my bed and hops up to sit

cross-legged against my feet. He's got a horrible trail of bruises across his right cheek that disappears into his hairline. Battered and discolored but okay.

"It's good to finally see you awake. You had me so worried," he says and gives me a huge smile before ripping into the pudding. "Man, I get hungry when I'm worried."

I work my throat and a scratchy voice comes out that doesn't sound like mine. "How long was I out?"

"About two days," he says around a huge spoonful. "We've been sitting here waiting for you to come to so I could soundly scold you for scaring the crap out of me."

"And for stuffing me in a closet," Charlie says sourly across from us.

My lips tug into a smile. "Yeah, well, I was protecting you."

"I could have helped," he argues.

"How? As a human shield?" I scoff. "Because that's about all you were capable of doing at that point. You fell unconscious the second we teleported inside."

He looks away and mumbles something under his breath. Hawk smirks and winks at me.

Images flash through my mind of that horrible night. There was no time to think about any of it then, but now there is. I consider the fact that Charlie's teleportation hardly hurt at all when it had brought Hawk to his knees, how Zeta grimaced every time she took a taste of my blood, how that . . . that *force* pushed out of me and seemingly paralyzed the lamia in Scholar's labs. The implications are staggering and my heart starts to hammer which, unfortunately, is announced loud and clear by the stupid heart monitor. The boys both stare at me so I lay back and study the ceiling, trying not to think too hard anymore but I can't get the thoughts out of my head.

What's in my blood is so much more than strength or a potential cure for the werewolves. If I can do all that, what else am I capable of?

"You okay?" Hawk says and prods my foot.

"Yeah," I say hoarsely. "It's just been a crazy week, that's all."

All our talking must wake Celina because she jerks to and basically screeches when she sees me. Her ears stand straight up and she launches herself out of her chair to wrap me in a hug. My breath catches in my throat.

"Oh, Phoenix!" she says and starts blubbering on my shoulder.

"Ouch," I croak. She hastily draws away but leaves her velvety hands on my shoulders.

"I've been so worried! They brought you all here and you were unconscious and I *told* them, I told them tell me everything and don't you dare leave a single detail to the void! They tried to keep me out but . . ."

Celina keeps rambling on and I just smile. She leans in for hugs a few times while she talks as if to reassure herself more than me. Hawk sits on the end of my bed chuckling.

I'm so distracted by Celina that I don't even realize Jefferson and Melody have entered the room until Jefferson's directly behind Celina. Seeing them both alive sends another wave of relief through me. Celina scoots over so Jefferson can approach my bedside. He gives my upper arm a gentle squeeze.

"Still alive?" he says gruffly but his eyes crinkle as a ghost of a smile crosses his face. "It's good to see you awake, Phoenix."

"And I'm glad you didn't get bled dry by the vampires."

He scoffs and rolls his eyes. "I might be getting old but I'm not *feeble*."

Celina gets up so Jefferson can take the chair and he sinks down to close his eyes like he's been having a long, trying day. On the other side of the room Melody has a private conversation with Charlie over one of the books at his bedside. I catch a few of his whispers—he's rather excited about the plot.

"I'm sorry I wasn't here before," Jefferson sighs. "We were taking care of a few fanged loose ends in Duluth and Moose Lake."

"More vampires?" I ask.

He nods and casts his gaze at Melody. "There were a few stragglers but we made quick work of them."

"And the selkies?"

"Several injured but they'll all pull through. Well . . . almost all of them."

"Right." I swallow and glance at Celina who's running her velvety hands through my tangled hair with a soft smile.

I wet my lips before I ask my next question, afraid of the answer. "And the lamia? Epsilon?"

Jefferson shakes his head and a fervent nervous energy wraps around my lungs, making me breathe faster.

"She disappeared," he says solemnly. "Must have ported past the barrier and fled. I guess our *friend* was too much to handle and scared her off."

"Who?" Celina prompts but the curiosity in her faces dies when Jefferson and I stare at her. I don't know what she sees in our gazes but her ears flatten against her head. She pats my knee and clears her throat. "I'll leave you to rest."

The faun trots out of the room and I turn back to Jefferson. His beady eyes narrow as they study me in return.

"And what about our friend?" I ask. I remember Scholar's last words to me. She said she'd come find me. Or maybe I dreamed that . . . or was hallucinating or something.

"Vanished," Jefferson says, a tinge of anger to his words. "My best guess is she needed to get away from the attention, and went after that lamia. But speaking of our mutual friend, who was supposed to be hidden and never revealed—" He sneaks a glance at Melody and Charlie who are too engrossed in a particularly thick book to bother paying attention to our conversation. "How did you find out about Scholar? What did you do?"

A familiar twinge of guilt twists my stomach. Because of the secrets Hawk and I keep, we forced Scholar to disappear. We brought a war to her doorstep. I owe Scholar for everything she's done, but I'm not ready to give up my most devastating secret yet.

Hawk turns pale and hangs his head like he's tired of lying. Before he can make the mistake of revealing what happened to Duke, I give Jefferson a half-truth that we can all handle.

"We got impatient," I say quickly. "Well, *I* got impatient about . . . well, you know. I went to the library dead drop and lied, said we had an emergency and needed to meet."

Jefferson runs a hand down his face, then through his hair before he lets out a long sigh. "Phoenix—"

"I know what I did put her at risk," I say and toss Hawk an angry glare when Jefferson's focusing on his hands, warning him not to speak. "I'm sorry."

"One of these days your impulsiveness is going to be the death of you." Jefferson shakes his head.

I drop my gaze to my bandaged hands, still aching and sore from punching holes in Scholar's floor and wielding that shovel in Duluth. "I know," I say in a small voice.

"You're just lucky Scholar was your companion in that fight," Jefferson continues. "She's probably the only one—apart from a majestic—that could haul your butts out of that disaster and stop those lamia from gutting you both. Next time you won't be so fortunate."

He doesn't know. No one knows except Hawk and Scholar—and Epsilon. Scholar didn't stop those lamia from killing us. I did. Jefferson's been in on the secret of my blood, but at this point my lips are sealed until I can talk to Scholar again.

A brooding silence fills in the spaces left by our conversation until Hawk clears his throat and tosses a broad smile at everyone in the room trying to lift the tension.

"So, have we missed anything in Moose Lake?" he asks lightly. "Has the city managed to function without us?"

Jefferson gives a slow nod of his head. "Nothing major. Deputy Graham has everything handled. I think Ashley's dog went missing—" I do my very best not to react too strongly. "—and there was some freak fire, but other than that . . . oh! The school called wondering where the two of you ran off to. Guess you've missed too much school."

I'll still stuck on the part about Duke, Ashley's dog buried out in the snow, and can't force myself to pretend to care what the school wants. Hawk, however, manages to let out an exaggerated groan and rolls his head around his shoulders.

"Great," he grumbles. "So, we stop a massive vampire attack and a pair of supposedly extinct lamia, and we still have to go back to school and get in trouble for saving everyone?"

"No need to fret," Melody cuts in. "I took it upon myself to invade their offices, flash my FBI credentials, and sort the whole thing out. They won't call in the truancy officer now that they know you're a couple of undercover agents working a massive sting operation. You won't have any more trouble from that old bag of bones—what was his name?"

"Principal Tippy," Jefferson interjects.

Well, that certainly manages to elicit a reaction from me. Hawk and I both bark out a laugh. I can only imagine Melody blowing through like a storm and coming down on the principal and his snippy secretary. If only I could have seen it myself. At least that's one less thing to worry about.

Jefferson rises from the chair and gives my knee a single pat. "As soon as you're on your feet, we've got work to do," he says in low conspiratorial tones.

He doesn't elaborate but beckons to Melody. She sets down the book she and Charlie had been gossiping over and joins Jefferson at the door.

"I'll come round again later," she announces to the room. "I've got a few loose ends to settle with the selkies before they head out now that their charge has disappeared. You keep healing up, chaps."

We all chant our goodbyes and then it's just the three of us. There's too much to think about, too much to agonize over, but I'm too tired to do any of it. I need some mental peace and quiet.

I slide my legs off the bed but when my feet hit the floor, my knees buckle and the cold tiles ice my feet. Hawk's at my side faster than I can see him move and holds out his forearm so I can brace myself against it. He's clearly recovering well—freakin' werewolf healing powers.

"Where are you trying to go?" he asks.

I nod towards Charlie's bed. "I need to get up and move my legs. And I really want to see what all those books are."

"Hey, who says I'm sharing?" Charlie says sharply but then smiles. Guess he's finally warming up to us.

Hawk helps me walk carefully to the other side of the room and I sit in the open chair next to Charlie's bedside. Hawk perches on the end of the bed, despite Charlie's protests, and proceeds to burrow through the books, holding them out for me to see the covers. Whenever one catches my eye, he passes it over so I can read the description on the back.

Charlie runs both hands through his caramel hair, as if agonized we're laying our hands on his miniature library, but a smile seeps onto his face—I don't think he even realizes he's doing it. Hawk gives me a grin and tosses another book at me. I catch it with a grimace and stick my tongue out at him.

After a minute of silent shuffling, Charlie gazes over the books and picks up one tucked under his elbow like he had been harboring it from our curious reach. It's a well-worn sci-fi story and he looks at it like an old friend. He taps the spine of the book in his hand and looks like he wants to say something but the words are too hard to swallow.

"Try this one, Phoenix," he says at last and holds it out to me.

I grin and toss the book in my hands back to Hawk to take the one Charlie's offering. He grimaces at the rough handling.

"First names?" I say and hold a hand over my heart. "Hawk, did you hear that?"

"I think we finally made the friend circle!" Hawk says and holds out his fist so I can bump it with mine.

"So, are we just first-stage friends? Or are all friends the same?" I ask and Charlie's face puckers into a frown. Despite that, his eyes are bright and humor dances there. "How do we reach the mystical rainbow island of besties?"

He laughs and shakes his head, turning a book over and over in his hands. "I owe you." He pushes out the side of his cheek with his tongue and brushes his thumb over the pages of the book. "You hauled me out of that building on your back. You saved my life."

"And you got me past that dragon's barrier to save this ginger idiot." I cock my head towards my brother. "I'd call us even."

After that, we fall into a comfortable rhythm and Charlie actually joins in the conversation. We talk about books, movies, the creatures we've met in our adventures, and all the things normal friends would talk about. We sit in a loose group, each grabbing a book for ourselves, and challenging each other to finish first. Food comes and we act like the typical goofy teenagers we are—except Charlie who's legally a young adult.

When the lights go out and Charlie's asleep, Hawk sneaks over to my bedside and pulls out the pendant around his neck to show me it's still there, then presses a finger to his lips, winks, and slinks back to his own bed.

The next couple of days we're stuck in the medical ward recovering. The doctors and fauns tell me I'll have scars around my neck from those stupid bites and maybe across my cheek from the lamia's claws, but other than that, I'll make a full recovery. Hawk's discharged early but is confined to our side of Underground which is the furthest away from where Dasc is being held. My brother still manages to slip away and return with food or candy to share with the rest of us.

Melody and Celina come to visit frequently, bringing in treats and news of what's going on outside our seclusion. Through them we learn of the battle that unfolded on the eastern seaboard with the leviathan. Well, battle makes it seem like a fight actually occurred. As soon as Draco flew in, the leviathan disappeared into the depths of the ocean. Agents are still searching for it. Its appearance and that of the lamia has shaken the legendary community. Monsters thought to be long extinct have returned, and everyone is scrambling to figure out how and why. Then another big question looms. What else might come back?

The leviathan isn't the only thing that can't be found. Melody informs me there's been no sign of Scholar or Epsilon but I know they'll surface sooner or later. Scholar said she'd come find me. As for Epsilon, I hope she never finds me again.

At long last, we're discharged from the hospital and there's a general sense of relief between us all. Melody walks us out and treats us to lunch at a seafood restaurant topside—we would have gone to the market in Underground but Hawk isn't allowed that close to the penitent cells where Dasc is being held captive. So, instead we act like a normal group of friends discussing movies and books over tilapia and biscuits.

When it's time to finally part ways, I find I'm loath to

say goodbye. Now that we've become friends with Charlie and Melody, I'm sad to see them go back to Duluth. Melody gives us both hugs and warns us to take care of ourselves. We promise and she slips away to start up the SUV. Once it's just us and Charlie outside, he clears his throat and turns the goodbyes awkward fast by falling silent.

"You all right there?" Hawk asks and leans against the SUV, getting a good coating of salt along his back.

Charlie nods slowly. "I'm not good at this part."

"You mean making things seriously awkward?" I say. "Because I think you've nailed it."

He crinkles his nose at me but we all laugh.

"It's not goodbye," I say. "I'm sure we'll end up helping each other again. And then we'll be going through the trials together this summer."

Hawk holds out his hand and shares a handshake with Charlie before saying, "And we'll have to return the books we stole from you at some point, too."

"What?" Charlie's eyes go wide and he instantly starts to dig through the duffle bag slung over his shoulder bulging with the books he kept with him in the hospital. "What did you take?"

I give him a wicked grin. "I guess you'll find out once we're done reading them."

"Oh, come here you big boob," Hawk says and pulls Charlie into a hug. When Charlie's face goes deep red, I burst into laughter and can't stop until my brother lets him go and Charlie wheels towards me like I'm going to attack him as well. Instead I thrust out my hand. He looks at it with relief and gives my hand a single firm shake.

"You're not so bad, Charlie," I say.

A smile spreads on his face. "Likewise."

"Stay safe out there. Now, go get 'em unicorn." I give him a good slap on the shoulder, which makes him stumble from the force, and he climbs into the SUV next to Melody. We wave as they pull away—Hawk fake crying as he waves a napkin he took from the restaurant—until they disappear down the road. We stand in the chilly winter air as the familiar noises of Minneapolis surround us. I soak it in and let the cold brush my face.

"Guess it's just us again," Hawk says.

"I guess so," I say and tilt my head in his direction until our matching green eyes find each other. "Listen, there's something I need to tell you. I'm sure you noticed how I managed to stop Epsilon from killing you."

"It was kind of hard *not* to notice," he admits.

"I've never done something like that before," I say quietly. "My abilities have been strictly strength and whatever it is that helps you with the werewolf disease. But lately it's been more than that and stopping the lamia. When Charlie ported me past Scholar's barrier, there was nothing of the intense pain you felt. And before that, I think I stopped a berserker from, well, berserking in Underground during the interrogations."

I heave a sigh and struggle to find the words I'm searching for. My brother waits patiently for me to put my thoughts together.

"I don't know what I am," I say at last. "But I'm getting stronger. Whatever's in me is more than a potential werewolf cure, Hawk. I don't know what I'm becoming."

"What are you saying?"

"I can't keep lying to the IMS. I can't keep this to myself."

He shifts his jaw back and forth before he says, "I want you to promise me something."

"Depends."

My response earns me a glare.

"Don't do anything rash," he growls. "Scholar said she'd come back to find you, so wait. We've bought ourselves time." He pats the top of his sternum where the blood pendant lies beneath his jacket. "I'm good. And after all the warnings from Scholar and Jefferson, I think it's best if we let Scholar figure this out first."

"You know, what I've become—everything we've done—it isn't going to stay hidden forever."

"I know." He sets his hand on my shoulder. "But when we need to, we'll handle it. Together."

I set my jaw. That, at least, is something I can get behind.

"Together."

25

Jefferson sits behind the wheel as we head out in a van like the one on our last visit to La Crosse. This time Hawk sits across from me along with three other agents and a cooler between our feet containing the head of Zeta. It's the key to Jefferson's plan, one he managed to convince the director to let us try. The last time we went I was all nerves. I'm still nervous but there's a certain calm I've managed to achieve. I've defeated my share of vampires and stopped a pair of lamia. I can do this.

Once we reach La Crosse, Jefferson, Hawk, and I get out to place the red ribbon on the bridge to signal the vampires that we want to meet. It's a long shot but if this works, it's going to save a lot of people. We wait in a stoic group on the other side of the bridge for what seems like hours before another one of the agents buzzes us to let us know that a vampire made contact and placed a black ribbon.

"It's show time," Jefferson murmurs and we make for the

warehouse where everything went to crap last time. We're better prepared for any kind of assault this go around. Not only do we have the agents we brought with us, but there's a slew of agents hidden all throughout the warehouse district and the building itself where the meet is about to go down. We won't make the same mistake twice.

Despite what happened before, a pair of vampires still come to our meeting in the same place we slaughtered a group of their kind. This time it's a wizened crone of a man and a slender woman as his bodyguard. Jefferson and Hawk both come in as my seconds despite the one bodyguard rule. We aren't playing by their rules anymore. They need to know we mean business. Dasc wanted me to deliver a threat, so it's time I do.

"Is red the color of war?" the lead vamp asks and they take off their sunglasses to reveal their bloodshot eyes.

"It's the color of the blood I'll shed in victory," I respond with the required phrase. "Although, technically the color of that blood would be *black*."

I open the cooler at my feet, and kick it over. Zeta's head rolls across the floor and comes to rest at their feet. Thin trails of black goo line its path. The vampires' fangs come out and they stumble backwards. In unison, Jefferson and Hawk draw machetes from hidden pockets in their jackets. There's unbridled fury running through me and I let these monsters see it in my stance, the curl of my fists, the fire in my gaze. The lead vampire looks towards the door but two other agents in disguise block the opposite exit. The walkway overhead creaks under the weight of a dozen boots as more agents make themselves known.

"Oh, and that other group of vampires you sent to surround the building," I say and cock my head. "They couldn't make it to the party."

The two vampires crouch slightly, flexing their hands and baring their teeth like the monstrosities they are. Their eyes jump around the room looking for an escape or an enemy to attack. When no one moves to strike them down, they focus on me. I cross my arms over my chest and glare.

"You're not going to kill—" the vampire starts but I cut him off, a tactic Jefferson suggested earlier that I use.

"Here's what's going to happen. We're going to let you go so you can pass on a message to the rest of your filthy friends." I take two steps forward and the vampires actually lean away from me. "This little uprising of yours is going to end *today*. Step foot on Minnesota soil again, so much as touch a single strand of fur on a werewolf's head, and we'll chop you into pieces like we did the lamia."

"You're . . . granting us mercy?" the vampire asks, clearly not trusting my word or perhaps thinking me weak.

I move closer until I'm towering over him. "We're not going to put a bad dog down when he can still be useful," I growl. "But if you don't put your leash back on, we aren't going to offer your kind a second chance. Do you understand?"

He doesn't speak but nods. I grab him by the collar of his jacket and lift him up until we're eye to eye. The bodyguard doesn't move to stop me but tenses.

"I *said*, do you understand?"

"Yes," he breathes.

I drop him to the ground.

"*Then get out of my sight!*" I bellow and point to the far door.

The pair scamper to their feet and the agents step aside to let them trip in fear out the door. I'm breathing hard and clench my fists to stop them from shaking. There's five beats of silence once the vampires are gone.

"Remind me never to get on your bad side," Jefferson says gruffly behind me.

We're quick to leave the area but a number of agents stay to patrol the city in case the vampires change their minds. However, word apparently spreads fast of our encounter. As we navigate to Underground, a number of calls come in saying the vampires spotted along the border and in Minnesota have begun to retreat and retreat fast. Jefferson pats me on the back, Hawk keeps nudging me in the ribs, and the other agents toss me smiles. We did it.

It's with great relief when we reach Underground and are able to pass along the good news to Director Knox. It could be an effect of the lighting but I swear I see pride in the director's eyes.

Then there's only one last step to take, and this time Hawk can't go with us.

"I'll be waiting right here," he says and sits with Celina near the entrance to Underground. "Go get 'em, Nix."

I nod and let his confidence fill me up and Jefferson's rage harden my skin. Together Jefferson and I walk through the familiar corridors of the penitent cells. The white hallways stretch on forever until I stop in front of the door glimmering with a dragon's barrier where Draco waits in his usual black suit.

His intense, calculating gaze sweeps over me. "You've caused quite a stir."

Scholar's warning echoes in my head that the IMS is not

to be trusted, Draco in particular. But after everything that's happened, I've decided I can't afford to lose my trust in people. If I hadn't trusted Charlie or Melody or Jefferson or the selkies, where would I be now?

"Are you ready?" he asks.

"More than I've ever been," I say and mean it.

The barrier drops and I walk inside to find Dasc waiting for me chained to the table in the center of the room. His blue eyes narrow, trying to read me past my outer layer of hardened rage and experience that's come with chopping the heads off dozens of monsters. I take my seat easy as you please and lean back in my chair. I watch Dasc for a long time, studying him as he studies me.

Dasc survived the impossible. Witty's gone on about his healing abilities. He's lived for centuries. He's a force to be reckoned with, but I wonder what the power in my veins could do to him. Would he wilt in agony like the lamia if I push out that force? Would the magical disease flowing through him evaporate so he could be killed?

"You've changed," he says quietly. "What's happened?"

"Care to explain why two lamia were looking to kill you?" I ask casually.

His reaction is subtle but it's there. Dasc, the almighty alpha of the werewolves, shrinks in on himself in fear. His eyes dart around on the table as if he's drawing up imaginary scenarios and countermeasures with the information I've given him.

"Maybe they were old friends you screwed over? They're about as old as you, right?" I offer and rap my fingers on the tabletop. "All this talk about a 'she.' *She's* trying to kill you. *She's* starting up a war. Was it a lamia all the time? Or . . ." I rest my clasped hands on the tabletop. "Is something even more powerful than the lamia pulling the strings?"

The flick of his eyes to mine and away again tell me I'm right.

"There are bigger monsters than you, right?" I say, quipping the same line he said when he tried to kill me in Moose Lake all those months ago.

"You don't know what you're dealing with," he says darkly. "You don't—"

"You know what?" I say over him. "I'm done playing games. You can spin your poetry for someone else who cares. I made your bargain. I owe you a life debt. Then I also went and slaughtered a bunch of vampires, saved the werewolves, and scared the rest of the vampires back into whatever hole they crawled out of. My end of the deal is done."

"Who killed the lamia?" he asks.

I tighten my jaw and think of that powerful force that surged out of me, stopping the lamia in their tracks long enough for Scholar to chop Zeta's head off and to scare Epsilon into fleeing.

There's nothing Dasc can gain from knowing part of the truth, anyway. "My brother and me."

He falls silent and I shake my head, disgusted.

"That's it?" I snap. "More question games? Well, you can forget it. I hope you rot in hell."

Fury rages through me. People have been hurt and killed because the lamia came to Minnesota to find Dasc. Scholar wasn't even their original target but because of me, she got thrown into the mix and is now in the wind. She had been my best hope for turning my blood into a cure. It's all gone and that's on Dasc. I sweep my chair back and make for the door.

"Wait," Dasc says and gives a defeated sigh. "I'm going to need a map and something to write with."

"Why? So you can write your madman rantings down? I'll just burn them for fun."

Those wretched blue eyes pin me at the door. Every century of cold calculations, heartless murder, and years of watching the world die around him shows through in those eyes. The eyes of a monster. The eyes of a being who's lived far too long.

"We made a bargain, Phoenix Mason," he says. "So, I'm going to honor our deal. Get me a map of Scotland. I'll lead you straight to Genevieve Barnes."

ABOUT THE AUTHOR

Bethany Helwig lives in a small town in Minnesota. When not working as a paralegal, she writes fantasy novels, composes music, tries her hand at art, and enjoys the madness that comes with participating in various fandoms.